i

Published in 2017 by FeedARead.com Publishing

Copyright © Judith Arnopp

A CIP catalogue record for this title is available from the British Library.

Cover design by Covergirl

Edited by Cas Peace
www.caspeace.com

Dedication

The Beaufort Chronicle is dedicated to my parents,
Doreen Lily Robson, 1923 - 2015, and Victor Ronald
Robson 1920 - 2016.

Thank you for showing me the way.

Other books by Judith Arnopp:

The Beaufort Bride: Book One of The Beaufort Chronicle
The Beaufort Woman: Book Two of The Beaufort
Chronicle
A Song of Sixpence: The story of Elizabeth of York and
Perkin Warbeck
Intractable Heart: The story of Kathryn Parr
The Kiss of the Concubine: A story of Anne Boleyn
The Winchester Goose: at the court of Henry VIII
The Song of Heledd
The Forest Dwellers
Peaceweaver

The King's Mother

Book Three

of

The Beaufort Chronicle

Judith Arnopp

The King's Mother

I have been here before. It is just two years since I bore the train of Anne Neville as she followed her husband to his stolen throne. I remember quite clearly the finality of the crown of England lowering on to the usurper's head. But Richard was not God's chosen king. He won the throne through duplicity, and stealth; some say infanticide. There are few left to mourn him now. His supporters, those who refused to swear fealty to Henry, have been punished.

The last Yorkist coronation was a murky affair, a dirty dealing concealed beneath a mantle of white. This time things are different. Today the sun is bright and Westminster Abbey is clothed in Lancastrian red. The choir evokes God's praise for the rightful king, and the good Lord shows his hand and blesses us, blesses my son as he claims his rightful place, making me proud.

All eyes are fastened on the crown as Thomas Bourchier holds it aloft like a great jewel. My throat closes with unshed happy tears, and I hold my breath as time seems to falter. On the dais, Henry, his chin level and his eyes unfocussed, clutches the wooden arms of the coronation chair.

1

No one moves. I scarcely breathe. There is not a sound in the abbey; all eyes are upon the new king, each of us ready to be the first to cry out in glory at his name.

The choir sings out loud as the Archbishop shuffles a little closer and lowers the Confessor's crown to my son's head. As the golden diadem blesses his brow, the sun seems to grow stronger, shining through the iridescent windows, infusing the nave with light. Around me the congregation rises to their feet, bareheaded before their king, and the abbey of Westminster resounds with my favourite name.

Vivat Henry! Vivat Henry! Vivat Henry!

I have been waiting so long for this. There were so many times I thought it would never happen. I bite my lip, tears gathering on my lashes, obscuring my vision. I do not blink them away but, consumed with pride, I throw back my head and let them fall.

Outside the crowd throw their caps into the air and call their blessing on the king. The air rings with great joy. My son brings hope to England, an end to discord, a new dynasty heralding peace. As I follow in Henry's wake in the procession back to Westminster Hall, I squint into the bright sky and smile at a conglomeration of pigeons that flies up from a rooftop.

The assembly stand as we take our seats on the dais and I cannot help regretting that the dowager queen is not here to witness my triumph. I am the first lady in the land, the days when I served the greatness of others have passed forever. Joy consumes me, my heart is fit to burst with happiness. When next I visit my confessor I must remember to seek God's forgiveness for such vanity.

Thomas and Jasper join me at the table, I crane my neck, seeking sight of my son. He was so long in exile

2

that I have not yet grown used to raising my eyes and seeing him there before me. A wave of joyful pride washes over me when I locate him.

He is in conversation with the Archbishop of Canterbury, the old man leaning close to catch the quietly spoken words of the king – *my son, the king* – how well that phrase sings in my head. How easily it trips off the tongue. *My son, the king! The king, my son!*

Henry places a hand on the archbishop's shoulder, and Bourchier takes out his kerchief, mops his forehead before bowing as low as his old bones will allow. Henry watches as the old man takes his leave, before turning and making his way to the dais, his hair lifting lightly at the swiftness of his movement. When he comes close, I force myself to stop watching him and stare instead at my tightly clenched fingers. As he takes the chair beside me, Henry places his hand on the table and I am transfixed by the coronation ring that glints on his knuckle. It makes me smile.

He covers my hand with his. "Well, Mother, our day is here. Our trials are over."

"I am glad I have lived to see it, my son."

His mouth stretches into an answering smile, his brown eyes tawny in the torchlight, reminding me of his father's. "The ceremony went smoothly. I half feared the old man might drop the crown, or trip over his robes."

Irreverent laughter rumbles in Henry's chest but I do not reprimand him. "I have sent him home," he continues. "It seems he is ailing."

"Ailing?" I stare at the door but the archbishop has already left. Henry shrugs and picks up his cup.

"Some fever that has been plaguing him."

A shiver of fear runs through me.

"Fever?" I murmur, my eyes still riveted to the yawning door of the hall. Henry turns toward me.

3

"Mother, why are you repeating everything I say?"

I force a smile, and laugh uncertainly.

"Am I? I am sorry, my thoughts were far away."

I disguise the frisson of fear, draw my mantle closer about my shoulders. My thoughts were with the rumours of the pestilence that is reported to be sweeping across the country; lurid stories of men, women and children taken suddenly ill with a burning fever, dying quickly of sweat and exhaustion.

My informants say that some are claiming it to be God's judgement on what they see as Henry's theft of another's crown. But God is on *our* side. He has been all along. My son is no usurper; he killed the counterfeit king to bring back justice and peace to England! *He is no usurper!*

The phrase echoes in my head. In my mind's eye I see Richard falling on the battlefield, my brother-in-law, William Stanley and his men, drawing in for the kill, and Gloucester's limp body thrown across the back of a donkey for all to mock.

Henry's supporters cast scorn upon Gloucester's carcass just as Margaret of Anjou's men cast scorn upon his father's. There was no paper crown for Richard of Gloucester but he was dishonoured all the same. I shudder violently and slop wine on the cloth.

"Mother, are you ill?" Henry grips my hand and guides my cup to the table. "Would you like to retire?"

"No." I force a smile, raise my chin and assume a serenity I do not feel. "I am fine, Henry, just anxious for the meal to begin. I did not break my fast this morning."

As I reach for bread and begin to tear it into sops, Thomas leans across to take possession of the wine jug.

"Nice to see you have an appetite at last," he winks. "You could do with some padding on those bones, wife."

I send him a stinging look before turning my attention to the tray of capon a boy is placing on the table before us. I transfer one to my trencher and begin to pull it into small strips of flesh, occasionally placing a morsel in my mouth, chewing it well as I have learned to do, to give the appearance of making a hearty meal. Beside me Thomas needs no such artifice and attacks his food as if it is likely to be his last.

Jasper stands and raises his wine cup. "To the king!" he cries, and the assembly rises noisily to its feet, shaking the rafters with their praise.

It was like this before. At Gloucester's crowning I remember the Duke of Norfolk riding into the hall on a charger to declare the beginning of the feast. I recall the squeals of the women, the delighted cries of the youngsters, and the solid certainty of those gathered at the top table where I stood at the side of Gloucester's queen.

They too believed themselves secure. Yet a few months later their infant prince was dead, the queen herself sick unto death and soon to follow him to the grave. Already, on his coronation day, the king was sliding down the slippery slope to disaster. Gloucester's enemies were present at the feast, myself among them, their false applause rattling these same rafters. King Richard's biggest mistake was to be blind to a man's capability for deceit. He should never have placed his trust in them.

Henry and I must be sure to learn from that.

I cast my eyes about the company, examining the flushed faces of our so-called friends. They devour the food we place before them, lift their wine cups to call good fortune upon us but how many of these men love my son sincerely? How many are merely waiting for an opportunity to slide a knife between his pale ribs?

I was among the traitors that day two years ago. I stood by quietly at their crowning but I resented Anne, who was so pallid and weak a queen, and her husband whose pretended reluctance to accept his nephew's throne was as clear and as malodourous as a corpse at a wedding.

I smiled upon their crowing even as I plotted to bring my son home. I held the hem of the queen's coronation robe, followed her down the aisle at Westminster and raised a cup to her husband's long and healthy life, just as this company are doing now. Was that a sin? Is it a crime against God to fight for justice? My confessor assures me it is not but I am never sure.

As I watch the faces around me, each one concealing a potential enemy, my stomach rebels against the food I have eaten. I push away my plate, grope for my cup and drink deeply, my heart banging, my ears ringing, my mind screaming of danger.

Despite the scarlet clad guards that ring the hall, any one of these people could be an assassin. I put out a hand, my fingers finding the purple velvet of Henry's sleeve. Surreptitiously I grasp it, rub my thumb into the thick rich nap, and close my eyes to pray for God's protection.

Coldharbour House

The dowager queen and her daughter Elizabeth come to my apartment a few days later. We have an unspoken rule that my former subservient position in their household is forgotten, or at least ignored. They must now defer to me, and they do so with no outward sign of resentment ... although I am sure it is there.

They take a seat close to the hearth and listen patiently while I describe the events of the coronation. I cannot conceal my pride, I can hear it ringing in my voice, as plain as a bell calling all sinners to prayer. I suspect I am boring them. Elizabeth cradles her empty wine cup in her lap. She sits very still, poised, and apparently enthralled at my tale.

I imagine they resent being left out of the coronation proceedings. Elizabeth must feel slighted, and I know from those I trust among her household women that she worries Henry does not intend to carry out his promise to make her his wife.

In truth, we have little choice; the Yorkist faction, what is left of it, make it clear the union of the two houses is the only way forward. Without the appeasement of Edward's daughter, our reign will become fraught with discontent and England has borne enough of that. And, if her mother is anything to go by, Elizabeth comes from good breeding stock.

The dowager queen signals my servant and he comes forward to refill their cups, offers a plate of pastries. Both women put up their hands and refuse the food, both preferring to sample the wine.

"It is a shame, of course," the former queen remarks, "that the coronation was not postponed until after our children were wed. A joint crowning is always so much more pleasing to the common people."

Elizabeth jumps slightly and turns to her mother. Her face is hidden from me but I would swear she frowns to deter the dowager from continuing. I keep my expression bland, maintaining a gentle smile on my lips.

"But, just imagine, Elizabeth, a coronation all of your own – how much nicer that will be. The eyes of the

7

world will be upon you, and Henry will play no part in it. It will be your day, and your day alone."

"Indeed, madam." She is quiet, meek but I sense iron beneath her pliable exterior. I well remember the necessity of hiding my own emotions beneath acquiescence. I too was forced to dissemble, and I did so for so long that it has become second nature to me.

Her mother has no such sensibilities.

"When do you imagine the wedding between our children will take place, My Lady?"

Our eyes meet. She retains much of her youthful beauty. Her face is an open question, her brows delicately raised, only the slightest of nerves is visible. She imagines that as parents of the king and queen we shall be equal but I have seen too much of her cunning. Her ceaseless plotting against Gloucester, her shameless intrigue and duplicity. We can never trust her. Despite our past alliance, I will never allow her to hold power again ... and neither will my son.

"My son, the king has been occupied with other, more important things. A king has many duties, affairs of the heart have to take a back seat."

I hold her gaze and my smile steady. Kingly duties had never hindered her husband from consorting with whores but I had not intended to remind her of that. She does not bite, and refrains from reminding me she is familiar with the duties of a king but she shifts uneasily in her chair.

"Let us not pretend it is an 'affair of the heart' Marg ...My Lady ... we both know it is state policy."

My smile widens, my eyes turn to her daughter.

"Oh, I am sure Elizabeth's heart is involved also."

Elizabeth has the grace to blush. She puts down her cup and links her fingers in her lap.

"In truth, Lady Margaret, I have scarcely exchanged more than half a dozen words with the king, and then only in public. Indeed, I have no idea if he intends to fulfil his promise at all."

Silently I applaud her courage. She grips her hands together so hard the tips of her fingers grow pink. She looks away, her cheeks flushed, a gentle glow of perspiration on her brow. Pretending indifference, she hides the import of her words beneath a shrug of the shoulder. She keeps her head turned from me, feigning interest in the song of my musician who quietly strums his lute in the corner.

"My son always keeps his promises. He vowed before God to put down the usurper and unite our houses by making you his bride, and I am certain he intends to honour that promise. You must be patient."

In truth I have been curious myself. Henry is indeed preoccupied but I have watched him on the few occasions that he and Elizabeth have met. He keeps himself apart from her, although polite when they meet he pays her no more attention than any other women at court.

Of course, there are plenty of young girls who go out of their way to attract his attention but Henry does not seem to notice them. As far as I am aware, he has no mistress, possibly because his mind is habitually distracted by matters of state.

Henry's priority is to rectify the wrongs of his predecessors; he has no time for dalliance. Yet, I have seen him glance at Elizabeth, follow her progress from the room when he thinks no one is watching. Is he nervous? Unschooled perhaps in the art of love? I must ask Jasper when I see him next. I wonder if it is an area of his schooling that has been overlooked. The situation between them cannot continue; I will do all I can to remedy it but, for now, I turn the conversation to other matters.

"I have been considering your other daughter, Cecily. Now her marriage to young Scrope is to be annulled, we must look for another, more illustrious suitor for the future queen's sister ..."

The dowager sits forward, clears her throat.

"Her marriage to Scrope was never to our liking."

"And who can blame you? We can find her someone better – I have been considering my half-brother, John Welles. They are not strangers, and she will not get better than a Viscount..."

"Your brother? I know John quite well ...I believe he and Cecily have met several times at court. He is an upright, well respected man."

Perhaps this is the way forward. It might be wise to convince the dowager and her daughter that I already consider them family. My smile widens as I play the benefactor.

"I intend to invite Cecily to join my household. There the two can meet informally and I will be there for propriety's sake ..."

I pause mid-sentence, suddenly aware that young Elizabeth's poise is breaking. "Is anything wrong, Elizabeth?"

She turns toward me, blinded by unshed tears. She gasps before she speaks, places her long delicate fingers to her breast as her breath catches in her throat.

"I – My Lady, should I not be wed before Cecily? I have been passed over ... all my life ... marriages arranged for me have always come to nothing. T-to see Cecily wed before me is ... is asking too much."

I laugh, but not unkindly.

"Oh Elizabeth, my dear. Cecily and John will not be joined immediately! I have yet to bring her to my

10

brother's attention. I am sure Henry will have honoured his promise to you long before then."

"But when? He shows no sign of desiring it."

"I promise I shall speak to him."

Before she can retort that I should not have to intervene, I reach out, grasp her wrist but she pulls away and dabs her nose with a kerchief.

"Oh, I hope so, My Lady. I really hope so, or I fear I shall die an old maid."

December 1485

Jasper, recently wed to the dowager queen's sister, Catherine Woodville, is away from court with his bride, and I am to dine with my son, the king. It is the first time the two of us have spent an evening alone since his crowning.

I dress with care, choosing my favourite dark red gown. On the table are a pile of books I promised him; both of us take pleasure in the pursuit of theology and I am glad indeed to have someone on whom to practice my Latin. Once the maid has adjusted my sleeves, I click my fingers at the page and he hitches the books beneath his arm and prepares to light my way to the king's privy apartments.

Henry is standing at the hearth when I enter. He lifts his head, a half smile lightening his habitual frown.

"Mother," he says, coming forward to take my hands and kiss my cheek.

"How was your day, Henry?" I ask as I settle into a seat.

"Quite trying, Mother. You will recall there was a meeting of parliament?"

"Oh yes, so there was."

I indicate to the page to place the books on the table and leave us. He bows low, backs toward the door and makes his exit. Henry brings two cups of wine and we drink for a while in companionable silence. I am loath to bring up the subject of his marriage and in the end there is no need for me to do so, for he speaks suddenly with a hint of annoyance.

"Thomas Lovell, obviously urged and supported by his peers, asked when my marriage to Elizabeth will take place ..."

I sit up straighter, alert for his next words but he does not continue and I have to prompt him.

"And what answer did you give?"

He shrugs, avoids my eye.

"I said I am willing. It was, after all, part of the agreement if they backed my bid for the throne, but I did not set a firm date." He stretches out his legs, lies back in his chair and stares at the flames in the hearth. "No more parliament now until the end of January."

I can see he is attempting to change the subject but having come this far, I refuse to be deflected.

"You should speak to Elizabeth, Henry. The people expect it and it will quieten those who favoured York – dissent should be avoided at all costs."

He looks at me, his eyes more grey than blue in the firelight.

"I know that, Mother."

"It is not that I expect trouble, I just feel it would be expedient to do all we can to avoid it."

"There is the question of her legitimacy."

"Then reverse the bastardy placed upon her by Gloucester, it is in your power to do so."

"Yes, I know." He ponders for a while, taps a finger on the arm of his chair. "I would be happier if we knew the fate or the whereabouts of her brothers. I am

12

loath to legitimise her and in doing so invalidate my own claim."

"Do you expect the boys to pop out of the closet or something, Henry?"

His eyes crinkle at the edges but his amusement is short lived. He leans forward, speaks more urgently.

"But what did happen to them, Mother? Are they still living? I have had the royal palaces and prisons searched from top to bottom yet there is no sign of them, and no sign of their bodies either. Someone must know of their fate."

"All we can do is appear certain of their deaths. We must act as if there is no question of their survival. Elizabeth and her mother are as mystified as you and I; I am quite sure they are not hiding anything. You could offer Elizabeth sympathy at their violent end, use it as a ploy to win her friendship."

He gets up suddenly, stands at the hearth with his back turned to me. I lean forward, tug playfully at the hem of his tunic. "Henry," I say placatingly. "Surely you cannot dislike her. She is very fair. The people love her ..."

"And perhaps that is the problem ... perhaps I would prefer it if the people loved her a little less."

The logs in the fireplace crackle in the silence that falls between us. I swallow an obstruction in my throat.

"And love you a little more?"

He fidgets, avoiding my eye like a boy who wishes to run off and play, his face almost sulky. "They will come to love you, Henry. Once you have wed their York princess, filled the royal nursery with sons, and set the country on an even keel they will worship you. If you ignore her common born grandfather, Elizabeth is of good fertile stock and we need an heir."

Silence again apart from the scratching of a mouse in the wainscot, or it may be a bird at the window.

13

I clear my throat, and fiddle with the tassel on my girdle as I await his reply.

"Do you think she is chaste? I have heard rumours ..."

I wave my hand dismissively.

"Oh Henry, there are always rumours. I would lay my life on her purity. She is ambitious and too aware of her own value to squander her chastity. If you are referring to the old story of an intrigue with Gloucester, I would swear it was false. I was there at court, you remember. Gloucester was a complex man but I saw him with his wife. He was devoted to her."

"Even at the end? They say she was sick for a long time ..."

"Henry, if you doubt Elizabeth's virtue perhaps you should put it to the test. Court her, try to lure her to your bed, if you can ... but do not be surprised if she refuses you."

"I am the king!"

I cannot disguise my amusement.

"Kings hold little thrall for Elizabeth; she is the daughter of a king. She wants to wed you, not bed you. I wager she will resist your overtures until she is sure of you and your union is blessed before God."

Henry quirks an eyebrow.

"Is that a challenge?"

A curtain opens and a servant quietly approaches to place a tray of dainties on the table. I watch as he replenishes the wine then, as the boy retreats, Henry laughs, breathily down his nose.

"Oh Mother, if you are right and she resists me, I will give you a brace of manors of your own choosing."

I stand up, reach out my hand and we touch palm to palm, his fingers tight about mine.

"We have a wager." I say, looking him squarely in the eye before breaking into a peal of laughter.

The question of the missing York princes continues to nag at me. King Edward's sons, last seen playing on the Tower green, have long been dismissed as dead but rumours of their survival are persistent. Some people whisper of an escape during the chaos of Buckingham's botched rebellion, others claim they were alive and well until Henry took possession of the Tower.

I know full well the latter is a lie, so I also tend to dismiss the idea of their escape. I try not to dwell on what may have become of them, the horrible possibility of infanticide. Since the day of his birth, when I swaddled young Richard's flailing new-born limbs and handed him to his mother, he has held a special place in my heart.

My thoughts drift back to the dark days after the death of King Edward when the dowager queen had hastened to sanctuary with her children. Gloucester, already in possession of the young King Edward, tempted her to place Richard in his care, to keep his brother company while he awaited his coronation. The two boys stayed in the royal suite at the Tower and it was shortly afterwards that the nightmare began.

Slowly the boys were seen less and less and after Gloucester took the throne, they ceased to be seen at all. It makes me shudder to recall the day I first heard the rumours that they were dead. It was Buckingham, after his arrest for treason, who spread the news that Gloucester had had them killed. I recall my horror at the time; the disbelief that Richard of Gloucester, the once doting uncle could stoop so low. But it was not long before I began to suspect that the perpetrator of the crime was not the king at all, but the man who began the rumour. The man who shortly afterwards died a traitor's death.

If the boys are no longer on this earth, why have no bodies ever been produced? What earthly good are two dead princes to anyone if their death cannot be proven? It serves no-one, least of all my son.

For long stretches I forget about the matter but every so often the question mark that hangs over their whereabouts comes back to taunt me. I hate to admit it but Henry's claim to the throne is tenuous; his security rests entirely upon his marriage to Elizabeth and, in order to secure her hand he must legitimise her. In doing so, he places her brothers' claim above hers. What if they *are* still living? Hidden away somewhere, growing stronger every day, growing swiftly into men, secretly biding their time, learning prowess in battle? If that were the case, then their existence could spell peril for the House of Tudor.

Westminster Palace - 18th January 1486

Having taken a surfeit of roast peacock, I belch quietly into my kerchief and look on with something akin to horror as a tray laden with fruit tart is placed before me. I cannot take another mouthful of this rich fare and shake my head at the offering. Beside me, Henry has no such delicacy but tucks into his food as if he has not eaten in a month. His bride, Elizabeth is more restrained. I noticed she ate little of the meat course and now toys with her pastry without interest. She is probably worried about the coming night as a chaste girl should be.

I look about the wedding hall with satisfaction. The deed is done. Henry and Elizabeth are wed, and the houses of Lancaster and York are finally united. With this

16

royal union comes peace, and now, surely, everyone will be satisfied.

As the platters are removed, a minstrel enters with a harp. He perches on a low stool and begins to pluck at the strings, the music flooding the hall with languid peace. I sit upright in my chair, the twisted stem of my wine cup cool beneath my fingers, a smile of contentment on my face. I have fought long and hard for Henry's crown and now his marriage provides us with the means to reinforce our reign with an heir. I close my eyes, the music of the minstrel flows delightfully over me as I beg God to bless this union and make it fruitful.

After the minstrel, a troupe of players present a pageant that features a dragon and a knight. My mind drifts and I watch with half an eye, clapping at the end. Next comes a trio of dancers who leap and twirl as if they are hoisted on strings. As the entertainment is rounded off by a trio of fools, and our energy dwindles, the time approaches for the royal couple to be put to bed. We drink a toast to the king and queen, the cries of the company gratifyingly loud in my ears.

Henry's gentlemen usher him away with great ceremony while a blushing Elizabeth is escorted to the royal apartments to be made ready. I accompany her giggling group of women, eager to give her my blessing and perhaps, if I am able, comfort her that the trials of the marriage bed are nothing to be feared.

With much laughter and some subtle bawdry her finery is removed. A fine linen nightgown is placed over her head and tied at the neck. She stands before the hearth while her hair is freed from its bonds and brushed to a sheen. The outline of her body is clearly visible through the thin stuff of her attire, making it clear my son has won himself a prize indeed. I turn away, embarrassed at the line my thoughts have taken. I remember always.

On my own wedding night I was full of fear of what was to come but, to my great relief, Edmund left me alone in the huge bed and slept in his chair. There must be none of that between Henry and Elizabeth who is sufficiently old enough to bear a child.

When she is fit to be presented to her husband, we escort Elizabeth to the bridal chamber. The king has chosen the glorious painted room favoured by Henry III as his own. The doors are flung wide in readiness, and I prepare to gently urge the nervous bride over the threshold but my encouragement is unrequired. Elizabeth's step does not falter when she sees the vast four poster bed that dominates the chamber. When her women have removed her outer gown, she climbs blithely onto the mattress, lifts her arms while the covers are tucked about her and smiles directly at me, her cheeks pink with triumph.

A twist of envy wrenches at my gut. It is such a short time since Henry and I were reunited and now this girl, this beautiful girl, will take precedence over me. I have lost my position, my influence with my son and possibly some of his love. The knowledge sits heavy in my breast.

One of the women makes a saucy joke and amusement rumbles up from deep in the queen's belly. I watch as she covers her mouth with her hand as she tries to contain it, but then she gives a shout of laughter, reminiscent of her father's.

I frown and give a little shake of my head to warn her. This is no time for levity. I have no time for the tradition of rude celebration, a royal bedding should be a time of solemnity. When she notices the severity in my eye, her merriment is doused and she sobers, her eyes turning expectantly toward the door.

The sound of footsteps grows louder, the murmur of excited voices herald King Henry's arrival. The door is thrust open and my son enters, quietly ... his nerves more visible than those of the queen.

Henry's nightgown is finer than many men's court clothes, his thick velvet nightcap and robe are embroidered with gold thread. On his feet a pair of soft slippers and above them an expanse of hairy calf. I remember those legs in his infancy, when they were soft and hairless. I recall kissing his toes, blowing raspberries on the soles of his feet to make him laugh. My heart twists. The man before me is no longer my child. He is Elizabeth's husband. I am close to tears as I watch his gentlemen remove his robe. I blink them away, and don a wide false smile as he moves toward me with a flush of embarrassment in his eye. He takes my hands and kisses my cheek.

"Mother." His voice buzzes in my ear. I try not to cling to him as I wait for his servants to draw away from us so that we might have private speech.

"My son," I murmur, placing the cup of my palm against his face. "God is with you this night. Go, fill her virgin womb and provide us with a fat Tudor prince."

He laughs, his blush deepening. Kissing my other cheek as he whispers a reply.

"The deed is already done, Mother. I am afraid your wager is lost."

My mouth drops open. I stand transfixed as he climbs into bed and plants a hearty kiss on his wife's lips. My surprise is so great that I forget to pray when Bouchier steps forward to make the sign of the cross and bless the royal bed. Somewhere nearby a choir boy begins to sing, his voice high and pure and all the while my mind is ringing with the news. Elizabeth is already with child. I am going to be a grandmother.

19

I still have not moved when Jasper takes a handful of petals from a bowl and tosses them high into the air. They flutter down upon the counterpane and settle like blood upon the snowy sheet. The cheers of the court ring loudly in my ears as, with jovial din they begin to filter from the room.

But I do not move.

"Come, Margaret," Jasper says as he takes my arm. "Our king and queen have a job to do."

He urges me from the room, the door closes behind us and before I know it, I find I have been escorted back to the hall. Jasper eases me into my seat, and I look about the wreckage of the feast, suddenly tired, suddenly devoid of energy.

I have little wish to linger. Now the bride and groom have departed, the ceremonious part of the celebration is over and the company will descend into drunken ribaldry. For a little while I try and fail to show interest in Jasper's conversation. He talks of his new life, and I am glad he is content with his lot, and happy with his chosen wife. I cannot bear to think of Myfanwy whose heart must be well and truly broken at his marriage. She will not care that in marrying Catherine Woodville Jasper's prosperity increases and the ties between York and Lancaster are tightened.

I try to banish memories of the past and with my mind still clinging to the news that I am to be a grandmother, I signal to my women. Surrounded by great pomp as is my due, and with my head as high as I can lift it, I retire majestically to my room.

As I am prepared for bed I begin to recall aspects of Elizabeth's behaviour over the past weeks that should have alerted me to her condition. Her usually rosy cheeks have been pallid lately, her appetite reduced to that of a sparrow. I had assigned her megrim to anxiety about her

20

forth-coming marriage, supposing some delicacy over her approaching wedding night. I never once suspected she was already debauched.

With a sniff, I acknowledge to myself that she is little better than her father – I just hope she never strays from the marriage bed as he did. The Tudor bloodline must *not* be contaminated. I sigh, and look dejectedly about the chamber. My eye running across my possessions; the locked coffer of treasured jewels, my fine collection of books, my book of hours still open at the page I last read. My pens are neatly laid beside a sheet of parchment, my needlework with the thread spooled ready for me to take it up again. All is familiar, my things as I left them, where they are supposed to be. But then my eye falters and travels back to a box of trinkets, a pile of deeds and papers.

I rise from my seat, take up a parchment and unroll the list of prime properties I had marked as possible winnings from my wager with Henry. A waste of time. He has made me a laughing stock. Disappointed, I make to tear the list in half and cast it into the flames but something makes me hesitate and instead of destroying it, I tuck it away for safekeeping. There will be other opportunities.

My bedtime drink of camomile is hot. I sip it slowly, the tip of my tongue protesting. It will be sore in the morning. Allowing it a few minutes to cool, I take another sip, and absorb the full meaning of Henry's news for the first time.

I am going to be a grandmother. Soon, there will be a Tudor heir in the royal nursery – and, if the queen is anything like as fertile as her mother, he will be the first of many. A king can never have enough sons.

I close my eyes, a slow smile spreads across my face. Grandsons. If anything can make up for the misery of separation I suffered when Henry was taken from me, it will be grandsons. Royal grandsons who will soothe the ache of those barren years as nothing else could do.

I settle back into my pillows and amuse myself by imagining how they might look. Maybe they will be dark haired like me, or fair like Elizabeth, red like Edmund. Whatever the shade of their hair or the hue of their eyes, I will cherish them, teach them, guide them through their tender years as I never could my own son. I begin to make a list of names in my head. Henry, or Edmund perhaps, or John, in honour of my father.

April 1486

"What do you think of this, Henry?" I unroll the plans I have had drawn of the improvements to Coldharbour House. The king leans over the table, draws the candle close the better to see by. As he studies, I watch him unawares, noticing for the first time that there are hints of grey in his hair. With a twinge of fear, I remember he is not immortal ... and neither am I. But there are many years ahead yet. I close my eyes and beg God once again for a strong boy child to secure our line.

"This part will be very fine. I like that idea ..." Henry breaks my reverie, drawing my eye to follow the line of his finger.

"Yes, I have planned it so my apartments look over the gardens to the Thames. That way the scent of the roses should overcome at least some of the river's stink."

We are still laughing when a loud knocking falls upon the door and a messenger hurries in. It is clear from

22

the strong equine odour that he has ridden hard and fast and come to us straight from the stable.

"Ned!" He is a man now, the features of the boy obliterated by strong bones and facial hair. As soon as I recognise him, I move forward to greet him. "What is it? What brings you to us in such haste?"

"My Lord Jasper sent me. Humphrey Stafford and his brother Thomas have broken sanctuary, Lord Lovel with them. They have split, the brothers riding north, Lovel ... we know not where."

As if a spell has been cast upon his features, Henry's laughing face hardens quickly into stone.

"Give me the letter."

Ned hands it over, gives a sheepish look in my direction before turning dutifully back to his king. I draw Ned closer to the warmth of the fire.

"Have you heard from Myfanwy?" I ask. "Does the Lord Jasper still visit her?"

He shakes his head, glances around as if to ensure that no one can overhear.

"The last time they had a fight, a falling out. He has not visited since and the last letter he had from her she told him she was ailing. 'Sick unto death,' she said. I have heard nothing since and My Lord does not confide in me."

My jaw drops, my head suddenly echoing with the noises of the hall. Myfanwy cannot be ill, cannot be ailing! Not Myfanwy, she is young ... like me.

And suddenly I realise that I am no longer young. My bones ache for a reason, and the wrinkles on my face are not just due to worry but to age.

"Oh ... I will write to her. I shall write straight away ... as soon as I am free." My throat closes, and I shake my head to dispel the tears that are gathering on my lashes. Whether those tears are for Myfanwy or myself I am not certain.

Henry gives a loud explosion of anger, drawing my attention from the past. He is furiously pacing the floor, his face pink with irritation. With Jasper away from court it is my duty to step into his shoes. I push away my personal grief and hold out my hand. He presses the crumpled paper into my palm.

After Bosworth, Lovell and the Stafford brothers, three of York's most fervent supporters, fled into sanctuary. Out of our reach, their existence has eaten away at our peace of mind but now ... now they are at large, they are even more dangerous. The remnants of the Plantagenet following might soon come out of the shadows and band together against us. These traitors must be apprehended, placed in the deepest darkest cell until justice can be taken. Nothing must stand in the way.

"Jasper is in pursuit, they are headed north."

"They must be captured, Henry, and at once. They must be put to death – as the traitors they are."

"I am aware of that," he replies, his tone unusually terse. He turns abruptly to Ned.

"We shall prepare to ride out. Take some refreshment and be ready to join me."

As Ned bows out the door he sends me a sympathetic look but I ignore it. I cannot think of Myfanwy now. Henry is my priority. I pour the king a cup of wine and hand him a plate of pastries.

"You are going nowhere without first eating something or you are likely to faint on the way."

He huffs in annoyance.

"So the kingdom must go hang for the sake of my stomach," he snarls before slumping into a chair and taking a savage bite of pie. I know his rage is not against me but against the traitors who would harm our rule.

Men are very much like children. Beneath their rough ways, and their fearless attitudes they are just small boys playing a game of war. I fold my arms.

"I do not know what the rush is. If I know Jasper he will already have them under lock and key. Your journey may well be wasted."

I cannot admit that I want him to remain in the safety of the palace, and let others do the dangerous work. I think Henry should continue with his intended progress into the north country, not throw his plans in the air for some wild goose chase ... I am deluding myself. The truth is, I cannot bear the return of the old fears that are rising within me. I cannot give voice to the ever present terror of betrayal.

Any one of the king's retinue could harbour secret loyalty to York. Since the crown was placed on Henry's head I have been on constant alert for traitors. I scan each room I enter, searching out seemingly friendly faces that may be concealing a secret agenda or hide an assassin's blade beneath their cloak. Sometimes I wake sweating in the darkness, the nightmare vision of a stealthy shaft of steel thrust suddenly, and fatally, between the ribs of my king.

As seems to be my destiny, while Henry rides forth with a band of men, I wait and pray. In the morning, my knees worn red-raw with kneeling, word comes that the Staffords have been taken but Lord Lovel somehow managed to evade capture, disappearing it seems from the face of the earth.

I sit down and write of it in my journal and somehow, the flow of my pen opens something in my mind, clarifying my inner thoughts. This rebellion, short lived and unbloody, failed to raise support from the old adherents of Richard III. I dip my pen in the ink and write a few more lines. To rally an army you require a figurehead. It was lucky they lacked a Plantagenet prince to follow. Had one been available, would the outcome have been the same?

I bite my lip, remembering the missing princes. Surely they are dead, buried in some secret place in the deepest confines of the Tower. They can offer no threat to us now but ... there are others. What of little Warwick, the half-baked idiot son of George of Clarence? On his own he poses little threat but, were he ever to fall into the hands of our enemies, he may prove dangerous yet.

June 1486

"Arthur? You are going to name him Arthur?" I look with astonishment from Henry to Elizabeth. "I imagined you might choose to name him Edmund after your father."

"I prefer Arthur, and Elizabeth agrees. We should choose a new name for the future king of a new dynasty."

"You could have named him for your father to the same end; there has never been a King Edmund before."

Elizabeth, who is sewing near the window, keeps her head down, concentrates on her needle. Henry sighs, perches on the corner of the table.

"King Arthur is an inspiration, Mother. I am told we Tudors are descended from him. I would like to remind people of that. Arthur is a good name, a strong name, a name to inspire fealty."

"Suppose Elizabeth gives you a daughter, do you intend to call her Guinevere?"

Even Elizabeth raises her head and smiles at that. Henry chuckles, his face merry, his eyes sparkling and seeing him so happy, I forgive him everything. It matters little what the boy is to be called, and Henry is right, Arthur is a good name. There will be other sons we can name in honour of his father. I turn my attention to my daughter in law.

"The arrangements for your confinement are all in hand, Elizabeth. I have given a list of our requirements to the priory, all will be as it should be. Oh ..." I cock my head, listening. "...I suppose that is your mother arriving?"

Elizabeth puts down her sewing and stands to greet the dowager. I make a mental note to remind her this is no longer necessary – as queen there is no need for her to pay respect to anyone. Not even me.

"Elizabeth." The dowager kisses her daughter before turning to greet me. We touch cheeks and murmur a greeting before resettling in our seats. Henry, after a few guarded pleasantries with his mother-in-law, pleads an engagement and makes a hasty retreat. As his footsteps dwindle away the dowager turns to the queen.

"How are you feeling now, Elizabeth? Has your ... erm, your little inconvenience passed?"

The queen opens her mouth to respond but I reply on her behalf.

"The queen is very well now. Dr Lewis advised us on a remedy and things are now regulated. He says she is doing very well and the child is thriving."

Elizabeth is indeed blooming. Now the sickly early days are passed, she resembles a plump peach, her first pregnancy quite unlike my own. For the duration of my pregnancy with Henry I was listless and sickly and out of sorts. But Elizabeth is lucky, she suffers none of the hardships I was forced to bear.

I remember as always when I was a child in a strange land, widowed and afraid, bumped around the country in a hateful litter, beset by enemies – afraid of my own shadow. Elizabeth exists in comfort. She is secure, cherished and her every need catered for. She cannot fail to produce a bonny son. There is no excuse not to. I must begin to think of him as Arthur. His health is the important thing, his name is secondary, and if Henry favours Arthur, then Arthur it shall be.

News comes that Lord Lovell has emerged from hiding again, undeterred by Henry and Jasper's previous show of strength he has managed to raise a small army near Middleham, the stronghold of support for the former king.

Again, Jasper proves indispensable, riding forth with a great army, stopping short of battle to offer pardons to those who yield and lie down their weapons. A few men sheepishly surrender and offer fealty to Henry but Lovel, sensing his ship is sinking, sneaks off in the night before we can lay hands upon him, evading capture as he did before. Humphrey Stafford makes a desperate attempt to seek sanctuary at Abingdon but Jasper and Henry are done with leniency and haul him out and send him hastily to the block.

To rid my mind of these ugly things I concentrate on womanly concerns, ensuring the plans for the queen's forthcoming confinement are all in place. A healthy son will slay the hopes of York and everything must be perfect for the coming of the first royal Tudor prince. Everything must be as different from Henry's birth as it is possible for it to be.

The king has decreed that the birth of his son should take place at Winchester but the castle there is old. It is draughty and ill-appointed, so we arrange for her to be confined instead at the nearby Benedictine monastery of St Swithun.

As the time approaches, I instruct Elizabeth on the intricacies of childbirth, the traditions and etiquette

28

of royal labour. To my great chagrin, her mother, the dowager queen, whom Elizabeth desires to be with her, whispers her own advice into her daughter's other ear.

Like me, Elizabeth Woodville bore at least one of her sons in perilous conditions. I gave birth to Henry in the freezing fortress at Pembroke in war-torn Wales, and she brought forth her son, Edward, into an uncertain world, in the chilly damp confines of the sanctuary at Westminster. We are both determined it shall be different for Elizabeth - there will be no danger to the throne, or to the health of the child and the mother. Not this time.

While the dowager and I excitedly prepare for our first royal grandson, Elizabeth keeps to her apartment, feasting calmly on dainties. In between snacks, she sews tiny garments with her chubby pink fingers. The voices of her sisters rise and fall as they keep her company. Every so often they issue small bursts of laughter which are stifled when I raise my head to warn them that over-excitement is not beneficial for a woman in gravid state.

As the time approaches for the court to remove to Winchester, the trunks are packed, the household goods piled onto carts, the horses made ready. With great reluctance I make the great sacrifice of offering to travel with Elizabeth in the horse litter – a mode of transport I have abhorred since I travelled in one while carrying Henry all those years ago.

The journey is tedious and vastly uncomfortable, necessitating us to make frequent stops along the way. The queen needs refreshment. The queen needs the close stool. The queen needs to rest. What could easily have been covered in a day, stretches into three and by the time we arrive in Winchester, the September evening is already drawing in. Tossed and broken as if I have just weathered a great storm upon a broken ship, I yearn for a warm bath and a soft mattress to lay my aching bones upon. No one is happier than I when the priory of St Swithun comes into sight.

Winchester – September 1486

The prior's house is more than adequate for our needs and after a swift refreshment the servants make haste to ready it for the queen. The great hall which is to serve as the queen's chamber is hung with rich arras tapestries, all except one window but even that is heavily screened to protect her from drafts. The bed is made up with sheets from Rennes, two long pillows, two square and a counterpane of scarlet, furred with ermine and bordered with velvet. The pallet bed on which the child will be brought forth is similarly prepared. The mid-wife is summoned in readiness and I, and the queen's mother are lodged in rooms close to the queen. When we show Elizabeth to her lying-in chamber, she looks resignedly at our preparations.

"It is very fine," she says with no sign of pleasure. "It is all very fine, indeed." She turns away, a hand to her brow. I step forward, signal to one of her women.

"The Queen is exhausted, help her to retire. She must be rested for the birth."

She submits obediently and the dowager and I retire to the ante-chamber.

"Elizabeth looks overly fatigued," I remark as we ease ourselves into chairs. "Do you think her strong enough for the birth?"

The dowager raises her eye brows.

"My daughter is merely weary from the journey. It has given her a headache or some such malady. She will be well enough by morning. She is made of sturdy stuff, being of my blood, bringing forth children is second nature to her."

I read the unspoken sneer behind her words. While the dowager has borne many children and successfully raised most of them to maturity, I have but one. There was a time when her words would have injured me but now I can smile and lift my chin for it is my son and not hers who sits firmly on the English throne. I rummage in my pocket, bring forth a tiny linen cap I have been working for the new prince and bow my head over it.

I make a run of small stitches before looking up to find the dowager is watching me. Her face is serene, showing no sign of disappointment that her sly arrows have missed their mark.

"I do hope it is a boy," she says at last. "We are sore in need of another prince."

It is the one subject the dowager and I can agree upon.

*

I had imagined myself offering comfort, holding Elizabeth's hand, and soothing her brow while she strained to bring forth my grandson but the reality is very different. From the moment the agony begins to bite hard, she loses control – she rages against the pain, tosses on the mattress as if possessed by demons. I remember how it was with me. I have never forgotten my shock at the sudden ferocity, the naked primitive baseness of childbirth. At first, risking a smack at Elizabeth's flailing hands, I take hold of her arms, shout instructions for her to calm down. She must remember she is a queen bringing forth a prince, not a hoyden birthing a street brat.

31

My heart twists with pity at the sweat beaded face she turns toward me. Her mouth is down turned in agony, her eyes unnervingly wild.

"Hush, all will be well, Elizabeth" I reach out, smooth back her hair and then she spurns me, cuts me to the heart.

"I want my mother!" she wails. Her words douse me like a bucket of cold water. I step away from the bed and allow the dowager to take my place.

Perhaps it is natural that a mother should be the one to ease the travails of a daughter, for Elizabeth Woodville's silky tone soothes the queen as mine could never do. She strokes her daughter's head, bathes her forehead with a cool cloth while, rejected and impotent, I bite my lip and frown.

According to the physicians a child is supposed to come after twenty contractions of the womb but that was not so when I birthed Henry. It is not so for Elizabeth either – the candles are burned low but still she twists and strains. Her face is puce with effort, her cheeks streaked with tears yet she seems to be making little progress. I begin to fear for the child – my grandson must be born safe and sound. No ill must befall him.

Thoughts dart through my mind – is there is some herb I have overlooked that may open her, ease the child's passage into this world? I wrack my brains, trying to remember every old woman's tale I have ever heard for occasions like this. A memory stirs, or perhaps it is instinct but it is an idea I am impelled to act upon.

"Open the doors!" I order suddenly. "And the chests and cupboards – loosen the ties on the queen's girdle."

The women gape at me. I flap my hands at them.

"Go along, hurry up, do as I say!"

32

I am unsure how it can help but it surely cannot hurt. I am driven by the certain knowledge that if it fails, our only recourse will be to summon the royal surgeons to cut the prince from her womb.

A gust of air sweeps through the room as the dowager takes her daughter's hands and hauls her to her knees. Elizabeth groans, but somehow she manages to follow the midwife's instruction to squat like a mendicant. There is nothing royal about our queen now. She could be a beggar maid giving birth on a dirt floor. The rich velvets are tarnished with gore. Her hair is lank about her shoulders, her gown damp with sweat and the words that escape her lips are more suited to a bawdy house. The habitually regal dowager crouches beside her, also spattered in blood and birth water and I would give all I have to put aside my dignity and take her place.

"Now, push Elizabeth!" the dowager demands, bearing her teeth as if she would labour with her. "Push, push like a daughter of York."

I have no time to be offended at the name of York, for no sooner than her words are spoken then Elizabeth emits a squeal, puts a hand between her legs. She looks up sweaty and triumphant.

"The head. His head is born!" she cries. The midwife nudges the dowager unceremoniously out of her way.

"Lie on your back again, Your Grace. We must slow the child down. It will not do to have him come too fast."

The queen lies back with her knees akimbo and breathes hard, as if she has been running up a hill. Her eyes are fastened on the midwife, her fingers entwined with her mother's as she follows every instruction. She lowers her chin to her chest, and her face engorges with blood as she embarks upon another push. In a great flurry of activity, wetness spurts across the room and the shoulders are born. As my grandson is thrust into the world, I step forward and see him lying like a gasping fish on the finery of his mother's bed.

"It is a boy!" The midwife turns and beams a gap toothed smile. Despite the immense joy in my hammering heart, I force myself to keep calm, and my expression serene.

"As I knew it would be," I say, moving slowly forward to watch as the midwife cuts and ties the cord. Elizabeth and her mother embrace, the queen weeping. The midwife lifts the child, hesitating as to whether she would be wiser to pass him to me, or to the queen. I entrap her with my eyes and as if bewitched, she decides it is better to upset the queen than the king's mother, and places him in my arms.

Ignoring the dowager's snort of outrage, I cradle our heir, Henry's son and lift him so I might be the first to anoint his brow with my lips.

"My grandson," I whisper, as he struggles to squint into the light. "Arthur, who shall be our Prince of Wales and heir to the Tudor dynasty. I bid you welcome."

His body feels solid in my arms, his legs thrust strongly, and his pink mouth opens wide, showing his gums and a tiny quivering tongue. I must hand him over to his mother. He does not belong to me - not entirely.

Reluctantly, I pass him into Elizabeth's keeping and watch as she soothes him, places him instinctively to her breast where he latches on greedily. He is lusty for life, hungry for sustenance, eager to grow and to learn, and lay hold of his inheritance.

King Arthur shall be a virtuous king – I shall see to it, for with my guidance and his father's example we shall make a strong ruler of him. I close my eyes in thanks.

34

Oh Edmund, I hope you can see this; you would have been so proud.

Messengers are sent out to spread the news of the queen's safe delivery of a prince. Despite the incessant rain, bonfires are lit in the city streets and the pavements throng with people giving voice to their joy that an heir has been born to us.

In the cathedral, the choir sings a *Te Deum*, the soaring voices filling me with gladness but also bringing a painful lump to my throat. Arthur's birth strengthens us, and marks the dawning of a new age, an end to the wars, the beginning of an unsullied and peaceful era. He is a prince of promised peace and we are at last secure.

I envisage the line of my descendants spreading into the future in an unwavering path – a line of kings such as England has never yet seen.

Eventually, I have to cease my thanks to God, rise from my knees and return to the priory where Henry and Jasper are gathered with the king's councillors in the hall. I hurry through the cloister garden in a sudden shower of rain that dampens my face, beads of moisture clinging to my veil. My son looks up when I enter.

"Mother. There you are, we are waiting to start."

I disguise my slight pique at the reprimand behind a smile, and take comfort that the king has delayed the meeting for my sake. He is as eager as I that I should be part of his council. He acknowledges my quick mind, my extensive knowledge of how a court should be run. I remove my cloak and hand it to a maidservant and, as she hurries away, shaking raindrops from the fine thick velvet, I take a seat at the table, close to the king.

A fire snaps and crackles in the hearth where the logs glow red and black as the flames consume them. A man enters with a tray of cups and a welcome flagon of malmsey. Resting my elbows on the table, I clasp my hands together, intertwine my fingers and turn my thoughts to the business in hand. In the corner, waiting to take instruction from the king, a scribe is sharpening his pen.

"The arrangements for the christening will have to be brought forward. It is not wise to delay."

Henry and Jasper exchange glances, Jasper gives a small nod. Henry shuffles a pile of papers, scratches a few words with his quill.

"I had thought the twenty-fourth would give us plenty of time."

"Can Oxford get here by then? Should we not delay? He has a long journey to reach us."

I am eager that John de Vere's unswerving loyalty to our cause be rewarded by his appointment as Arthur's god parent. Henry looks up, dismisses my advice.

"No need, Mother. I believe he is already on his way."

Winchester – 24th September 1486

Elizabeth reluctantly relinquishes the prince into Cecily's arms and watches as he is wrapped in a cloak of crimson cloth of gold. He snuffles as the ermine tickles his nose until she tucks it back from his face, unable to resist running a finger along his silken cheek. He stretches his mouth wide in an attempt to cry but as we stand in line ready for the procession to the cathedral, he relaxes against her, relapses into tiny snores. The ushers nudge one another and smile at the snuffling sound issuing from their prince.

As we make ready to pass through the door, I glimpse Elizabeth watching from her bed, her face pinched and white. Until she is churched, the queen cannot leave confinement – it is the way of things. Having been brought up in the royal palace, she is well aware of the procedure but it does not make the short parting any easier to bear. With a touch of pity, I send her a bolstering smile.

"He will soon be back with you," I promise. "Try to sleep while we are gone."

A blast of trumpets and the procession begins. In the queen's absence I am first lady of the land. I take my place ahead of Cecily and Arthur, and with the queen's brother, Dorset, and John of Lincoln following on behind, we process slowly to the cathedral. In the queen's great chamber we are met by Edward Woodville and, beside him are Lord John of Arundel and Master Audley who are to bear the cloth of estate.

With many lords and ladies behind us, we venture slowly outside into the inclement weather. I look up at the watery sky just as the rain, that had briefly ceased, begins again. A cold drop lands on my cheek and I brush it off as if it is a tear but, from the look of the angry clouds, I fear we will all be wetter before the day is done.

The crowd is standing hunched against the chill, but as we draw near they straighten up and ignoring the weather, begin to call out in good cheer. We parade forward upon a red carpet, spotted with puddles. As the moisture seeps into my shoes I allow no sign of discomfort to show.

Despite the dismal day, the people are in good spirits, they wave their arms above their heads, releasing the stench of musty, damp garments and unwashed bodies. My heart warms. Some of them may be ragged and of little account but they are Henry's subjects and as such they are worthy of my notice. Their faces remain a blur but their approving voices blast loudly in my ears, their love for us bringing comfort. Regardless of the increasing rain that dashes against my cheeks like a fistful of gravel, I lift my chin and smile.

The west door of the abbey yawns before us. We pass a double line of the king's yeoman, and proceed into the shadow of the building, through the narthex where we shake off drops of rain before entering the nave. I can feel my ancestors watching proudly from Heaven as slowly we process along the aisle, between soaring gothic columns, toward the altar where the dowager is waiting to receive our grandson.

I was reluctant to her becoming Arthur's Godmother but Henry and Jasper assured me it was seemly. I am the last person to argue with etiquette. But, as baby Arthur is passed into her arms, I cannot help a twist of envy – an unchristian emotion for which I hastily beg forgiveness.

It is because of Henry, I tell myself. I was deprived of his childhood and it is only natural that I am loathe to share my grandson with others. I am overwhelmed by the strength of my feelings toward him but hopefully they may become less intense once he is joined in the nursery by other children. Perhaps, when there are more royal children, I shall grow used to the claim of others upon them.

The voices of the choir rise and fall. During a lull in the singing, John of Lincoln moves closer to my side, the shoulders of his cloak darkened with damp.

"I am informed my Lord of Oxford is but a mile away, shall we wait?" he whispers. I smile and nod in relief. I had feared he would not arrive in time. We can wait a short while for the sake of so loyal a subject but I quickly grow weary.

My knees, which become more troublesome by the day, are weakening, the familiar ache made worse by the damp inclement weather. I daubed them well with an infusion of dandelion and white willow bark before I left Coldharbour but regardless of that, pain bites like the dart of a devil. Surreptitiously I shift from one leg to the other. The dowager catches my attention, lifts her eyes peevishly to the vaulted ceiling. She has never been one for patience and, seeing her lack strengthens my resolve. I straighten my legs, surreptitiously stretch my back and calm my features, as if the delay is not in the least tedious.

An hour passes, the choir having exhausted its repertoire, begins again, while behind me the assembly fidgets and coughs. I crane my neck, seeking out Jasper who, on catching my eye, reads my unspoken request and goes in search of the king.

As protocol dictates, Henry is concealed from public view, seated behind a screen from where he can view the proceedings in comfort. After a few moments Jasper returns and resumes his stance by the font, wrists crossed at the hip, his eyes straight ahead. I sigh inwardly and resume my fidgeting from foot to foot. If Oxford does not arrive soon I will have to insist upon a seat, and I am loath to admit to such weakness, especially in front of the dowager.

What with the rain and the delay, the whole ceremony is beginning to feel doomed – I whisper a rapid prayer to dispel any hint of bad omen and begin to recite passages from Leviticus in my head.

Behind me, Prince Arthur stirs, his sudden squawk sending a ripple of surprise through the gathering, as if he has woken us all from private dreams. Cecily rocks him, croons softly until he falls asleep again. This is ridiculous. We have been waiting little short of three hours. Henry should do something. We can bear no further delay. It is quite unlike Oxford to be so unpunctual and quite unforgivable for him to keep us all waiting so long. There are limits to our gratitude even for one whose loyalty has been so enduring. I cannot imagine what is keeping him!

Arthur's cry increases to a fractious scream. He is probably craving his mother's teat. In desperation, Cecily hums a soothing tune that seems to be having little effect.

The tall curtains part and a cleric tiptoes across the nave and whispers in Jasper's ear. Close by, I hear Lincoln clear his throat and swear beneath his breath. Dorset snorts disbelievingly in reply. Turning stiffly, I impart my frostiest stare and they lapse into repentant silence.

Jasper, whom I assume has been in conference with the king, returns. He skips up the three steps to stand before the altar where he clears his throat and addresses the congregation.

"There will be no further delay. The king has instructed that his step-father, My Lord, the Earl of Derby, be appointed as the Earl of Oxford's proxy. The ceremony will now proceed."

My husband steps forward, tugs at the front of his tunic and fiddles with his cuffs before approaching the font. He bows courteously to the dowager and beams at the people gathered. With quiet amusement I recognise his proud surprise, his appreciation of being included in the ceremony and acknowledged as step-father to the king.

The prayers begin. There is a rustle of anticipation as the crowd strains to glimpse the child as he is carried to the font and his robes are loosened. Cecily transfers him to my husband's arms and Thomas looks down at my grandson with an incongruous, doting smile. I feel a little rush of pride.

John Alcock, Bishop of Worcester steps forward, raises his hands and begins to intone a blessing. The anointing is about to proceed when a commotion disturbs the tranquillity of the nave. Rapid footsteps sound on the tiled floor behind us as Holy water trickles from the tips of Alcock's fingers.

We turn as one to face the travel stained figure of the Earl of Oxford hurrying down the aisle. He whips off his hat, flicks moisture on the tiled floor.

"The roads are abominable; I have traversed torrents and flood to get here."

Thomas's ego deflates, his face falls and sharing his disappointment, I send him a look of sympathy. Oxford nods a hasty greeting to those closest to him, throws back his cloak and opens his arms to receive the prince. Arthur, who had finally begun to fall asleep, roars louder in protest at yet another change of plan. Oxford's chilly damp tunic must be a sharp contrast to Thomas' dry warm velvet. Our prince screams in fury and, as his forehead is anointed by holy water, he yells all the louder.

The bishop raises his voice above the din as another prayer follows. Obediently, I lower my head but for once, I have had my fill of praying. My lower back is craving the comfort of a chair, and my ever suffering knees are glad indeed that the end of the ceremony is in sight.

Cecily, wiping away a sentimental tear, takes possession of the bawling prince again. She bounces him, croons in his ear, and bears him off toward the shrine of St Swithen where we all take some much needed spices and hypocras.

Amid merriment and music, respects are paid to the bawling prince before Cecily bears him hastily back to his mother for nourishment. As his plaintive wails recede into the distance, the company sighs in relief and the mood relaxes. Thomas, recognising the tight set of my

41

jaw as an expression of pain, plays the part of a perfect spouse, offers me his arm and escorts me to a chair. I sink gratefully against the cushions and accept his offering of a cup of wine.

"Well, Margaret, what a fiasco!" he comments. I sip warm sweet malmsey and smile up at him.

"All was well in the end," I reply. "It will make an amusing story to relate when Arthur is old enough to appreciate it."

"Our young prince didn't seem to relish the experience of being welcomed into God's church."

Laughter bubbles in my throat as I begin to appreciate the farcical morning we have just experienced. Thomas places one hand on the back of my chair and looks about the room, his eye settling on Henry who is in conversation with Oxford. I follow his gaze.

"Were you very disappointed when Oxford turned up at the last moment?" I ask.

Thomas looks askance. "Who me? No, not at all," he lies.

As evening approaches and I am looking forward to the comfort of my apartments, I am summoned to the queen's bedside.

She is flushed, small droplets of sweat adorn her brow and her hand, when I take it, is burning. Angrily, I turn upon her woman.

"She has a high fever. Have the physicians been summoned?"

"Of course, My Lady, they are on their way. I thought they would have been here by now."

Another of Elizabeth's women brings a bowl of water and begins to dampen her mistress' brow. I look down at my son's wife; she is restless, her legs ever shifting beneath the sheet. I tug at the covers, tuck them tightly about her neck but peevishly she thrusts them back.

"You must keep warm, Elizabeth. We must burn the fever from you." As I tuck the bedding back around her, I speak loud and slow as if she is deaf, or stupid. She whimpers and fretfully tries to free her arms from the sheets. 'Make sure she takes plenty of fluid," I instruct the nurse. "Has the king been inform ..."

As I speak, the door is thrust open and Henry enters with the physician at his heels. While the doctor fusses around, holding the queen's hand, pulling her lower eyelid down, assessing the colour and taste of her urine, Henry stands impassively at the foot of the bed.

Does he care? I wonder. Does he realise how many women are taken by childbed fever? He stares at her for so long I have to cough to get his attention. He jerks his face toward me, smiles whitely, nods in approval of our efforts before turning and leaving us to the task. As he reaches the door the child stirs in his crib, his thin wail startling in the quiet of the chamber. Henry halts, turns his head to speak over his shoulder.

"Remove the child at once, the sickroom is no place for a prince."

I watch the king go. Part of me wants to run after him, to probe his feelings on the danger his queen is in, but duty makes me stay. If I had the charge of nursing her I would administer feverfew, lady's mantle, or perhaps pennyroyal, and sorrel to soothe her immoderate thirst. The doctor does none of this but instead murmurs about 'bad humours' and orders her to be bled. I watch as he brings forth a bowl from his bag, turn my head away as he makes the incision but my eye is drawn back in time to see Elizabeth's blood flow thick and red.

Can this be right? She still bleeds excessively from the birth, surely her constitution requires strengthening,

43

building up, not lowering. Perhaps I should speak out but he is the doctor, I am just the king's mother. I cannot know everything, although the bumbling medic before me can surely not be better informed than I.

After a few moments Elizabeth quietens, drifts off into a deep sleep. The physician, satisfied that his treatment has had the desired effect, gathers his things and prepares to leave.

"I shall return at dawn, My Lady, to ensure the queen continues to thrive. In the meantime, instruct her women to keep her covered, and ensure she drinks on the hour. I shall lodge close by, should I be needed again."

I could demand that he stay but he inspires little confidence – a village wise woman would do better. I allow him to leave and when he has gone, I have my seat moved closer to the bed. For many hours I sit beside Elizabeth, watching, fearful that her breast should cease to rise and fall.

Women die in childbed all the time. Wives are replaceable but Elizabeth is not. Although there are many who would crave to take her place as queen, it is only Elizabeth who binds the loyalty of York's adherents to us. She is the one who underpins our stability, prevents the old strife from breaking out again. As much as I hate to admit it, even to myself, we need Elizabeth, far more than she needs us.

She must survive.

An hour before dawn, the queen still tosses and turns, her forehead burning to the touch. I can either summon the physician back or take matters into my own hands.

I call my man forth from the shadows, send him to the prior with a list of ingredients, urging him to make haste. When she has recovered I will insist that Elizabeth studies the art of medicine. My physic garden has kept my body fit and my mind active – I swear by both the cultivation and administration of medicinal herbal lore.

While I wait for his return, I order the fire be fed and the window opened. The servant looks at me askance, fearful of the harmful night air but I ignore him. The cool fresh air has never injured me. It seems to take forever for my man to come back. He offers up the basket with a bow and I take myself into a side chamber and begin to prepare a remedy. As soon as it has sufficiently cooled I return to the bedside and slowly spoon the concoction into the queen's mouth. She grimaces, spits it out and I do not blame her for the taste is foul indeed. Leaning forward, I speak loudly into her ear.

"Elizabeth, it is Margaret, the king's mother. You must take this medicine; you need to get well, for the sake of the child and for the sake of Henry, and of England."

A tear trickles from her eye and for a moment I fear my words have not penetrated her fevered mind, yet just as I think she is too far gone to care, her eyes open a slit. I support her head, hold the spoon to her lips again and, this time she obediently opens her mouth and swallows the bitter mixture with a gulp. When the bowl is empty, I offer chamomile and lemon to take away the bitterness and she falls back on the pillow.

"Sleep now, Elizabeth, you will be better in the morning."

I hope I am right. Just to be sure, I kneel at the queen's bedside, praying for God's mercy until I can stand the pain in my knees no longer. Then I get up and pace the floor quietly so as not to disturb Elizabeth's slumbering women. Opening the shutter, I stand alone at the window and watch the lightening sky as it turns from grey to pink. When I can clearly discern the shingles on the opposite roof, I return to the bedside where I sit and count her breaths.

Morning is a long time coming. At first light the doctor returns in a flurry of cheerful complaints about the chill of the dawn. He leans over the bed, feels Elizabeth's brow, opens her mouth to look at her tongue, and pronounces the fever broken. Since I am in no mood to exchange words with a charlatan, I allow him to claim the credit but make a mental note to advise Henry to engage another physician at his earliest opportunity.

Satisfied that the queen is now enjoying a restful sleep, I issue a list of instruction to her yawning attendants and return to my apartments. Too tired to eat, or even pray I bid my woman help me disrobe so I may retire to my bed.

I sleep deeply and for much longer than I intended but when I eventually return to the queen's chamber, I find the dowager has taken my place at her bedside. Elizabeth is propped up on pillows, her face is wan, and her expression languid but she appears to be fever free and aware of her surroundings. The dowager looks up when I enter, her face creased with anxiety but she does not relinquish her seat. My eyes fall upon their clasped hands. Elizabeth Woodville's greeting is rude and taut with anger.

"Why was I not summoned? I am the queen's mother and should have been called at once."

In truth, I had not given her a thought, all my care had been for Elizabeth. My wish was to save the queen, and preserve Henry's wife so she may provide him with future sons. My concern had been only for the mother of the future Prince of Wales. I had given no thought to the dowager queen.

"There was no time," I prevaricate. "The physicians and I attended to the queen. There was such a crush of people, I did not tarry long myself.'

Why am I lying? Why can I not confess how afraid I had been? There is no shame in sitting up all night with one's daughter in law; why do I wish to keep my care for her a secret?

Elizabeth tries and fails to pull herself up on her pillow. She falls back, her eyes narrowed as if she is trying to see through a thick mist.

"I had the strangest dream," she says, frowning in her effort to recall it. "I remember now ... I was in danger of falling from a very high place. I called for you, Mother, but you did not come. M - My Lady, the king's mother was there instead, she held tightly to my hand and would not let me fall ..."

Our eyes meet and she smiles at me. I wonder how far she can determine dream from reality.

*

I draw my shawl closer about my shoulders and move nearer to the hearth. It is almost June yet the weather has made a sudden retreat back to winter. I am tired of spending so much time indoors and long for the balmy summer days in the gardens. I have made detailed plans of the changes I wish to make to the grounds of Coldharbour and am doing my best to get Elizabeth to show an interest in improving those at Westminster too. But the queen remains lethargic. She sleeps too much and tires at the slightest exertion, although I have made sure she takes rhubarb and ginger twice a day.

While we wait for Henry and Jasper to return from counsel, Elizabeth and I discuss the plans for her coronation which Henry promises will take place before

47

the year is out. She lowers her needlework to her lap, puts a hand to her brow, alerting the healer in me.

"Have you another headache?"

"Not a bad one, just a dull throb. It will pass."

"Would you like me to send for an infusion of camomile?"

She smiles, the bones of her face strained. "Would you? That might help."

I get up and ring the bell to summon my woman and as I do so Henry comes in, shaking drops of rain from his cloak.

"It is surely not raining again?" I exclaim, clicking my fingers at a page to help the king disrobe. "I had hoped we had seen an end to it."

"Not in this country, Mother. I swear I have seen more wet weather here than in all my years in France."

I turn from the table and hand him a cup of wine.

"Yes, well England has other benefits that the king of France can only dream of."

He nods a greeting to his wife and settles himself in my seat.

"And what might they be?"

"Oh ..." I rack my brains trying to think of something but am happily relieved of the need to reply by Jasper who bursts suddenly through the door.

"Henry, Sire – I have had tidings from Ireland."

"Ireland?" Henry turns in his seat to face him, his brow lined with questions. "What news can that be?"

"A boy, Your Grace, has turned up in Dublin claiming to be the Earl of Warwick – the people there are hailing him welcome."

As Jasper continues his tale, explaining how the lad with hair as fair as a Plantagenet has managed to capture the hearts of the Irish, Henry's face grows dark, his eyes narrowed in thought. When Jasper reaches the end of his report, Elizabeth sits up straight, frowning though her megrim.

"Warwick? But my cousin is lodged in the Tower. How can this be?"

"I do not know." He frowns into his cup.

"Is it not strange, Your Grace, that it comes so soon after Lincoln's disappearance from court?"

"That fact had not escaped me, Jasper." Henry rises, slams his wine cup on the table. I look from one to another, following their line of thought.

"You think John of Lincoln is involved of this?"

Lincoln was the nephew and named heir of King Richard, his nose firmly put out of joint by Henry's accession. Although he swore fealty to us and accepted a position in our court, he has been restless, unhappy. We should have seen his defection coming.

Henry breathes heavily down his nose and looks at me for a long moment as he processes his thoughts.

"I suspect so, and I would not be surprised if Lovell had a part in it too but we should not jump to conclusions, I suppose."

Jasper issues a humourless laugh.

"I would say the matter is plain. Lovell has been at large for weeks, and then Lincoln, his erstwhile ally and companion also makes himself absent from court without a by-your-leave. They have to be at the heart of this, this … this … treason!"

"But, Henry …" Elizabeth leans forward in her seat, her needlework fallen to the floor. "If they are indeed behind it, they cannot be working alone. Where would they find men to fight for them, who is funding them?"

Their eyes meet. Elizabeth's are wide, her face pale; Henry's cheeks are red, his mouth set in a thin red line. I realise I have seldom seen him so angry.

49

"A very good question, my dear. A very good question indeed." With no further word he turns on his heel and storms to the door, throws it open.

"Wait, Henry!"

Jasper leaps to his feet, drains his cup and hurries in Henry's wake. Elizabeth, forgetting etiquette, grips my sleeve.

"My Lady Mother, how can this be? Who is helping them, and who is this boy in Dublin?"

"Henry will discover his identity. You may be sure of that. He is an imposter and will soon be dealt with. Do not worry. The king has spies throughout England and in Ireland too – word will come soon enough. I suspect your aunt in Burgundy is elbow deep in the matter."

"Aunt Margaret? Of course, she was furious after the death of Uncle Richard but it all seems to have happened so quickly. Who can the boy in Ireland be?"

I leave the repeated question unanswered, but I can tell she is wondering about her long lost brothers – Henry's rival. She has not yet realised that should one of her brothers return and attempt to usurp Henry's place, he will also usurp Arthur's. I make no reply but her question resounds in my head. Who is this boy – this Irish imposter? We know it cannot be Warwick but ... who else could it be? The stories of a boy with bright Plantagenet hair imply connection with Edward IV but what connection?

My hand creeps slowly to my throat, my fingers icy on my own skin, and I shiver suddenly as a log subsides in the hearth. Something feels terribly, terribly wrong.

Jasper's tidings have destroyed my peace of mind. As we dine in the great hall my eyes settle on the different faces gathered. I am constantly considering their loyalty, their possible defection. Apart from John of

50

Lincoln, our court is intact but should this boy's claim take hold of men's hearts, they may begin to trickle away one by one and rekindle the war between York and Lancaster we all hoped was dead. The boy in Ireland must be captured and stopped, for his very existence jeopardises the security of my son, and also the joy of my heart, my little prince, Arthur.

Elizabeth continues to ail until well into the new year. What should be a time of peace is beset with worry for her health, and anxiety about increasing political unrest. Lincoln, whom we had once thought reconciled to our reign, has now taken refuge at the court of Burgundy. Rumours persist that he is raising an army, funded by Duchess Margaret, to invade our shores and replace my son with a counterfeit Earl of Warwick. Henry and I know beyond doubt that young Warwick is held fast in the Tower of London. Whoever Lincoln is parading as the rightful heir is an imposter, a counter in a game of power but we hold the trump card. If required, the real Warwick can be produced but ... and there my confidence plummets.

The real 'Warwick' is dim-witted and plain, their false claimant to the name is not. He is princely, with Plantagenet bright hair and the confidence to match it. The public is fickle. If they can be persuaded the boy is indeed one of the long lost princes of York they will shun the genuine Earl and follow the imposter.

"We will stop them, of course," Henry says when we are alone together. "They are doomed to failure."

"Well, no one would want a child on the throne again. I am surprised at Lincoln. He fooled me into believing in his loyalty to us."

"Mother, I very much doubt Margaret of Burgundy intends to crown the boy. He is but a figure head, a romantic notion of a wronged prince. When – if –

51

they were to win a battle against us, he would no doubt die an untimely death, leaving the way free for Lincoln himself to rule."

"Lincoln!"

"You will remember our defeat of Richard at Bosworth destroyed Lincoln's future as king also. He was Gloucester's nephew, his natural heir…"

"I know that, Henry. I need no lesson in ancestry. I had hoped he had put that behind him. I hoped his loyalty was unfeigned."

Henry snorts derisively. "I think loyalty is genuine only until such time as the crown comes within a man's reach."

"In that case … none in our court are truly loyal."

"Exactly, Mother, sad as it is."

Kenilworth May 1487

The sun, that has been so tardy this year decides to show its face at last but there is no time to idle, no opportunity to enjoy it. We are thrown into a frenzy of preparation for battle; orders are issued, lists are compiled and the bailey begins to fill with laden wagons. I watch from Kenilworth's highest tower as the men make ready for the muster at Nottingham. Despite the barely suppressed jubilation of those untried in war, and the sunshine that glints dazzlingly on their armour, the sight reminds me of darker days; days of conflict I thought had passed.

I can almost smell the approaching battle, sense the fear, the anticipation in the air. The faces of our seasoned warriors are dark with intent, their actions measured and determined amid the chaos of preparation.

I follow the path of a young squire, laden with his master's armour, hurries to do his bidding. He dodges past a groom who battles to hitch a pair of panicked horses to a baggage cart. Once they are firmly tethered, a man leaps into the seat, takes up the reins and, weighed down with supplies, the wagon creaks slowly across the bailey, a dog darting from beneath the wheels, just in time. I hear a shout and look up to see Jasper seeking Henry in the melee.

Jasper has grown stouter since his exile ended and his greying hair is bright in the sunshine. Henry lifts a hand in response to his call and I watch them navigate a path through the confusion, coming together by the forge. Jasper places a hand on Henry's shoulder, speaks rapidly into his ear, embellishing his words with rapid hand movements. My son's face pale and drawn, testament to sleepless nights and work heavy days. He is biting his lower lip, either from nerves or anxiety to be on the road.

Henry is no war monger. He does not have his father's hunger for battle, a greed that Jasper still owns. Henry does not look for glory; he yearns for security and peace in his realm. His unsettled youth has left him with a longing for stability. I wish for it too. I am sick to death of war. I close my eyes against a sudden image of Henry struck down, a gash in his side, his life's blood seeping into England's soil. I send up a prayer for his protection.

"Preserve my son," I whisper to the ever present Lord. "Whatever happens, bring him home, save his dear soul."

Too soon, they are ready to take their leave of us and I descend from my eyrie and join Elizabeth at the entrance to the hall. Henry sprints up the steps to bid us farewell. He slides an arm around her waist and clasps her briefly to him, his lips grazing her forehead. I look on and she has the grace to blush when she sees me watching. When it is my turn, I cling to his hands, lean in close so that only he can hear my words.

53

"Stay out of the fight, Henry. You are indispensable. You must preserve yourself for the sake of England, for the sake of your son and future sons."

I do not mention my own need of him. His grip tightens on my fingers.

"Do not worry, Mother. I have no intention of putting myself at risk. I shall crush this imposter like a beetle beneath my heel and then return as soon as I may to continue my rule."

But my mind is not appeased. Does he think Edmund rode to fight William Herbert with the intention of dying? Did Harry ride off to Barnet with thoughts of death? And Richard of Gloucester: when he made his last charge, was it in the certainty of victory, or defeat?

I keep my dark thoughts to myself. I have absolute faith in God. He will bring my son home where we can continue our quest to bring peace to England. God will spare him so he may complete the task he has begun.

I allow no hint of my simmering fear to show as, with a last wave, Henry climbs on his horse and flashing me a jaunty smile.

"I will see you anon," he calls, before raising his arm and calling to his household knights to ride out. United in anxiety, Elizabeth and I link arms and retreat into the warm security of the keep. I blow my nose, denying tears by feigning an approaching cold. The torture of waiting begins afresh.

It is agony not knowing how the king and his army are faring. If I were a man I would order my horse saddled and ride off to join them. But, most powerful woman in the kingdom or not, I am forced to wait here and tolerate the constant questions of Henry's queen. Her voice echoes in my head until I feel like screaming, or speaking out in anger, banishing her from my presence.

But, as always, I endure it. I have withstood worse than this.

But, on the day the men clatter back into the bailey, jubilant at their victory, I realise I should never have been afraid. I am in high spirits as I watch Henry leap from his horse and see at once he is quite unscathed. He looks up at the hall where Elizabeth and I are waiting. His expression is one of undisguised triumph and he hurries toward us with a newfound confidence in his step.

"Mother."

He kisses my cheek, retains my hand in his while he greets his wife. She clings to his sleeve, words that nobody heeds falling from her lips. Close behind Henry comes my husband, Thomas for whom I have quite forgotten to fear. He places his hand on my shoulder, smiling a welcome but when he opens his mouth to speak, Jasper hurries up the steps with a child at his side – a half-grown boy of some ten years old.

"Who is this?" I ask but Henry, his hand on the small of my back, urges us inside.

"I am need of refreshment, Mother," he says, "and a warm soak. I shall tell all while my bath tub is filled."

While wine and victuals are brought to table, Henry and Jasper begin to tell the story, one filling in when the other gives pause.

"Lincoln is dead? You are quite sure?" I ask. Henry wipes his mouth on the sleeve of his jerkin.

"Quite sure, Mother. I saw it with my own eyes ... although, in some ways, I could wish he was not."

"Why? So he can stir further dissent against us?"

He puts down his cup, his eyes serious.

"No, but were he alive we could persuade him to tell us who else was involved in this uprising. Who carried messages, and who spent coin upon it? Lincoln did not fund it, that is for sure. The miserable priest – Simons -, who seems to have been the boy's protector, is also dead. I would give a lot to know the truth but hopefully Lovel will soon be apprehended..."

"Lovel escaped unscathed again? He is slippery – and seems to have a knack of evading capture!"

"Indeed: but not this time. My men are hunting him, they will find him for certain."

"And this boy ..." We all turn in the child's direction. He is huddled close to the hearth, his eyes huge and round, his so-called Plantagenet bright hair, tarnished with mud and damp with sweat. "This is the child they paraded as the son of York? He looks like a beggar and ... there is some disparity in age, surely?"

"Yes." Henry gets up and moves toward the boy who cowers away as if fearful he will feel the blow of the king's cuff. "Miserable little whelp but I hold no grudge against him. It is clear from the looks of him that he was a pawn in a bigger fool's game."

"Throw him in gaol and be done with him." I sniff and brush my hands briskly together as if I have touched something foul.

Henry is silent. The moments pass, only the dry wheeze of the young boy's terror can be heard until the king turns away.

"No." Henry says. "I shall make an example of him but not in that way. I shall put him to work in my kitchens as befits his status and there, all that see him shall know his pitiful tale and mock him for it."

The boy, Simnel, does not take his terrified eyes from the king's face. I feel a twinge of pity for him. Henry is right. Poor young fool, his only crime is in the shade of his hair, and possibly the taint of bastard Plantagenet parentage. Perhaps it would be kinder to throw him in gaol as I suggested than condemn him to a life of mockery, but Henry is king. His will is mine.

Later, when my woman is brushing out my hair, Thomas comes to my apartments. It is many months since we have been alone together. At first, I fear he has come to claim his conjugal right, which I am long past desiring. I stiffen and signal for my veil to be replaced to cover my hair before I rise and move toward him.

"To what do I owe this honour?" I ask politely.

"Oh, nothing. Do not fear, Margaret, your virtue is safe."

His eyes sweep over me without admiration. It is hard now to recall those brief heady days when we took delight in our marriage bed. That passion was borne of loneliness, fear and desperation. Before Henry was King I needed the comfort of a man, a strong man whose status and authority would help put my son on the throne. Now I am the King's Mother and powerful in my own right, I am in need of no-one, and avoid intimacy. His coming this evening is unsettling. I purse my lips and silently wish him to the dogs.

I watch as he pulls out a chair and sits down. He has a bruise on his forehead and a long scratch on his cheek.

"You were in the fight?" I ask belatedly as I take a seat as far from him as is polite. I smooth my skirts, the crimson velvet soft between my fingers.

"No, I was part of Henry's guard. These wounds are the result of an excitable young mount, unused to the din of battle. You should be grateful I persuaded the king to stay out of it."

"Indeed, I am. Tell me, what do you make of this boy, Simnel; who do you think he really is?"

"I think he is a nobody, some sprat spawned on a bawd by George or Edward perhaps but of no import. He will be happier in the kitchens."

"Were there many losses?"

"I didn't stop to count them but yes, there were heavy losses on both sides."

Silence falls while I pray for the souls of the departed. When I raise my head, Thomas yawns and stretches, showing an unhealthy coated tongue. I avert my eyes.

"Perhaps, while this victory is still fresh, Henry will give some thought to Elizabeth's coronation. Once she is crowned, York's old adherents may be appeased and begin to accept us."

"Her mother speaks of nothing else."

"The dowager is a constant source of irritation. I do not know what can be done with her."

Thomas leans forward. "I have heard that our dowager queen possibly knows more of this recent affair than she cares for us to know."

"What do you mean?"

"I mean that perhaps ... she and her older sons are in some way complicit."

I shake my head. "What sort of woman would plot against her own daughter, her own grandson? That is a ridiculous idea!"

"Is it though, Margaret? She would gain much ... at your expense."

The die has been cast and his words will not leave me alone. All night I toss and turn, the thought of Elizabeth Woodville's possible involvement in treason against us robbing me of sleep.

Farnham

58

The queen languishes for weeks, overseeing the raising of her son from her sick bed but by Christmas, although still suffering from the occasional malaise, she has resumed full duties at court. We leave Winchester at the end of October and reside at Farnham where the prince's household is to be established.

A large personal staff has been engaged, with his own chamberlain, a lady governor, a nurse, and several rockers to soothe the royal cradle. I have advised the king that Arthur's staff should be liveried as befits the household of a prince and readily, he heeds my suggestion.

Garbed in their fine velvet, they swear solemn oaths of service to the chamberlain, and then pledge fealty to Henry and to Prince Arthur. Every month, Henry and I meet with John Alcock, Bishop of Worcester and Peter Courtenay of Exeter who are to advise us on the prince's upbringing. His education is vital. He must become the most learned prince in Christendom; a patron of the arts and learning. There is so much to be remembered, so much that must not be overlooked.

Every morning the prince is brought to the queen so she may inspect him and rest assured that he is thriving. He is a lusty baby; gaining weight quickly and Lady Elizabeth Darcy who has been set in charge of the royal nursery says he is already ruling the roost. The women appointed to rock the cradle report that he sleeps light and wakes often, demanding to be fed. In the back ground his nurse concurs this, complaining loudly of sore dugs to all who will listen.

I had hoped that Elizabeth would recover quickly from childbed and soon be able to announce the arrival of a brother for little Arthur. Henry may have his heir but a king needs more than one son. A boy who will one day be king requires brothers to support him and champion his cause, help him strengthen his hold on the country. There can never be too many sons, or daughters for that matter, who will marry and forge strong alliances. If the nursery is to increase in stock, Elizabeth must recover soon. I continue to dose her regularly with raspberry and nettle leaf, and red clover to restore her fertility.

Arthur is perfect. I visit as often as I can, startling the nursery staff by cradling him on my shoulder, patting his back until his wind is broken, offering advice to the nurse. Tradition demands that the soon to be anointed Prince of Wales should reside away from court in his own household and, in a few days, we will be leaving him here at Farnham.

It will be no easy parting and I am sure I will grieve as deeply as Elizabeth. It would be easier for all of us if another prince was already budding in the queen's womb but there is no sign that relations between her and the king have yet been resumed.

On the day of our departure the queen emerges from the nursery after bidding farewell to her son. She is red eyed but resolute, and I watch with some admiration as she mounts her horse and takes up the reins.

Although it is almost thirty years since I was forced to leave my own son behind yet I remember well the pain of it. Now, watching as my grandson is left in the care of trusted strangers, I reflect how my grief would have been tenfold had I been able to foresee the future.

From the day I wed Harry Stafford, I enjoyed only snatched moments with Henry but I knew he was safe. Even when he fell into the hands of the Herberts, I trusted Anne Deveraux to have a care for him. My real sorrow did not begin until after Edgecot when he fled into exile with Jasper. Had I known then we would not

60

meet again for another fourteen years ... I would not have born it. I pray Elizabeth is more fortunate.

Westminster -1487

I pull up short on entering the queen's apartments unannounced. She is sitting at the hearth with her mother; they look up, almost guiltily, at my approach. I incline my head politely and join them as if I am invited and not in the least irked to see them there together. I have tried very hard to get closer to the queen but in truth her mother is always in the way. My friendship with her sister, Cecily, is far easier. I always feel as if Elizabeth is harbouring a secret resentment, or keeping something from me.

The dowager looks down her nose. "I was commiserating with Elizabeth on her separation from little Arthur. I was fortunate in that Edward never saw the necessity of separate households for our children. We kept the royal nursery close to us at all times."

King Edward never saw the necessity for many things. He flaunted his mistresses under his queen's nose, blind to the shame and upset it caused her but I refrain from saying so. Instead, I ask after Arthur's health, for I know Elizabeth receives news of him each day.

"He is very well, Lady Mother. Lady Darcy reports that the colic has passed and he grows stronger by the day. He can already sit up unaided."

"He is like his father in that," I beam as I launch into a story of Henry's early days. "Shortly after he learned to sit, I was forced to leave him in his uncle's care. I was so glad when he learned to pen a letter. They were so precious to me. In fact, I have some of them still. They are yellowed now, and wrinkled with much reading."

"I should like you to show them to me some day," the queen smiles. I beam in agreement while the dowager shifts irritably in her seat. I note with some satisfaction that the queen has regained most of the weight she lost after the birth and a vital glow is returning to her cheeks. If this continues Henry will soon be tempted back to the marriage bed and we can begin to hope for a second prince.

"None of my children suffered from colic." The dowager announces, as if colic is some failing of the mother. "It may be Arthur gets that from Henry also."

"I do not recall *the king*" I emphasise pointedly, "suffering from it greatly either but I am given to understand it is commonplace at the three month stage."

"Perhaps you misremember, or had ceased to care for him before he began to suffer."

She is infuriating. I long to stand up and smartly slap her self-satisfied face but I must remember who I am. I am no longer her minion to be rebuked but I am risen too far above her to lower myself. I refuse to enter into her squabble.

"You may be right."

It takes all my strength to appear so agreeable but it is clear from the two spots of colour on her cheeks that my reticence is infuriating her. I make a mental note to speak to Henry. I am tired of her flaunting about the palace as if she is still queen.

I wish I could banish her from our presence as one would exclude a tiresome dog from the room. If only she would retire from court of her own will.

Woking –September 1487

The queen's eyes are red from weeping. I make my excuses and retire to Woking for a few weeks while she

62

comes to terms with the fact that her mother has suddenly taken it upon herself to retire to Bermondsey Abbey. The queen's brother, Dorset, now occupies rooms in the Tower of London. Henry and I are certain both the dowager and her son were knee deep in the conspiracy to rob my son of his throne.

In her desperation to believe the imposter Lambert Simnel was in fact her long lost son, the dowager worked against the king, and her own daughter! She is both unfit and unsafe to be allowed her freedom but we draw short of imprisonment. Let her hatch her conspiracies at Bermondsey where she is out of our sight but under the watch of the loyal Cluniac monks. Our court is well rid of her influence, and so is the queen.

Yet, I am not entirely easy with her banishment. Elizabeth Woodville was, after all, once my queen, my mistress and, for a short time, my friend. I am inwardly shamed of my concurrence in her punishment but I hide it well.

Henry, mistakenly believing he can salve his wife's tears with riches, removes the dowager's goods and chattels and bestows them on her daughter. But still the queen quietly weeps and, sometimes the mood at court is so demoralising, I feel like joining her.

In search of peace, I retire to Woking for a few weeks. As I walk beside the moat where dark brown trout slumber in the still green waters, I remember happier days when Harry was still alive. It takes me a little while to realise that at the time I had not known I was happy. Perhaps happiness is a feeling that can only be enjoyed in retrospect, perhaps it is something we never truly recognise while it is here.

A flurry of small birds in the thicket pulls me from my dreaming, and somewhere a blackbird begins to sing, ethereal in the sunshine. I close my eyes and sigh, allowing the strain of the past weeks to dissipate. I realise that, despite my vast household, I am a thousand miles from my troubles here. I must remember to be grateful.

My life as the King's Mother is very unlike my old one but also different to how I imagined it would be. I have little time for idleness, and leisure is a luxury. Whereas once the days passed as slow as a snail across the garden path, these days I seldom have the ease to work in the gardens. I miss the contact with the soil, being in tune with the turning of the season, the cyclical changing of the year. Nowadays I can only snatch moments.

Before I return to the hall I pass through the gardens, pluck a rose and hold it to my nose to inhale the light heady scent. Noticing a green fly clinging to the stem, I take my kerchief and squish it before turning my attention to others that are infesting my favourite blooms. These green flies, once in residence, quickly multiply, feasting upon the sap until the blooms fail and the plant is destroyed. I detest these parasites even more than I hate slugs and snails – at least the latter do not attack my roses.

I become so involved in my task that I forget what I am supposed to be doing and the sun is high in the sky when I recall that I had been on my way to a meeting. Reginald Bray is waiting to discuss the improvements to the solar. I look at my spoiled kerchief and tuck it guiltily into my sleeve as I hurry along the path. A gardener struggles from his knees to pull his forelock and wish me good day. I smile blithely and call a bright hello to Henry Parker as I pass him by. But I feel better already and know I was right to return to Woking.

Perhaps I will stay longer than I had intended, or maybe I will take a short tour of all my properties. It is several months since I have been to Lathom, which is also currently undergoing vast improvement and expansion. There is no real need for me to travel directly back to court, Henry can manage without me for a while, he always has the benefit of Jasper's advice. But I cannot tarry away from court for too long, for the queen's coronation is set for November and I must be there to ensure the arrangements are in place and things are carried out correctly.

<u>Westminster Abbey – 25th November 1487</u>

I enter the queen's apartment where Cecily and her cousin Margaret are assisting Elizabeth with her toilette. She is almost ready, and there are just the finishing touches to apply before we set off for the Abbey. I stand on tiptoe in attempt to see over the heads of the women who are overseen by the Duchess of Suffolk, the queen's aunt. Belatedly noticing my presence they murmur apology and greet me with deference. The duchess reveals no resentment for my part in her sister, Elizabeth Woodville's removal from court. Cecily, who has become almost a friend since I took her into my household and arranged her marriage to my step brother, is especially warm in her welcome. She curtseys low, as if I were a queen before drawing me into the conversation.

"My Lady," she says. "We were just admiring the workmanship on the queen's gown. Is it not fine?"

Running my eye over the vision that stands before me, I move closer, merging with the women to examine the exquisite needlework on the royal sleeve.

"It is lovely," I say. "Just as it should be."

The queen's ladies are dressed similarly but not identically to Elizabeth. The air in the room is perfumed with the fragrance of youth – the girls shine with robust fertility. Anne, one of the queen's younger sisters turns from the window, her voice quivering with the excitement of the day.

"The sun is shining," she says. "I am so glad for you, Elizabeth. It would never do to be crowned on a drizzly day."

Cecily looks up from lacing the queen's sleeve.

"I think mother was crowned in the rain. Father used to say that it did not matter for she shone so brightly, the sun was not required."

The girls laugh, sobering one by one as they remember their father and happier days. One or two guilty looks are cast in my direction but I smile blithely as if their longing for the past is not casting me back into obscurity.

The queen sighs, her expression suddenly sorrowful. It is clear she is missing her mother and no doubt wishing she were here to witness the triumph of her day. Seeing she is close to tears, I dispel the sudden gloom with a clap of my hands, gaining the full attention of the room.

"Now, are we ready? Let me look at you all."

The queen blinks rapidly and pulls herself together, beckoning her sisters and cousin to her side. With a great rustle of fine fabric they stand straight and tall for my inspection. Elizabeth is quite perfect, her mother's ethereal beauty that I always found too brittle, is softened by the earthiness of her father. Elizabeth seems to glow and I cannot recall ever having come close to such flawlessness before. The gown of white cloth of gold suits her perfectly, the ermine furred mantle cascades from her shoulders, pooling like water about her feet. Her hair is left loose, covered only by a coif of the new style, cross laced with a network of golden cord.

66

"You are quite, quite lovely, Elizabeth," I say in spite of myself and as I signal for Cecily to come forward to fasten the ties of the purple velvet mantle about the queen's shoulders, I wipe a trickle of moisture from my cheek. I am becoming sentimental in my middle years.

"Keep your heads up and remember to smile and wave to the crowd as we pass."

I twitch the skirts of my gown and lead the procession down the stair to the lower hall where I bid the queen farewell and go by another route to join my son at the abbey.

As is tradition, Henry and I are invisible to the congregation. We are screened from view but able to see all that unfolds below. I have just settled in my seat when a blast of trumpets alerts us to the entrance of the queen. I lean forward the better to see.

Elizabeth follows the bishops through the nave, her head high, her chin level but her cheeks are burnished with emotion. I watch with detachment, assessing her, anxious should she make a mistake but, as always, I find little to complain of. She has been raised to be a queen and attended to her lessons well.

She succeeds in hiding her nerves. Although she must be anxious, her hands do not shake, her knees seem not to tremble. To the onlooker it might be something she has done every day for the whole of her life. Pride stirs in my breast and not for the first time I acknowledge, but only to myself, that she is a worthy queen for my son.

The voices of the choir fill the roof, soaring to the heavens, belittling those of us gathered in God's presence. Beside me, Henry leans forward, his elbows on his knee, a slight smile playing on his lips. I wonder again about his feelings for her. In public they are courteous; he is always deferent and she always receives him with smiles, accepting his attentiveness as her due. She has never said a word against him, but of course, she would never speak ill of him to me. Only a fool would do so.

I would pay much to know the true state of affairs between them. When they are alone, do they laugh? Is their marriage bed warm and boisterous, or is it cold and dutiful? And if it *is* joyous, why is Elizabeth not already with child again?

I have placed women among her household servants, some might call them spies. Their duty is to report to me any sign of a morning megrim, or lack of appetite that might signal the announcement of another pregnancy but there has been nothing. I cannot fathom why a man and woman of good age, having borne one healthy son, have not yet conceived another. I must consult my physician, he may know some remedy or some way of ensuring another child is begotten before the year is out.

The music stops, the assembly shuffle and cough as the bishop prepares to request God's blessing on our gathering. Since the queen was born of York, I had thought this day would irk me but instead I find I am strangely touched by it. Women of our position, in our time, are tested, sometimes to the limit. I am testament to that. I find myself proud of the way she conceals her inner uncertainty, her fear of taking a wrong step or muddling her words and applaud her at each stage of the ceremony that passes without mishap.

The clear tones of the archbishop's voice pulls me from my reverie and I watch as Cecily assists the queen to prostrate herself at the altar. A prayer follows. I close my eyes and call down God's blessing, repeating the much muttered prayer, asking that the queen may soon be fruitful. One son is not enough; not nearly enough.

At the archbishop's signal, Cecily helps her sister to rise. Elizabeth stands straight as her bodice is loosened and her upper body exposed to allow the Archbishop of Canterbury to anoint her on the forehead and between her breasts. She does not flinch from our eyes and I realise she is braver than I would be in her place.

There is not a sound in the abbey as all eyes are upon the queen as she is seated upon the royal throne. Everyone holds their breath as the crown of England is lowered onto her head. Then, after a moments pause, we erupt into spontaneous, joyful ovation.

I find myself standing, applauding and calling out as loudly as the rest, although she cannot see and certainly cannot hear me above the hubbub. Her wish, and that of York's old adherents is fulfilled. Elizabeth is crowned queen consort and hopefully that will bring appeasement and peace to England.

All the queen need do now is prove herself fertile again and give my son another boy. Her prime duty is to fill the royal nursery with princes and princesses to secure our Tudor line. I shall not rest easy until it is so.

<u>Westminster Palace - January 1488</u>

The coronation has wearied me so I retire to Coldharbour House, where I am far enough away to enjoy some respite from court but close enough to return should the need arise. I spend my time in contemplation. Communing with God and searching my soul to ensure I am following my prescribed path.

I also find the time to catch up with correspondence. As duty dictates I deal with matters of state before I turn my attention to the more pleasurable ties of family and friends.

My man comes in to replenish the fires in my parlour, stacking them high while I pen a long overdue

69

letter to my dearest sister, Edith, whose son Richard is to marry the queen's cousin, Margaret.

Soon after Henry's accession I turned my mind to arranging the best of marriages for my closest kin, and young Margaret, the daughter of the hapless George, Duke of Clarence, is an ideal match for my nephew.

As always, I have one eye on the future. I know my grandson will need strong family alliances when it is his turn to be king. Margaret's marriage to my nephew is satisfying to all, tightening the bonds between York and Lancaster just as securely as my son's union with Elizabeth. Our family must band together against outsiders, form a strong iron band to protect the Tudor rule. Both Richard and Margaret seem content with the arrangement and I hope for Richard's sake that his affianced bride is more fertile than her cousin, the queen.

The queen's fertility, or lack of it, is beginning to dominate my thoughts. Another son is vital to our continuing security yet every month the queen bleeds and the royal cradle remains empty. I am at a loss as to what I can do about it.

On a bright chilly January morning, I accept the king's invitation to break my fast with him. Henry tears a strip from a loaf of still warm bread and shows me a list of dignitaries he plans to invite to the Easter joust. I cast my eye over the names, frown and shake my head at one or two, and offer more suitable replacements. As he scores black lines through those I have rejected and scribbles a fresh name in the margin, I take the bold step of quizzing him as to the state of his marriage bed.

"I can barely wait for the news of another grandson. I hope it will come very soon." I say, my own bold words making my heart beat a little faster.

Henry looks up, suddenly flushed and startled, but he gives me no answer. Instead, he deftly deflects my curiosity by turning the conversation to Collyweston, the manor he knows I have craved since I first lay eyes upon it. He places a document before me – a deed detailing the extent of the grounds, the vast estates and properties that are parcelled with it. The only requirement for the property to become mine is his royal seal. My palm grows moist as I contemplate taking possession of it.

My quest for a grandson momentarily forgotten, I take up the document and pore eagerly over the description of a sumptuous hall, well-stocked forests, and rivers teeming with fish. There is the making of a fine chapel, extensive gardens and a park, all of which can be further improved. I am desperate to transform the whole property into a palace. Collyweston is a place such as I have always dreamed and Henry, in thanks of my past services, is gifting it to me. My happiness is brimming over but I am careful not to allow too much joy to show in my words. Coolly I smile my appreciation.

"I shall send Master Bray at your earliest convenience so you may discuss the terms," I say. "I trust him to work in my best interest..."

"... surely, Mother, you can trust me to do likewise." Henry is half laughing, half serious, waiting for me to turn the matter to levity.

"You can never be too sure," I jest, tapping the side of my nose. "I have learned to trust no one. I have been cheated once too often before."

Henry's answering guffaw wakes his fool who has been dozing at the hearth. The little man yawns and stretches, climbs to his feet and waddles to the table. He rubs his eyes, cocks his head to his king

"Cheating is a game," he says, "and every game has its cheats. Show me a cheat and I'll show you a fool, show me a fool and I'll show you a cheat ..." The punchline as we both know is *Show me a fool and I'll show you a king* but he knows better than to take the joke so far.

He rolls up, clutching his belly at his own poor wit, while Henry and I exchange glances, neither of us prepared to put his wit to the test in case he is too wise for either of us.

"Peace, my good fool," Henry says, "be so good as to leave me with my mother. We have business matters to attend to."

As the fool skips from the room, I clutch the deeds of Collyweston to my bosom. I am reluctant to part with them now they are in my possession. I look at my son, so tall and handsome even at this hour of the morning and recall my quest to know the state of his marriage.

"How is Elizabeth?" I ask, as if the answer is of no great import.

"Not pregnant, Mother, as far as I am aware. How is your husband?"

He has turned the table so sharply that for a moment I fumble for a reply beneath his penetrating stare.

"He is well, I imagine," I manage at last, although in truth I have not seen him for a week or more. My spies inform me that he is spending more time than is seemly with one of the queen's women, a woman young enough to be his daughter.

I do not care. He cannot hurt me by it for I am done with such things. The older I become I find I have less desire for bed sport and, although I hold no grudge against him, I often resent the shackle of a husband. I dislike how Thomas struts about court in his role of 'father to the king' when in fact, he barely knows Henry at all.

72

Henry's accession has provided me with my heart's desire. I not only have my son home in England but he is in the securest position I could wish for. His status as king makes me a powerful woman, and it irks to share my glory with Thomas. I have no need of a husband, either in my bed or at my table. Were I a widow I would be totally free to make my own decisions, run my own households, and issue my own orders.

Henry shuffles his papers, places them in neat piles about his desk, before holding out his hand for the deeds. I take one more lingering look before reluctantly handing them back, keeping my eye on them as he places the parchment roll with the others. I suppress the desire to ask if he is going to sign it now.

"Mother, if you are not completely happy ... in your marriage, I mean ...there are ways to free you from it."

So, Henry has heard the rumours of Thomas' indiscretions too. There is little at court that escapes him. I wonder if my marriage is the talk of the taverns.

"Divorce, you mean? Oh, no I would never ... that is quite against God's plan."

He puts down his quill and replaces the lid on his ink pot.

"I was not thinking of divorce. Mother ... there are other ways." He stretches, hides a yawn behind his hand and sits back in his chair. I am grateful for his concern.

"Thomas is not a – difficult husband. Luckily, I outrank him socially and he is happy for me to do as I wish but still ... his potential authority, his legal precedence over me rankles. I confess I wish he were not so ... obvious in his indiscretions. I would be rid of him if I could."

Neither Henry nor I acknowledge out loud that now our cause is won, my spouse has ceased to be of use to us.

"Perhaps there is something, less drastic than divorce that can be done. I shall think on it, speak to my advisors on the matter. Now, Mother, would you care to accompany me on a walk around the garden? When I took the air yesterday, I noticed some small white flowers beneath the hedge. I am sure you will be able to enlighten me as to their name."

Had Henry been raised in my company, he would not have to ask. I rue his lack of knowledge of common English things but an excuse to walk in the garden with my son is not something I am prepared to forego.

I slide my hand into the crook of his arm and we make our way from his chambers into the dazzling winter sunshine.

November 1489

I weigh the coin in my hand, throw it up and deftly catch it again. It gleams in my palm like a promise. A golden sovereign, struck with Henry's enthroned image is on one side and the Tudor rose on the other, overlaid with Henry's coat of arms. It is a proud moment, our Tudor dynasty affirmed in gold is the culmination of a good year.

I cast my mind back over the last two years and realise I have enjoyed the kind of peace I have hitherto only dreamed of. My son is finding his feet, ruling as a just and honest king. He has pardoned the old adherents of York who have sworn fealty, and forged new and exciting alliances with the European heads of state. The most rewarding of these is the Treaty of Medina de Campo between England and Spain. As part of this agreement provisions in hand for a marriage between little Arthur, soon to be named Prince of Wales, and Caterina, the daughter of Ferdinand and Isabella. It is a worthy match and proof of Spain's confidence in Henry's rule, their acceptance of our new dynasty.

There was a brief dark hour in April when the north rose up against Henry's new war tax and the Earl of Northumberland, sent to contain the unrest, was hauled from his horse and cruelly murdered by the mob. Henry's anger against the perpetrators knew no bounds and for a while I feared a return to the old days of unrest and bloodshed but the revolt was quickly contained. However, although peace has now resumed neither Henry or I have forgotten how easily trouble flares up. What makes it more difficult to swallow is the fact that the uprising had more to do with the north's lingering affection for Richard of Gloucester, than resentment of Henry's taxes.

The queen, being second cousin of the murdered duke, was distraught at the news but God has a way of sending comfort in difficult times. Elizabeth's grief is lifted by the realisation she is, at last, with child again. Instead of looking sorrowfully backward, she now looks forward to greater joy in the future.

Relieved and glad of this long awaited announcement, I insist that the queen follow the guidance laid down in the Book of Royal Protocol.

She has been confined to her chambers for almost a month and any day now I expect to receive news of another grandchild – a brother for Arthur, a little Duke of York to strengthen our cause.

"Her name is Margaret..." Henry lays the new-born in my arms. Entranced, I place my finger in her palm and she clutches it, the candlelight glinting on tiny shell-like nails. I bend my head toward her, brush my cheek against the whisper of her hair and inhale her sweet, new scent. My head swims as memories of Henry's birth flood my mind.

I was half dead when they first let me hold him, a child myself, but the love that filled me in our first moments together has never left – not even when they took him from me. I realise now, I had almost given up, almost resigned myself to old age but now, holding Henry's daughter, I am invigorated, the chill of encroaching dotage washed away by the maternal euphoria that floods my being.

This child shall not be taken, this child, this girl, my namesake will never know the hardships I have suffered. I shall see to that. I vow silently to God who watches over us that she shall know only security, only happiness, only love.

Gently, I stroke her cheek and she turns her mouth toward me, hungry for nourishment, greedy for life. Reluctantly, I tear my eyes from her and look at her father who waits anxiously at my side, ready to return her to her mother. Slowly my mouth stretches into a smile that encompasses both Henry and Elizabeth.

"She is beautiful," I say, surprised to discover my voice is husky with emotion. "And she is very strong. You have done well, Elizabeth."

I do not want to pass her back to them. I need to hang on to the moment, stand in the shaft of sunlight that has found a way through the confining curtains and silently adore the latest addition to our Tudor family.

I rock her gently, whisper my pledge of protection and love, and place my lips on her forehead once again.

Henry clears his throat and, reluctantly, I let him take her. She squawks as she is deprived of the warmth of my body and my arms hang limply at my side. I feel bereft.

"Margaret – Margaret Tudor" – the name echoes in my mind as I visualise her growing up. Our shared name will surely create a bond between us. Margaret and I shall become friends, allies. I shall speak up for her when she falls foul of her father's favour. I shall spoil her with pretty gowns and fine books, coach her in herb lore and healing. Little Margaret shall become a mirror image of myself, and we shall form an unshakeable union that none shall ever break.

Placentia Palace - October 1490

Henry and Elizabeth invite Thomas and I to a private supper where we are joined by Jasper and his wife, Catherine. It is to be an intimate meal with friends, and Henry has ordered his servants away and bidden his guards to wait outside the door. As a mark of the informality of the occasion Henry pours our wine himself. With a smile and the suggestion of a wink he hands me a cup. Immediately I am on the alert, knowing instinctively he has something up his sleeve. I know better than to enquire of it, he will reveal all in his own time. I turn to Elizabeth who is seated at my right.

"I saw little Margaret today, my dear. She is growing apace, and crawling everywhere now. Her poor nurse is quite run off her feet."

Elizabeth smiles her slow, pretty smile and launches into praise of her first born daughter.

"She is very forward, grabbing at everything within reach. Yesterday, while I nursed her, she broke the string on my pearls and scattered them all over the floor."

Catherine leans forward. "I remember my daughter Anne doing that to me," she laughs. "I suppose one should really question whether small children and pearls really go together."

We laugh, the men looking on, politely bored with our talk of babies. But lately we have had a fill of politics and this is to be a family occasion. I pluck a grape from the table and pop it into my mouth.

"I have found a woman who makes the most exquisite lace," the queen continues, delving in her pocket to produce a sample. "I have asked her to make me a quantity of trimmings. Would you like some, Lady Mother, when she delivers it?"

I take the sample from her, smooth it across my fingers to examine the quality of the workmanship.

"It is very fine," I say, passing it to Catherine who holds it closer to the fire and bends her head over it. "I should very much like some. I have ordered new linen and it will make the perfect embellishment, perhaps we should put your woman in touch with mine. They can work together ..."

My attention is taken by a servant entering quietly and passing Henry a message. Immediately, I am on the alert, sensing trouble. He bows out, closes the door silently. A log slumps in the grate and Henry's hound lifts his head, looks wearily about the room before sinking his chin on his paws. I turn back to the queen, half-heartedly resume our discourse. "We could have similar garments made for our next ..."

"Damn!"

Our conversation forgotten, we look up.

"What is it?" I ask. Henry and Thomas exchange glances as Jasper gets up, puts his cup on the table and takes the message that Henry passes to him. As he reads it, his chin drops, his eyes search for mine. I put up a hand, clutch at my throat.

"What is it?" I ask again, the domesticity of the evening spoiled before I know the reason. Henry is staring out through the window, although it is pitch black outside and there is nothing to be seen.

Jasper passes the paper to Thomas before looking up.

"It's that boy we've heard rumours about. He is no longer keeping a low profile but has the audacity to declare before the Burgundian court that he is in fact Richard of Shrewsbury, calling himself Duke of York and the rightful heir to his late father's throne."

Elizabeth draws in a sharp breath, I turn in time to see her wine cup fall, hear the clatter as it rolls away to the hearth. She is on her feet, and a deep red stain is spreading across her skirts. We exchange glances, her face is parchment white, her eyes dark hollows. Catherine takes her elbow to steady her as Jasper continues.

"He is reported to be Plantagenet in looks as well as demeanour. Tall and blonde, with the elegance due to one of royal birth but ... he cannot be who he claims, of course. It is all a falsehood ..."

Catherine cuts across her husband's speech to address the queen.

"Sit down, Your Grace, you are unwell."

Elizabeth allows herself to be lowered back into her seat, her trembling fingers clutch the stem of a fresh cup of wine but she does not drink from it. She looks up at me with a mixture of hope and dread.

"Is it him?" she whispers. "Could it truly be him?"

"No. How many more imposters must we be forced to put down? Of course, he is not the Duke of York."

My voice is harsh as I deny it but my certainty is feigned. In truth, we know not who this man is. None of us know the fate or the whereabouts of the queen's brothers. That is a truth that died with Richard of Gloucester on Bosworth Field.

I push away the possibility that the imposter is the queen's brother. That boy is dead. I cannot allow my mind to dwell on the memory of the child whom I virtually brought into the world. I shake my head in an attempt to erase the memory of his new-born cries, his shaky first steps, his baby tongue trying to form the name 'Margaret,' that somehow emerged as 'Maga.' This latest imposter is not that child.

Elizabeth's voice breaks into my reverie.

"But my aunt Margaret ..."

Before I can reply, Henry turns from the window, his face furious and hawk like.

"Margaret of Burgundy hates the very name of Tudor. She would dress up a monkey and call it York if she thought it could unseat us."

Belatedly, he tempers his words with a tight smile and Elizabeth subsides, gives a weak humourless laugh. "Yes," she says. "Yes, you are right, of course, Henry. But I cannot help wondering ..."

I watch the king move to her side, take her hand in his as he perches on the edge of the table.

"My dear, this man is very unlikely to be your brother and you must make it clear to everyone outside this room that we have no doubts on the matter. The man is an imposter ... a would-be usurper of all we hold dear. Think of your son, our dynasty, our future. We must never, ever let anyone think you doubt he is false. We must not allow this pretender to undermine our rule, our security or our happiness."

The evening is spoiled. Elizabeth is quiet and fretful, Henry distracted, leaving it to Jasper to try to entertain us, and Catherine and I attempt to continue the conversation as if nothing is amiss.

For the next few months we act as if nothing has happened. Our grandeur at court increases, I insist upon the tightest security, the most extravagant show of stateliness we can manage. I trust nobody and no one, not the lowliest toad of the gutter or the highest noble in the land shall be given cause to report that we are in any way unstable.

At night, when my court clothes are removed and I climb into my high bed, the anxiety returns. All night, it crouches like a demon on my pillow, leaving me exhausted but unable to sleep, my peace of mind scattered like a handful of chaff in the wind.

Souvent me souviens is my motto. *I remember often.* Never will I forget the long journey I have taken to be where I am today. Without those scars I would be weak. The trials and torments of my life have led me here. I will never forget. I will never let go of the past for it has shaped me, and made me strong.

All my life I have suffered insecurity. I went into Wales a scared and vulnerable child, I emerged a determined woman with a battle to fight. When King Edward died I was on the cusp of winning Henry's rights, of gaining permission for his return from exile and his reinstatement. The king's death cast me back but I was not beaten.

I had to begin my quest again, under a new king, and befriend a new queen. I never really believed I would achieve all I have today but here I am, The King's Mother. I am not prepared to let anyone take that status from me – especially a counterfeit son of York. England is for

Henry, and for Arthur when we are gone. Our Tudor line will continue. I have seen it in a vision, our line stretching into the future in an unbreakable golden thread.

<u>Sheen Palace - February 1491</u>

Henry invites me to look over the drawings for his planned improvements of the palace. I stand beside him and examine the document he has rolled out on the table. He taps a fingernail on the parchment.

"See here, Mother? I intend to extend this area, and install glass in the windows here to allow light in. The whole effect will be uplifting ..."

I bend closer to the table, unwilling to admit my eyes are growing dim as I age.

"These rooms were used by Margaret of Anjou – I remember visiting her here with my mother."

"The repairs and renovations made then were shoddy. I plan something much grander, much more innovative. You see this area of timber framed apartments here ... I intend to rebuild them in stone."

"How long will this all take?"

"Well, we will not be spending Christmas here for a few years but I expect to see changes quite soon. It will be the rival of any palace in Europe, the crowning achievement of our reign."

I look at him, fuelled with enthusiasm at this new project and my heart swells with pride. There are some who accuse him of parsimony but he spends money wisely, he does not fritter it away. Besides, I have ever viewed frugality as a virtue. If he were extravagant his detractors would not hesitate to label him a profligate. King Edward may have prided himself on his wife's habit of never being seen in the same dress twice but there is more virtue in mending and rewearing a gown that cost a king's ransom than in casting it off.

The queen, brought up in the excessiveness of her father's court is surprisingly enough equally as careful with her personal expense. Her worst extravagance is her charitable work. She lends so much coin to her friends that she often leaves herself short and is forced to borrow to get through the month. Although she often leaves herself without enough coin, most of her allowance is spent on gifts to the needy, benefices to the church, relief for the poor.

She and Henry are selfless monarchs, their concern for the welfare of the people seldom seen in royalty. I think Henry deserves this small indulgence. A palace to mark his time as king, a landmark in England that will stand long after we are gone. A building such as Sheen will last forever, a monument to my son and his heirs. My mouth stretches wide with pleasure.

"It will be quite perfect, Henry. I have really benefitted from the improvements I have made to Collyweston and Woking. I will send my architect to you so you may discuss your plans with him and see if he has any suggestions for further improvement."

He places his hand on the small of my back and ushers me to the open door.

"Where are we going?"

"I was on my way to join Elizabeth in the nursery. She has something to tell you ..."

I cannot help speculating as he takes my elbow and guides me along the corridors. The queen must be with child again. It can be nothing else. I had noted she was pale but had put it down to the cold we have all been suffering.

The guards throw open the doors. Elizabeth looks up from the floor where she is playing with Margaret.

The child looks up, holds up her arms to me and I sweep her into an embrace. She is fat and warm and smells of milk. Her cheeks are red and her chin well daubed in dribble. When she smiles she displays the erupting tiny teeth responsible.

"I have some salve for her sore cheeks, Elizabeth. I will have it sent to you, and I will have something prepared for her gums too."

Elizabeth rises to her feet, sits in the nearest chair.

"I think this is the last of her teeth to come. Poor Margaret has suffered with everyone."

"Hmm well, it is best she gets used to suffering, it is a woman's lot."

"Good grief, Mother." Henry quirks an eyebrow. "We are cheerful this morning."

Keeping Margaret on my knee, I settle myself into a chair, stifling a groan. This cold, damp weather plays havoc with my knees and lately, despite the remedies I take, the ache is creeping to other parts of my body. I have no intention of allowing anyone to notice this, not even the king.

Margaret engages me in a clapping game, I bounce her on my knee and catch the queen's eye over her daughter's head.

"So, Elizabeth. Henry says you have news for me. I hope I have guessed right as to what it is."

She flushes, pink and pretty and very much like her father.

"I am sure you have, lady mother. The physician says we can expect a new arrival before the summer is out. Perhaps in June, or July."

Pleasure rises within me, it moistens my eye. I swallow a tight knot of happy tears and give her the benefit of my widest smile.

"Let us pray for a son this time, a king can never have too many sons."

<u>Greenwich - June 1491</u>

My third grandchild arrives bawling furiously on a hot morning in June. When the messenger arrives to tell me the queen's pains have begun, I hurry to the palace so as to be on hand to greet him. When they place him in my arms, Elizabeth is still lying, exhausted and sweat drenched, on the truckle bed where she has given birth. While the midwives clean her up and remove the detritus of the delivery, I make acquaintance of this large, blood-smeared baby.

I draw the blankets over his naked body and rock him, quietly humming the soothing song that never failed to quieten Arthur or Margaret. This child is unmoved however and continues to protest loudly against the injustices of the world he has just entered.

"Sshh, little man," I croon. "There is nothing in God's creation that deserves such a fuss."

His limbs thrash beneath the blanket, his heart-breaking cries reverberating through his body, his mouth a wide open cavern, his tongue red and trembling between pink, toothless gums. If he were not so new to the world, I would swear it was a fit of temper. I look over to Elizabeth who, her nether regions bound, is being helped back into bed by the midwife. The queen has already made it clear that she wishes to feed her son before handing him over to a nurse in a day or two.

"I think he must be hungry, Elizabeth," I yell over the infant's din. "Are you ready to take him?"

She nods, eagerly reaches out for him and I lay her son in her arms. Her head droops forward as she

85

exposes a breast and the child latches on, suckling ferociously. The resulting silence is blessed.

"Good gracious, I have never heard the like!" As I sit at her bedside and watch them together, the Madonna like scenario is not lost on me. She glances up, tucks a strand of hair behind her ear.

"You were right, lady mother, he was indeed hungry."

"Men are born so," the midwife buts in. She pauses at the foot of the bed, her arms full of soiled linen. "They live out their lives hungry for something, and leave it as hungry old men."

"But this child," I say, leaning forward to lay a hand protectively on the infant's foot, "is a prince of England, and shall want for nothing. He has no need to rage."

"That's as may be, My Lady, but you mark my words, with a temper like that, if he is not given what he wants, he'll stop at nothing 'til he gets it."

The child is not yet an hour old and this silly woman thinks she can predict his character. I sniff my displeasure, flick my fingers at her in dismissal, and turn back to the queen and my new grandson.

Elizabeth winces. "He has a mighty suck! I pity his nurse; her dugs will be raw within the week." She eases his mouth from her nipple, making the child squawk again, hastening her efforts to transfer him to the other breast. "I wonder where Henry has got to. He has been summoned, I expected him before this."

"He will come as soon as he can. Just look at the child, see how tightly he holds on to the neck of your chemise."

"His grip is strong. I think he will be a great horseman, and strong with the sword ..."

"But, surely, as second son, he will be intended for the church? England is ruled by church and state after all. He will be Arthur's line to God."

A question flutters across Elizabeth's brow but then she gives a little shake, as if clearing her mind of worry.

"Well, there is time to decide that. We might discover he is more suited to a layman's life…" She breaks off as the doors are opened and Henry hurries in.

"I was hunting," he says, breathlessly throwing off his cloak. "I came as soon as I heard."

He leans over the bed, one hand resting lightly on Elizabeth's shoulder. "They told me it is another son. Thank you, wife, you have done well."

"And a hearty son he is too." I lean forward into their domesticity.

"He is certainly eager for sustenance," Elizabeth winces. She draws him away and he lets her nipple fall with a pop. The three of us look at him and he scowls back, his eyes slitted, sleepy from a surfeit of food and releases a loud pocket of wind. Elizabeth lifts him to her shoulder, rubs his back and he drools excess milk down the back of her shift.

"Have you thought of a name? I ask, settling more comfortably into my seat. "Edmund this time, perhaps?"

Elizabeth, resting her face against her infant's head and inhaling the scent of his hair, replies, "I thought Henry might be nice. It seems to suit him somehow."

The king and I exchange glances. Neither of us can find an argument with that.

<u>Woking - June 1492</u>

After a sleepless night I wake with a head ache and surprise my woman by requesting a tray so I may break

87

my fast in bed. "In bed, My Lady?" she asks, slowly recovering her surprise. "Of course, I will see to it at once."

While she scurries off to dispense orders to the kitchens for a light repast, I lie back on the pillow and frown at the ceiling. I am definitely out of sorts, full of aches and pains such as I usually only suffer so acutely in winter. I make a mental note to dose myself with a tonic of comfrey and liquorice. The morning is too bright to be maudlin. Once I have eaten and my stomach is settled I will get up and set about the day as usual. I am not in my dotage yet.

When the fire is set I ask that the shutters be drawn back to allow the sunlight to stream into the chamber. A bird is singing just outside the window, sweet and sharp against the backdrop of the noise from the stables, and the clang of the blacksmith's hammer in the forge. After a lengthy stay at Woking, I am due back at court tomorrow and despite my slight megrim I will not be sorry to go. It does not do to be too long away from either the government of the country or the smaller politics of the nursery. I am taking the first bite of my breakfast wafer when the door opens and a message is brought in.

"What is it?" I ask crossly.

"A message from court, My Lady, from the king."

I put aside my tray and hastily open the letter. As I read the words, my world tips a little as I am reminded of our shared human frailty, my own mortality.

Elizabeth Woodville, the dowager queen, the woman I served with all semblance of meekness and friendship, has died in retirement at Bermondsey Abbey. I am summoned to attend on the queen at my earliest convenience.

Souvent me souviens. As I am dressed, memories flicker through my mind. Elizabeth, young and very fair, treating me kindly after a close encounter with a mob at the palace; Elizabeth welcoming me to her court, to her innermost circle, embracing me as a friend when I was friendless. Later, after Gloucester took the throne, Elizabeth, afraid and stricken with grief, fleeing to the sanctuary at Westminster.

With the future of her sons in peril, we plotted Gloucester's downfall, sealing our pax by pledging her daughter to my son. What happened to our alliance? When did my trust in her falter? When did we cease to be allies and instead became rivals? Was it after Bosworth, when our children were joined? I am suddenly swamped with guilt that I allowed mistrust to come between us, and used my power to have her sent from court.

With the news of her death still wavering between my fingers I suddenly see myself clearly, and I deeply dislike what I find. It was envy of her relationship with the queen that drove me to urge Henry to act against her. Elizabeth, a dowager queen, has died in poverty because of me – her years as Queen of England belittled, her position of Mother to the Queen demeaned. I let the missive fall onto the bed covers and cover my face with my hands; hands that are soon moist with guilty tears.

But moping never does anyone any good. It is too late to alter the past but I can change the future. I resolve to be a better person, a kinder, more thoughtful individual. When my toilette is complete, I hasten to the chapel where I light a candle and pray for the dowager's soul before I set off to offer comfort to her daughter, the queen.

Elizabeth's women are sitting apart from her, whispering in a huddle while the queen waits alone at the window. She does not turn at my approach and I am forced to clear my throat and speak her name twice before she hears me. Her head turns slowly, revealing a wan, tear-stained face. She struggles to speak, her voice grating with grief.

"My Lady, how good of you to come." The hand that grips mine is cold, her fingers trembling and uncertain. I notice the lace on the kerchief she clutches is frayed and torn. Broken by her grief, my throat fills with suppressed tears, robbing me of words but I draw her into my arms. She stoops to return the embrace, her pregnant belly like a hard rock between us.

"Where is the king?" I manage to ask.

"He was called away but promises to return. Oh, Lady Margaret, I feel so alone now. When I think I shall never see her, or seek her advice or hear her merry laughter again ... It will be a strange and cold world without her – Oh, I do not think I can bear it."

I ease her into a chair, my hand strokes her silken hair, and her head falls against my breast.

"Oh you will, Elizabeth, my dear. We are all stronger than we think, and you will find the courage you need for the sake of your children. All of us are more resilient than we realise."

The door opens and Cecily hurries in, followed by their younger sister, Anne, both showing signs of recent weeping. "I came as soon as I ..." Cecily begins until she sees me and drops a curtsey. "Forgive me, My Lady, I am quite distraught."

The queen leaves the comfort of my arms and falls into a huddle of misery with her sisters, excluding me. They are united in grief; a family in which my presence is not required. After a few moments, I leave

90

them to their mourning but, before I go, I press a small vial into the hand of Elizabeth's woman. "Make the queen and her sisters an infusion of camomile. It will help to soothe their sorrow."

"Yes, My Lady." She bobs a curtsey and I notice the tip of her nose is red, her eyes looks sore. The Dowager's death has touched her also.

"The queen is close to confinement," I say. "This level of grief is not good for either her or her child. We must try to persuade her to go to bed. See to it that she rests while I will go and discover the whereabouts of the king."

The palace is hushed, as I pass swiftly through the corridors, I notice courtiers huddled in small groups. They are always gossiping, and court scandals spread as rapidly as a plague. As I pass they turn toward me, deferentially lower their heads, their whispers following me as I hurry to Henry's apartments. The guards at his door stand aside, the portal opens and I sweep through, entering the king's warm and fragrant sanctum.

I find Henry with his ministers discussing the emperor's recent acknowledgement of Perkin Warbeck as King of England. It is an outrage and an insult that needs to be dealt with but Henry must put the needs of his wife and his unborn child first.

"The queen is in need of you, Henry," I say, my voice sharp with unspoken recrimination. "I am not making light of the situation overseas but Elizabeth is extremely distraught. It is unhealthy both for the queen and the child. I have sent for the physicians, hopefully they will persuade her to rest, offer her something to help her sleep."

"I was with her this morning, she seemed quite calm when I left. It is natural she should be unhappy."

"Unhappy, yes but not wretched. I did not like the look of her complexion just now. I hope the company of her sisters will aid her recovery and not aggravate the hurt."

He shuffles the papers on his desk, striving to hide his irritation at my intrusion. Usually we are in complete accord but the dowager's death has shaken me, opened my eyes to my own mortality. I need to attempt to rectify it by providing proper care for her daughter. What will become of this family, this realm when I too am no longer here to ensure it is properly run?

I feel as if Death sits on my shoulder, nudging me, reminding me of my lengthening years, his habit of striking when we least expect it. I sigh, recalling the many times I have suffered bereavement: husbands, uncles, my mother, my brothers, my friends ... It is never easy.

"Whatever her mood when you last saw her, she is not calm now, Henry. I feel she is on the edge of ... despair." I answer more sharply than usual. "And she needs you. I fear for the safety of the unborn child."

Jasper rises stiffly from his seat, picks up his cap and makes his bow.

"This matter can wait a while, Your Grace. We can speak of it later."

He bends over my hand, we exchange smiles and he quits the room with the rest of the council in his wake, leaving my son and me alone. Henry gives a gusty sigh as he rolls up a parchment map, places it with others on the table. He snuffs a candle sending a thin trail of smoke wafting like a wraith between us.

"Very well," he says at last. "I will go to her. Will you join me?"

I shake my head. "No. It is you she needs but I will wait on her later on in the day. Elizabeth Woodville will leave a large void in the queen's life; I hope perhaps in some small way, I may be able to fill it."

1494

The king is magnanimous and allows the queen to have the naming of our new-born princess. With very little hesitation she chooses Elizabeth, not after herself but after her mother. I bite back the stab of envy; after all they cannot christen every daughter after me.

She arrives in July. Unlike her brother, she is so fair she at first seems bald, her face is delicately boned, her fingers perfect and tiny. While young Henry is rapidly growing into the replica of his grandfather, Edward IV, I suspect this girl will grow to be more like me, small and birdlike.

With three children in the royal nursery, and Arthur, Prince of Wales thriving in his own household at Ludlow on the Welsh border, we are as secure as a monarchy can be. Were it not for one nagging threat that refuses to be extinguished, life would be perfect.

The pretender is still at large overseas, making outrageous claims of Plantagenet lineage. Henry's spies have discovered his real name is Perkin Warbeck, and he is a lowly commoner hailing from Antwerp. His outrageous and persistent declarations of injustice and negation of Henry's crown casts a shadow over our reign, and causes friction between the king and queen.

Political relations between England and Burgundy are strained to breaking, and the duchess Margaret, as the boy's maternal aunt, champions his cause, pouring money into his pot and calling on the heads of Europe to support his claim.

Quietly furious, Henry sends an embassy to remonstrate with Maximillian and Philip about the behaviour of Margaret but he receives little response. "She is an independent sovereign," the ambassador tells us. "Her conduct is outside of our control."

In response Henry forbids all commercial enterprise with Flanders, orders all Flemings to leave our shores. The trade market is transferred to Calais. Although consequences are felt on both sides, Maximillian and Philip still refuse to dismiss Warbeck from their lands. Riots and attacks break out and the alliance between us and Spain falters, teetering on the edge of breakdown.

Although it seems the whole of Europe is against us, Henry and I never let our lack of ease show. My son is furious but his anger is nothing to mine. It is a strain to keep it hidden and remain calm, and treat the threat as ridiculous. God willing, the day we lay hands upon the pretender will come soon ... and God help him when we do.

I am at Coldharbour House when Henry comes unexpectedly to see me. It is late in the evening and I have just come from the chapel, ready to partake in a light meal before I begin my evening toilette. I look up, startled when he is announced.

"Are you alone?"

He nods and comes toward me, his greeting kiss instinctive, no more than a brush of lips on my brow as he clutches my wrist. I notice his hands are cold.

"Come, join me at the hearth. The night is chilly. I hope you are not the harbinger of bad news."

"No, no. I have just been thinking ... about this boy, this ... imposter."

I sniff and straighten my back, containing my irritation between my clasped fingers...

"In my opinion we are all thinking far too much about him. He is nothing more than a - a – a wasp that must be swatted and forgotten. He has no real power."

I speak the words strongly, decisive in my negation of the danger.

"Yet the Emperor Maximillian has proclaimed him the rightful king. His following is growing and his persistence is unsettling the Spanish. My negotiations for the union between Arthur and Caterina are foundering because of his continuing liberty. Ferdinand and Isabella refuse to send their daughter to England until he has been stopped ..."

He pauses and, sensing he has more to say, I wait for him to resume.

"He is illusive, the men I sent after him cannot get close enough. He is ringed around with supporters – some of them lately members of our own court."

"Who?" My voice is sharp as a knife edge of fear deflates my carefully constructed certainty. We must not let this man undermine our security, our hopes for our dynasty.

"I have a lengthy list in my apartment, most of them old adherents of York but not all – some of them I had thought to be my friends. I suspect my own steward, Fitzwalter, is involved, and Sir Robert Clifford – although, I still have some hope of drawing him back into the fold."

"At least Charles of France is losing interest in the pretender now that his attention has been taken by his intended invasion of Italy."

"Sometimes it feels they are all against us, Mother. They treat me like some low-born knave. They spurn me: Burgundy, France, and the Holy Roman Emperor. Warbeck is not doing as badly as we pretend. He is steadily working toward invasion and one day he just might succeed. If our realm is to be defended against him, I must be sure of those around me."

"God is on our side, you can be sure of that, Henry." I place a hand on his sleeve but he pulls away, irritated as he sometimes is by my implacable faith.

"God is sometimes slow to act, Mother. My own life is testament to that. I cannot depend wholly on Him, I need the support of men on Earth not just Heaven."

He turns back to face me, lowering his voice so I am forced to lean forward the better to hear.

"Mother, what do you know of the movements of your brother-in-law, William Stanley?"

I sit up, surprised at the question.

"What do I know of his movements? What do you mean?"

Henry inhales deeply, pushes back his velvet cap and ruffles his hair. The uncertain distrust in his eyes is painful to see.

"I think he is involved somehow. I suspect he is in communication with Warbeck and is part of the plot to unseat us."

"William Stanley? But he fought for you. His actions on the field helped to place the crown upon your head at Bosworth. Why would he turn his coat now?"

"I do not know. Perhaps he feels he has not been sufficiently rewarded. Perhaps now I am king he dislikes my rule. Perhaps he is bored, seeking adventure or advancement in a new Yorkist court. My men have questioned his retainers, his son ... I am told he has a vast fortune stashed away ... enough to finance a rebellion."

"Sir William is many things but he is not a fool. You are king! If he wished for advancement, he would work to secure your hold on England, to strengthen your cause, not weaken it."

"Unless of course, he believes the claims of the imposter and his old adherence to the heirs of York was never really broken. He was loyal to Edward – I suspect it was just Gloucester's actions that rankled ..."

Silence crackles between us, my eyes are fastened to his face and suddenly I realise Henry has passed his prime. My son is not yet old but the strain of kingship is showing. There are lines upon his brow and around his eyes. I should have realised it before but I have heard it said one never sees one's own children as fully adult.

I swallow the sudden need to embrace him, halt the advancing years that, in making him middle aged, will make me elderly. I drop my voice to a whisper, although the servants have all been sent to bed long since.

"And ... do you also have doubts?"

He rubs his chin, his fingertips rasping on his beard. He opens his mouth to speak, closes it again but suddenly his doubts and fears spew forth in a torrent.

"I *know* his life, Mother. I understand it for I lived one just like it. I too was exiled and alone in a foreign court, among people I couldn't trust. I too longed to come home to England, to reclaim my rights, and mix in the company I was born into. Supposing he is who he claims to be? That makes him my brother-in-law, kin to my wife, uncle to my children yet I cannot let him live. If he is an imposter then I will have no qualm in taking vengeance for it but ... if he is indeed Richard of York I cannot allow him to set foot on English soil – I must have him killed before Elizabeth or anyone else sees and recognises him and transfers their allegiance from me to him."

"So you *do* believe he is who he claims to be!"

"No, I do not. I will not allow myself to believe that at all. I am no soothsayer and I cannot judge who he is or predict what will happen but I know I must do all I can to keep him as far from my throne and my family as I can, even if it means killing a royal prince."

My indrawn breath is loud in the silence. I reach out and after a moment Henry places his hand in mine, our fingers lock together.

"You are the only person I can wholly trust, Mother. I can speak in this way to no one else, not even Jasper now he is ailing. I have no wish to add to his worries ..."

Jasper too has been feeling his age, recently spending more time at Thornbury than at court. His thoughts have slowed and his sword arm is hampered by rheumatism. Henry sorely misses the astuteness of his wisdom at council. It is my duty to step in and advise the king in Jasper's stead. Pushing aside every trace of lingering doubt, I assume a confidence I do not feel.

"We will beat this imposter, Henry; for that is what he is. He is nothing but a thief come forth to steal what is rightly yours. We must continue to act as if he is of little concern to us. As I have said before, he is a fly, an insect, to be swatted in one swipe and a pest no more. Your spies may yet eliminate him before he leaves Europe, but if he does come, I swear we will put an end to his claim the instant he sets foot on our shores."

Henry attempts a smile. "I would still like you to discover what you can about William Stanley – perhaps you should watch your husband too."

"Oh, Thomas would have no truck with traitors. He gains too much pleasure from being seen at court as the 'father of the king.'

"That is as maybe but watch him anyway. Maybe invite him to supper, ply him with too much wine and promises ... discover what he knows. Brothers sometimes confide in one another – I understand there is an unwritten trust between them."

Many times in the past I have felt insecure, set about by enemies but never such as now. Perhaps it is because I now have so much more to lose. Sometimes, it is as if Henry, Elizabeth, the children and I are isolated in the dark, surrounded by monsters. If we stray too far from each other, we might be snatched, undermined, taken down and devoured.

As the days turn to weeks every curtain seems to conceal an assassin, each footstep rings with danger but we dare not let our insecurity show. To reveal our fear would empower our enemies, lend strength to their pretentions. And so we attempt to disarm those we suspect with reward and good fellowship.

We greet would-be traitors with wide smiles, laugh loudly at their jokes, applaud their courtly wiles and shower them with favours. Henry and I do not make the queen party to ours fears, or our suspicions. Although her brow is often knotted with concerns of her own she is better left in ignorance. If I could read her thoughts I suspect they would be with her lost brother and the identity of the pretender overseas. I have trained myself not to think of the possibility of Warbeck and Richard of Shrewsbury being one and the same but it is clear to me that the queen has not.

But it cannot be all doom and gloom. When June finally chases away the chills of spring, I join the queen and the children for an afternoon in the gardens. It is good to feel the light summer air on our faces, see the young prince and princesses tumbling like puppies on the greensward under the watchful eye of their nurses. When the weather allows, they relish the freedom of the jewelled mead, rolling down the grassy banks, running races back and forth while we applaud them. The afternoon takes me back to my own nursery days when I played with my own siblings at Bletsoe.

Young Margaret and Henry are great rivals, each doing their best to outstrip the other while little Elizabeth, who is still at the tottering stage, trips over her long skirts and runs hurrying to her nurse to have her sore palms kissed. Henry, noticing her plight, abandons the race and comes after her. He offers her his hanky to dry her eyes and when her tears are staunched he takes her by the hand and leads her carefully back to the game.

Henry enjoys no longer being the baby of the nursery and gladly plays the part of a concerned older brother. His relationship with his sisters is curious; he often wrangles with Margaret who is as argumentative as he, but he is gentle and considerate toward his more pliable little sister. As the pair run away toward the outer edges of the enclosure their voices drift in the warm sunshine and I am almost happy. My contentment as ever tinged with regret that I knew few such afternoons with my Henry.

A musician is seated a little apart from us, is quietly strumming his lute, just loud enough to entertain but not drown out our desultory conversation. Tapping her foot to his tune, the queen takes out a kerchief she has been embroidering. I watch her needle flying in and out of the linen and, as she sews, Elizabeth regales the ladies with a tale of a joust she attended once at her father's court.

As her story gathers pace, she abandons her sewing and leans forward enthusiastically painting a pretty picture. She describes a hot June day, a host of pretty ladies in the stands and a mysterious knight who rode in to challenge the king's champion. I play little part in the conversation although I think I recall the day she speaks of. I was in attendance on Elizabeth Woodville,

100

half of my attention on my duties to the queen, the other part wondering on the whereabouts of my exiled son. For me, the memory of that day is tainted with anxiety and uncertainty but for Elizabeth it held all the unstained bliss of childhood. Those insecure days are gone now and it should fill me with gratitude to be where I am now but, although Henry and I have gained our heart's desire, the danger and insecurity has not diminished. It has, if anything, grown stronger.

I am growing sleepy, lulled by the sound of the queen's voice. My head is hot beneath my headdress, an ache beginning in my temple. I close my eyes and relax back in the seat but the sound of a branch snapping in the small copse that rings the garden. Tiredness is chased instantly away. I leap to my feet, click my fingers at the guards who immediately respond, rushing to the boundary their swords at the ready.

"Henry, Margaret, bring Elizabeth here at once."

Prince Henry looks up, mouth open, his face flushed ruddy by the heat of the sun and mercifully, for once he does as he is bid. While the women form an easily breached defence about the queen, I draw the children close to my skirts. Our breath arrested, the women and I stand like sentinels as the guards stealthily approach the hedge. When their red tunics disappear from view, the queen and I edge closer together, groping for each other's hands.

"We should return to the palace." The queen's voice is little more than a whisper but I can hear her terror and realise our attempts to exclude her from our fears have failed. She is well aware of our precarious security.

"No, we must not move, not without the guard."

We wait, each flying bird a possible missile, each breath of wind an assassin's footstep. Little Elizabeth wriggles, trying to break free from me but I hold her fast in an iron grip. She begins to cry, loud plaintive sobs that float out across the gardens.

"Hush," I scoop her into my arms, balance her on my hip, the weight of her increasing the ever-present ache in my lower back as I jog her up and down. She smells of warm summer grass and sweet baby sweat; beneath her hood her hair sticks to her forehead, and there is a streak of mud on her cheek.

"What do you think it is?" Prince Henry reaches out and clasps my skirts and I look down, smiling encouragement.

"It is probably just a deer or a rabbit."

"Then why are we frightened?" His brow crinkles, as he cuffs the end of his nose on his sleeve.

"Oh, we are not frightened," I reply, bombastically, "we are just interested."

He exchanges glances with Margaret who raises her eyes heavenward in disbelief.

"Can we continue our game now, Grandmother or do we have to wait here until the guards have caught the rabbit, or the deer or whatever it is?"

I open my mouth to answer when a cry goes up in the wood and something comes leaping through the undergrowth, a pale streak bounding the hedge into the garden. The children cry out.

"It is Hector! Look he has caught a rabbit. Mother, look it is Hector! Father will be pleased he has been found."

The king's dog, lost on the hunt two days ago, has returned, filthy and dishevelled after his adventures. Disregarding his filthy state the children fall on him and he laps up their welcome. Elizabeth begins to laugh shakily while I breathe a sigh of relief and whisper a hasty thanks to God for our deliverance.

"Come, take the beast to the stable and have him bathed." To the loud dismay of the children, a page hurries to do my bidding, dragging the bedraggled dog off to be made clean again.

I look about the garden, considering the proximity of the woods, the vulnerability of the palace gardens. I have learned a lesson this day. It could have been a spy or an assassin sent forth to destroy the treasures of our royal nursery.

There can be no more such afternoons, I promise myself. I will warn the queen, issue orders that she and the children are to be kept indoors for the good of the realm.

<u>February 1495</u>

I do not mourn the passing of January. Lately our rule has been beset by deceit and treason and the coming months can only be better. At the end of November last, seventeen men were arrested for treason against us. Some of them were men of standing, men we thought we could trust: Fitzwalter, Mountford, Thwaites, Ratcliffe and Daubeney and other men of status. There were churchmen too among them, men of God who claim they genuinely believe Warbeck to be the Duke of York.

They languish in the Tower now, undergoing questioning, stripped of their estates and possessions. They must serve as an example of the fate of all those who trespass against us.

Late January on Tower Hill, Henry finally takes his vengeance and blood is spilled. I pray for their damned souls, and beg God to reveal to us all such black hearted villains for they are traitors all.

For several weeks Henry and I isolate ourselves from our court. We are distrustful of everyone; our halls seem to be full of potential traitors, enemies concealing their hatred for us behind congeniality. But this cannot last. We have to show ourselves unblemished by recent events. We must not allow ourselves to be affected by those who plot against us, for that way, they will win.

Thomas comes to Coldharbour House seeking solace, asking for advice.

"The king expects me to preside over my own brother's trial? Is this some kind of test? A punishment perhaps?"

He is haggard, his chin unshaven, drips of wine on his linen. I wonder what it was that made me cleave to him all those years ago, in my time of need. Today he is unstable, unattractive and unkempt. My instinct is to push him away, turn my back on him in his trouble but ... the disgrace of his brother could taint us both. He must put aside his self-pity and act like a man, a soldier. I square my shoulders and look him in the eye.

"It is true your brother has aided the pretender, sent forth spies to ascertain his true identity. It is also true that William has sworn never to raise his hand against a son of Edward IV. Therefore, your brother admits he is a traitor and a danger to both of us."

"Robert Clifford could be lying ... perhaps he has some grudge ..." I silence him by raising a finger, wagging it beneath his nose. "I have taken the council of the king's advisors, there is no doubt. You must preside over the court, if only to demonstrate to the world that you are true to our king or your brother's death ... as death it will surely be ... may bring you down with him and pour disrepute on the sanctity of our marriage. I will not be tainted by the inconsistencies of your family and ... if you wish to be saved Thomas, you must do as I say. Exactly as I say."

For a long moment our eyes are locked. We have travelled a long way together; fought our way from the obscurity of York's rule to a status of great power beneath the reign of my son. Both of us want to maintain that position. At length Thomas releases a great shuddering breath, collapses onto a stool and rakes his fingers through his thinning hair.

"I cannot help but think of my mother ..." He looks vanquished. I take a step forward and he looks up, the whites of his eyes shot with blood. I raise my chin, and keeping my lips tight, I look down my nose. "You must be strong in this, Thomas."

"But Margaret, she will never forgive me ..." With a cry he grabs my wrists, drags me close and throws his arms about my waist, sobbing into my belly. I bear it for a while until my sympathy outweighs the repugnance I feel. Tentatively, I place my hand on his hair while he gives way to a fit of weeping. Only a statue would not feel some touch of pity.

Thomas makes love like an old man. Gone is the masterful thrusting passion of his youth and in its place a gentler, questing search for security. I endure it as I have endured so much and in the morning I wake regretful, and disappointed in myself. While Thomas snores on, I creep from the bed, my bones protesting at the indignity they have been forced to suffer. I must pray. I must rediscover my former self-esteem and trust that Thomas will not seek to undermine it again.

The chapel is cool and welcoming. I enter as a sinner who has sought bodily comfort within a marriage I seek to leave. For a long time I pray, asking for guidance, begging for strength. It is not often I leave the chapel with my questions unanswered but this morning God remains silent. Unable to bear His mute frigidity, I quit the cold

105

quiet sanctuary and meander back along the dimly lit passages that lead to my apartments.

February is always bitter but it is colder this year, perhaps it just seems that way because I am older. Drawing my shawl closer about my shoulders I pass into my rooms with my head high, unsure of meeting my husband again so soon. He looks up when I enter and I notice there is colour in his cheeks where there was none before and his eyes are less shadowed. It seems he has benefitted from our liaison far more than I.

"Margaret," he gets up and pours me wine that I accept silently, without looking at him. To my humiliation I feel my cheeks suffuse with blood. He laughs gently.

"I should thank you, wife ... for your bolstering words ... and your comfort."

His hand falls heavy on my shoulder and he begins to stroke my upper arm. I turn my head, see those calloused fingers, the neatly trimmed nails, the hair growing thickly on his wrist. Quite uncharacteristically, I am at a loss for words and he fills the silence. "I can do it if you think it is the right thing. Stand in judgement against him, I mean."

I shudder and pretending it is the February chill bothering me and not his proximity, I move away toward the hearth to hold out my hands to the flame.

"It is the only thing to be done, Thomas. There is no choice," I say. "Sometimes we have to put our personal feelings aside, sacrifice our friends, our families and act for the sake of the realm. You are not the first to do it and you will not be the last."

He follows me to the hearth, leans on the mantel and looks down at the flames, frowning into the blistering logs as if they are the fiery coals of hell.

"No," he says when he at last looks up. "I will not be the last."

*

I wake early and go to stand at the window. There is snow in the air, the sharp bite of it making my nose tingle and sending an army of goosebumps marching across my skin. I wrap my shawl around me and retreat toward the hearth where my woman is preparing a bowl of frumenty.

"This will comfort you, My Lady." She places it in my hands and I sit for a while allowing the warmth to penetrate my fingers. I take a spoonful, smile my gratitude but my thoughts are far away.

Today my brother-in-law is to die a traitor's death, hung and quartered like a commoner. He has fallen from the heady heights of Lord Chamberlaine, to the ignominy of a felon's death. This day is surreal, like an impenetrable dream from which I cannot wake. Horribly torn between loyalty to my son and pity for my husband, for whom I thought I had long since ceased to care, the day hangs heavy.

I spend even longer at chapel than is my habit. There are so many souls to pray for in these sorry times. But I leave my misery in God's lap and return to the hall somewhat stronger and prepared to show support for Henry's actions.

The guards at the door stand to one side and, lifting my chin and squaring my shoulders, I pass into the King's chamber. Reginald Bray is standing at the window watching a flurry of fat snowflakes. He turns when he hears my footstep, his face opening in pleasure.

"My Lady," he bows low and shows me a seat near the fire. "I had not looked for you this morning."

"Good morning, Reginald. Where is the king? I hoped to speak to him before the business of his day begins."

107

"Alas Madam, he has ridden out earlier than is his habit."

I bite my lip. I should have guessed. I resettle myself on the stool.

"Was my husband with him?"

"No, My Lady, I do not believe so."

I frown into the flames. Where is Thomas? I find my thoughts are with him, more constantly than they have lately been. Bray brings me from my reverie by asking if he should call for refreshments. I stand up and shake my head.

"No, no thank you. I shall call upon the queen. Some feminine company may help me to pass this sorry day."

He bows again, gratifyingly low and escorts me to the door.

"I shall inform the king on his return that you were looking for him."

"Thank you. That is very kind."

Elizabeth and I share a companionable few hours but afterwards I have no memory of our conversation. The whole time I was with her I was fretting about Thomas, visions of the atrocities inflicted on his kin running through my mind as if I had witnessed it. I take my leave of the queen and her ladies just before the Sext bell rings, hurrying to my chapel to say one more prayer. When I emerge, a figure steps from the shadows and I cry out in sudden alarm.

A hand falls on my arm, a friendly voice speaks my name. "Thomas, you startled me. How – how? Is it done now?"

"Aye, it is done."

I make the sign of the cross, whisper a hurried prayer for his brother's soul.

"Was – was it ... very bad?"

108

His breath in my face is tainted with wine and lack of sleep. He pulls off his cap and twists it, shedding seed pearls that scatter to the floor.

"It was bad, yes but ... at the last minute the king showed some mercy and by grace of God commuted the sentence to execution. He - William did not suffer ... overmuch."

"We can take some comfort from that."

"My heart is heavy, Margaret. I am going to ask the king's leave to take a short tour of my estates. Would you accompany me ... as soon as the weather breaks?"

I agree for his sake. Despite the cold, the court seems stifling, and I long to get away. I am confident the king will have no objection for as long as Thomas is in my company, Henry can be sure that he is not stirring up an uprising in vengeance for his brother's death. I nod my agreement and show my teeth in a semblance of a smile. I have neglected my holdings in recent months and it will be a relief to escape the claustrophobia of court for a time.

Thomas and I break our journey for a few days at Jasper's castle in Thornbury. When night is not far away I suggest we halt at a nearby priory but he insists there is not much further to travel.

I could protest about my aching back, my frozen fingers, the nagging throb at the base of my skull but instead, I concur and the journey continues.

We have not travelled far when heavy clouds rush in bringing icy rain that flies in our faces, as painfully as a fistful of pebbles. Thomas moves his mount closer to mine, raising his voice above the wind and gesticulating ahead.

"Not long now. Thornbury is just over the next hill."

"I am glad to hear it," I shout back over the hubbub of the weather. "I have lost all feeling in my fingers."

He nods and smiles, baring his teeth and screwing up his face against the driving rain. It is clear he has not heard me but I do not persist in my complaint although every bone of my body is shrieking in protest. It takes all my strength to remain upright in the saddle and as we struggle for the last mile, Thomas at last recognises my plight. With an exclamation of surprise, he takes my horse's reins.

"Just hang on to the saddle, Margaret, I will lead you. Honestly, we have but a little way to travel."

And through the rain which is rapidly turning to sleet I at last see the welcome lights of Thornbury Castle glimmering in the rapidly falling dusk.

Thornbury's ostlers have taken refuge from the weather and we ride into the empty bailey. Soon, they appear, as if from nowhere, to take charge of the horses. I fall from the saddle into Thomas' arms, lean heavily upon him as he assists me up the steps to the hall. They are steep, each one sends pain crashing through my lower back and hips and the warm blast of the fire on entering is welcoming indeed. Catherine hurries forward.

"My Lady," she takes my elbow and assists me to a chair while Thomas unties his cloak. "We have been so worried. I was just about to send out a party to look for you."

"Oh," I say, struggling to project my voice through frozen lips. "There was no need to worry. I was perfectly safe with Thomas. He is not one to let a little thing like the weather stand in his way."

Thomas casts a sideways glance in my direction, recognising the hidden rebuke at his refusal to heed my suggestion and pause our journey sooner.

"We are here now, and glad to be so," I continue, unwrapping the cloak from my head and attempting to loosen the ties. Seeing my struggle, Catherine reaches out to assist me then, remembering who I am, she pauses, draws her hands back to her sides.

"May I help you, My Lady? Your fingers must be frozen."

"Please do, your assistance is most welcome. Where is Jasper? Surely he is not out in this."

"No, he is ...resting but I am sure he will come down as soon as he receives news of your arrival. He will berate himself for not being down to greet you."

"Oh ... no need for that. I am glad of a few moments to thaw out. A drink would be most ..."

"Oh, do forgive me, My Lady." She snaps her fingers and a page comes forward with a tray of mulled wine. The spicy aroma wafts about my head as I cup the vessel in my hands.

The pain, as my fingers start to regain their feeling, is akin to bliss, and I welcome the drink more as a conduit for warmth than to quench my thirst.

Catherine orders warm water to be taken to my chamber so I can wash and rest before supper. Our servants are sent to prepare our rooms, lay out our possessions and make ready our clothes for the evening.

As we cross the floor toward the stairs our voices echo in the vaulty roof, our footsteps loud upon the flagstones. Standing at the bottom, one hand on the bannister, I wish with all my heart that the guest chambers were on the lower floor. But, summoning my strength for the assent, I place one foot on the bottom step and begin to climb as if I am ascending a mountain.

When at last I cross the threshold, the chamberers make haste to quit the room and, making straight for the nearest chair, I plump down and bid my

111

woman help me remove my shoes. I flex my toes and rest my head on the back of the chair while she massages my feet to restore the feeling to my frozen extremities.

"I need to lie down. While I recover my breath, look for my pot of arnica salve. I would have you rub it into my bones so I may get some rest."

She hurries to do my bidding and I lie my head back, close my eyes ...

When I descend to the hall for supper, the men are already gathered at the hearth. Thomas is standing with his back to me; beside him an elderly man has a hand on his shoulder and is speaking into his ear. Thomas throws back his head, his loud guffaws disturbing the hounds asleep at his feet.

"Well, My Lords, something seems to be very amusing."

They turn toward my voice, Thomas' face still stretched with lingering humour. As he wipes away a mirthful tear the gentleman beside him speaks and my heart jolts so painfully, it is all I can do not to cry out in shock.

"J-Jasper," I stutter his name, quickly recovering myself, careful not to display my dismay at his altered appearance. He is old ... shrunken and ailing; a sorry shadow of the soldier he once was. Illness, whatever it may be, has hit him hard, stolen his prime and left an empty husk. He takes my hand, draws me closer and kisses my cheek; a liberty only he would dare to take.

"How are you?"

Inwardly, I curse myself for the insensitive question. It is clear for anyone to see that his days on this Earth are numbered.

"Oh," he shrugs his shoulders and a glimpse of the old Jasper peeps from behind the rheumy eyes of this old

112

man. "I am not as sick as I was. This time next year I will be back in the saddle."

Without meeting my eye he turns away and picks up his cup. "I had hoped you would come in the summer months, Margaret. The gardens Catherine has planted are coming on nicely; I am always telling her about yours at Lamphey. Do you remember the roses that sprawled over that old stone wall near the fish ponds? What was the name of that rose?"

"I am afraid I do not remember," I say, grateful that he has shifted the conversation to something less heart-breaking than his health. "It was white, was it not, with the softest hint of yellow in the centre?"

He nods vigorously while Thomas looks on with raised brows. Thomas has never once deigned to speak to me of horticulture. Jasper leans closer, places his gnarled hand on mine, his fingers curling about my wrist as he draws me from the company that we might speak alone.

"I would have returned to court when I learned of the recent troubles but ... well, you can see ..." He pauses, changes the subject. "I am very proud of our Henry. I always knew he would rule well but the way he has handled the recent trouble at court has far exceeded my expectations.

Ever delighted by praise of my son, I beam back at him. "He is an exemplary king," I say, "and it is you I have to thank for it. Without your guidance and protection through those years in exile he may never have survived. In his father's absence you have been the perfect uncle, and the perfect brother-in-law to me. Had you not offered us refuge at Pembroke all those years ago... well, I dread to think what may have happened."

He squeezes my hand a little tighter.

"Ah, Margaret, I only regret we could not find you better midwives; you should have been mother to a

113

whole litter of little Tudors. That would have been the life you deserved. I rue the way your motherhood was spoiled by the vagaries of war."

"I have no regrets. Not now the outcome has been all we could wish for. The royal nursery is recompense for the loss of Henry's childhood; I see very little of Arthur but my grandchildren, Margaret and Henry and little Elizabeth salve my aching maternal heart. We have hopes of many more in the future, for the king and queen are young yet and Elizabeth seems to be as fertile as her mother."

"Have a care of them, Margaret. Never be complacent. Trust nobody. There are spies and ill-doers all around us."

"I am aware of that. Even William Stanley, the king's own Chamberlaine ...my own brother in law! I could scarcely believe it when it was discovered."

Jasper coughs, the phlegm breaking in his throat making me wince. "And your man, Thomas, he holds no grudge for it?"

"I do not think so, not openly, although he is sorrowful of course. Who would not be? But his loyalty to us is sound. Now, look, the supper is being brought in and I expect you are famished as usual."

We gather at the table as the candles are brought forward. The shadows of the torches leap and dance upon the walls, as I smile at the welcome sound of wine filling my cup. I take a napkin and shake it out, spread it across my lap and sit tall in my seat, watching as the feast is laid before us.

May 1495

As the end of May gives way to the promise of June and all the delights it holds, news arrives of the passing of

Cecily Neville. I place the letter gently on the table and hurry to the chapel to pray for her and light a candle.

Cecily is freed now from the sorrow of her latter years. Once she rode high, and like me was the mother of kings, but Cecily was affected badly by the struggle for power, the ensuing war that plagued us all. The first of her sons to die was Edmund of Rutland who perished long ago at Wakefield. Then the disgraceful end of feckless George, whose lust for the crown culminated in sentence of death, signed by the hand of his own brother.

They say that Cecily never forgave King Edward for the death of her favourite son. Then, with her family decimated by war, she made one last attempt to secure the throne for her family. Never a friend to the Woodvilles, she upheld Gloucester's claim that Edward IV's marriage to Elizabeth Woodville was invalid and, in doing so, made bastards of her own grandsons. I wonder, knowing all that came afterwards, if she lived to rue that day.

After Bosworth, when she heard the news that her last born son had been vanquished by mine, her appearances at court ceased and she spent her declining years in total retirement at Berkhampstead. Did Cecily, like me and so many ageing people, live in the past, rueing the decisions she made, the mistakes that led to ignominy for her offspring.

Perhaps she was able to take some comfort from her granddaughter's marriage to the king and the knowledge that after all, her great grandson will one day rule over England. I hope so. Poor proud Cecily. She is deserving of my prayers.

I finish my devotions and climb from my knees, clinging to the altar rail while the feeling returns to my feet. Age is like rot, it creeps upon us slowly, insidiously, invisibly consuming our youth and vigour until finally ... we crumble and become nothing. Nothing but dust.

It takes a few moments for the feeling to return to my limbs and I am able to walk. I force my carriage upright, lift my chin and chase away the grim thoughts of infirmity and death. I clear my throat, and make my voice decisive.

"Come," I say over my right shoulder to my waiting women. "I must make ready to visit the queen. She will be grieving for her grandmother. Between us we must ensure Cecily is buried as befits the mother of a king."

I find Elizabeth in the garden at Windsor. She is sad and pale, her eyes showing signs of recent tears but she seems resigned to the loss of her grandmother.

"I am grieved of course, but Grandmother was seventy years old," she says. "I hope I shall enjoy so long on this Earth."

I hook my arm through hers and accompany her along the path.

"We must ensure she is buried with all pomp ..."

"No."

The queen pulls her arm away, turns to frown at me, for once stubborn in her desire. "Grandmother would not have wanted a burial in the capital. She made it quite clear that she desired a simple ceremony at the Church of St Mary and All Saints in Fotheringhay, and an internment with my grandfather. They were happy at Fotheringhay once upon a time."

I bow my head in acquiescence and as we resume our stroll, I ponder where I shall be laid when the time comes. Since he was the father of the king, I would prefer to be with Edmund at Carmarthen rather than with Harry at Pleshey, or with Thomas, wherever he shall fall. Perhaps I should make note of it in my will …

"Lady Mother? Did you hear me?"

The queen's voice calls me from reverie. I give myself a little shake.

"I am sorry, Elizabeth, my mind was far away. What were you saying?"

We are admiring the budding roses when Henry's servant arrives, summoning me to the king's presence. I cannot help but feel a little annoyed at such an abrupt directive but obediently I take my leave of the queen and follow in the man's wake.

I find Henry in conference, the chamber crowded with those he trusts the most. It is clear that some matter of import has occurred because everyone is speaking at once. Before I begin to thread my way through the throng, I crane my neck to locate the king. Usually, the gentlemen would part to let me through and it is their failure to do so that alerts me to the severity of the situation.

I force my way to Henry's side. He is sitting at a small table, pen in hand, idly scratching a grid of squares, like a portcullis, onto a scrap of parchment. I have seen him make the same marks on paper before. I have learned it is an absentminded revelation of his inner sense of entrapment. He looks up at the sound of my rustling skirts.

"Mother." Belatedly, he attempts to rise but a wave of dismissal sends him back into his seat. I place both hands on the desk and lean toward him.

"What is the urgency, Henry? What has happened?"

He pushes a carefully folded paper toward me, I open it, shift closer to the candle the clearer to see the hastily written scrawl.

"It is from my informant. Warbeck has set sail from Vlissengen with a small army, headed, so my intelligence believes, to Ravenspur."

I hastily scan the letter, my mind struggling to absorb the information, before passing it back to Henry.

"It is as well we know. We can be prepared, have our troops lying in wait for him to disembark. The sooner he is in our custody the better."

"I have already deployed our troops. I need you to be on the alert, ready to accompany the queen and the royal children to the safety of the Tower ... should the need arise. I have already increased the guard."

Across the room, Thomas's voice rises above the others, insisting on the need for haste. "There should be no delay. We must secure the whole of the eastern coast at once. We cannot be certain where they will land..."

He is unaware that I am watching him. I recognise his determination to prove himself unquestionably Henry's man. I hide a smile. He is shouting his loyalty from the rooftops. My husband values his position, his role as the king's father, his status as husband to the king's mother and he is eager that all should know it. Henry and I share a silent exchange, he inclines his head and with an answering smile, I take my leave of him and return to the queen.

Finding her apartments empty, I locate her at last in the nursery, where I should have known she would retreat to seek solace. I join her by the window where she is reading to young Henry and Margaret. As I take a seat among them I recognise the tales of King Arthur and am struck by the cycle of life; habits, memories, passed from one generation to the next. We all pass on small details of

118

days gone by to our young in a vain attempt to inject a little of our own selves into a future we will not share. The queen enjoyed the stories as a child, I remember her telling the same tales over and over again to her brother, Richard of Shrewsbury, whose ghost has now come back to haunt us.

Little Elizabeth slides from her nurse's lap and climbs onto mine where she makes herself comfortable on my hard, flat bosom and pokes her thumb into her mouth. A warm and fluid emotion settles around my heart; my breath slows, my soul grows calmer. My arms slide around the tiny body and I close my eyes, acknowledging God's blessing. I thank Him for this child. I thank Him for them all.

Elizabeth reads on. Lancelot, the flawless hero has been unhorsed and forced to continue his journey on a lumbering cart. The queen's voice falters, she puts a hand to her throat and coughs gently, her voice hoarse with over use. "I need a rest, and a drink," she says. Henry sits up indignantly.

"But Mother, you were just getting to the best part!"

He folds his arms, his mouth a sullen pout, thunder gathering on his brow. Elizabeth ruffles his hair.

"I will carry on in a little while. Look, your Grandmother is here, we can share a drink together. Why do you not show her your new sword?"

Miraculously his expression clears. He leaps from his seat and hurries to the corner of the nursery and begins rummaging through his box. I tuck little Elizabeth more securely into the curve of my arm and speak over her head.

"The king instructs us to be ready to move to the Tower – should the need arise. You should order your servants to make ready for a sudden departure."

119

Her eyes widen, her brows lift in question but I am reluctant to continue with Margaret leaning on her mother's shoulder, listening to our every word. I am saved the need to embellish my news when Henry leaps between us brandishing a brightly painted wooden sword. He makes a sweeping chivalric bow.

"I am the King's champion and none can best me!" he shouts, setting about the shins of his mother's page. The wounded boy lets loose an agonised groan.

"Henry!"

It is the first time I have heard the queen raise her voice. Dislodging Margaret from the comfortable perch at her side, she rises swiftly, crosses the floor in two steps and snatches the sword from Henry's grip and smacks him on the bottom with it. "Apologise at once. That is no way to treat members of our household."

The injured page's face is red but whether it is from embarrassment or suppressed pain I cannot tell. Henry is scowling again. He mumbles a resentful 'sorry' and, energetically rubbing his sore behind, slumps beside Margaret on the window seat. Elizabeth conceals the confiscated sword beneath her cushions and sits down again, immediately resuming her former poise.

"You may go and have your leg seen to," she says to the page, and the boy bows before limping stiffly from the room, a hand to his shin.

"You must never behave like that again, Henry. You are a prince and obliged to set an example for lesser gentleman to follow. I am very displeased with you."

Sheepishly he gets up, moves closer to squeeze between his mother and Margaret, earning himself a scowl from his sister. "I'm sorry, Mother."

The Queen's arm slides around his shoulder and shortly afterwards she kisses his ruddy hair.

"I should think so, too."

As much as I love him, Henry needs a firmer hand. He is apt to run wild in this nursery of women and girls. It is time we looked about for a tutor to instil in him the requirements of a prince. I keep my face straight, let him see my displeasure but inside I know I would not have acted any differently to Elizabeth. Had I been allowed a share in my own son's childhood, I would have found it difficult to chastise him too. Our sons are precious and we love them, even in their bad behaviour. To this day, I tend to make excuses for the king's worst actions.

Little Elizabeth stirs on in my arms, her thumb slips from her mouth and she begins to cough. Instinctively, I sit her up, pat her on the back. When she is done she snuggles back on my lap. I place the back of my fingers on her forehead.

"She is very hot, Elizabeth. Has she been unwell again?"

"Yes. Her nurse says she was awake coughing again in the night. I have asked the physicians to look at her this afternoon."

"I have little faith in them. I will prepare a concoction myself to ease her throat when the coughing begins. It will aid her rest, and sleep is a great healer."

The doors open suddenly to admit the king. Elizabeth and I both turn in unison, our faces wide with pleasure at his unexpected arrival.

"Henry," I say. "I thought you would be in council for the rest of the day."

He kisses my brow, moves toward his wife and I turn away as he gives her his salute.

"I could not wait to escape. I have changed my mind since I spoke to you, Mother. Why should we allow the imposter to interfere with our decisions? I think the royal progress should go on as planned. The queen and I will travel north; I suppose your invitation for us to visit with you at Lathom still stands."

"Of course. Thomas and I will be delighted. We have made so many improvements you will not recognise the place."

"Is it safe though, Henry? Suppose the invasion was to be succe ..."

Henry holds up his hand, arresting her speech.

"We will set watchers all along the coast, and deploy our troops and ships. The pretender will not set one foot upon our lands."

"When do you plan to leave?" I toy with the tassel on little Elizabeth's sleeve, wanting but reluctant to remind them of her ailment. It is always a wrench for Elizabeth to leave the children and I do not want to make it any more difficult.

"Soon. First we must travel to Combermere Abbey in Shropshire, then to Holt and Chester, and then on to your manner at Lathom. You will have ample time to prepare for our arrival."

"I shall look forward to it. Hopefully the business with the pretender will be concluded by then."

"We can but hope, Mother."

Lathom – 4th July 1495

Henry and Elizabeth's visit with us at Lathom is the jewel of the summer. They arrive with just a small entourage and we dine intimately as if we are a normal family, providing me with the first taste of life as it might have been had Edmund survived. I picture him here in Thomas's place, imagine his pride in his son and the growing family. It should be him leaning on the mantel discussing diplomacy with Henry. Perhaps he is watching us. I hope that in some way he is aware of Henry and proud of all I have achieved in his absence.

Elizabeth's voice calls me back to the present.

"The new physician I engaged for Elizabeth writes that he is pleased with the improvement in her health. She has some difficulty breathing at night time and is weakened by it, but he has hopes of a full recovery. He sees no reason she why she should not thrive."

"It is strange that she does not improve in the summer months, most children ail in the winter but rally with the arrival of the warmer weather." I let the thought hang in the air. Elizabeth shakes herself, smiles her serene smile.

"I will be glad to return to Sheen. I miss the children so dreadfully when we are away and it has already been some weeks."

"I imagine you do. I know my exile from Henry was like a physical pain, as if I had a wound that refused to heal."

Henry looks away, discomforted by my sentimentality but the queen reaches out, her palm warm on the back of my hand. I look down at the contrast of her young firm skin against my own, which is wrinkled and marred with age spots. She squeezes gently and blithely changes the subject.

"Henry and I are soon to have our portraits taken. The sittings begin shortly after we return to London. I have never been painted before; have you?"

I look up, surprised at the question.

"No. I have never really thought of it." I have never had the leisure for such things. My life has always been governed by war with little time allowed to contemplate posterity.

"Oh but you should! I think it is imperative that you do. Henry will require one for the palace, and you should get another to hang here at Lathom. Why not commission one for each of your houses?"

"I shall give it some thought."

A portrait of myself will never be a thing of beauty. My visage is not likely to grace a canvas in the same way as the one of Elizabeth Woodville that hangs at Windsor – a thing of grace and diaphanous elegance. But it is a good idea. A portrait of me would illustrate my intelligence, my influence and position and my dedication to God and the church. I will follow up Elizabeth's idea and take steps to see it done when we return to the capital.

The men are admiring the solar window we had installed last spring; Elizabeth and I join them to watch the last rays of the sun as it sinks into the west. I love this transitional time of day when the light changes, the birds fall silent and the warmth of the sun lessens. Outside the garden is couched in shadow and behind us, my servants are lighting the candles, altering the mood of the chamber.

We settle down before the hearth where a small summer fire has been laid. Henry holds out his cup and as my man steps forward to refill it, the door opens and Reginald Bray comes to whisper in my ear.

"A messenger has arrived, My Lady, from London. He appears to have ridden hard."

"Well, show him up. Do not keep the king waiting."

We are all sitting upright and expectant in our seats when the man slides into the chamber, his cloak coated in dust, his face pale with lack of sleep. Henry stands, with one hand resting on my shoulder.

"What is it, man?"

"The pretender, Your Grace. His ship landed a small force at Deal on the Kent coast. There were casualties but our army routed them easily and they got no farther than the beach. But the pretender ... he I am afraid he escaped, Your Majesty."

I wince at the profanity uttered by my son and we are suddenly all on our feet, the men speaking all at once, preventing me from being heard. I subside, to wait for them to calm down and it is only then I notice Elizabeth is silent. She is standing very still, her eyes closed and her lips are moving, as if in prayer. This action, more than any other, convinces me that she does indeed harbour the suspicion that the imposter may be her brother. Whether she wishes him well or not, I cannot tell.

Henry, deprived of laying hands on the Pretender, takes out his frustration on the rebel's accomplices. One hundred and fifty nine men are railed in ropes and marched to London like horses drawing a cart. The Tower and Newgate prison is soon full to the gunnels; all are arraigned and condemned. One hundred and fifty are hanged, and their leaders executed, their heads tarred and set high upon London Bridge. There they will be left until they rot.

With this small victory our position is strengthened. Ferdinand and Isabella are slightly appeased, yet while the pretender is at large, our satisfaction remains incomplete.

The royal visit to Lathom is over too soon but the progress has been carefully planned and the allotted time with us has passed. On the morning of their departure the queen seeks me in my chamber.

"Thank you for your hospitality, Lady Mother. I am very loathe to leave and only wish it was to return to Eltham. I miss my little ones so very much."

"It has been a pleasure, my dear but I have learned the hard way that our best experiences are usually short lived. Take comfort that had you stayed too long the visit might well have grown tiresome – for us both."

She laughs gently, glances shyly from beneath her lashes.

"Lady Mother, I would tell you, although I have not yet shared my suspicion with the king, that I suspect another addition to the nursery ... in February perhaps, or maybe early March."

Her face is pink with pleasure. I stand up and embrace her, laughter and triumph dancing in my heart at the prospect of another grandchild to cherish. There is usually something good to throw the bad into the shade.

"And to think I thought your lack of appetite was due to the failings of my cook!"

"Oh no, madam, your cook's skills are unsurpassed. I was wondering if he would share the recipe for the ..."

We leave the room, my hand in the crook of her arm, for a final walk about the garden before they take their leave of us.

October 1495

I am always happy at the end of summer when the diseases and megrims that seem to infest the banks of the river cease to plague us. It has been a long hot season and deaths among the peasantry have been higher than usual. With the king and queen still on progress and Thomas embarked on yet another tour of his northern properties, I return to Coldharbour House. As soon as I have dealt with numerous small problems that have sprung up in my absence, I take my barge downriver to Eltham to visit my grandchildren.

September has been hot and thundery, with sudden heavy storms and flooding. The river is swollen, the air fetid and beneath my veil I am sweating as no Christian female has the right to. Every so often I bid my serving woman to mop the moisture from my forehead.

"I wish I had selected my other veil, this one is far too thick for this inclement weather."

"There is another in the luggage, My Lady, you can change once we reach Eltham."

"I feel I am being boiled alive." I wrench at the neck of my gown, while she flaps the fan a little more vigorously. We pass a family of ducks, some dabbling in the water, others stretched languidly on the bank. I lie back on the cushions, close my eyes, the thick green scent of the river stirred by the slow splash of the oars. Thank Goodness we have only a short distance to travel. I will soon be within the thick walls of the Palace away from the discomforts of the sun.

Before the barge has finished bumping against the jetty, I am on my feet, attempting to disembark. Behind me the women scramble for their belongings and following in my wake.

"I will refresh myself before I visit the nursery. Hurry and bring me water, my face feels thick with grime."

The royal apartments are quiet. I take a seat near the window, pull off my veil and loosen my hair. Soon my woman appears, pours water into a bowl and with a soft cloth blissfully removes the megrims of the journey.

I had fully intended to visit the nursery this evening but it has been a trying day and it is not as if the children are expecting me. I dine lightly and sink gratefully into bed at the first sign of darkness. Shooing all but one of my women away, I ask for the candles to be extinguished and close my eyes. A good night's sleep will restore my energy and I can enjoy a long day with the children tomorrow.

It is barely dawn when a sound awakens me. I sit up and frown at my woman who is slumbering in a chair at the hearth.

"Whatever can that be? Go and discover the cause of it please."

Straightening her cap, she scurries away. For a few moments I lie in wait but a creeping suspicion comes upon me; a sense that something is terribly wrong. I climb from bed with a muttered complaint and search out my shoes that she has tidied away out of sight. I am still struggling with the buckles when she returns. Her face is devoid of colour, her eyes wide and wild, confirming my fears.

"What is it?"

From the expression on her face I know I will not like her reply. As tension creeps to my shoulders, I brace myself for words that I cannot bear to hear.

"Elizabeth ..."

My heart skips a few beats.

"The queen? She has miscarried?"

"No, not the queen My Lady, the baby – *little* Elizabeth!"

I shall be haunted until the end of my days by the memory of my journey from the royal apartments to the nursery. Hampered by my improperly fastened shoes I stumble along the corridor, dread washing over my shoulders as, swallowing the need to vomit, I rush headlong toward despair, toward misery, and soul destroying truth.

The double doors loom before me where a pair of white faced guards stand aside to allow me to pass. I take three fearful steps into the room.

The women of the nursery stand ringed around a single figure kneeling in the centre of the floor. Through a fog of grief I recognise Elizabeth's nurse, Cecily Burbage. She has her back toward me. Her head is bowed, her hair flowing like water from beneath her nightcap. Jutting from the crook of her right elbow I can just see the tiny feet of my granddaughter. Feet that used to run across the room toward me, feet that recently hopped and skipped and danced. Fragile, fairy feet that are now stilled, feet that will dance no more.

One of the women looks up, startled to see me there. She glides toward me, like a wraith, a ghost bringing confirmation of all my fears.

"We cannot persuade Cecily to move, My Lady. She must have been there for hours –none of us were aware of ... what had happened. We just found her ...like this."

In the silence of the room Cecily begins to hum a lullaby.

Pain is lodged in my throat, solid, immoveable, like a rock. It takes all my strength to speak through it. Stepping deeper into the room, I place my hand on the nurse's shoulder and speak her name.

"You must get up now, Mistress Burbage," I say, my eyes fixed on the marble blue face of my granddaughter. "You must give the child to me. I will take care of her."

Cecily's head turns stiffly, her blank eyes revealing no recognition. The usual awe I inspire in these women is absent. Death has come to Eltham and disempowered me. Disempowered all of us.

Reluctantly she allows me to remove Elizabeth from her arms and, on stiff and groaning limbs I carry my granddaughter to the window.

Through the open shutters I hear the church bells ringing Prime, calling the devout to prayer, just as they do every day. But for the first time in my life I cannot find the words to speak to God. My heart is like a great slab of stone that has been baked dry by fire and cracked asunder by the sudden onslaught of ice. Shards of misery stab at my soul, a ripping pain in my heart, yet outside the palace, nothing has changed. For ordinary people, today is just like any other, the universe does not care that an insignificant princess of England, our little Elizabeth, has been taken most cruelly into God's keeping.

With pain wedged in my throat I pen a message to Henry and Elizabeth and send it post haste to Sheen. As the messenger rides away I picture them receiving it. On recognising my hand they will anticipate a comfortable letter, replete with domestic news, the progress of the garden, the delivery of the sumptuous embroidered velvet Elizabeth and I have been waiting for. They will not anticipate news of an event as devastating as my letter contains but there is no way to soften it. I would give all I have not to have to send this letter.

I imagine the queen's face falling as she drinks in the dreadfulness of the words. She will put a hand to her belly, her new child within might leap in response to his mother's sudden shock. And then my son, my Henry will notice her reaction and take the letter up, run his hand through his hair as he absorbs the horrid truth.

Recently he has negotiated with King Francis for a marriage between little Elizabeth and the one year old dauphin. Little Elizabeth should have been a queen of France – a figure of import, not a tiny unremembered corpse laid low in a marble tomb.

The king and queen make a hasty return to Eltham, each reacting to their personal tragedy in different ways. Elizabeth gathers her bewildered children to her breast and weeps with them. I wish I could do the same but I am drawn to my son's side. He needs me as never before, although he will not admit it. He refuses to bow down in grief and instead he buries himself in duty.

He sits alone in his chamber, his sorrow channelled into planning the most elaborate funeral that he can. No cost is to be spared. His infant daughter must have everything he can provide, every extravagance she would have enjoyed had she lived to adulthood. Dry eyed but torn, he orders the Princess Elizabeth be brought from Eltham to Westminster Abbey in a chariot drawn by six horses. She is to be laid in a grey Lydian marble tomb with a black marble cover near the altar and close to St Edward's shrine. An effigy of Elizabeth in copper gilt is to be placed atop it and an inscription with the words:

Here, after death, lies in this tomb a descendant of royalty, the young and noble Elizabeth, an illustrious princess. Atropos, most merciless messenger of death, snatched her away. May she inherit eternal life in Heaven.

I do all I can to lift the spirits of the royal couple and the children. It does not do to wallow in one's grief but ...oh, my own heart is broken and ... it is hard. Prince Henry is bewildered, bereft of his favourite playmate and young Margaret's white face is shuttered with stubborn, unshed tears. While my son buries himself in matters of state, Elizabeth stares listlessly from the window, one

131

hand stroking the rise of her womb, her needlework abandoned on the floor.

After a few weeks, although the pain does not abate, our family grows accustomed to little Elizabeth's absence. There are just two children in the nursery now. Elizabeth's cot is carried away, her clothes distributed to the needy. Henry and Margaret are subdued, missing their noisy young sister and only Arthur is unaffected. He only met her but once or twice and, of course, in his own household in Wales, the tragedy must seem less immediate.

"At least it was not one of our boys," Henry mutters, making Elizabeth and I gasp. But I understand what he means. With two sons we are secure. Two boys is a goodly number for a king; an heir and one to take his place should the unthinkable happen. God forbid that the unthinkable happen.

The king, searching for a day of joy, takes steps to make Prince Henry the Duke of York, neutralising the claims of the Pretender casting scorn upon Warbeck's claim to be the lost son of York. The ceremony is lavish yet our hearts are not in the celebrations that follow. For many weeks I am at a loss as to how to restore them; I fear their former vitality will never return.

Despite her sorrow, Elizabeth's health continues to thrive. Her pink cheeks and widening girth belie her ready tears. With a child kicking lustily beneath her ribs even she finds the strength to rise above the loss. It is her duty to move forward and she will not let it wear her down. Slowly, by degrees, she takes up her needle again and begins to fashion tiny bonnets and swaddling cloths for the new baby. Secretly I hope for another girl to replace Elizabeth but then I remember we are no ordinary family, and remind myself of our need for more boys. Arthur and Henry may be thriving but one can never have too many sons.

As winter's bite takes hold and preparations are in hand for the Christmas season, I order small New Year tokens for the children. For the king I wrap up a book of hours, and purchase a bejewelled and embossed needlecase for Elizabeth, cunningly wrought from gold. Even the meanest of my household will receive some small token and although he will not be attending court, I have not forgotten Jasper. Carefully folded in my clothes press is a collar on which I have laboured long, embroidering it with red roses, picked out in gold. But, before I can present him with it, news arrives from Thornbury. Tidings that takes us by surprise and hits us ... hard.

With a breaking heart I fold the collar away out of sight, unable to look at it yet unable to part with it. Jasper –there are so many memories. In the beginning he was kind to me, considerately filling the awkward gap between Edmund and I that neither of us knew how to cross. Even while he courted Myfanwy he found time for me, although I was little more than a child. He never dismissed me as plain, uninteresting and gauche but encouraged my interests and boosted my confidence by concentrating on the small talents I possessed.

I remember dear Jasper, taking me in at Pembroke when Edmund was killed, giving me his best chamber, and after Henry was born helping me avoid the indignities of a political marriage arranged by the king. I have him to thank for my happy years with Harry Stafford, and I have no doubt that had Jasper not been there to oversee Henry's safety and whisk him away to exile across the sea, we would not be where we are today. *Souvent me souviens* – I will remember ... often.

I can never forget Jasper, striding through life, refusing to lie down beneath York's rule, refusing to give up the campaign, shrugging off battle wounds, tirelessly plotting and raising support for Lancaster. It was Jasper's determination that won through, that placed us on the throne of England and shaped Henry into the king he is today.

Although in recent months he has been too ill to attend court, he leaves a gaping hole. He was Henry's chief advisor and there is no one to replace him. Henry has no higher, wiser authority to turn to now. There is only ... me.

Christmas 1495

Coming so swiftly on the heels of the death of little Elizabeth and Jasper, Christmas is a muted affair this year. Henry is much taken up with affairs of state, furious to learn that the Pretender, after boldly sailing to Ireland and laying siege to Waterford, has now been welcomed at the Scottish court.

"James is trying to provoke me," the king storms. "He has been helping the Pretender all along and never had any intention of forming an alliance with us. Look how he has stalled and prevaricated over our proposed match with Margaret and now ..." Henry pauses for breath, ruffles his hair and stares at me with fury in his eyes. I stifle the desire to smooth his fringe and straighten his collar. I stiffen my back, fold my arms before me and draw my lips in tight.

"Henry, sit down. You are working yourself into a frenzy of anxiety and that never helps anything. We must assume a total disregard for James' antics with the Pretender. If you let your anger show it will strengthen his cause – we have always given the world the impression that Warbeck is nothing more than a troublesome pest. We must have faith and be resolute. That is our strength."

"But James seems to believe the Pretender really *is* Richard of Shewsbury! He has thrown great banquets in his honour, clothed him in damask and velvet and encouraged a match with some kinswoman of his. Everywhere the imposter goes he is hailed as the rightful King of England, welcomed with open arms and worse of all … Ferdinand and Isabella now believe his lies."

He hands me a letter, I scan the script, frowning at the sentiment.

"They are stalling. It does not mean the match between Arthur and Caterina will never happen. All we need do is smooth the way. I can understand their reticence to send her across the seas while an imposter is at large and the threat of invasion is in the air. Send them our assurances the threat will soon be neutralised, tell them we shall not rest until it is done. We need to force a wedge between Warbeck and his affluent supporters – leave him isolated – close off his escape route by befriending his allies."

"You make it sound so simple, Mother."

He sits down at last, furrows of trouble still marring his brow but he is calmer now.

"Nothing in life that is worth doing is easy, Henry, and securing our dynasty for England is certainly worthwhile."

Poor Henry is pale, the skin beneath his eyes smudged with worry. "Have you been sleeping?" I ask suddenly and he looks up at me, a brow raised questioningly.

"A little, but poorly due to … one thing and another."

"I advise an infusion of chamomile before bed. It relaxes the body and soothes the mind. I take it myself, regularly."

He gives a short huff of amusement.

"Yes, Elizabeth has told me you served everyone chamomile when you visited them at the sanctuary when she was a girl. She described you as a tiny angel of light bringing hope into their darkness."

I feel my face reddening with embarrassment.

"Elizabeth said that? Goodness ... I was as afraid as everybody else ... terrified in fact. I had no idea if our plot would prosper or fail. It was a terrible time but we ... the dowager and I ... could only cling onto the vague hope that one day it would be over."

"And here you are ... The King's Mother."

"Yes, and one day we shall look back on this troublesome pretender to your throne and wonder what all the fuss was about."

"I hope so." He gropes for his cup and takes a mouthful of wine, sloshes it around his mouth before swallowing. "I am uncertain of Elizabeth's thoughts on the matter. I do not know what she feels ..."

"Have you asked her?"

"No. No, I haven't. I am afraid of her answer."

"She ... none of us can know for sure who he really is but I am quite sure Elizabeth will do her duty. Even if the Pretender should prove to be her brother – which I hope he is not – she knows her duty and will place your cause and that of her sons above that of a long lost sibling."

We fall silent while Henry scratches a few numbers into the margin of his book, dips his quill in the ink pot before writing again.

"I must go," I say, rising from my chair. "I shall continue to pray for peace in our realm, Henry, as I always do, and light another candle for Jasper's soul."

"He is such a loss to us."

Henry's voice is bleak. He is isolated, slow to trust, quick to suspect treachery. I wish with all my heart I was father, not mother to him. If I were Edmund, I could serve him ways that a woman cannot. I place a hand on his shoulder, stroke the thick velvet nap beneath my fingers.

"All shall be well, my son. We are God's beloved, and He watches over us."

When he makes no reply I take my leave of him. As I pass quickly along the corridors I think of my son siting alone in his opulent chamber, guarded by men he does not fully trust, in a realm he cannot quite believe belongs to him. *Send him peace*, I pray as I hurry to the chapel; *send him peace of mind that he may rule well.*

<u>Sheen Palace – March 1496</u>

Early in the year Henry signs a treaty with Phillip of Burgundy and other parties. It is known as the *Intercursus Magnus*, a treaty that not only salvages the Flemish and English wool trade but which also forces the dowager duchess, Margaret of Burgundy to accept our position on the English throne and to cease her support of the Pretender, depriving him of support.

With our realm strengthened against Warbeck and the arrival of a healthy princess in mid-March the country celebrates with much needed joy. The king and queen decide to name her Mary and from the start she is a lusty thing.

She is as demanding and loud as her brother Henry had been and stronger than Elizabeth ever was. As

I cradle his daughter for the first time Henry comes to look over my shoulder and we admire her together. She is sleeping, her eyes sealed shut, her lips performing an unconscious sucking action, as if she dreams of milk and a full belly. I run a finger over her down of red hair.

"She is quite, quite perfect, Henry," I say quietly. "You and Elizabeth have done the country proud again."

We both look toward the bed where the queen is slumbering on propped pillows.

"You selected my wife well, Mother," he says. "She is everything a king could require."

"Well, she was bred to be a queen and, since she offered the bonus of acceptance by the adherents of York, I knew she was the perfect match for you. When Arthur becomes king, the mix of York and Lancastrian blood in his veins will see all friction between the houses at an end forever.

"And not a moment too soon."

Mary wakes, stiffens in my arms, arches her back and opens her mouth to protest at her great hunger. The nurse hurries forward, bends the knee to me before holding out her arms to take the child.

"There, there little one. It can only be an hour or two since last you fed..." she says as I pass my granddaughter over.

"Thank you," I say, as she takes herself to a secluded corner and unleashes a breast. She has her own child at knee, an infant who needs the teat less often than a new-born. I watch as Mary snuffles in search of sustenance and as I look, I become aware of Elizabeth also observing from the confines of her bed. It is hard to see another woman nurture your child. I recall the pain well, just as I recall the agony of leaving him behind when I left to marry Harry. I approach the queen and sit at her bedside.

"Your daughter is lovely, Elizabeth, a welcome addition to the nursery."

"She will never replace Elizabeth."

"No, nothing can replace her but we will love Mary for herself, and she will aid our recovery, help the children heal. Henry in particular seems to miss Elizabeth."

"They were so close. He doted on her ... as did we all."

I hear the grief in her voice as she remembers her lost daughter and understand her tears are not far away. I squeeze her frozen hand.

"Prince Henry will soon forget and, while that sounds cruel, it is better that he should. I hope this new sister will soothe him. I think she will come to resemble him more closely than his sisters."

"She certainly seems to share his hunger and outrage."

We laugh gently and I lift my hand which has remained unconsciously covering hers.

"Well, make the most of her while she is with you. She will be moved to Eltham soon enough and you will soon resume your duties and re-join the king at court. You have been missed, Elizabeth, your churching cannot come soon enough. Our court lacks gaiety without you."

"I am lucky to have you there in my place. I must be sure to quickly regain my strength in time for the summer progress."

"Yes, you travel south this year, and are visiting the Isle of Wight, I believe. Have you been before?"

The conversation drifts to other things and when I am convinced her mind has strayed from the discomfort of another woman nursing her new-born, I take my leave. I am tired out by the day and still yet to attend supper in the hall. More and more I find myself weary of court life;

if it were possible I would retire to the country for the summer but I have duties here and need to be on hand should the king require me.

1496

A year of uncertainty, a year of stress for the king as the Pretender grows stronger. The king prepares for invasion on the Scottish border. Our northern counties are on full alert, armed to the teeth against attack and early in the year Henry sends his ships northward.

At court we know not who to trust; the specious masks of our hidden enemies obscure our worthy supporters. Even as we prepare for war, we do not give up hope of avoiding outright war. Embassies are sent to Scotland in June and again in August to propose peace, sealed with a marriage between James and our eldest granddaughter, Margaret but King James declines to discuss it. Our emissaries send news by stealth but even the loyalty of our spies is suspect and we cannot be sure that the intelligence they provide is flawed.

To our relief, anxious to win our friendship and gain our support against France, Ferdinand and Isabella now reject the claims of the Pretender. King Charles of France tries to scupper our links with Spain who is his enemy, by proposing we set aside the Spanish treaty and instead agree a marriage between Arthur and the daughter of the Duke of Bourbon.

The alliances and enemies of Europe swirl in a great maelstrom in my head. As the tables turn, and allegiance shifts, the union between Arthur and Caterina becomes crucial to Spain. They are eager for the marriage now and for us to become part of the Holy League against Charles. All we need do, they say, is to lay hands on and dispense with the Pretender without delay. Even the

Pope presses us to take up arms against France but until the matter of Scotland has been settled, we are reluctant to do so.

The hall is crowded, everyone is eager to witness the foreign dignitaries visiting our court. Our nobles dressed in their finest robes gather to attend the extravagant entertainments Henry has laid on to amuse our guests.

The Spanish ambassador, de Puebla, is all smiles. When the pageant comes to an end, as the applause begins to die down, he fawns over me, leaning over and speaking to me as if I am a child and not a woman approaching her fifty fourth year. My ire is piqued, making me tight-lipped in the face of his oily attentions but I have put up with worse things for the sake of Henry and our realm.

"Such exquisite hands you have, My Lady," de Puebla croons, "such pretty long fingers."

I do have pretty fingers, it is true but I do not need assurances of it from a buffoon. I remove my hand from his, resist the impulse to wipe it on my sleeve. He is, no doubt, unused to negotiating politics with women and believes the only way to win my support is through flattery. I wonder if he uses the same tactic on his queen, Isabella.

Sniffing my displeasure I allow my woman to help me into a chair but he is too thick skinned to notice my dislike and does not have the tact to move away. He hovers beside me, irritatingly pointing out details of the dance now taking place before us, as if I cannot interpret the steps for myself.

"I have seen nothing to match the grandeurs of your palace, My Lady," he enthuses. "No, not even in Seville."

I raise an eyebrow. "Indeed, I understand the courts of Seville to be unsurpassed in the Christian world."

"Oh, not like this! They are nothing like this!"

I can bear no more of his insincere flattery.

"I am short of stature, Ambassador, not of intellect. I shall speak plain. Truly, false praise will gain you nothing with me. I suspect your spies have informed you of my influence with the king and you harbour hopes of winning his favour through me. If that is so, those reports are quite incorrect. Henry makes up his own mind. I may hold strong opinions but, trust me; my views hold no sway over him whatsoever."

He has the grace to blush and bluster for a few moments before fumbling for the dregs of his dignity. I forestall his intention to speak again.

"Now, if you will forgive me, I see the queen is trying to attract my attention. Do excuse me."

There is nothing he can do but stand back and let me pass. I rise to my feet, allow him to briefly take my hand again before I move away, all my fury imprisoned in the set of my shoulders.

"Lady Mother," the queen greets me. She summons a chair be placed beside hers and I take my place. "Are you vexed? I saw you in conversation with the ambassador from Spain. Is he not obnoxious?"

"Oh, indeed he is! And quite oblivious to the fact that a female is capable of any wisdom. He imagines the path to Henry's good will can only be traversed through praise for my 'pretty fingers'. Clearly, he could see nothing worthy of admiration in my face or figure."

She laughs at my indignation and I relax, glad to see the return of her former pink prettiness. There are shadows of course, I expect there always will be. I imagine every bereaved mother lives with the memory of her dead child alive in her heart. Sometimes, if I look very closely I can almost glimpse little Elizabeth peering from behind her mother's eyes. I take a deep breath and will the sadness away. One must not be morbid. I force my mind back to the path of politics.

"All this nonsense will be worth it once England has joined with Spain. Once we have ousted the Pretender and made our peace with Scotland, Arthur and Caterina can be wed and we can turn our attention to the business of extending our line further."

Elizabeth pulls a face.

"It seems so strange to think of Arthur ever fathering a child. He is growing up far too fast. He is still a boy, all that is far in the future."

"Princes do not have the leisure of a lengthy childhood, you know that, Elizabeth. Henry had to put aside youth when he was very young ... when he was ..."

" ...Taken into the custody of my father. I know, but he says Herbert treated him fairly."

"Anne Deveraux made sure of that. She was like a mother to him while he was with them and treated him as one of her own. It was small comfort to me, but comfort nonetheless."

"God forbid I should ever be parted from my children."

"Amen, Elizabeth, Amen."

"So, the Pretender has won himself a pretty bride, I hear." Henry has crept up unawares. Elizabeth and I turn at the sound of his voice as he takes a seat between us. "I hope she is barren. We do not want a whole nest of little vipers to deal with. Blast James and his meddling. It was better for England when the Pretender was wandering the courts of Europe. Anything rather than having him camped on our own doorstep."

He presses the tips of his fingers together, looks out across the hall, his brow lowering.

"Smile Henry," I murmur, "the eyes of Europe are upon us. Do not let the ambassador take a story of royal insecurity back home to his masters."

Obediently, he raises his head, clicks his fingers to instruct the musicians to play louder. Elizabeth sits up, grasps Henry's hand.

"I would like to dance, Henry. I wish you would dance with me."

"I am not a dancing man, my dear, you know that. Anyway, the musicians are tiring now, it is almost time for Skelton's poem to be read."

The queen subsides, disappointed but not dismayed.

"I am probably too weary anyway," she says. "Poetry will be more restful. Oh, look, Lady Mother, the ambassador approaches, mayhap he wishes to play court to you again."

"What's that?" Henry looks up. "Play court to my mother? What the devil?"

"Just a joke, Henry," Elizabeth laughs. "The ambassador was trying to get to you via the good graces of your mother." She waggles her fingers. "Apparently our lady mother's fingers are unsurpassed in Christendom."

"Indeed," Henry growls as de Puebla approaches and executes an extravagant bow. "I wonder what he will have to say about mine," he smirks from the side of his mouth.

My lips twitch with amusement that I only just manage to suppress.

The threat from Scotland becomes all encompassing, consuming all of Henry's attention. While

144

our kingdom is in peril of invasion I make sure the court is run with strict attention to protocol. I enforce rules on everything, from codes of conduct to forms of dress. A show of pride and majesty will help to convince everyone, not just ourselves, that my son rules by the will of God. There is much strength in appearances and we cannot afford to let standards slip.

All through the summer the situation with Scotland hangs like a jagged blade above our heads. As war becomes inevitable Henry's tax collectors are kept busy, their efforts raising both funds for the approaching war and the resentment of the people. It is mid-September before the news that we have been dreading arrives and we learn that the Pretender has made his move.

I join the queen in her apartment but we are both taut with nerves, our conversation stilted and edgy. She fiddles nervously with her prayer beads while we wait for an audience with the king. Henry has been closeted away for hours with his counsel. When the door finally opens and he joins us, I am shocked by his hollow cheeks, his shadowed exhausted eyes.

"Henry ..." The queen and I move toward him in unison. "What news is there?"

While I usher him into a seat Elizabeth flaps her hand at a servant, shooing him off to fetch the king some refreshment. Henry plucks a grape from the bowl but after putting it in his mouth, he spits it disgustedly into the hearth.

"There has been great devastation in the north, James has attacked our fortifications between the Rivers Tweed and Till, and caused great damage to Norham Castle."

I frown, bite my lip while Elizabeth gets up and begins to pace between the hearth and window.

"But it is not all bad news." Henry's hair is ruffled, his pallor wan as if he has not slept in days. "Our envoys report that James and Warbeck have fallen out. It seems the Pretender took exception to the violence."

He gives a humourless bark of laughter that is more worrying than his bloodless face. "They have parted company which weakens James' assault. We must wait and wonder while my informants garner more news."

"I am so tired of waiting! So fatigued from wanting this damned Pretender caught and dealt with."

"Hush, Mother." Henry's hand is on my shoulder, his face close to mine. I can smell the wine on his breath, the bitter disappointment of his heart.

"Oh Henry, it was never supposed to be like this. Our reign was supposed to be a glorious time of peace, the end of war! I am certain it will end that way and know that God is on our side."

"So He is. Wait and see, this is merely a test ... like Abraham and Isaac. One more hill to be scaled before we lay hands on the Pretender. Once he has been dealt with you will gain your dream of perfect peace."

"Oh, I hope so Henry. I do hope so."

"I know so. I have seen it."

News comes that the breach between James and Warbeck is irreparable and the Pretender has taken ship with his wife and left the shores of Scotland. While the depleted Scot's army limps home, Henry's spies urgently try to follow Warbeck's trail, attempting to predict his destination, judge where he may land.

Meanwhile, Henry raises levies for full scale retaliation on James and resentment among the populace increases. In late Spring columns of soldiers and munitions stream north toward the border while in the small Cornish parish of St Keverne, the tax collectors

146

knock on the door of a blacksmith, who refuses to pay his dues.

June 1497

Elizabeth and the children come to Coldharbour where, safe behind the town walls we await the outcome of the unrest in Cornwall. All it took was one dissenter, one fool to refuse to pay, leaving the king's men with no choice but to use force. Now, it seems, the whole of Cornwall has risen against us and a few days later news comes that 18,000 men are marching on London and have already reached Farnham in Surrey. The king has no option but to take up arms against his countrymen.

I have just finished my evening prayer when Henry's messenger arrives wishing to see me on a matter of urgency. He passes me a letter, I break the seal and unfold it, immediately recognising my son's hand.

I scan the words quickly and hand the paper back.

"Inform the queen; tell her to have the children made ready for a journey."

My women scatter, all but one who hovers at my elbow awaiting further instruction.

"Where are we going, My Lady?"

"The king orders us to take refuge in The Tower – make haste."

Elizabeth joins me within the hour. When the situation is explained she makes no fuss, asks no questions. Relieved to discover her so biddable, I take charge, sending out orders and instructions for the royal apartments to be made ready at The Tower.

Henry sends Daubeney to assess the situation and then he himself rides out, well armoured and stout of heart. The men of London hasten in his wake, willing and eager to fight with whatever weapon they can lay hands on. Every loyal Englishman sees it as his duty to defend the capital. With the peasantry of Cornwall up in arms, London is on high alert. The gates are closed, the walls are guarded and there is no safer place than behind the impregnable walls of the Tower.

The Tower of London has stood the capital in good stead for more than four hundred years and it is about to do so again.

The children are roused from their beds. Margaret, more aware of the dangers we face than her infant sister is white faced and silent. Obediently, she climbs into the saddle, takes up the reins, eager to reach the sanctum of the fortress. Prince Henry, seeing it all as a 'great adventure' straps on his wooden sword. His high pitched excitement echoes in my head, exacerbating the already palpable tension and fear that vibrates through me.

"Are the rebels coming, Grandmother?" Henry asks, "Do you think they will catch us? If we are captured, will they kill us?"

Margaret emits a stifled sob and Henry jerks round to face her but he is silenced only for a moment.

"I am sorry, Meg. I did not mean to frighten you. I am sure they will not catch us. Cornwall is a long way off and they will be tired when they get to London and want to rest. They will not have time to bother with us, we are just women and children. It is the king they want..."

"Henry, be silent." My voice thunders in the darkness and he subsides, casting fearful glances my way for the remainder of the ride.

And such a journey will forever be imprinted on my mind. I had thought I was above fear, believed my life so far had hardened me against imagining daggers in the dark. As we pass through streets shadowed by doubt and darkness, the doors of the houses that are locked and barred seem to hold unspeakable terrors. There may be hidden foes, the threat of an assassin's knife, and all that stands between my grandchildren and the looming threat is myself.

I know I am not alone in my fear. The queen, holding Henry firmly on the saddle before her, keeps silent yet her eyes dart from side to side revealing her stifled fear, her pent up nerves. Neither of us will rest until we get the children to safety and are at ease behind the confines of the Tower keep. I wish to God we had removed ourselves in the broad light of day.

The rain increases, the cobbles shine blackly in the dim light, and the Thames lurks close by, reflecting and magnifying the menace. As the outline of the fortress looms ahead, I crane my neck upward. Beside me, Elizabeth swallows audibly, and murmurs something I do not quite hear.

"What did you say?"

"I was praying. Thanking God for bringing us here to safety."

But there is still a way to go. Many layers of security lie between us and the inner keep, the sanctum of The White Tower.

"Save your prayers, Elizabeth, until we are safe within," I say, nudging my mount forward.

It is not the first time I have been in danger but then I had feared only for myself. Now the threat is aimed at my dear son's family and there is only my frail, weak body standing between my grandchildren and our foe. But God is on our side, I repeat to myself. *I know this*.

He has shown this to me many times.

Elizabeth's horse stumbles. "Keep a firmer hand on the reins, Elizabeth," I say. "Your horse needs to know you are in charge."

"My palms are sweating."

"Shush. There is no need to share that fact. Hide your fear. Remember, we are all as brave as we let the outside world know. If we feign valour, no one will be the wiser."

As we grow close to the Tower gate and our presence is announced a great clamour erupts and the portcullis begins to rise. We pass through the first gate, the temperature drops, the stench of the river wafts up and the queen shudders violently, looks around with fearful expression.

"Whenever I come here I cannot help but think of ...."

"Yes, I imagine."

Her brothers are no longer here, I can swear to that and I would give up the keys to my jewel house to know their whereabouts.

"Come," I say. "Not in front of infants."

Henry and Margaret are watching us intently, drinking in our every word. Their eyes flit from the familiarity of our faces to the slick wet walls of the keep that are black and awesome in their impregnability. I wonder how much they know. Servants gossip and the fate of the boys is still so uncertain. We cannot contain rumour and speculation. How much of their York family's history has filtered to them? How long until they start to ask the questions?

I look down at Mary, held warm against my breast. She is the only member of the party who is oblivious to the danger. Still in her night clothes, her cap is lost, her hair is tumbled, and her thumb, red and moist, has fallen from her mouth in her slumber. The weight of her body has sent my arm to sleep, and I can scarcely feel my fingers but I will not pass her to a servant to carry.

"I am surprised she has not woken," I say, in an attempt to turn our thoughts to domestic things.

"I think Mary will be one of those who can sleep anywhere, under any circumstances," the queen replies as she crosses the inner drawbridge.

I urge my horse after her and the others follow, the sound of our horse's hooves loud on the cobbles. Craning my neck I see shadowy faces at the windows of the royal apartments where I imagine the servants are making hasty preparation for our unscheduled visit. In the bailey, when a groom comes running, I pass the child to a waiting woman before climbing stiffly from the saddle. Thank God for bringing us safe and sound.

While Elizabeth does her best to soothe the children, I think longingly of my comforts at Coldharbour but, shunning the makeshift bed on offer, I spend the night on my knees, entreating God in his wisdom to preserve my son and our hold over England.

We deserve it. I have fought all my life, long and hard for the right of Henry to wear the crown. It shall not be taken. Again and again, I beseech the lord to send Henry good fortune, to smite those that rise against us and to let the Pretender fall into our keeping.

Once Warbeck is held fast in the Tower he will be powerless. He can rot there, a half forgotten story, a fiction told by old men to whom nobody listens.

I am standing at the window, watching the sky lighten to a pale grey dawn. A heavy dew has fallen, coating the window with moisture and clothing the world outside in a damp grey muffler of mist. It is difficult to believe it is almost the end of June.

Elizabeth stirs by the fire. She yawns and rubs her eyes.

"I thought heard a noise," she says. "What is it?"

I have heard nothing but, peering into the murky night, I see the flash of torches, men moving below to greet a rider at the Tower gate.

"A messenger, I believe," I reply, my voice belying the increased beating of my heart. "But it may not be for us. The Tower is a busy place, so many people coming and going."

But something tells me the news this messenger brings, be it good or bad, will determine our future. Henry has either won or lost and Elizabeth, the children and I shall either leave here in triumph, or creep away with our proud future broken and torn.

The messenger is wide eyed, limp with exhaustion from his wild ride. He fumbles for coherence as he hands me the ragged note. I tear the parchment open and squint at it by the light of a candle. Henry's words are difficult to read as if his hand was too weary even to wield the pen. After a moment I look up to where the queen sits expectantly, every sinew of her body alert for news, her lips moving in a silent prayer for victory.

"Henry has won," I say, and she relaxes so suddenly and completely that for a moment I fear she will fall.

"Oh thank God, Oh thank the dear lord."

*

Two thousand men lay dead on Blackheath Common, the ground steeped with rebel blood. As Henry makes a triumphant return to his capital the people call their appreciation. The king has turned the enemy from the gates of the city and redeemed his people from the threat of attack. It is the closest they have yet come to demonstrating love for my son and their affection is most welcome.

For days they clamour outside the Tower, a rabble of unwashed humanity, a stinking, uncouth assemblage of ungrateful souls. Yet, they cry out to us with love and gratitude and with all our hearts we love them and are grateful in return.

Cecily Burbage, ignoring the children's indignation at the piecemeal offerings for breakfast, is encouraging Mary and Margaret to eat. Prince Henry needs no such encouragement. We have not told the children of their father's victory or that he will be joining us for breakfast.

The king, unwashed and still with the filth of the battle field upon him, enters quietly and places his helmet on the table and ruffles Henry's hair. The children look up, leap from their chairs with Elizabeth and I just a step behind. He picks up Mary, kisses Margaret's brow and punches Henry lightly on the shoulder. When the children have lost interest and resumed their breakfast, Elizabeth is taken into the circle of his arms. Keeping my eyes averted, I reach out and clasp the edge of his cloak, screwing it in my palm, clinging to the reality of the fact that he is home.

I wait patiently while my son untangles himself and turns for my greeting. When he releases me from his arms, I smooth back his hair that is still mired from the battleground. Although he swears he took no part in the fight, it is clear he came close to danger last night, too close for comfort. But he is back, safe and sound and I thank God for it.

"You have done well, Henry. The rebellion was dealt with competently and quickly. Well done."

"There were many losses."

I shrug dismissively.

"Rebel deaths; traitors should not be mourned."

"They were my subjects nonetheless. Were it not for James and that damned Pretender, I would have had no need to raise the taxes and none of this uproar would have happened."

I turn away, a little piqued at his attitude. He should be thanking God for his victory, celebrating his triumph not regretting the loss of a few ... felons.

<u>September 1497</u>

As peace in the realm is resumed, Elizabeth and I take Prince Henry on royal progress to East Anglia where it is hoped his presence will instil loyalty in the wavering hearts of the people. Each town we enter is decked with the Tudor colours, and pageants and entertainments are laid on for our pleasure, it seems on every corner of every street. Although I am so exhausted I can barely keep my body upright in the saddle, I paint on a smile, wave cheerily to the crowd. Little Henry, mounted on his own pony, laps up the attention. He sits tall and returns their greeting in a proud, chivalric manner. He shows no fear of the multitude, no awareness of possible hidden dissenters but accepts the adoration as if it is his due.

Meanwhile in London, the king is wreaking justice on the ringleaders of the recent insurrection. But, in his mercy, he commutes the sentence of hanging, drawing and quartering and allows the traitors to be hung until fully dead before they are decapitated. Their boiled and tarred heads now grace London Bridge, and their other bodily parts adorn the city gates for all to see, as a deterrent to other would-be rebels.

Refusing to be defeated by the trials of travel, I behave as if nothing is amiss but Elizabeth, who is not so well schooled at disguising her mood, is tense and irritable. Too often after a long day of public engagements, I see her with her head in her hands, her forehead furrowed with worry. Thankfully, Henry is enjoying the experience far too much to even notice; he enjoys the players and the wild enthusiasm of the watching crowd.

"I think I might like to be a player, if I were not a prince," he announces. "It must be fun to strut upon the stage and pretend to be someone quite different to oneself."

His happy mood brings a smile even to Elizabeth's worried face.

"We are all playing a part, Henry. People are seldom who they pretend to be. We all have a secret self buried deep inside."

He thinks about this for a moment.

"Do we, Mother? Who are you then, when you are not being the queen?"

It is a good question. His innocent response makes me re-examine Elizabeth afresh and wonder who she is inside for her words have more than a ring of truth.

All my life I have pretended to be brave and very grand. Even today, I may look like a serene yet ageing countess in a sumptuous black gown absolutely certain of her own worth and position but inside I am floundering in fate's current. My skin is wrinkled and beneath my skirts my knees are inflamed and painful. My every smile conceals insecurity as I hope against hope the ebbing tide will not leave me cast up, parched and broken on the shore.

What sort of woman does Elizabeth conceal beneath her serene exterior? She is not just a Tudor queen; she is also a Plantagenet princess, just as she has always been. But who is her real self? Where do her loyalties really lie?

The threat of invasion has not passed and within days we learn that Warbeck, after escaping from Scotland and managing to navigate a passage through the ships we sent to intercept him, has disembarked at Whitesands Bay. He dares to taint our sacred soil with his traitorous feet, and marches across Cornwall, gathering traitors in his wake and has himself declared king at Bodmin.

The black hearted Cornishmen, uncowed by the recent punishment we bestowed, provide him with a warm welcome, applauding his declaration and cheering his promise to dispense with all taxes. His rhetoric sees his army of supporters swell, and they march on, finally attacking Exeter and taking possession of Taunton.

I make all haste back to London to find Henry tense of jaw, shadowed of eye and surrounded by advisers. He looks up as the men draw back at my entrance, allowing me a path to the king. I take the sheet of parchment he is holding and run my eye across it.

"What steps have been taken?"

Most men would shy from involving their mothers in business but most men were not born to me. He gets up, looks over my shoulder, rubs the end of his nose and squints at the paper I am holding, jabs it with his finger tip.

"Daubeney has him under surveillance, he reports the Pretender's every move."

"Good. Good; he will soon be ..."

"And meanwhile, James attacks us in the north."

I look up sharply, frowning at this latest news. I should have expected no less.

"Our border is well defended?" I frown, turning the statement into a question.

"Of course; and I have not yet given up on negotiating terms. It is just a matter of making a tempting enough offer."

I take the proffered seat, and after smoothing my skirts, accept a cup of wine.

"We will succeed. There is not a man on this Earth that cannot be bought."

"If we can afford his price," Henry smiles at me over the rim of his cup. "It is good to have you back Mother, although I sent you away to keep you from danger, you were very much missed."

"Sometimes, my son, it is better to be in danger than impotently fretting from a place of safety."

October 1497

September is an anxious month that turns as slowly as the autumn leaves into October. I begin to feel better, certain that my prayers will be answered and our fortunes are about to change for the better. The tension ebbs and flows, a tide that regularly shifts from futility to conviction. After a week of uncertainty Elizabeth and I receive the news that we have been waiting for.

Henry writes from Taunton that Warbeck's army is depleted. His men, traitors all, are deserting him in droves and the Pretender's decisions are becoming increasingly erratic. The imposter is losing control, losing hope and very soon, I pray, he shall lose moral completely and give himself up to our mercy.

Shortly after dawn, as I return from prayer I find a messenger has arrived from the king. I unfold the crumpled grubby sheet, holding my breath to steel myself against bad news.

We have him! Henry writes. *He is no prince, but a lowly, pale-faced whelp with no more dignity than a dog from the gutter. You will be astounded when you meet him that anyone could have been taken in by his claim to nobility.*

I release a breath I had not realised I was holding. It is not Richard, praise God. Had it been he, I cannot imagine how I would have found strength to deal with it. Such good tidings are long overdue. I lift my eyebrows and sit down near the window, looking without seeing across the gardens. *Thank God*, I think. *Thank God and all his saints for this news.*

I turn my attention back to Henry's letter, bending my head to decipher his enthusiastic scrawl.

I also have another in my custody, one Catherine Gordon, the short acquaintance of whom assures me she is a gentle creature who has been horribly misused by both James and the Pretender. She shall return to court in my company where I have promised a place shall be found for her in Elizabeth's household.

Elizabeth, having lately returned from the shrine of Walsingham, invites me to view the portraits lately made of us. The artist has made a good likeness of the queen; she stares back from the canvas, plump and fair, her fingers idling toying with the stem of a white rose. She looks placidly into the distance, her thoughts probably on children and domestic matters. My portrait on the other hand, is less pleasing. It is as well I have never been given to vanity.

"I look very terse," I comment, peering closer at the deep furrow between my brows, the dissatisfied parallel lines that flank the mouth. "Is that how I really look?"

Elizabeth's laugh is silvery, reminiscent of her mother's.

"I think the black gown and veil make you appear sterner than you are. Perhaps you should remember to smile next time you sit."

"I think I should stop wearing black. My objective was to focus on piety, the book to indicate my learning – I had no intention of presenting such a dour picture."

"You must have another made, Lady Mother, maybe wearing your dark red gown and gable hood. Red is a much better colour for you."

"Well, luckily vanity has never been a particular vice of mine. I shall have to be wary of ever being painted again. Has Henry seen it? What was his opinion of it? I note the artist has captured the king's face almost perfectly. I would like a copy of this one for Woking."

I lean closer to the portrait of my son, a smile playing on my mouth as I study the familiar hooded eyes that he inherited from me, and the mobile lips bequeathed by his father. "He is such a handsome man. His father was too, although I think Henry resembles me more than Edmund."

"He did not look very handsome on his return from Bodmin. I think he is suffering from strain and lack of sleep. He is having some trouble with his eyes, did he tell you?"

"No." I frown at her. "What sort of trouble? A sty or something?"

"No, not a sty. He complains of blurred vision and headaches. I told him he needs to stop poring over those accounts of his, or use more candles when he works long into the night. I do not know why he does not engage a man to do more of his accounting for him. Never once in my life did I see my father totting up a row of figures."

I do not reply but find myself suddenly liking her less. It is always so when she makes veiled criticism of my son. It is her duty as his wife to find no fault in him and not be constantly comparing him to her profligate father. I never once complained of Edward or Harry ... or, perhaps I did.

I have a sudden memory of the small irritations of Edmund leaving his sword on my prayer desk, of the long, embittered arguments I had with Harry when he was determined to abandon Lancaster and fight for Edward of York. I loved him anyway, despite our differences, why should it be any different for Elizabeth?

I give myself a mental shake and smile, turning my thoughts to the matter in hand.

"Well, I think the portrait of me will be better hung behind a curtain but it will do. Yours and Henry's are fine enough to grace the palace, I must have copies taken for Coldharbour."

The queen leans toward me.

"Have you seen him yet? The Pretender? Henry is reluctant for me to meet him. Do you know why?"

I shake my head.

"He has not confided his reason to me but I understand there is little to admire. He is clearly not your brother but an underling, a nobody. The king is right to display him at court as a kind of curio. It might teach the rogue to keep his place."

"My women say he is good looking, but not as handsome as my father was. I – agree – it is not my brother, after all."

"Were you hoping that it was?"

"N – no, not hoping, of course. I would not want anything to undermine our rule or that of my sons but ...

160

oh, I would give up much to know the fate of those little boys."

I stoop and leave a kiss on her brow.

"My dear, so would we all and it must be much harder for you. Rest assured the man in Henry's keeping is an upstart, a chancer, nothing more than that."

"And I must wait and wonder about Edward and Richard for the rest of my days."

The queen does not attend the festivities. She pleads a headache and Henry invites me to take her place as his companion in her absence. The hall is hung with finest arras, so many candles and torches are lit that, were it not for the deeper shadows at the periphery of the chamber, one might mistake night for day.

At the sudden blast of trumpets, the crush of people cease their conversation and part as the king and I enter, my fingertips nestled in his palm. I am reminded of the day long ago when I followed my mother's skirts to be presented to the old king, Henry VI. I can still remember the soft feel of the velvet between my fingers, the way her heel peeked every so often from beneath her gown, revealing a lick of white kirtle. Today, I follow no one. I am at the front of the procession, my hand held lightly by the king. And now, that king is my own son, the old king's namesake.

As we pass through the throng the courtiers fall reverently to their knees. Henry escorts me to the high table, assists me into Elizabeth's canopied chair beside his throne. I settle into the seat, cast my eye about the hall, noting who is present … and, more importantly, who is absent.

Turning to make some remark to Henry I find his attention is taken with a woman on his right hand side.

161

Surreptitiously, I lean slightly forward in my seat to discover her identity.

Henry is attentive, watching her hands as they dance between them, animating her words with long, bejewelled fingers. Fingers that from time to time come to rest briefly on her beaded bodice, deflecting his interest from the movement of her lips to what lies beneath.

The king shifts in his seat, leans a little closer. I hear his nasal laugh and watch his left hand tighten on the arm of his chair.

She must be the Gordon woman but I can discern no sign of grief on her pretty, alabaster face. A shadow of unease falls over me, making me reach for my mantle and draw it close. When the servers arrive Henry indicates that his guest should be served first. I frown; this is high honour indeed for the wife of a pretender. Acting as if I have not noticed her, I show no desire to be introduced but her face is burned onto my inner eye.

She inclines her head in thanks, and laughs. It is a pretty, high pitched sound that pierces my breast with a feeling I recognise as jealousy. Unable to draw my gaze from them, I see the king's smile falter. It quivers, his tongue briefly flicking into view, moistening his arid lips, his eyes narrowing with something I can only interpret as desire.

I force myself to look away, reach out for my cup and gulp a mouthful of wine that stings my eyes and makes me cough. My woman darts forward as I grope for my kerchief, and feebly pats my back, fussing and twittering in my ear. Sharply, I hold up my hand in a silent signal for her to desist and she falls back to resume her place behind me, her hands folded.

The king has noticed nothing of my plight. All his attention is on his quarry. Fury rumbles in my gut,

162

indignity for Elizabeth's sake. I press my lips together and look scathingly upon those gathered in the hall, defying any one of them to give one sign of gossip. This will never do. Elizabeth should be here; the king's fascination with this woman must be nipped in the bud. I shall see that it is done.

I say nothing of this to Elizabeth but she will hear soon enough for the whole court is buzzing at the king's infatuation. While the women look on in scandalised indignation, the men nod appreciatively as if glad their king is showing signs of male vigour. I do not know and dare not ask the nature of their relationship but Henry should keep to his marriage bed. It is heirs we need, not bastards. No good ever comes of ill-begotten children. Has he learned nothing from the chaos brought upon us by the illicit behaviour of King Edward?

Everyone at court addresses Catherine Gordon as My Lady Huntly, ignoring her marriage to the pretender, and the son she has borne to the traitor. Warbeck is present in the hall but not as a guest. He is dismissed as an underling, a laughing stock of the highest degree. How must he feel to see his dearly beloved flirting so outrageously with his enemy? I can only surmise he is broken by it for he wears a face as long as a sheep.

In the weeks that follow, I carry on as if nothing is amiss. I would never allow the world to see the injury Henry's behaviour is causing me for any questioning of his conduct would amount to criticism. All I can do is pray, and hope that he tires of her soon. She is one of those fine fair types who blossom early but rapidly set seed and fade prematurely into a fat and overblown old age.

Henry must be aware of my disapproval but he makes no attempt to mend his ways. His pursuit of her, if indeed she has not already been caught, makes him a laughing stock. The king dances, he *dances!* His hesitant steps as ludicrous and inelegant as an underfed, performing bear. He who so seldom graced the dance floor with his queen is now a besotted middle aged fool. My pride is so injured by his cavorting that I can barely watch, but, in truth, the pain in my heart has more to do with the bad feeling that is inflating between us than his masculine weakness. We have never been at odds before.

Sheen Palace - December 1497

By the approach of Advent Katherine Gordon has become a familiar presence at the side of the king. By now, Elizabeth is clearly aware that she has a rival but she is careful to betray no hint of jealousy. She treats the newest member of her household no different to the others; showing neither favour nor disfavour. If she resents the way the king has put aside his habitual sobriety and forgotten his lifetime's objection to dancing and gaiety, she does not reveal it. She hides her feelings so well that the court has no clue there is any breach between them. But I sense a shadow and set my informants to watch them. Soon they report that the king visits the queen's chamber but rarely.

I had hitherto dismissed the queen as a pretty, pleasant member of our royal family. For all her York blood, I was pleased with her fertility, her robust health, her willing obedience but now my opinion of her rises. Her conduct at this difficult time is flawless. She is strong, not just of body but of mind and for the first time I come to appreciate that the trials she has suffered in her life are not dissimilar to my own.

Raised from birth as a princess, a future queen of France, she was then cast low by the vagaries of war,

164

driven into sanctuary, not once but twice. Many times she went in fear of her life, in fear of her future. After the death of her father when her brother's throne was stolen and she was bastardised, her mother and I were drawn into conspiracy against the usurping king. Had the dowager and I failed then ... her life, all our lives, would have been very different. Elizabeth was there all through it, shut away from the world, her future bleak and undetermined, yet she showed nothing but quiet resilience. I have never acknowledged how strong she is before.

For the first time my opinion of my son is marred. I do not criticise him openly, of course, but it hurts to realise he has defects, like the rest of us. Over the years I have made him an icon of perfection and I am disappointed in his all too human flaws. His mind should be on begetting future sons, strong supporters of their brother's crown, not wasting his seed on some pretty traitor's wife. I had thought him better than that. I had thought him pious and dutiful. Now, I see he has the failings of every other man but ... I love him still.

The Christmas festivities approach. Elizabeth orders new clothes and for the king's new year's gift, a jewel for his cap with a pearl as large as a hen's egg. She herself has a new gown and a fine new hood. Even I am intrigued by the new fashion for headwear that is emerging and order a hood with a peak at the front like the gable of a house roof. The queen and I shall appear at the Christmas feast similarly dressed, a sign of our unity and friendship.

"How are the negotiations coming along?" Elizabeth asks.

"Negotiations?" Henry is involved in so many dialogues with different nations that I am unsure to which she refers.

165

"With Spain, of course. Surely if the wedding between Arthur and the Infanta is to go ahead, Caterina should come to our court soon."

"Oh, I think they are still reluctant to send her. The presence of Warbeck at court is not pleasing to them despite the fact he is under house arrest and poses not the slightest risk."

"Arthur asked about her in his last letter," she says. "He is worried about the living arrangements at Ludlow after they are wed."

"They are too young for the marriage to be consummated if that is his concern. I know only too well the damage it can wreak on a girl if she is bedded too soon."

"And I am not yet ready to be a grandmother," she laughs, hiding her mouth behind her hand, the jewels on her pretty fingers winking in the candlelight.

Christmas Eve is the last day of fasting, tomorrow the feasting and merrymaking will begin. The children are eager, finding it difficult to sit still, small skirmishes breaking out between them. Henry is the worst behaved of all. He squirms in his seat, fidgets with his eating knife, inadvertently overturns his finger bowls and flicks his napkin at Margaret who cries out in pain.

This is too much, my patience runs out. I turn my head sharply toward him, silence him with a look and he subsides into his chair, the picture of remorse.

He has already been told that if he misbehaves he will miss tomorrow's mummers play and since entertainments of any kind are high on his list of pleasures, it is a heavy penalty indeed. For the rest of the meal he is mute, eating heartily of the meagre offerings. I myself partake lightly of the food, knowing that tomorrow's surfeit will see a return of my intestinal complaints.

166

I relax back in my chair as the dishes are removed and music begins to play. Prince Henry, already forgetting my warning, leans forward in his seat, elbows on the table and his chin in his hands. Beneath the cloth his feet are tapping, keeping time with the melody. He turns to me with a beaming face, "I like this tune," he says, our former disagreement forgotten. "Do you know what it is called?"

"You will be able to enquire of the musicians afterwards," I say. "Now, sit up and straighten your back, a prince never ever slouches."

Obediently he stiffens his spine and continues to tap his toes in rhythm with the song. I hear the scrape of a chair as the king rises to his feet and leads Catherine Gordon onto the floor. The company applaud and stand back to watch their monarch dance. Catherine has the grace to blush pink and I curse her for her prettiness, her youth and grace.

The queen reveals no sign of resentment. With great skill, she ensures the smile remains on her lips, her head tilting from side to side with the music. Prince Henry's surprise, however, is undisguised. His mouth has fallen open, his eyes full of indignation on his mother's behalf.

"Why is Mother not dancing?"

He swivels in his seat, leans across me to speak to the queen.

"Mother? You should be dancing. Would you like to partner me? I know the steps."

I fully expect Elizabeth to frown and instruct her son to be quiet but to my surprise, after the briefest hesitation, she graciously inclines her head.

"That would be my pleasure, sir."

Henry, his breast as proud and pouting as a pigeon's, rises to his feet. The court bursts into uproarious applause as the six year old boy leads the queen onto the floor. As is his habit young Henry steals the show; he dances with grace, throwing the king into the shade and, for once, I am glad of it.

Of course, the children have been instructed in the dance as part of their schooling but I had no idea Henry was so accomplished. Compared to his father's clumsy lumbering he is as light footed as a deer. When the dance ends and another begins, he bows with all the elegance of a courtier, takes his mother's hand and hops and trips through the steps without a single mishap. The queen keeps her chin high, her cheeks blazing with pride, love for her son evident in her teary eye.

The applause, when the dance ends, is deafening. I watch the young prince drink in the admiration of the gathering, see his courtly acceptance of their acclaim. I want to applaud with the rest but I keep my hands tightly clasped in my lap. As much as I love him, the child should be curbed. So much exuberance, if given full rein, can only end in a fall. When he leads the queen back to her seat, I remain expressionless, although he seems not to notice.

"Did you see us, Grandmother? Were we not elegant?"

"Indeed you were, child, if you think such a term should be applied to the upstaging of the king."

His pleasure melts, he looks apprehensively toward his father who is now assisting the Pretender's woman into her chair. Henry turns anxiously back toward me.

"Was I wrong, Grandmother? Have I been impertinent? Will the king be displeased with me?"

"You will have to wait and see." I turn my face from him and leave him to stew, contemplating the error of his ways. I know he means well but he must learn to

168

think before he acts. His invitation to his mother to dance was to salve her honour. He loves Elizabeth beyond measure but he would have been wiser to consider the reaction of his father.

A lengthy evening of entertainments follow and I am not sorry when the music slows, the musicians begin to wilt and the promise of bed is not long away.

The children are hurried off to the nursery a little after nine and the queen retires a short while later. Against my inclination I linger at the feast, watching and wondering if the king will follow in the wake of his wife, or trail like a dog in heat after her lady in waiting.

My relief is great when he does neither but instead joins a crowd of gentleman who have gathered for a game of chance. I see Thomas among them, deep in conversation with John de Vere and John Morton. Henry calls for more wine and candles and I realise he does not intend to retire for the night just yet. I sweep toward the gathering, they pull off their caps, bow from the waist, my female presence muting the male topic of their conversation.

"Ah Mother," the king says, taking hold of my shoulders instead of offering me a seat among them. "Are you off to bed? You are wise, we should all do likewise. Tomorrow will be a long day – up before dawn to hear mass." His lips are warm on my brow when he stoops to kiss me, robbing me of the opportunity to linger.

It is mortifying to be ordered abed by my son. I cling to his sleeve for a moment, relishing his closeness, wanting to put right the ill-feeling that has risen between us of late. But, knowing myself bested, I force a light-heartedness I do not feel and bid them all good night.

In my warm welcoming chamber, as I tolerate the ministrations of my women, I think back on the evening. I see again Prince Henry, dancing so well, seemingly part

169

of the music, the godling of the feast, the lord of the dance. I smile as I recall the fine figure he cut but it would never do to inform him of it. I have a feeling that should he ever discover his own attractiveness, he would become too full of his own worth for his own good. I make a mental note to speak to Elizabeth and the king; we must call a meeting with his tutors. The boy needs curbing. He must not be allowed to get out of hand.

The place between sleeping and waking is a curious one. I seem to float, half dreaming while the events of the day and the promise of tomorrow waft like a drift of dandelion seed in the darkness. At first, when the distant shout intrudes upon my slumber I do not stir. But then the voice comes again, closer this time; a loud and urgent cry that is full of fear and I realise it is not part of my dreaming.

"FIRE! FIRE!"

Fire is a thing we all dread. We have all heard stories of flames ripping through homes, destroying possessions, taking lives and livelihood, burning all in its path; the personification of evil.

I sit up, swing my legs from the bed, and hobble on stiff ankles to the chamber door. Before I can grasp the handle it is wrenched open and my manservant cannons into me, almost knocking me from my feet.

"My Lady!" he yells, without apology. "There is a fire in the king's apartment. It is out of control, and we are to evacuate the palace!"

The king's chamber adjoins mine. I can smell the stench of scorching cloth. I turn my head to the open door where a flickering tongue of flame is already licking at the tapestries and smoke creeps serpentine along the floor, filling the corridor with choking fumes, bringing only death and disaster.

"The king is rescued? The children have been taken to safety?" I ascertain, calmly reaching for a heavy robe to cover my nightshift.

"Yes, My Lady; there is no time for that. You must come quickly."

My women, still in their night rail, run before me like so many startled hens, I follow in their wake as calmly as I can, my young rescuer grasping the cuff of my gown to hasten my passage. As yet, I can see no further flames but I can smell the fire, thick and acrid in the air, and the boards are warm beneath my slippered feet.

As we approach the outer door, the frigid night hits me like a wall. We hurry though a crowd, where men's voices ring loud in my ears and women are weeping, and servants rushing to and fro. A man runs past, his hair singed, his cheek smudged with soot. He roughly barges into my escort, water slopping from his leather bucket and drenching my gown below the knee, soaking my slipper.

Outside, huddled in my robe, my women form a protective ring around me. I tilt my head to look up at the flames leaping from the king's chamber window, the belching smoke collecting in a thick cloud above the palace. It is like some dreadful nightmare from which I cannot wake. I cannot move, my mind is paralysed. In all my years, all the trials life has laid before me, this is my first experience with fire.

Close by a window shatters, glass explodes, showering to the ground and peppering the spectators below. Women scream and we leap back as one, amid cries of dismay, shouts of fear. Everyone, even the bravest of us, dreads fire. It has no respect for kings and princes.

The flames must have taken hold in the royal apartments, close to my son as he was sleeping. I scan the

171

crowd for a sight of the king and almost miss him. Henry stands hunched and diminished within the ring of his protective guard. Someone has wrapped him in scorched brocade, his scalp is clearly visible, shining white through his uncovered hair. With a shiver of dread, I remember he is growing old, and his heir, Arthur is as yet, very young. Had God not watched over us and the king had perished this night, England would once more be in the hands of a youth. And we are all too aware of the inherent risks of juvenile rule.

Horror at what might have been swamps me, weakening me, robbing my knees of strength. I begin to pray, my lips moving but issuing no sound. I thank God for sparing us and, as I pray, the suspicion of attempted regicide germinates in my mind. Treason.

I push through the crowd who, on realising my identity, part to allow me passage to the king. Elizabeth is already at Henry's side, the children nearby, clinging to the skirts of Nurse Cecily and Elizabeth Denton. I run my eye over them, assessing their health, noting their terror but thankful they are safe and uninjured. On seeing me, Margaret comes running and I allow her the comfort of my bosom before turning to the king. Cradling her close, I speak over her head, a hand to her ruffled hair.

"Are you well, Henry?" I ask, hearing my own fear. "Is the queen unharmed?"

He shuffles forward, wincing at each step and I realise he is barefoot. "We are all safe," he says. "God be praised."

"Amen," I say.

"A..." Before he can echo my prayer, a deafening rumbling erupts from within the palace and our attention is drawn back to the fire. One wing, that a short time before had been a fine example of architecture is now a smoking pile of rubble, Henry's elaborate apartments in ruin.

"What was that?"

"A wall collapsing, I suspect," Henry replies looking bleakly up at the column of smoke, ash and debris that rises high in the sky. His hand slips into mine and relief washes over me. Having come so close to losing him, our recent disagreement now seems shallow. Pointless. We must never fall foul of one another again. I squeeze his fingers and without looking at him, I whisper. "Thank God you are safe, my son."

Although the heat of the fire is intense, the frigid winter air nips at our ankles, our thinly clad bodies begin to shudder with the combination of shock and cold.

"We must get the children inside," I say, regaining control of the situation. "Come along, let us take refuge in the old manor, the moat will hold back the fire and stop it from spreading."

We are a sad, sorry troop as we hurry to the yawning safety of the neglected hall. It has been standing empty for some time and is unwelcoming and icy cold. The walls are bare of tapestries and the fire sulky in the hearth. But my family are made of stern stuff, while lacking the niceties of a royal palace, we will make do. Beset with draughts, we huddle about the meagre flames, glad when blankets are produced by the thoughtful wife of the steward. The children are exhausted and still snuffling with fear as they are shepherded off to sleep in strange beds.

While our household staff does their best to make us comfortable, Henry, the queen and I cradle cups of warm mead and regard one another with hollow eyes as we absorb and try to make sense of the events of the night.

173

"Do we know what happened to ... Per ... to the Pretender? Did he come out safely?"

Henry and I turn at Elizabeth's question. The king tilts his head.

"I believe he is safe in custody, why do you ask?"

"Oh – I was just thinking, trying to establish everyone's whereabouts. I would hate to think anyone had perished ... even a traitor."

I wonder at her concern. Has she seen Warbeck? Has she dared to defy Henry's orders that she should keep away from him? Her face is pale, possibly due to the shock of the evening, possibly due to the awkwardness of the conversation, possibly due to a hidden truth. I purse my lips, narrow my eyes as I try and fail to recall seeing the Pretender during the upheaval of the disaster.

"We will know more in the morning," I say, "when they bring us a full assessment of the damage."

"We will have lost - priceless things – a small fortune in tapestries alone." Henry's face is dark, his brow lowered, his lips tight as if he blames someone, as if it is a judgement on us all. The queen draws in a short, sharp breath.

"Henry ... surely you do not suspect villainy?"

"Well, we have to consider it. The fire started in my private chambers, in my wardrobe. There are plenty of men who would like to see us wiped out and we do not have to look far to find the prime suspect. What better time to torch the palace than when we've all gathered for the Christmas feasts?"

"But ... surely, no one would ... Henry! Not the Pretender ... what about the children!"

Bad temperedly, he shrugs deeper into his blanket, his face wrinkling in disgust.

"Pah, everything reeks of smoke. I need a bath and fresh linen. I am going to bed."

174

He rises and stalks out of the room, rudely forgoing to bid us goodnight. In the silence that follows I can hear Elizabeth's distress, sense her restlessness. At last, she turns to me.

"What do you think, Lady Mother? Could it have been arson? Would anyone dare?"

Understanding the threat to the dynasty we have created, her eyes are wide with fear, for her children, her husband, for herself last of all. Although my own heart is beset with uncertainty, I cannot exacerbate her suffering. If she is to function properly in the days to come I must set her mind at rest.

"No, I doubt it very much. In all likelihood it was a careless servant, a neglected candle flame, a forgotten lanthorn. These things happen ... even to people like us."

The king quashes rumours of arson by declaring the fire an accident, no act of malice. While the queen mourns the loss of the palace in which she spent most of her childhood, Henry loses no time in making plans for the rebuilding.

"I will make it bigger and better," he says, showing me the drawings he has made. "All of red brick, I thought, with many chimneys, and windows and a long gallery here ..."

His eyes are full of enthusiasm, his mouth taut with repressed pride. "And our new building shall be rechristened. I shall call it Richmond, in our family's honour."

"That will be a fine thing, Henry. Your father would be proud. I like the way you have placed the royal apartments overlooking the inner courtyards as well as fine views over the park and gardens ..."

"Yes, the gardens. I hope to borrow your expertise when the time comes, Mother."

"I shall be honoured!" I clasp my hands together, glad beyond measure that the dispute between us is at an end. What does it matter where or whom he spends his nights with, as long as he does his duty with the queen, and we are friends again.

<u>Westminster - 1498</u>

Apart from some unrest in Wales, which Henry quickly quashes, the early part of the year passes quietly. This newfound peace is welcomed by all and our happiness is doubled in February when Elizabeth gives birth to another son. This time, to my great delight, they name him Edmund.

As I hold the child in my arms, I close my eyes and think of his namesake, feel his presence more strongly than I have for many years. It is as if he is looking over my shoulder to lay his blessing on the child, proud of the dynasty we created together.

If only he had lived to ... no, I must not think like that. To wish Edmund back is to deny Harry, whom I also loved and also lost. Both men were equally as dear to me, yet it was Edmund who gave me Henry. It is to Edmund I owe everything I have.

Life at court continues, the queen, plumper and more placid than before the birth, is seemingly resigned to Henry's attentions to the Gordon woman. Perhaps she expects no less from a marriage, after all her father was a man of appetites. I dare say she was taught by her mother that it is something all women should learn to tolerate.

I am sure Thomas has never been faithful to me but, once I grew immune to court gossip, that fact has never troubled me. For the last few years he has not come to my bed once, and I am glad of it. Since my courses ceased, my desire for him, or any man, has dissolved completely. There is really little advantage to being his wife at all – I do not require the benefit of his status or security. Saving the king, I am the richest, most powerful personage in the land. What need have I of a husband?

With Arthur's marriage to Caterina becoming more and more certain, it will not be long until I am able to hold my first great grandchild in my arms. On that day, with three grandsons and a great grandson, our dynasty will indeed be secure.

The only blemish on my life this year is the Pretender whose presence at court continues to unsettle me. Knowing he is so close, and imagining his hatred for us, makes it impossible to sleep easily in my bed. I am convinced it was he who started the fire at Sheen. How simple it would be for him to take a candle and slyly set alight the draperies that surround the king's bed, or ignite the rich tapestries, or the silks and velvet in the wardrobe. But Henry dismisses my concern.

"The men I set to watch over him observe him keenly. I would trust them both with my life," he says, as if I am already senile.

"Well, I hope so, Henry, because that is precisely what is at stake. I would not trust the Pretender within an inch of my own apartments. He has spent his life in hatred of you; travelled Europe waiting and hoping for the chance to take you down, and now you let him sleep at the foot of your bed like a pet dog. It is akin to giving houseroom to the devil."

"Hardly, Mother. I told you, he is locked in, watched at all times by men I trust. One day he will make his move, but he will not get away with it. He will take his chance and it will be his undoing. I am ready and waiting for that moment."

"I pray you are right."

Henry looks at me from his familiar hooded eyes, his mouth quirked into a smile.

"I do not require your prayers in this instance, Mother but if it makes you feel better ..."

That evening the king brings Warbeck to the hall where a feast is laid in honour of several visiting foreign dignitaries. The Pretender, dressed in finery provided by the king, moves sheepishly after his master, stands quietly as he is examined, interrogated by the curious visitors to our court. He answers with words the king has provided, words that denounce his royal claims and damn him as a traitor, a chancer of the lowest degree.

Catherine Gordon sits at the king's side, her eyes on a lace kerchief she is twisting in her lap. She does not look at the imposter, does not smile or raise her eyes for the duration of the feast. When addressed by the king, she answers politely but she eats sparingly and makes eye contact with nobody. She is not always so quiet.

I have seen her throw back her head and laugh at some witticism of the king. I have seen her tease him, extort money from him in a game of chance. Only in her husband's presence is she silent and pale and tortured. I cannot decide which is the real Catherine and which the dissembler.

I cease my examination of her and let my eyes wander about the hall, watching for other members of our court who may be harbouring sympathy for the plight of the imposter. If I see one look of pity, one kind smile I shall insist the king take action. Henry is too trusting. With the aid of friends, a prisoner without chains is likely to run. The temptation would prove too great.

When Henry embarks on a royal progress through Kent he takes the Pretender along with him. The palace seems empty without the king but I ensure things run smoothly in his absence, attending supper in the hall each evening and with the aid of Reginald Bray, oversee the rebuilding of Sheen. Henry has spent so much upon restoring the fabric of the building and replacing the priceless items lost in the fire that the people are punning on the name Richmond and labelling it instead, *Rich Mont.*

Looking at the pile of bills to be settled, I am not surprised. Richmond Palace will be a splendid edifice indeed, a worthy palace for my son and all the Tudor kings who will come after.

By the second week of June the king and his court have returned and I take the opportunity to retire for a time to Coldharbour. As the barge embarks on its short smooth voyage along the Thames I order the curtains closed to screen me from the other river traffic. My head aches and I am in much need of solitude, an escape from the concerns of court. For a short while I will have time to be myself and relax in my riverside garden. I have asked Cecily to join me early next week, and perhaps the queen and the children could join us later.

Last summer I began the task of instructing Margaret in the secrets of herb lore and, to my surprise, Prince Henry also showed an interest. This year I have commissioned books on the subject so that the children may indulge their studies once they return to Eltham. The next few months hold the promise of relaxation and precious time with my family which in a small way recompenses for the years I spent apart from Henry when he was the age my grandchildren are now.

I wake in the early hours to a silent house. It is not yet time to rise for morning prayer but through the open shutter, the horizon shows the promise of dawn. I am sure I heard a sound and lie awake, listening but apart from the usual simmering slumber issuing from my woman, I hear nothing. I relax again, let my head sink into the pillow and seek sleep, counting my blessings, and thanking God for all I have.

And then the sound comes again. I sit up, slide from the bed, cross to the window and peer out into the shadowy courtyard. Figures are below, their voices muted, their horses sidestepping, the harness jangling in the silence of the night. I watch as they hold a brief conversation with the guard before being escorted toward the house. News from court at this hour can only be ill. My heart begins to beat a little faster and I put a hand to my throat.

"What is it, My Lady?"

My woman comes to stand beside me. I can smell the sweat of her bed, her tainted breath.

"I do not know. Help me dress."

A few moments later, clad in a loose housecoat, Reginald Bray shows a messenger into my parlour. Both men bow but I bid them rise, impatient at their formality in the face of my tension. I hold out my hand for the letter while Master Bray in his usual calm and quiet manner relates the news contained within.

"It seems the Pretender has escaped, My Lady."

"Escaped? From the king's wardrobe? How so?"

"It seems a window was inadvertently left ajar and he took advantage of the lapse. The king is confident of capturing him quickly. He wanted us to be on the alert ..."

"In case the villain ventures here to murder me in my bed?"

180

"Oh, I doubt that, My Lady. I understand the king has sent messengers to warn them at Eltham also. It is better to err on the side of caution."

"Indeed it is." I turn sharply to the servant waiting by the door. "Order my barge made ready. I must travel to Westminster and discover for myself the events of this night as they unfold."

My plans of a peaceful break from court are in ruins. I should never have left. It seems every time I absent myself something happens to call me back.

"My Lady, I am sure there is no need. The king has all in hand ..."

"My presence might be required. The queen may be in need of comfort."

The queen of course has a vast retinue of women to offer her comfort should it be necessary but I will not be deterred. This news has chased away my fatigue and my blood is surging beneath my skin, filling me with a need for action. Calling my women from their beds, I have them dress me for a chilly river journey.

Dawn lies upon the Thames in a damp, drear mist. I drag my furs about me and peer through the curtains at the river. Despite the early hour, it is already milling with small craft, boats darting hither and tither. Reginald Bray, who insisted on accompanying me, sits opposite concealing any notion that he would sooner be in his bed.

"It is busy for this hour, is it not?"

"I suspect, Madam, that word has got out and they are in search of the felon. No doubt a hefty reward will be offered for he who is fortunate enough to apprehend him."

"No doubt."

I huddle deeper into my cloak, my mind wandering to Henry. What will he do now? The Pretender has proven himself untrustworthy. This could mark the beginning of another lengthy hunt. At large, Warbeck can do untold damage to our rule, our foreign policies that have so lately begun to prosper. Europe was just beginning to accept our reign and view our hold on the country as stable. I shift irritably on my cushions. Henry should have heeded my advice. A bird may sing sweetly, seemingly happy to be fed on seedcake and worms yet, should you just once leave open his door, he will fly straight for the nearest tree. Our Warbeck bird has flown and it could cost us dearly. This crisis could so easily have been avoided had the king heeded my warnings. Henry should have shut the Pretender away in the Tower and forgotten him, as I advised.

Without giving the guards time to announce my presence, I stalk into the privy chamber. The king and his ministers turn at my intrusion. Henry rises from his chair.

"Mother, what are you doing here? You should be in bed. We can manage perfectly well."

He kisses me swiftly and I sense but ignore his annoyance.

"I would not have slept a wink after hearing such news. Besides, if you did not require my presence you should not have sent a messenger."

"It was to warn you, I didn't expect …"

"No matter. I am here now." I pull off my gloves, throw them on the table. "Tell me what has happened and what steps have been put in place for his recapture."

"London is on high alert, all roads from Westminster are picketed, and men are out searching. They seem to think he is headed upriver."

182

"We must hope he has not already taken ship. By God, Henry, when he is recaptured he must be brought to account for this … and his inept gaolers too."

The king presses the tips of his fingers together and watches calmly as I pace the floor. A smile plays on his lips, a smile that arrests my attention. I cease pacing, return his stare and realise he is in possession of some facts that I entirely lack. I turn to the gentleman present.

"Would you excuse us, gentlemen I would speak to the king alone."

They turn as one to the king who nods his permission, and they take their leave, one by one bowing over my hand before departing. Henry and I sit is silence listening to their voices fading as they move along the passage. I turn to my son and fold my arms across my stomach.

"What is it you have not told me, Henry?"

He opens his hands, palms upward, his ink stained fingers splayed, concealing nothing.

"There is no need for panic. I told you, all is in hand. I am confident he will be returned by morning."

I cast my eye to the window.

"It is morning."

"Then we should be hearing something very shortly."

We lapse into silence again. I sit beside him, watch him sign his name on a few bills and then the door opens and a messenger enters, bows low before the king as he hands Henry a letter. For a few moments he frowns over the script, then tosses the paper on the table, sits back and surveys me smugly.

"There, you see, I was right. The pretender has been apprehended at Sheen. He took refuge in the Charterhouse where the prior offered him shelter. He now has him held fast under lock and key - Why are you still here?" Henry turns to the messenger who flushes red and shuffles his feet.

"If it please Your Grace, my master wishes to know what should be done with the prisoner. Should he be brought here to Westminster?"

Henry taps one finger nail on the table while he considers it. "No," he says at last. "Have him sent straight to the Tower."

1499

With the Pretender behind bars, life at court becomes more relaxed. The name Warbeck that was once at the forefront of everyone's mind is soon no longer mentioned. Nothing now stands between an alliance with Spain but still Ferdinand and Isabella continue to stall. What more can they want? The king has triumphed over all rival claimants to his throne. Warbeck, a proven traitor and imposter is locked up, never to emerge from the Tower again. The royal nursery is replete with children, three sons is more than any king can reasonably ask. There are barely any left alive who can claim even a tenuous right to our throne. The Spanish reluctance to form a union with us is both infuriating and insulting.

As the Spanish alliance seems to be floundering once again, Henry makes preparation to travel to Calais for a summit meeting with Philip, the young Archduke of Burgundy where Henry hopes to secure an alliance by joining Prince Henry in marriage to Philip's infant daughter, Eleanor.

"Perhaps when the Spanish see Philip is happy to align himself with us it will give impetus to the union of Arthur and Caterina," I remark when Henry informs me of his plan.

"It will not hurt to let the Spanish believe we are also considering spurning Caterina and contemplating a match between Arthur and the archduke's sister instead. Ferdinand has dallied long enough, perhaps he will strap on his spurs if he fears we are abandoning our plans of an alliance with him."

"Henry, you are not seriously going to ..."

"No, Mother. I have no desire to risk the alliance with Spain. I have fought for it too long but it might be wise to let Ferdinand and Isabella sees that we have other options."

Early in the year reports reach us of a few cases of plague affecting the southern parts of the country. By late April it has reached the poorer parts of the city. Our informants bring word of bodies in the streets, people dropping like flies. Often the pestilence seems to take those in their prime, while the young and the very old survive. I send out extra monies for the poor, spend longer on my knees begging God's mercy, and order my household to add the afflicted to their prayers.

After sending the children away from the sickness, to the rural palace at Hatfield, Henry and Elizabeth bring the date of their departure forward and, on the day they set out for Calais, I take refuge at Collyweston.

The plague takes swift hold of the city, the number of dead rising as the heat of the summer increases. Although I am certain Henry has the sense to think of it himself, I write to him, advising him not to return but to extend his duration overseas. We should not think of visiting the south eastern part of our realm until the danger of infection has passed. Henry writes to me in great frustration.

No sooner are we freed of the Pretender than pestilence offers the Spanish yet another excuse for refusing to send their daughter to England. Is there no sign of the plague abating? How long must I endure this?

I share his impatience. The alliance with Spain is imperative for our continued economic growth and political stability. Henry has already begun to make improvements to the royal palace as part of the Infanta's advent. New windows, statues and carvings of dragons, roses, greyhounds and portcullis now adorn Westminster Palace. It would all be such a huge waste of expense should the negotiations fail at this late stage. I increase my daily entreaties to God for an end to the suffering of our people. But we are forced to play a waiting game. In the face of contagion we are all rendered powerless and there is little to be done about it.

And then as summer heat reaches its zenith we receive news from Hatfield that throws our troubles into the shade. The Spanish can do as they please, the pestilence can take half our population but it will never match the desolation, the heart shattering grief of little Edmund's death.

Fifteen months is no age at all. Edmund was such a merry soul, the most contented of all the royal children. Everyone loved him, from the gardener's boy to the king. Perhaps it is true that only the good die young. Perhaps God was jealous and wanted him as his own. But it is so cruel. Edmund was barely walking, barely able to form his words and now he is gone; forever to languish in my heart like some half formed thought, a painful memory of an unrealised dream.

As I grow older I realise our lives are nothing but a collection of memories, flawed recollections of a time and place that will never come again. Once life is extinguished those memories die with us and we become nothing more than an imperfect jumble of half-recollected stories in the minds of our children.

Little Edmund had not been given time to form his own memories and will last only as long as Elizabeth, Henry and I can remember him. Then he will be snuffed out, a tiny flame that flared for a brief moment in the dark.

"I have a letter from Cecily." The queen looks up at my news, a glimmer of interest showing through her sadness.

"Is she well?"

I move closer, take a chair at her side. Cecily has been absent from court for some time after the death of her daughter, the second to die tragically young. We are pitifully short of cheerful news.

"I am afraid not," I reply as gently as I can.

Elizabeth jerks her chin questioningly.

"It takes time to recover from the loss of a child. It is even worse when that child has lived long enough for us to recognise their laugh, understand their humour, and know their sorrows and fears. Perhaps she should come to court so we could mourn our losses together."

I had thought I was done with weeping this morning before I left my chamber. I clear my throat which is curiously tight, reluctant to bring more sadness upon the queen. She has enough of her own.

"It is not her daughter this time, Elizabeth ... it is her husband ... John."

My words startle the queen from her self-pity. She starts visibly, grasps my sleeve.

"John Welles? He is ... dead?"

I incline my head, my heart overflowing with grief.

"Oh, Lady Mother, he was ... your brother ... I am so sorry."

I pat her hand, as though I am the one comforting her and try not to remember my half-brother John as a child, a toddler running in my wake, trailing toy soldiers and swords. After I was sent away with Edmund I saw him seldom but never forgot him. As soon as Henry won the throne, I secured my brother's marriage to Cecily, thinking it a good thing. But for poor Cecily at least, it has brought only grief. After the crushing death of her daughters, she is now widowed and entirely alone. However will she bear it?

"I shall write and ask her to come to my house at ColdHarbour. She will perhaps find it easier to return to court in slow degrees from there."

"I shall write to her too, emphasising my need of her comfort. She is too proud to come to me for her own sake."

The queen remains lethargic throughout the summer, even the arrival of her pale, grief raddled sister fails to rouse her sufficiently. They sit like lost souls, speaking only of the dead and a past that will never be recaptured. They are too young for that. They are barely past their prime. They should be looking to the future not regretfully backwards.

The queen does her duty of course, as she always has, but she is sad, pale and wan. When I dose them both with herbal infusions and advice, they accept my ministrations obediently but with little warmth or appreciation. Where Cecily does her best to appear to be rallying, it is almost as if the queen has no wish to recover but I refuse to give up.

"Drink it up, right to the dregs and you will feel much better."

She lowers her cup.

"What would be the point? When I recover to full health and Henry gets another child on me I shall only live in fear, waiting for it to die. I do not believe I am destined to have any more children. I am growing old and Henry takes his pleasure elsewhere ..." Her voice breaks. I lean forward and retrieve the cup before she spills the carefully prepared infusion down her skirts.

"It is normal to feel grief Elizabeth but you must not let it define you. Do not let it eat you up. You are young enough yet, there will be more sons. I am sure the king's interest in Catherine Gordon is no more than friendship. A man needs the company of young women to keep him virile. It is no reflection on you."

"I know you do not believe that, Lady Mother but I am grateful for your wish to offer comfort."

"It does not do to wallow in one's grief, Elizabeth. Imagine if the king were to do so; imagine if he were to neglect his duties because of his sadness. To add to his personal grief, since the death of John Morton Henry has been without his chief administrator, his favourite cardinal, his friend ..."

Elizabeth stands up. "I know. I know and you are right. I shall make more effort." To prove her determination she snatches the cup from the table and gulps it down. "There," she says. "Now I shall be better in no time."

She is as good as her word. After that day it is as if she has folded her grief away and hidden it at the back of a closet. She attends all her duties, projecting a placid and serene countenance to the court. Always generous, her donations to the poor increase, often leaving her short herself, forcing her to borrow funds.

189

Cecily's presence aids her recovery. She is there when the queen needs a face she can trust, someone in whom she can confide. I must confess to a little envy of their companionship but it is a sacrifice I am willing to make. Together, I am satisfied, they will heal the faster and I am glad to take the opportunity for a few weeks to myself at Coldharbour.

I have not forgotten Henry's suggestion that I take a vow of chastity. When he does not mention it again, I raise the subject myself when we are sharing a meal together. He puts down his cup.

"I had thought you had changed your mind, or that it was just a whim. Have you spoken to Thomas about it?"

I incline my head.

"Our marriage is no longer ... our relations are merely spiritual. He has no objection."

"Supposing you should ever be widowed. You may wish to form another, beneficial marriage."

I purse my lips.

"I will not, Henry. You are the only man in the kingdom to whom I am socially inferior."

He laughs and hands me a brimming cup of malmsey wine.

"Quite right. I momentarily forgot. There is nothing to gain from a husband ... apart from companionship perhaps. Have you considered that?"

I shake my head, sip my wine.

"I have you and Elizabeth, and the children keep me occupied. If I find myself in need of spiritual guidance or support I can rely on Reginald Bray to provide it."

He draws some papers from his desk, makes some marks upon a page.

"We shall see that it is done, Mother. If you are quite sure..."

"I am sure."

Thomas has been a good husband and I have no regrets but within the month, while I remain wed to him for life, I am freed of the ties of matrimony. I can now devote myself to prayer and the royal children. It is refreshing. I feel different from other wives. I have a husband without the inconvenience – it is rather like enjoying a surfeit of good wine without the resulting headache, or a profusion of green apples without becoming bilious.

It has been a long sad summer and I am not sorry to see it end. The harvest is in, and in my gardens the trees are denuded of fruit. The apples and quince are stored and the soft fruit preserved to nourish us in the coming winter. I am strolling among the thinning flowerbeds when I hear a footstep on the gravel behind me. I turn sharply, my face opening in pleasure.

"Ned! What are you doing here? I thought you would be in Wales, preparing to hibernate for the duration of winter."

"Oh, I came on an errand and could not leave without calling on you. I hope it is not an intrusion, My Lady."

"Never. Never." I beam at him as we progress between the straggling remains of the lavender beds. With a twinge of sadness I notice the grey in his hair, the slight stoop to his shoulder. He sees me looking and straightens up, thumps his chest where the arrow once lodged.

"I get no trouble from it at all now, My Lady, although I still suffer from breathlessness in the colder months."

"I suspect you always will. How is your wife?"

"She thrives, as does our granddaughter."

"Ah, little Joan. When she is of an age I shall find her a position in my household, if that be your wish."

"I shall think on it, My Lady. I hope the king is thriving, I was sorry to hear of the loss of the prince."

I stoop to pick up a forgotten pear but when I turn it over I see the wasps have got to it first and I toss it back into the long grass.

"A sad time for us all but we are recovering, and soon we are to have a royal wedding. Now he is fourteen, in a few months' time the marriage between Arthur and Caterina is to take place via proxy. Then the Infanta will embark for England. I look forward to welcoming another granddaughter to our land, and once they are of an age, I hope for many great grandchildren too."

Silence falls and I know we are both remembering that night so long ago at Pembroke when my birth pangs began and he helped me to my bed, and called the alarm. Had he not been there I may have lost Henry and all this ...would be nothing.

"Ned, if you ever desire to return to court, come to London or enter my household, you would be most welcome, and your lady wife too."

He backs off a little, shakes his head.

"Oh no, My Lady, thank you all the same. I am happier in Wales where a man can breathe properly and the earth beneath my feet is soft and green." To make his point, he stamps his foot on the hard baked clay and laughs, giving me a glimpse of the boy I once knew. My helpmeet and friend.

"I would not be here if it were not for you, Ned. I owe so much of it to you. I wish I could repay your service in some way."

"You have! The holding you gifted me is more, so much more than I ever dreamed of and we are happy there. Contentment is a prize indeed."

He is right. Contentment is everything. I wonder if I will ever achieve it. He scratches his nose.

"They are saying in the taverns that the Pretender is to be hung. Is that true?"

I raise my head.

"I have heard nothing. Surely, I would know if it were the case."

"Just gossip then, My Lady. They are saying Warbeck conspired with the Earl of Warwick to escape, and a ship was arranged to take them overseas. There was some huge conspiracy to overthrow the king ... if it were true, you would know, would you not?"

"Yes ..." My mind drifts, in the back ground I can hear Ned's voice but make no sense of his words. My attention is not regained until I realise we are in the stable yard and he is taking leave of me. I smile and kiss both his cheeks, making him blush, reminding me vividly of the Ned of old.

"Take care, Ned. Safe journey." I raise my hand and watch him mount his horse. He settles himself into the saddle, salutes me like a soldier before riding away. The dust thrown up by his horse has not even begun to settle when I turn on my heel and hurry to find Henry.

I find the king at leisure, his feet on a stool and a bowl of cherries at his side. The uncharacteristic relaxed demeanour immediately alerts me to some change in fortune. I nod to a servant to fetch me a chair and perch on the edge, keeping my back straight and a hand on each knee. I do not speak for so long that Henry begins to squirm beneath my gaze.

193

"What is it, Mother? Why are you looking at me like that? You look as if you are sitting in judgement."

"I want to know what you have been concealing from me. Why did you not tell me of the Pretender's repeated escape attempt?"

"You had retired from court. I thought you needed a rest, a break from intrigue and diplomacy."

"They seem to be one and the same thing. What of Warwick? Is it true he was involved? Why would a simpleton involve himself in a plot against us? The last I heard he was more interested in animals."

Henry shrugs. "I only know what my informants tell me. Warbeck was apprehended half way over a wall. How he escaped the confines of his cell is anyone's guess. Warwick, whom they tell me has formed a relationship with the pretender, was apparently also at large in the Tower grounds. It does not take much to figure out they were in league with each other."

"And your plan?"

"Plan?"

"How do you intend to deal with them?"

"Warbeck will hang like the lowborn felon he is and ... I haven't decided about Warwick. He is a high risk prisoner – Isabella and Ferdinand would be happier if he is dead. We can tolerate no more threats to our crown."

"On what charge?"

"What charge? Teason, of course."

"You will execute an idiot; an anointed earl, whom you know is innocent, to appease the niceties of the king and queen of Spain?"

"If I have to."

"And Warbeck, have you considered ...?"

"What?" He leans forward, his former relaxation abandoned. He is tense now, his fingertips pressed together, his brow furrowed and the lines that flank his mouth cut deep, as in stone.

"If Warbeck is indeed the Flemish imposter you claim he is, he cannot be committed for treason against us. Since he owes us no allegiance to you as his king, his crime is not one of treason. You should invent another charge."

Henry slumps back in his chair, his face dark, his mouth a slash of bitterness. For a moment he looks defeated and my heart leaps with compassion at his dilemma. He is a God fearing man yet he has to keep his hold on England firm, he must strengthen his claim. We must erase all threats to our throne, even if it means descending to duplicity.

"But ..." He looks up, our eyes lock, the moments before I speak again stretching so long as to last forever. He begins to bite the skin around his fingernails. As I watch him I come to realise there is no other way.

"Most people are not politicians," I say at last. "And I suppose those that do realise and try to speak out against it ... can be silenced."

November the twenty third blows in cold with high white clouds that scud like ships across a wild blue ocean. After an extra hour in the chapel, I take a small repast before sitting down to write in my journal.

This day, the Pretender, Perkin Warbeck, the common born son of one John Osbeck from Tournai, died by the rope for treason against our realm.

But I do not write of Edward, the seventeenth Earl of Warwick, the innocent who was executed alongside him for crimes against us.

195

Sixteen years. It has taken us sixteen years to reach this day and we celebrate it with great ceremony. A few weeks ago Caterina, the Infanta of Spain landed on our shores. After enduring a perilous overland journey, beset by the fierce heat of Spain, when her ship finally set sail she was driven back to port by heavy storms.

Henry, fearing she will never reach us alive, sends forth his most trusted captain, Stephen Butt, who escorts her safely to our shores. She eventually lands in Plymouth on the second day of October and the king, impatient to finally lay eyes upon her, breaks protocol and rides with Prince Arthur to see her for himself.

The queen and I are left behind to wait and wonder what is happening and how the meeting is progressing. On their return we allow them no time to refresh themselves but demand to be told all about it.

"She is a good looking girl," Henry says. "With a very fresh and healthy figure..."

Ripe for childbearing, he means. This is good news indeed.

"Unfortunately she has little English but a proud and regal bearing."

"You found her to your liking?" I ask Arthur, who blushes awkwardly at my question and glances, shyly at his mother before replying.

"I found her all a future queen should be ..."

"Apart from her sad lack of the English language," the king interjects. "I would have thought Isabella would have made sure she could at least communicate with us on arrival. It is not as if they have not had the time."

"She has a few words," Arthur says defensively. Elizabeth and I exchange sly smiles while Henry gives a curt laugh.

196

"Ha, she has 'please' and 'thank you' and 'verrry 'appy' but I'm not sure that will take her far at this court."

I flap my hand at such negativity.

"She will learn, Henry. You must remember she is very young and young minds are fertile and quick. I swear she will be fluent by Yule."

"And Arthur can have fun teaching her," the queen leans forward, teasingly squeezes her son's knee. She is looking brighter than I have seen her for many weeks and I take it as a sure sign that the union with Spain is good for all of us. Now the pretender has gone, the deal with Spain is soon to be sealed and we can look to the future. I pray God our troubles are over.

A few days before the wedding Caterina makes her entrance into London and I get my first glimpse of her. The crowds are out in force and she presents a pretty picture upon her little white mule. Every window along the street is adorned with flags and greenery, the air rings with music and joy. On her journey Caterina is entertained with pageants, poetry and song of which she will understand very little. How foreign it must all seem to her, how extraordinarily raucous the common people must seem to a girl of such reputed piety.

Elizabeth, Arthur and I watch from the window of a haberdashers as the Spanish retinue ride past. After much discussion it was agreed that Prince Henry should escort her into the city. Despite our careful coaching on the etiquette of such duty, I watch him like a hawk lest he misbehave. He is now ten years old and still not wholly reliable.

As always, he plays to the crowd, taking off his feathered cap and waving it in the air, increasing the roars of delight. He turns to Caterina and says something which she probably cannot understand but with a wide smile she emulates him, and the crowd scream louder. She has won them over already. They are eating from her dainty gloved hand.

"What a curious hat." Elizabeth leans forward the better to see, directing my gaze to Caterina. She wears her hair loose so it flows down her back, and the crown of her head is covered with a coif the colour of carnations, and topped with a small cap, rather like a Cardinals, but very prettily laced with gold.

"Perhaps they are the style in Spain," I remark, rather more concerned with what is inside her head than what adorns it.

"Oh, look! look!" Elizabeth is pointing, her face open in surprise, her eyes wide. I follow the line of her finger. In the midst of Caterina's entourage are a group of blackamoors, all finely dressed and riding as proudly as their mistress. The rich hues of their garments contrast gorgeously with the deep dark tones of their skin. They are beautiful, alien and fascinating; their exotic looks drawing much notice from the crowd.

"Do not point, Elizabeth."

"Oh but they look so fine ... so curious."

"Their land is just cross the sea from Spain. I imagine they are commonplace there."

"That one carries a trumpet, look. Perhaps they are the Infanta's musicians."

"Perhaps ... Look, Henry is standing in his stirrups now! Oh, did he not listen to any of our instructions?"

"But, Mother, the people are loving it. Listen to their cheers."

Later in the afternoon a very weary looking girl is brought to the royal apartments at Baynard's Castle. As she makes her way toward us my eye is drawn to the curious way her skirts sway as she moves. She curtseys to the king and queen, her body stiff and unnatural. At first I think there is some ailment that hampers her movement but when she lifts her face to us I realise she is riven with nerves. I am suddenly reminded of my own youth, and recall the terror of entering a strange household, in a strange land...

Compared to Caterina's journey, Wales is more akin to an adjoining room than venturing abroad. How must it feel for her? I am told it is hot in Spain, an arid land of desert and oranges. How miserable and damp our bleak November must seem to her; no wonder she appears so pinched and despondent. With a rush of pity I think perhaps we should have delayed her arrival until the spring.

"You are welcome, Caterina," I say in Latin, and she hesitates for a moment before realisation strikes her and she replies likewise, her voice strangely accented but sweet.

The queen guides us toward the hearth where Caterina holds out her hands and shudders. "You must find it very cold," says Cecily with a friendly smile, hugging her own torso and rubbing her arms to demonstrate the meaning of her words. The queen intervenes, indicating Caterina's skirts.

"Tell me, Caterina, how do you make your kirtle stand out in such a fashion. It is so graceful, the way they move as you walk. It is as if they are performing a dance of their own."

The Infanta frowns, unsure of the queen's question and I attempt to repeat it in the Latin. As understanding spreads across her features, she lifts the hem of her skirt to reveal a neat shoe and white silk stockings. She turns up the hem of her petticoat and shows us a stiff hoop of willow or some similar wood that makes it stand out like a bell. The ladies, forgetting their former shyness, exclaim in wonder, move closer to examine the cunning design and begin showering Caterina with questions. Although the princess must feel as if she is under siege the awkwardness has passed. The Infanta, the queen and her sister will soon be firm friends.

Elizabeth, Henry and I watch the wedding ceremony from a private closet. Prince Henry, Duke of York, proudly leads the bride to be joined with his brother. In silver tissue embroidered over with golden roses, he keeps his chin high and plays the gallant. I can see his lips moving as he quietly encourages Caterina on their journey along the aisle. From my advantaged position, the couple seem very small, unready for the duties their future holds. Arthur as king of England, Caterina as his bride and the future mother of English kings and Henry, who will be the king's right hand. And, unless I live to be more than a hundred years old, I shall not be here to witness it.

I switch my attention to Caterina whose person is swathed in white satin, laced with gold, her strange bell-like skirts swaying and catching the light of the thousand candles. Beneath a rich coronet and veil, in testament to her purity and fertility, her hair flows loose. It is red-gold in colour, her pale skin giving no indication of the hot sun beneath which she has been raised. I watch her keenly, alert for any mistake, but she deports herself impeccably, the perfect partner for our perfect prince.

As I would expect, Arthur deports himself equally as well. Only I, his grandmother who knows him so well, can sense his inner nerves, his intense desire that nothing should go amiss. Unlike his brother, who seems completely relaxed and relishing every moment of the occasion, Arthur is all too aware of the duty laid upon him as our heir.

He is anxious of failing, of disappointing his father, of being judged inadequate. Weeks ago he confided his worries of the approaching marriage. He has had little dealings with women, so I have arranged for the couple to stay at Coldharbour House after the wedding. This will give them time to become acquainted but I have made it quite clear there is to be no consummation. Not until they are both a little older.

Prince Henry passes Caterina into the keeping of his brother and together, the prince and princess climb the steps to the red carpeted platform where the ceremony is to take place. The voices of the choir soar as Henry Dene, the archbishop of Canterbury steps forward to read the solemnisation before leading them to the great altar.

After mass, the royal couple are blessed by the king and queen and then they process to the door. Cecily bears the princess's train, bringing back memories of the day I bore Anne Neville's when she was made queen. This is a proud day for England and for Henry as the House of Tudor joins with the king and queen of Spain.

A hundred ladies and gentleman follow in their wake to the church door where Arthur dowers Caterina with one third of his income as Prince of Wales. When they emerge into the sunshine, the waiting crowd roars with delight. Trumpets, shawms and sackbuts blare out as Prince Henry conducts the royal couple to the Bishop's Palace where a great feast has been laid out.

This morning I awoke when it was still dark, my mind running over the arrangements of the day, searching for a forgotten detail, a tiny mistake that could cause disaster this day. There must be no ill omen, nothing to make the crones whisper of evil portent or impending doom. But it seems I left no room for error. God was on our side, and the wedding was faultless, the day as bright as midsummer. My head may ache from fatigue and the sound of cheering but we could not have wished for more.

I eat little of the rich fare placed before us. Instead my attention is on the delivery of it, the deportment of the servers, the offerings of the cooks, and the behaviour of my grandchildren at board. I notice Caterina also partakes sparingly of the banquet; perhaps the food is strange to her pallet or maybe her appetite is depleted because her mind is on the coming night. The king, unwilling to provide Spain with any room for annulment, insists that the pair be bedded although the consummation is to be delayed.

When the feasting draws to an end, amid cheers and cat calls, Caterina is taken away to be made ready to receive Arthur into her bed. Shortly afterwards, with bright blushing cheeks, he too is escorted to the nuptial chamber to perform his dynastic duty. I do not join them. I have little taste for the bawdiness that will surely follow. It is just the sort of vulgar hilarity I have always deplored. As Arthur is carried off amid great merriment, he searches me out across the hall, casts a desperate look in my direction. *What am I to do?* he seems to say. *So much is expected of me.* I lift my arms and clap with the rest. It is the only answer I can give.

The door closes and I am left alone with the servants and a few lingering revellers. I survey the wreckage of the hall, my mind still with Arthur and Caterina as they begin their married life together. *What can he do?* I ask myself. *What can any of us do?*

The wedding celebrations continue for so many days that I am soon sickened of the surfeit of pageants, tournaments and banquets and long for the tranquillity of my own home. Coldharbour House has been given over to the newlyweds but the idea of a trip to Woking winks enticingly at the back of my mind. I cannot leave court just yet for it seems we are entering a time of matrimonial celebrations. In a few days we are expecting envoys to arrive from Scotland to make the arrangements for King James' marriage to Princess Margaret. I hope to God it is an easier match to arrange than the Spanish one.

Margaret, having witnessed some of the preparations for Arthur and Caterina's wedding, is torn; eager for the finery and fuss that will surround her yet not ready for a husband and reluctant to leave England. I noticed her envy as Caterina was made ready for church and knew she was thinking of her own forthcoming nuptials. From now on Margaret will enter centre stage. She is seated with the queen, Caterina and I as we prepare to watch yet another pageant at Westminster Hall.

Arthur and the king are further along the table with young Henry. I hear the Prince of Wales' shout of appreciation as a stage with a fully rigged ship is wheeled into the hall. Next comes a castle which is clearly supposed to represent Castile, atop it sits a Spanish lady who, judging from the pretty red hair, is the Infanta.

Caterina's eyes open wide as men dressed as marvellous beasts draw the stage into the centre of the hall by the means of huge golden chains. Suddenly the room fills with mariners and girls in sea green costumes. The movement of their dance makes the whole ship seem to bob on the waves. Caterina claps her hands when she recognises herself being courted by 'Hope' and 'Desire' and her laughter rings out. It does my heart good to see her relaxed, so at home in our midst.

So much expense, so much extravagance for a few hours entertainment. Henry has emptied his coffers to stage such a show. I try to calculate the costs, my mind wandering ... I do not wake from my reverie until the musicians begin to play and I realise the dancing has begun.

When the music starts Arthur is partnered with his aunt Cecily who, recovered now from her bereavement, skips about the floor like a woman half her age. Then Caterina and one of her ladies take their turn to dance, and after that Prince Henry partners his sister, Margaret. As is my habit, I do not dance but I applaud and smile, craning my neck to see if the Scottish envoys are impressed by their future queen's particular grace.

Henry and his sister perform two basse dances and then, to my horror, Henry, presumably growing too hot, throws off his robes and dances in his jacket. In the throes of delight he has completely dispensed with etiquette, forgotten my repeated warnings of how he is to behave. Mortified, I clench my hands together tightly but can only look on in alarm as he jumps and bounds like a puppy, leaping higher than anyone has the right to. Thankfully, the company explode with appreciation, clapping and calling out in glee, encouraging Henry in his exhibition. Hearing the applause he leaps higher spinning mid leap and landing, light as a feather, to take up the steps again. Oh dear, they really should not encourage him; his conceit will know no bounds.

I glance again at the Scots envoy, imagining the stories they will take back to their king, but I see only pleasure on their faces, their applause as appreciative as the rest of the company. I am at a loss to understand it.

The king and I exchange glances, he raises an eyebrow but it is unclear if he is displeased or not but there is no doubting the queen's opinion of her errant son. She leans forward, her laughter bright and merry, her eyes awash with glad tears. Momentarily, she stops clapping and rests her fingers on my arm.

"Oh, Lady Mother," she gasps. "He is so much like my father!"

With Arthur making loud claims of his prowess 'in Spain', the newlyweds seem to be well matched. He is attentive to her in company, while she, like any gently bred princess, smiles and blushes each time he addresses her. I long, quite inappropriately, to know what passed between them last night. I hope my instructions were adhered to.

As preparations are made for their departure to Ludlow where they are to take up their seat as Prince and Princess of Wales, I watch the pair together. They play at chess, walk in the gardens, their heads close together whispering whatever it is that young people whisper together. I am satisfied they will do well enough together. All the hard negotiation was worthwhile and when the time is right, I am confident that the couple will be blessed with many sons.

In December, a few days before Christmas, the pair take their leave of us. Ludlow is a long distance from London but Arthur has almost reached his majority. It is time for him to be in charge of his own household, preside over the council of the Marches, and learn how to govern his principality. While he prepares for kingship his studies will continue under the jurisdiction of Dr

Linacre. He has so much to learn and I pray his young, pretty wife will not prove too much of a distraction.

The wedding has been so long in the planning that I can hardly believe it has come to fruition. The match was made when they were both in the cradle and now they are joined there seems to be an anti-climax. I look about for a way to occupy us in the coming months. Margaret's betrothal to King James is still some way into the future but I engage her and the queen and Cecily in the selection of fine materials for her wedding clothes.

Slowly the finery accumulates, the royal apartments littered with bolts of fine fabrics, half made sleeves, embroidered linen. A few days before the union is to be formally celebrated we are sewing in the queen's parlour, the conversation returning to the wedding no matter how I try to change it.

"What is he like, the King of Scots?" Margaret asks quietly of the queen.

"Oh, handsome, so they say. Brave and chivalrous."

She looks at her mother in disbelief.

"Have you met him?"

"I have not, but I know those who have."

My lips twitch but I keep my silence. I have also heard reports of his popularity with the women. Rumour has it that he has already fathered five illegitimate children but I am not going to tell Margaret that. The people of Scotland certainly seem to love him, his chivalrous style of kingship has won him widespread favour, and his court attracts poets and musicians from all over Christendom.

"Is Scotland very different to England? I have heard it is very cold …"

I can relate to her fears, of course, far more closely than the queen. Princesses can never expect to remain in the country of their birth. Elizabeth was fortunate – I know of no other king's daughter who has had that luxury. Margaret has been raised in the knowledge that she will one day leave us, leave England and embrace a new country as her own. We can only pray she will be happy, and well treated. I hope she is as lucky as I was with Edmund.

"We shall ensure your coffers are filled with warm clothing. Look ..." To distract her I show her the embroidered Tudor roses I am entwining with James' emblem of a thistle.

"How lovely, Grandmother," she replies. "The thistle and the rose ..."

<u>Richmond Palace – January 1502</u>

Entwined roses and thistles seem to be everywhere. The symbol is used all over the palace from the queen's kerchiefs to the royal bed linen and it is even used to decorate Elizabeth's great chamber where the proxy wedding between England and Scotland is to take place.

On the morning of the betrothal Margaret hides her tender years beneath a veneer of dignity and poise, and betrays no sign of nerves. She does not fidget; she does not bite her lip or tremble, and my heart swells with pride, and also regret that she must soon set out on her path alone. I well recall my terror the day I was wed to a stranger. I was younger than Margaret, unformed and inexperienced of the world outside the nursery but I quickly learned that there is more to life than warm possets and a honey tongued nurse.

But I have done what I can for my granddaughter. When Henry first consulted me as to the Scottish alliance

207

I made sure that her departure should be delayed for as long as possible and the union not consummated until Margaret is of suitable age. The Scots king is a mature man, lusty and greedy in his appetites but he must look elsewhere for satisfaction until my granddaughter is old enough to bear his attentions.

The gathering falls silent as the archbishop begins to speak, his voice echoing in the lofty chamber.

"Are you content without compulsion, and of your own free will?"

My heart skips in pity as Margaret gives her answer, loudly and with pride.

"If it please my lord and father the king, and My Lady, my mother the queen."

Her consent is given in ignorance of the man she is accepting. The Scottish king is not present. James Hepburn, Earl of Bothwell stands proxy for his master. He steps forward and links hands with Margaret and before God Margaret and England are joined unassailably with James and Scotland. The deed is done.

Trumpets blare as people rise to applaud the union. Amid the crowd Henry looks at me, his face triumphant, and my heart softens as I applaud louder. God willing, Margaret's future may be better than I fear.

Henry was the reward of my unasked for marriage and I did find happiness for a short while. I pray God my granddaughter is as fortunate. I step forward to join the king and queen, and merge my voice with theirs in celebration of the pinnacle we have mounted. Our family, our small realm is now united with both Spain and Scotland. We are stronger now, our enemies are vanquished and our Tudor dynasty is set to expand. Our future fortune is unrolling before us like a great red carpet.

Henry spares no cost in the period of celebrations that follow. Everyday there are jousts and pageants and feasts, all designed to illustrate our great wealth and majesty of our court. Now all foreign opposition to our reign is ended, we can afford to concentrate on pleasure – and, my goodness, we have earned it.

Margaret is not scheduled to leave our court until later in the year, and in the meantime I am determined to educate her in the ways of the world and try to prepare her for what lies ahead.

As queen of Scotland she is now of equal rank to the queen and I. She sits at the queen's right hand, walks side by side and for the first time is treated as a woman grown. Her wardrobe is replete with gowns for every occasion, her particular favourite a crimson velvet with white fur cuffs. She has sarcanet sleeves of orange and white.

"Which shall I wear while my likeness is painted?" she asks. "I cannot decide which becomes me the most."

Maynard Wewyck is taking portraits of the king and queen and Margaret to be presented to King James as part of the wedding gift.

"Perhaps you should ask Master Wewyck, he may have a preference but I favour the red. It is regal as befits your status."

She looks at me for a long moment. "I sometimes forget … that I am a queen and must leave soon. My attention is on trivial things like clothes and jewels when I should be spending as much time as I can with my family. I know I shall miss you all when I am gone."

"Oh, we can exchange letters, and there will no doubt be opportunities to visit," I reply, as if we do not rue her leaving us at all.

"But … that will not be quite the same, will it? I am leaving everything I love behind and going into the unknown … like that adventurer Mr … Mr Cabot who has gone off overseas in search of new lands. He has no more idea than I of what awaits him. It is … quite terrifying."

She is plucking her petticoat, twisting it in her fingers. I reach out and still her hand.

"You will be a great queen, Margaret. You have the blood of kings in your veins, the quick, fertile mind of a politician and you are beautiful. Remember your origins, your nationality but never be seen to place them before the good of your adopted country. You are Queen of Scots and must act like it. Your own desires must now take second place. In a few months you will feel at home. Women are strong, remember that. Say it to yourself before you sleep. 'I am strong. I am queen. I am a strong Scottish queen and I will survive."

From her expression I have offered little comfort but she firms her chin and nods. "Yes, Grandmother, I will remember that always."

I should add a codicil perhaps, should strife ever divide us from Scotland, it would be as well to have an ambassador there, someone to prioritise us above the country she marries into. But I do not speak of it. Hopefully that day will never come. Instead I turn the conversation to a topic that is precious to all our hearts.

"I wonder how Arthur and Caterina are settling in at Ludlow. Hopefully they will be firm friends before the day comes for the marriage to be celebrated fully."

She flushes, ducks her head to avoid my eye, focussing her attention on her needle.

"Then, when a prince is born to them, there will be further reason to celebrate in England." I tilt my head back to catch a glimpse of lowering sky outside the solar. "I remember when there was nothing but war, nothing

210

but upheaval, death and dread. I will never tire of celebrating weddings and births and seeing our dynasty grow in strength and influence."

The conversation lapses into contented silence and my mind drifts back across the years, uncomfortable memories cushioned by the comfortable present. Margaret will never understand the insecurity of my past, when I had no inkling that I would ever be anything more than a woman in waiting to Elizabeth Woodville, born on the losing side, my royal connection broken, my destiny stolen, my family shamed. Now I am the King's Mother people say I am proud and overbearing but I have earned my place. I have fought hard and long and have every right to be gratified by my achievement. My family are now perfectly preserved against ill fortune and neither I nor my offspring shall ever bow the knee again. I am the mother and grandmother of kings and princes. For years to come they will speak of me and mine and thank God for the day we won our throne.

<u>Westminster Palace - February 1502</u>

I am reading quietly from my book of hours when I am disturbed by the sounds of weeping issuing from the queen's private chambers. I place a marker between the pages and go to investigate the cause. I find the queen, her head bowed over another who is weeping copious tears into the royal petticoats. Such a breach of etiquette cannot be ignored. I hurry forward.

"What is it, Elizabeth? Who is ..."

The creature in the queen's arms lifts her head to reveal a tear streaked face, parchment white, the mouth squared, made ugly by grief. Katherine, the queen's sister is barely recognisable but I know the cause without need for explanation.

211

"Katherine," I say with sinking heart. "Why are you here? You should be at home with your children; there is nothing the queen can do to help you. She has no influence in state politics."

"But he is innocent! William has done nothing..."

I hold up my hand to silence her and she hiccups into submission.

"The king's advisors think otherwise. They report your husband was seen many times fraternising with Suffolk and his cohorts."

Suffolk, cousin to the queen, has long harboured resentment toward us. There are some who believe his claim to the throne is greater than ours. He is a proud, unlikeable man who has tested our patience very dearly over the years. This past summer, sensing our good will was wearing thin, he left our court and fled overseas, taking refuge in the court of Maximilian, the Holy Roman Emperor. His existence now casts the last remaining shadow over the peace in our realm.

Recently, Henry ordered a sermon be preached at St Paul's Cross condemning Suffolk as a traitor and now is paying close attention to his friends. William Courtney, Henry Bourchier, and other members of our court are known to have dined with Suffolk shortly before his defection. We suspect they bide their time, plotting an invasion, and other dishonourable schemes to steal our crown. Henry's decision to arrest and hold them fast within the Tower keep is the only course he could take. Self-preservation is always wise and traitors are better imprisoned away from the eyes of the world, out of harm's way. The traitor's wife, on the other hand, is a problem the king will leave to the queen and I to solve.

"Get up, Katherine," I say. "He is not dead yet."

She dabs her red nose with a kerchief that comes away with strings of snot and dribble. I turn my face from her. She has my pity yet I have faced far worse things than her in my life without resorting to such a performance.

"He will be attainted, that is all." I have to raise my voice over her continuing bawling. "He will be lodged in the Tower but the king has no designs on his life."

No doubt she is remembering Warbeck and Warwick whose lives Henry also promised to spare but who both died a traitor's death after all.

"I will be a pauper!" she wails. "What will become of me and my children? How will we survive? He has done nothing wrong!"

Elizabeth leans forward.

"Dear Kate, do not weep. I will help you. I cannot intervene in the king's business but I have my allowance, I can spare you a little coin. And I will speak to the king, beg his mercy ..."

"Much good that will do you," Katherine sniffs, ignoring the gentle kick she receives from the queen in a subtle plea for silence.

"And I will take the children into my care and upkeep. I can find them a guardian and a governess."

Katherine quiets a little, sniffs her thanks, dabbing her nose with her ruined kerchief. Elizabeth glances toward where I stand with my back to the window rigidly clasping my own wrists and trying not to empathise with a woman so deep in trouble. Her utter despair illustrates my own strength. Had I been so weak Henry would have rotted in a European court, exiled from his lands, a nobody with a hopeless cause. The queen smooths her sister's hair, reaches for her fallen cap and places it reverently on her head.

"I will order rooms to be made ready for you, sister. You will stay here in the palace under my protection. Everything will come right, you will see."

She summons Cecily forward and without being asked, she leads her weeping sister away. As they depart Elizabeth and I exchange glances.

"It is horrible, quite horrible," Elizabeth breathes.

"It is always so when treason is discovered."

"Courtney always seemed such an amiable man. Of what is he guilty? Sharing dinner with friends? He may have done so in ignorance of their private schemes. He has never seemed in the least discontent with us ..."

I laugh humourlessly. "You do not believe that, Elizabeth. We have both been on the 'other' side. We both know of hidden plots and schemes. You appreciate, more than most, that Henry cannot afford to take risks. He must leave no untidy ends that may be used to strangle his hold on the country or threaten the well-being of his heirs."

Greenwich – February 1502

I have often noticed that trouble, when it arrives does not come alone. It heaps one trial upon another until it is impossible to turn, or to breathe. For days I am uneasy, expecting ill tidings, anticipating doom but on the day it does come, I am not ready for it. None of us are.

Elizabeth and I are preparing to join Henry for mass when a messenger arrives from Ludlow. He comes directly into our presence still mired from the road and passes a letter to the king. We pause, waiting for him to relate the news, expecting the usual descriptions of feasts or Arthur's prowess in the tiltyard. Henry opens the letter and frowns, and the first prickings of disquiet flutter in the outreaches of my mind. And when he looks up his lips are white, his eyes as dark as blood against his parchment skin. I know the news is ill before he even speaks of it.

"There is sickness at Ludlow," he says with a nervous glance at the messenger. "Both Arthur and his wife are ill a bed."

"What sickness?" Elizabeth moves forward, unceremoniously snatches the letter, her eyeballs moving rapidly as she drinks in the words. "May God have mercy, it is the sweat. We must go to them straight away."

"No." I step forward. My head is light, loud alarm bells clanging in my ears, perspiration breaking out on my brow and upper lip as I try to indirectly voice my fear. "You cannot put yourselves in danger of infection. If Arthur ... if they are mortal sick – we cannot risk – the king. If anything happens ... we ... the king must be here, to prepare ... young Henry."

"They will not die!" Elizabeth shrieks at me, her eyes awash with tears. "That is unthinkable. Arthur is sick, he will need his mother. We are not just monarchs, we are parents too. Henry ..." She turns to implore the king, but he has turned his back and is staring into the roaring flames. His shoulders are bowed, as if the weight lies heavy on them. He does not turn until she cries his name again and even when he does turn to face us, he will not meet her eye.

"Mother is right. We cannot go yet. We cannot risk contagion. It is hard but ... Mother is right. We will send our best physicians and he *will* mend. Once all risk is passed we will go to him."

"And suppose it is too late by then?" Her usually amiable pink face has turned hard and white, like stone, her words as cold as marble and there is no affection between them. Once, as the royal nursery filled, they were full of joy but slowly, as it began to empty and the little ones began to die, little Elizabeth, little Edmund, the love between them began to dwindle too. I had not

215

noticed until this moment that there is little left between them now but duty.

Henry spends more time with the younger prettier Gordon woman, than he does with his queen. Perhaps it is normal; perhaps all men drift away as their wives lose their youth, their mystery. But, if the worst happens, where will they find comfort?

They stand apart, staring at but not seeing each other. I had never thought Elizabeth could look so care worn or Henry so close to defeat. I must rouse them. Somehow I must resurrect their fighting spirit. I clear my throat and speak through the threatening veil of tears.

"You must not forget that Arthur and Caterina are young and strong. Remember how he shrugged off the measle when he was a boy? They will come through this, you will see. I suggest we dispatch the royal physicians and hasten with all speed to the chapel and pray for God's mercy. You are God's elect, Henry. I have faith that He will not inflict the worst upon us."

And so we pray long and hard. For almost a week we do nothing by entreat God's mercy: we go through the motions; we dine, we retire early and suffer sleepless nights. Although I have only just left the chapel, in the quiet of my chamber I kneel again and implore the Lord to show mercy, to spare the lives of those poor children. The good of England depends upon their survival.

Since sleep evades me I sit down and write a letter to Ferdinand and Isabella – they should know the peril their child is in. But I find I cannot write it. I cannot force my hand to form the words and, as dawn is breaking, I hear the sounds of muffled footsteps. I put down my pen and cock my head. Only on a matter of grave import would anyone dare disturb the peace of the king at such an untimely hour. I pull on a warm robe over

216

my nightgown and hurry along the adjoining corridor in the wake of the messenger.

I arrive in the king's chamber as the emissary takes his leave. I recognise the king's confessor and know without doubt that he is the bearer of ill news. The guard allows me to pass, his face expressionless, and his eyes curiously bright as I step into the gloomy chamber. The only light is provided by the fire and a single candle near the bed.

Elizabeth is in her nightclothes, her hair long and snarled from a restless night, she stares into the fire with blank eyes. Henry is by the window, looking out although it is still too dark to see. One hand nervously clutches and unclutches his nightgown in the region of his heart. Neither of them stir at my footstep.

"What news?" I say, my voice unintentionally loud and sharp. "Have tidings come from Ludlow?"

Henry turns toward me, the lines on his face deep cut, the sorrow and despair in his eye more eloquent than the words he cannot bring himself to utter.

My hand creeps to my throat, my eyes seeking out the queen. She has not moved. She is like a statue, her skin solidified by grief, her hair dry and lifeless, and her fingers claw like. Somehow, I manage to take a step toward her and lay a hand upon her frozen skin.

"Elizabeth? Come, come with me..." I cast a glance at Henry and he gives a slight nod which I take as permission to leave. In the queen's chamber her women creep unwillingly from the shadows, and I realise that news travels fast. While they hover close by, unsure what to say or how to act, I ease Elizabeth into a seat where she plops like a stone into a river. I begin to chaff her hands. A girl brings a hot drink, and a sponge to wash away the queen's tears but her cheeks grow moist as fast as she can dry them. Elizabeth clutches the cup in her hands and as the warmth begins to penetrate her frigid fingers and the softness of the sponge competes with her falling tears, she hurls the cup away, throws back her head and begins to scream.

It goes on and on. She is deaf to my pleas, or the begging of her women to stop, the requests to lie down on the bed. Elizabeth leaps from her chair, pushes us away, runs to the centre of the room where she folds herself in two as if she is broken. She tugs at her hair, wrenches her head to and fro so hard I fear her neck will snap. This is how it feels, I think. This is the reality of the news that I have dreaded all my life. Her son is dead. Her firstborn child, the lord of her hopes, of all our hopes. I want to scream with her for our boy has gone. The heir of England is dead, vanquished not in the glory of battle but by a slow, painful, dreadful sickness. It is insufferable.

Her screams continue until the door is thrown open and Henry strides in, somehow regal in his night attire. With a jerk of his head he empties the room of women. I hesitate at the door and watch as he takes his wife into his arms. She resists at first, pushing against his chest, straining to free herself from his embrace until quite suddenly she relents, her head flops onto his shoulder and she subsides, sobbing into his arms. He lays his cheek upon her hair, closes his eyes … and I leave them.

A crumpled message is somehow in my hand, as I read it the words swim about the page. Two days … Arthur has been dead for two days … I creep silently back the way I came in ignorance not half an hour since. Wanting only the solitude of my chamber I send my women away, sink helplessly to my knees, and cling to the *prie dieu*, begging God to heal the savage wound he has wreaked upon my heart.

The country mourns, requiems are sung in every church, in every city, in every town and hamlet. The walls are hung with black, voices are muted, the taverns are quiet, and we are, every one of us, laid low. The realm of England has been dealt a stunning blow; as a family we are all but slain. Despite his own recurrent health problems, Reginald Bray is in daily attendance on me, his calming tones reasoning as he suggests what should be done.

"Yes, yes," I say. "See that it is so." I have lost heart, mislaid my fighting spirit. My sense of invincibility is quashed.

As if Heaven has sympathy and the angels are weeping with us, Arthur's body is carried from Ludlow to Worcester in a veil of steady rain. The carriage bearing the royal coffin is mired several times, requiring oxen to be brought from the nearest town to pull it free. When the end of his final, pitiful journey is reached at Worcester, his funeral is joined by Tom Howard, the Earl of Surrey and Talbot, Earl of Shrewsbury. But the king and queen and I are too distraught to attend.

We remain at Greenwich, cold and comfortless, unable to find a single ray of sunshine on this the bleakest of days. On the very hour his body is laid low in his tomb, I look from my window as the rain begins to fall again. I look up at the grey leaden sky and wonder if the sun over England has been doused and we shall never see it again.

We are swathed in grief, disabled by sorrow, our tears falling as thick as blood, as bitter as aloes, as if there will be no end to it. A tailor creeps in to discuss our mourning clothes but I am too listless to care. I agree to anything just to be rid of his company. It is not until three days later when I first pull on my new funereal clothes that I remember there is another who must surely mourn

219

Arthur as deeply as we. At Ludlow, a place that will now forever be the castle of death, the ailing Caterina, Princess of Wales, is still recovering from the pestilence that claimed her husband's life. Someone must go to her and explain that she is now a widow, at the age of seventeen.

We are still in the depths of sorrow when a letter arrives from Ferdinand and Isabella asking for Caterina and the first instalment of her dowry to be returned to Spain. Clouded with confusion, it takes a while for the insult of that request to penetrate.

Henry stalls. *The Dowager Princess is still unwell, not fit enough to travel.* His real intention is to wait and watch her, discover if she is carrying Arthur's heir before he decides what to do with her. Both Henry and I are reluctant for further instalments from Spain to cease, both hopeful of discovering another reason for her to remain. As mother of the future heir Caterina would secure a permanent position at court. I begin to question my wisdom in forbidding the consummation of the marriage. Now, I hope with all my heart my instructions were ignored for, if she were pregnant we would have some hope of an heir and a continuing Spanish alliance.

We send mourning clothes to Ludlow, and Elizabeth orders tasty food to tempt the pallet of the convalescent princess. As soon as she is strong enough to travel the king orders a horse drawn litter to remove her from the tainted humors of the castle. The memory of my own young widowhood is as fresh as if it were yesterday.

May 1502

It is not until May that Caterina arrives at Croydon, where she lodges at the palace of the Archbishop of Canterbury.

220

A few days later the queen sends a page to enquire after her health. The question on all our minds is 'is she with child?' for until we know the answer, we cannot declare Prince Henry as the king's heir.

We try to look to the future but we are all so heart sore. A short time ago we had three princes. We were secure on our throne and the future of our dynasty was seemingly set in stone. Now our children are dying and two of our boys are gone, leaving our hopes in the hands of just one small, rather ungoverned ten year old.

"We are young enough, Henry and I, to have more sons..." Elizabeth's voice is roughened with grief, her lips twitching with nerves as she unconsciously destroys her kerchief, her finger tips probing the lace, enlarging the holes in the design. "We will put aside our differences, find comfort in one another and in doing so, fill the vacancies in our nursery. There is still time."

She looks lost ... desperate. I smile determinedly. "Yes, my dear. That is the thing to do. We must look to the future. The hour before dawn is always the darkest."

Inwardly, I berate myself for voicing platitudes but what else can I say? What can anyone say to make a difference at a time like this? Death seems so close, so immediate and threatening, as if there is no hope for any of us. The queen's kerchief rips suddenly, her forefinger thrust through the ruined lace. She rolls it into a ball and stuffs it up her sleeve.

"Prince Henry arrives this afternoon. Henry ... the king ... feels he will be better here, under his direct supervision."

"We will all feel better for his presence. He is such a bright, happy child, he is bound to cheer us."

But the child that arrives from Eltham is not his usual buoyant self. He comes listlessly into the chamber, performs a perfect bow in greeting but his bounce and vigour is missing. It would be more comforting were he to be naughty so we could chide him as we usually do. I would welcome a return to normality but the child is deflated and as dejected as the rest of us. He stands limply at Elizabeth's side as she clings to his hand and asks how he is faring.

"I am well in body, Mother but my spirit is sore." He gazes about the chamber, his eyes straying as if in search of something.

"What is it, Henry? Is something troubling you?"

He moistens his lips, the whites of his eyes and the film of sweat on his forehead gleam in the candlelight.

"Is it ... will I ... Am I to be the Prince of Wales now, Mother?"

The queen nods sadly. "You are indeed, my dear ... unless Caterina is with child."

"And a fine Prince of Wales you will make." I intervene. "It will be a great challenge for you and there will be new skills you must master. You must put aside your love of sport and music and apply yourself to kingship and government. Your father will instruct you, as well as your tutors. You have much to learn ..."

"But, Father will not die for years and years will he? I will not have to be king for a long time."

"Of course not, the king is in his prime. There is plenty of time for you to learn the intricacies of sovereignty."

He gives a wavering smile and sits down close to his mother's side, one hand on her knee. She drapes an arm over his shoulder, squeezes gently with loving fingers. He nuzzles his cheek against her velvet sleeve.

"So I shall be King of England and Margaret will be Queen of Scots. What about Mary, which country shall she be queen of?"

"We shall have to wait and see," I reply, interlacing my fingers and laying my hands in my lap. "But your father will secure a good match for Mary, maybe with Spain ..."

"She is too young to even think of it yet!" Elizabeth speaks sharply, her recent loss and the prospect of Margaret's departure to Scotland too fresh to even contemplate parting with her youngest child.

"Of course," I say to pacify her. "Mary's marriage is many years in the future. Now, perhaps Henry would enjoy a walk in the privy garden; it is too fine to be cooped up indoors."

The child nods agreement, rises to his feet and, remembering his manners, holds out his hand to escort his mother from the room. I follow in their wake and as we pass the king's apartments the door opens and my son emerges.

"Henry," I move toward him. "We are just about to take a turn about the gardens with the prince. Why do not you come with us? You have been too much indoors of late."

He nods his assent and I link his right elbow while Elizabeth takes his left. Prince Henry now walks a little behind.

After the dim interior, the sunshine is bright and we blink stupidly until our eyes adjust. We stroll quietly between the flowerbeds, the garden bustling with bees and birds.

"The medlar is blooming early," I say, plucking a white symmetrical blossom and holding it to my nose. "That promises a fine summer and a good harvest."

I offer it to the king who takes it, absentmindedly inhaling the subtle scent.

"We are in need of a good harvest," he says. "Any form of good news will be welcome."

223

The harsh daylight reveals the shadows below his eyes, and highlights the marks of anxiety on his brow. The lines that flank his mouth are cut deep and humourless. My heart twists with pity that my son should know such sorrow. If only I could erase it all and take us back to the time that was before.

That is the tragedy of humanity. As time passes we look backward to happier, kinder days yet every step we take moves us farther from them. We are marched relentlessly into a future we wish could be like the past. I am constantly harping on all the mistakes and decisions that cannot be rectified. If I could only go back a year, I would never send Arthur and Caterina to Ludlow. I would keep them close to court ... safe and well.

I have always imagined that once Henry was safely in possession of his throne, our trials would be trivial, or vanish altogether. I never envisaged anything as horrible as this.

Looking back, I remember thinking that losing Edmund was the worst thing that could ever befall me but trouble came thick and fast after: separation from my son, the vanquishing of Lancaster in battle, the death of Harry ... but if I have learned one thing it is that life is cruel. Fate waits for us to become complacent, grow happy again before it launches another attack, casting ever increasing troubles at our feet. Only a fool believes he is invincible.

Each dawn I wake to the knowledge that the coming day may hold disaster, failure, possible heartbreak, and possible defeat. Victory is never assured, and it is certainly never enduring.

The king blinks into the sun. "It is too bright out here. It is giving me a headache," he says, closing his eyes and pinching the bridge of his nose. "It is so damned cheerful."

I had thought his pale complexion was due to worry but now I see he is ailing.

"You are unwell?"

He turns his face from me to watch his son and only heir trying to catch a butterfly in his cupped hands. Elizabeth hovers close by, watching. She is smiling sadly, a flutter of fear on her features as if she dare not let him stray too far.

"I am not ill ... just tired." Henry says. "I have so many worries. What sort of king will the boy make, Mother? He has no training. His life has been one of leisure. Arthur had learned so much but Henry is like a pampered performing bear cub. I do not know if I can teach him all he needs to learn in the time allotted us. Arthur was ..."

"Irreplaceable." I finish the sentence for him. "But there is plenty of time. We must make the best of it." I detect the growing panic in my own voice as I contemplate the end of the king's life. Henry is growing old. He is very little younger than I, just thirteen years separate us, and he suffers so much anxiety, so much tribulation. He looks older than his years. I pray God that this does not reflect his state of health.

He turns his head slightly, smiles sardonically from the side of his mouth as the sun ducks behind a light cloud.

"Plenty of time, Mother, if I can persuade the boy to listen. He thinks he knows it all. Just how does one instruct a stripling boy who believes himself to be unflawed?"

"Life is a learning curve, Henry and the boy's tutor John Skelton has served him well. He is fluent in French and Latin, and his Spanish is improving. Erasmus was most impressed with him when he visited court last summer. Henry disports himself well in company and he is learning to curb his exuberance in public. A little more sculpting of his character is all that is required, and he must, of course, learn the rudiments of foreign policy and leadership. You are the only one who can teach him that."

Henry squints as the sun re-emerges, cruelly revealing the deepening crow's feet at the edges of his eyes.

"I am preparing to have him moved close to my apartments where he can accompany me about my daily business. If one needs to learn to swim there is no better way to learn than to be thrown in a river ...or so they say."

I allow myself a smile at his attempt at humour. "I approve your decision but you must also ensure he is allowed enough fresh air and exercise. You cannot incarcerate the boy indoors. Henry loves to hunt and that is a kingly pastime and one that is essential for his well-being. He also excels in the tiltyard, as well as tennis and wrestling. He should be allowed the companionship of boys his own age."

The king stares into the distance, avoiding my eye.

"Are you aware how many princes have been injured or killed at sport. He must be kept safe and I will not have him lead astray by the likes of those young hotheads Brandon and Compton, or the other fellow ... Richard Grey."

"A prince needs friends. He needs to learn how to conduct relationships, how to treat his underlings fairly and with respect."

"I had no friends, Mother, growing up in exile, always on the outside, always the boy with the empty title, no lands and no income."

Silence falls between us. I feel slighted, responsible for his sorry upbringing although I did all in

226

my power to right it. Jasper and I ensured he lacked for nothing and I fought hard to persuade King Edward to allow him home. And later, I bowed the knee to King Richard too for Henry's sake. I am injured that he shows resentment now when I have sacrificed so much.

"Indeed," I say at last. "But I am sure you would not wish such a life on your son. Henry is fortunate enough to be heir to a country he has grown up in, a country whose customs are second nature ... surely you do not resent that."

The king sighs, rubs the inner corners of his eyes again.

"No, Mother, I do not resent it. I am just ... tired. I will consult the physician about my blurred vision and perhaps give supper a miss this evening and take myself early to bed."

He reaches out, clasps my arm in apology and absentmindedly takes his leave of me. I watch him go.

Do not let this defeat you, Henry. Not when we have come so far.

Despite our grief, state affairs continue. Elizabeth, still conscious of her duty, buys warm clothing from her own purse and orders it to be sent to her brother-in-law, Courteney, who remains languishing in the Tower. Although beset by personal troubles the queen is not one to allow the needs of others to pass by unnoticed.

Despite our attempts to disguise our heaviness with genteel entertainments, the underlying mood at court remains heavy and both Henry and Elizabeth are ailing and sad. Physicians come and go from the royal apartments, visiting both the king for general tiredness and problems with his eyes, and Elizabeth for lethargy and an affliction of the stomach. But by mid-summer we are given cause for renewed hope when Elizabeth confides in me the cause. She is with child again and quietly terrified that it shall prove to be a girl.

"Girls are not entirely useless," I say by way of comfort but in truth, like her, I am horrified at the thought of a princess. It is a boy we need; now more than ever, we need a son to bolster Prince Henry's position, to strengthen our dynasty's future. But fearful as we are, at least there is now hope.

Tentatively the queen begins to fashion small garments, make arrangements for her lying in which should be some time in February or March. To divert her, we lay on lavish entertainments, including the minstrels and players that she loves so much.

Henry is eager to see her wide smile again and has largely ceased his 'friendship' with the pretender's wife. Of an evening I often find he and Elizabeth closeted alone, a musician playing in the corner as they amuse themselves at cards or dice. Often Henry comes away the loser and I am convinced he allows her to win a goodly portion of the monies to supplement her allowance which never seems to be sufficient. Elizabeth is charitable, which is a good thing, as long as one does not pauper oneself in the process.

By summertime it is clear that Caterina is not carrying an heir for England and young Henry is publically acknowledged as Prince of Wales. He has still not returned to his former high spirits, a clear indication that Arthur's death has affected him deeply. They met but seldom, and I suspect it has more to do with his own mortality and perhaps he is also cast down by the weight of responsibility laid so suddenly upon him. He needs the company of boys his own age and I often catch a bleak look in his eye, as if he longs to be outside in the fresh air rather than cooped up with his father and his tutors.

Henry presses the boy too hard and I make several attempts to advise the king of this but my son is afraid. He feels his age. The seventeen years of rule weighs heavy upon him, and he is determined the boy shall be properly prepared.

I, of course, can barely contemplate the day when Prince Henry must assume the rule of England. It will mean the end of everything I have lived for. My whole life has been, and still is, tied up in my son – I do not know what I should do without him. I can only hope I am the first to go. But ... oh, I am maudlin. I give myself a shake and focus my mind on the Queen's voice which has been droning on unheeded.

"I am sorry, Elizabeth, I misheard you," I say, putting a hand to my ear, pretending deafness rather than admitting to inattention.

"I have a whim to visit Wales," she says again. I look at her in surprise.

"Wales? Whatever for?"

"I think I will take Katherine and Cecily with me. We shall travel west via Woodstock ..."

"Alone, or is Henry to accompany you?"

"Alone, I think. The king is very busy with ... with important things ..."

She smiles sadly, as if ruing the knowledge that the king has more pressing business than cheering his grieving wife.

There is nothing I can say to deter her, I am unconvinced it is wise in her gravid condition but sometimes a woman's instincts should be respected. She makes the preparations but when Cecily is sent for, she is nowhere to be found.

"Have you seen Cecily lately?" Elizabeth asks me. "I think she has been absent ... for a few days now."

"I saw her four days since, when she accompanied me to mass."

It is unlike the queen's sister to absent herself without leave and I am quite cross that she should desert Elizabeth when she has need of her. Of all the York women, Cecily is the one I like the most – she is clever, amusing and devout; if I had been blessed with a daughter I should have liked her to be like Cecily but that does not give her leave to absent herself from court without permission.

"I shall send for her women and question them; they will likely know her whereabouts. Perhaps she is sick and in need of care."

I am with the queen when two of Cecily's women are ushered into our presence. They hover reluctantly near the door until Elizabeth beckons them closer. I lift my chin and look down my nose at them, making believe I am far taller than I am as I wait for the queen to speak.

"Do you know the whereabouts of my sister, Lady Cecily?"

The women rise from their curtsey, red with embarrassment, one nudges the other to make reply. The taller of the two steps forward.

"I believe Lady Cecily is gone from court, Your Majesty."

I step forward, cut through the queen's questions.

"Left the court? Without requesting leave from us?"

The girl seems to shrink into her own body, fear of me writ clear on her pallid face.

"That is all I know, My Lady. All I know. She did not say where she was going..."

So we are left to fret and fume. We can find no one who knows Cecily's whereabouts or whose company she is in. It is quite out of character for her to breach

230

etiquette in such a way and the queen should not be faced with such worry in her condition. Quietly, I promise myself to make my displeasure quite clear to Cecily on her return. In the mean time I turn my attention to other things.

It is several weeks before Cecily comes creeping into my presence. Although my instinct is to take her into my arms and thank God for her safety, I hold back my relief and turn a steely eye upon her.

"Where have you been? The queen has been quite distraught. It is lucky your unthoughtful behaviour did not bring on a miscarriage. Have you no regard for others? Did you not consider requesting leave of us?"

She turns dead white, her eyes dilated with something that resembles fear, and my anger turns abruptly into concern. I relax my tense shoulders, lean closer, peer into her terrified eyes. "Why are you trembling? I am not likely to bite you."

To my surprise she begins to weep, great tears gathering on her lashes, dropping onto her cheeks as if she is a baby. A baby! She must have got herself with child, only shame could bring on such a display of self-pity. I resume my former expression of displeasure. "Stop bawling and tell me what is wrong." I fold my arms, look dispassionately on her tears. "Where have you been?"

"I, Madam ... Lady Margaret, I beseech you to present my case to the king and queen. I fear I have brought their displeasure on my head."

"What have you done? Are you with child?"

"No!" She is indignant now, two spots of colour appearing on her cheeks.

"Then what? What crime can you possibly have committed against us that is so bad?"

"I – I have wed, My Lady, without royal permission."

My mouth falls open, a loud ringing in my ears as anger floods through me, outrage shaking my very bones.

"Married!" I bellow. "Married to whom?"

"Thomas Kyme," she whispers so quietly I can scarcely hear.

"Who?"

"Thomas Kyme," she speaks louder. "He – he is the son of John Kyme of Friskney."

"I have never heard of him."

"No, My Lady, he is … seldom at court."

"You have wed yourself to a commoner? A nobody, as if you are some … some trollop?"

"He is a man of small estate, My Lady but … a good man. You know yourself how hard they are to come by."

My mouth twitches involuntarily but now is not the time for humour. I stare at her discomfiture for a while and slowly come to realise that there are worse crimes, worse problems to face. I let my breath go, sigh deeply and allow a glimpse of compassion to show.

"You are in no small trouble, Cecily. It might be wise for us to speak to the queen, before we inform my son of your crime. He will be displeased, you can bank on that. I hope you are prepared for public disgrace, expulsion from court, the severing of relations with your sister?"

"I thought I was. Thomas and I are very much in love – but now it comes to it, my heart fails me at the thought."

At least Cecily is not dead, or injured; I should be glad that she has found love but she is of good blood and valuable marriage stock. It was her duty to marry at the king's pleasure, not her own. I sniff as I rise to my feet

232

and move toward her. For a long moment we stare at one another. I keep my face expressionless while hers is a battleground of emotion, bravado vying with remorse, tears with righteous anger. In the end, a memory stirs of the brief joy I knew with Harry and I find my anger softened. Placing a hand on her shoulder, I look from the window and recognise with a twinge of envy that such reckless love has ever evaded me.

Cecily's story is the stuff of romance, the recipe of minstrel's songs sung in halls across Christendom. Perhaps I grow soft as my dotage approaches but, hardly believing the words that issue from my lips, I whisper.

"If you are banished from court, you may come to me at Collyweston – you and this - this *squire* of yours. I would see what I can make of him."

Later in the queen's apartments Elizabeth stares uncomprehendingly at her weeping sister. I turn my face away, affording them privacy in this most personal of moments but I do not leave the room.

"How could you, Cecily?" the queen says at last, her voice hoarse with sorrow. "How could you do this now ... when everything about me is so bleak? You know you will be shamed; sent from court, banished? There will be nothing I, or anybody else can do to sway the king ..."

I watch from the corner, curiosity overcoming courtesy. Cecily covers her face with her hands, her shoulders judder. "Why did you do it? Why did you not come to me beforehand, Lady Margaret and I might have been able to intervene on your behalf but ... we can do nothing after the fact!"

Cecily sniffs and turns a tragic white face toward her sister.

"I wanted ... just once ... to choose for myself. Why should my marriage once again be for the king's benefit ...?"

I spring from my corner, injured by her inferred criticism of John.

"But ... You loved my brother! You were happy with him!"

Cecily has never given any indication that her marriage to my brother was anything but joyful. She turns to face me.

"Yes. I was happy with John but ... that was simply my good fortune. There is no guarantee I would be happy with another husband chosen by the king. I like ... I *love* Thomas. Should I not be allowed a little happiness? He is a good man, Elizabeth ... a gentle, *loyal,* humorous man whom I *choose* to spend my life with and he loves *me*!"

"That will hold little sway over the king! He will say you have debased yourself, given yourself cheaply to a commoner!"

Cecily swallows, lowers her head and then levels her chin and looks the queen squarely in the eye.

"And what do you think, Elizabeth? Are these the king's thoughts, or yours?"

Elizabeth's cheeks redden, "Of course not but why do you never think before you act? Why do you consider no one but yourself?"

"Not everyone is fortunate enough to marry a king. The best I could expect is some ageing widower with a houseful of children. I refuse to become a convenience to some balding, flatulent bore..."

"So you choose poverty over position? How long do you think your husband will bother with sweet talk and promises? How long before you are left kicking your heels in rustication while he discovers other pleasures?"

"We will not be paupers. He has lands and a small inheritance and I have monies ..."

"No. No, you do not, Cecily. Not anymore. I am as sure as I can be that the king will strip you of your estates, your income will be forfeit."

"But if you speak for us ..."

"Why should I? You have betrayed me! Brought shame upon ..."

Enough has been said. I put up my hand, my voice slicing through the queen's words.

"Let us not resort to anger. You will say things you do not mean and I would not have this tiny misunderstanding become a massive breach between you."

Taking Cecily by the shoulder I usher her toward the door but before we exit I turn back to the queen.

"I am not condoning Cecily's actions, Elizabeth, but the deed is done. It would be better if we stand united when the news is imparted to the king. We will leave Your Grace to ponder on it for a while and return in an hour or two. There may be little to be done by way of salvaging Cecily's lands or position but at the very least her position in your heart should remain intact."

As we quit the chamber the queen stamps her foot and lets loose an expletive that makes my ears ring.

As Elizabeth and I predicted, Henry is furious with Cecily. Heedless of our pleas, he strips her of her titles and lands and banishes her from court. As good as my word I provide refuge at Collyweston and wait for the king's fury to subside.

When I am shown into his apartments I enter breezily as though there is no conflict between us.

"How are you, Henry?" I kiss his cheek, tilt my head to assess his health but I am met with a frosty

235

frown. I decide to ignore it. "Hmm, you do not look well. Have you been taking the infusion I prepared for you? You look choleric; perhaps I should change the script and make up something to neutralise the ill humors."

He jerks away. "Stop it, Mother. I am perfectly well."

I fold my arms, tighten my lips and watch as he searches for something on his desk, dislodging a pyramid of rolls, sending them to the floor. He curses colourfully and without apology.

"What have you lost?" I ask.

"A paper I prepared. I thought, since we are out of sorts with each other it would make no difference were I to raise the matter with you now."

"What matter is that?"

"Woking."

At the back of my mind alarm bells begin to toll but I can not specify the cause. My son wants to discuss my beloved manor – the splendid home I created with my second husband, Harry. I have a sudden longing to walk again in the garden we created, run my fingers through the rich tapestries in the hall where we laughed, and revisit the bedchamber where we lay together.

"I have a mind to turn it into a palace for our private use ..."

My brows rise in surprise. When he says 'our' he means 'his' private use. He can have the use of any house in the kingdom yet he wants to take Woking from me. On some whim of his own, he plans to tear down the nest Harry and I created together.

"Not Woking, Henry! You can have any of my other palaces gladly, but not Woking ... it is my home."

"You will always be welcome, Mother, you know that, and I am offering you a life interest in Hunsdon in return."

236

"Hunsdon! I am not interested in Hunsdon, it has no place in my heart. Harry and I built Woking together; it is the place I go in search of solace."

"And when was the last time you visited?"

He places the tips of his fingers together, studies me with hooded eyes that are so much like my own.

"That is beside the point. I have been busy at court; worried for Elizabeth and the children, helping you with your foreign affairs ..."

"Mother, where I value your advice and assistance, I never intended to interfere with your leisure. You are free to leave court at any time."

I am stung. I had thought myself indispensable. But refusing to be drawn from the matter in hand, I turn the conversation back again.

"Regarding Woking. I will be hurt, immeasurably so, if you take it from me but there is little I can do if you truly wish possession of it. But you should be aware that it represents what little happiness I enjoyed while you were in exile. It formed my stability while I fought for your rights, your place in England. If, knowing all this, you still want it, then take it but I cannot give it gladly."

"Good." He smiles, but there is no pleasure in his eye. "I shall have the papers drawn up for your signature and Hunsdon will be yours."

I stand up, turning to leave without our customary embrace. "There is one more thing I would like before I sign, Henry."

"And what is that?" He puts down his pen, presses those finger tips together again.

"I would like Cecily restored. She is my friend and companion and your wife's sister. We both require her presence at court."

"As the wife of a commoner she cannot attend court. I have made my displeasure known. If I forgive her

237

we will have all the eligible women marrying where they please."

"At least restore some of her monies. She is of noble blood, used to fine things, a certain ... lifestyle. I think you have acted too harshly, Henry. I know what it is to be banished from court, twiddling one's thumbs in the countryside while life passes by ... it is not the sort of life I would wish on a friend."

"Then she should have thought before she jumped so hastily into a commoner's bed."

I move determinedly back toward him.

"My sources say Thomas Kyme is a good sort, no crimes have been laid against him. Be magnanimous and forgive them Henry, and I will sign the Woking papers without further ado."

He looks at me askance. "You drive a hard bargain, Mother."

"You do not have to welcome her back to court but I think, after a period of reflection, it would be noble of you to restore some of her properties, if not her status."

He picks up his pen again, makes some marks upon a page, ending the conversation, dismissing me and my quest.

Henry is changing. He is immoveable and sometimes, as he has shown today, lacking in compassion, even for his mother. Had I had the raising of him I think he would have been kinder or, at least that is what I tell myself. Suppressing the instinct to reveal the pain he is causing me, I take my leave ... without bidding him farewell.

I hate to be at odds with Henry and cannot determine what has come between us. I search my memory for some slight I have inflicted upon him, some unconscious insult that brings his displeasure down on

238

me. It is ridiculous to feel chastened by the actions of one's own son. It is not like Henry at all. How have I sinned against him? And then, the answer is suddenly clear. *He is ailing.*

Ever since the death of Arthur the king's actions have been out of character; as if the shock has shrunken his spirit, diminished his vitality. The insecurity of having just one living heir is eating him alive and there is nothing I can do to help him.

The queen is little better. Grief and disappointment, together with the megrims of pregnancy, leave her wan and tired. She complains of sleepless nights, feelings of nausea that steal her appetite and my attempts to doctor her take no effect. Poor Elizabeth is beset with trouble but will take no rest, or advice even as she plans her forthcoming visit to the Welsh marches.

<u>July – December 1502</u>

Elizabeth and her entourage set out for Woodstock in July. Henry, who is as concerned as I about the state of his wife's health, accompanies her for the first part of the progress. I remain at Westminster for a short time, preparing to leave for Collyweston where vast building works are underway but, shortly after Henry and his queen depart, word comes of the death of Elizabeth's nephew, little Edward Courtenay, the five year old son of her sister. I close my eyes and rail inwardly at this latest shock for the queen who has lately suffered blow after blow.

Infant deaths are commonplace but the pain of them is always intense. I spent Henry's youth in terror of him falling victim to some ailment or accident. I sit down and write letters of condolence, one to poor Katherine who still laments the recent imprisonment of her husband William Courtney, and one to the queen who is already so heavily burdened with grief.

I half expect Elizabeth to return home but instead she gives her sister permission to leave her, and continues on her journey. She writes to tell me of a planned visit to Raglan, where Henry resided in his youth under the care of the Herberts. I recall those days with a shrim of remembered insecurity – how glad I had been of Lady Herbert's kindness, yet at the same time, jealous of her motherly instincts. Poor Anne is dead now as are so many from those long ago desperate times.

I give myself a shake. There is no point in dwelling on the past, it is over and there are new and sorrier matters to worry about now. I force myself to focus my mind on Collyweston and the king's promise to visit there again soon.

Henry's last visit had been a great success when Thomas revelled in taking him to the top of a tower to show the improvements made to the parkland. But that was before our recent troubles. Now, with Arthur dead and just one ten year old son to succeed the king, the living spectre of Suffolk, terrifyingly at large on the continent, is never far from our thoughts. We are as vulnerable now as we have ever been.

Since Suffolk fled England for the sanctuary of Maximillian's court, many old adherents of York have flocked to join him. The Emperor resists all Henry's attempts to have him returned to England and the king has, on more than one occasion sought my council as to how he should act. Suffolk is out of our reach but his defection at least offers the opportunity for the king to take possession of his lands, and name him a traitor and a rebel against the crown.

Henry orders the arrest of Suffolk's friends and family, undermining the traitor's strength, deterring those who would support his rise against us. But so much more remains to be done.

"You must try to make peace with Maximilian, offer him money to aid his war with the Turks; he is always short of it. As much as you hate to part with it, the emperor is greedy, and a nice fat sum should ensure Maximilian places the traitor in our hands forthwith."

If there is one thing Henry values in me, it is my sage advice. After consulting with his advisers he does just as I say, even going so far as to convince the Pope to place the earl under a ban of anathema, condemning him and all who follow him, to perpetual Hell. Despite the emperor's promises that no further English rebels will find sanctum in his court he continues to procrastinate. Henry sends envoys and parts with vast amounts of money before he finally receives confirmation that Suffolk will be returned to England as a felon. I do not speak of it to the king but I have strong reservations that he will honour his promise.

As Christmas approaches Elizabeth begins her journey home, and returns from her progress looking not in the least refreshed from the trip. With a few short months left before the child is born, preparations are put in place for her confinement which will occur a month or so after Christmas.

February 1503 – Tower of London

We arrive at the Tower of London on a rain washed February afternoon. After a recent snow fall, drifts of dirty slush are piled in corners, a slick layer of mud underfoot in the courtyard. We climb from the litter and

241

take refuge in the royal apartments, where a fire keeps the worst of the chills at bay.

Our sojourn here is to be short for the queen's time is near and she wishes to be delivered of her child at Richmond Palace. I cannot tell her how worried I am for her health and fear that, as much as we all need and desire an heir, we should perhaps have waited until she grew stronger. The pregnancy has taken its toll. She is tired and pale, and my concern is deepened by her constant need to sleep. She says she cannot sleep at night yet I seem to find her dosing in her chair whenever I visit, no matter the time of day.

The queen's sister Katherine, recovering from her grief and stepping neatly into Cecily's role, settles Elizabeth into the royal apartments at the Tower. My own apartments are adjacent to the king's, close by the queen should I be needed. As soon as I have taken refreshment I hasten to the chapel where I ask God to send Elizabeth a safe delivery and if it be His will, bless us with a prince to strengthen our house. On my return I am surprised to see a travel stained cloak thrown over a stool and a large, muddy hound asleep at the hearth. I realise I have an unexpected visitor.

Thomas, having travelled from Collyweston to join me, lowers himself into a chair. "These rooms are damned chilly for all the king's improvements," he complains, as he gropes for his cup and takes a draught of wine. "How is the queen, not pupped yet?"

"No, Thomas, not yet. And how are you, My Lord? You look ... tired."

In fact he looks drained, his face bears a pallid hue and a film of perspiration beads his upper brow although he has taken little exertion. He is old now, and far from the hearty middle aged man I married.

242

"Oh, I am well enough, although this damned digestive trouble ..." He thumps his chest to indicate where the discomfort lies.

"Have you been taking ginger? It is an invaluable aid for such ailments. I can have some made up for you ..."

"Always fussing, Margaret. Why must you always fuss?"

"I merely desire to help. However, it is your prerogative to continue in discomfort. I shall say no more on the subject."

He reaches out for my hand but since I am seated outside the arc of his reach, he lets his arm drop. It hangs listlessly by his side.

"Oh, let us not be tetchy with each other, Margaret. It is an age since we were together."

"I am not tetchy, Thomas. I believe that to be you. I was indulging in spiritual contemplation until you barged in on my tranquillity."

"Do you want me to leave?"

I look at his pouched eyes, his heavy jowls, his protruding belly, and notice a button is missing from his doublet. A priceless item no doubt lost on the road, or on some tavern floor.

"No. There is no need for you to leave since you have only just arrived. If you were a small boy I would tell you to go out and come back in again when you had rediscovered a better frame of mind."

"But I am not a boy, although you have always treated me like one... always scolding, criticising..."

"That is not true!"

He has emptied his wine cup and is now wiping his lips on the back of his hand as he looks for a refill.

"Name me one time you treated me as man then."

I think for a while, my mind drifting back down the years as it so often does. I recall one small sweet memory and speak of it before I consider the import he may place upon my words.

"There was Lathom when you brought me a letter from my son ..."

In the silence that follows I recall the aching loneliness of that time when I was under house arrest and Thomas my only contact with the outside world. The letter he carried from my exiled son that Christmas had refuelled my lagging hope, and chased despair back into the shadows. The lovemaking that followed as reward for the risk he had taken was the most abandoned I have ever known. Even now my cheeks grow pink at the memory.

"Why Margaret! You are not such a cold fish as you pretend! I thought you had forgotten. Ahh, that afternoon, and others that followed, are the sweetest of my life."

"Really?" My ears are burning with embarrassment now. He struggles forward in his seat, takes my errant hand.

"Yes, really. You have been a good wife to me, Margaret. If we had not been burdened with all the troubles God has seen fit to heap upon us, I wager we would be among the happiest in the land. I have had no regrets despite the reservations I held before I took you on."

My breath is taken by his last few words; I stutter and almost choke in my haste to reply.

"Before you took me on? You make me sound like a wild horse, or – or a dog with the mange! What do you mean by that?"

He snatches back his hand as if bitten.

"Aside from your wealth, you were not a great catch. You were tiny, more like a child than a woman and barren too. If I had not already had sons enough, even your wealth would not have swayed me."

"Well, I hope I was worth the hardship after all."

Although Thomas and I have never been sweethearts I am stung by his honesty. It would not hurt him to soften the truth a little for the sake of my pride. He stares at me open mouthed.

"What do you mean? I already said I had no regrets!" He tries to get up but, hindered by ailing health, the movement becomes more of a stagger. "Honestly, Margaret," he breathes like a hard ridden horse, "there is never any pleasing you."

He has reached the door before I call him back. I have no wish to end his visit like this. "Thomas, come back. Let us begin again. We will speak of other things and put all discussion of our marriage to one side. It is past the time to worry about it now. Let me tell you about the queen's health, and Prince Henry's progress in the school room, or the alterations I have made to the gardens at Coldharbour."

"Hmmph."

He looks at me, just like the sulky boy I had promised myself not to compare him too, and returns to his seat.

"Pass the wine, Margaret, and have a cup yourself, see if it will loosen you up a little."

I pass him the jug and two cups and we are still bickering amiably when a page scratches at the door.

"If it please you, My Lady, it is the queen ... her travail has begun."

"Already? She has scarcely had time to settle in! The child is not expected for another week or so. Thank

245

goodness we had the foresight to engage the midwife early."

Alice Massey has delivered most of the queen's babies; she is a trusted and skilled woman for whose services we pay very well.

I rise to my feet, pick up a shawl and prepare to join the queen.

"Where are you going?" Thomas asks.

"To Elizabeth, she may have need of me ..."

"She has delivered enough babies; she should be able to do it unaided by now."

I look at him sprawled in my chair. He has no idea of the pain, the fear a mother suffers, although he cannot but be aware of the legions of women who have perished at such times. He is a cold unfeeling wretch sometimes.

"I will go to her, as I have before, in case she should require my presence."

I leave him in my chambers. As I sweep along the corridor I hear him call something after me but I cannot determine his words and have little care for his opinion. My grandson is about to be born, another small, perfect Tudor is about to grace our nursery.

The ante-room is crowded with women but nobody speaks. Instead they cluster together, listening open mouthed to the wailing of the queen. While I divest myself of my robe, the door opens and an under midwife hurries out, looks about the chamber, her eye halting when she notices my presence. She drops a curtsey.

"The child is coming quickly, My Lady, too quickly Dame Massey says. The queen is in great pain."

Fear lurches in my belly sending me hurrying toward the solid doors. I hesitate for a moment expecting them to open, but the guard are absent. I reach out a hand for the latch and push it wide.

The queen is on all fours, her hair plastered to her head, her mouth open in a great wail as pain assaults her again. She has clearly been suffering for some time. As I watch, she grits her teeth and bears down, sending a great spurt of birth waters that soak the midwife's skirts. Alice, catching sight of me, beckons me forward with a jerk of her head.

"Hold her hand, My Lady, if you would. It may help. I have never seen such an abrupt or speedy birth."

"Is the child alive?"

I take Elizabeth's hand and she clutches me like a drowning woman on a rope, her nails sharp.

"As far as I can tell. That is it, Your Grace, push gently ... gently, Your Grace. Let him come slow ..."

Elizabeth wails as, with a final effort a tiny wet creature slithers into the midwife's hands. She smacks it smartly, provoking a cry as thin as gossamer and I thank God that the child lives. Then Alice turns the child over and my eyes fall on the thick purple rope of birth cord. I search his gore smeared body for wrinkled testicles, a tiny manhood, but my joy drains away as I recognise the lack.

"It is a girl, Your Grace," Alice Massey calls to the queen whose needs are being met by the under midwife. "A bonny, beautiful girl..."

I stand up. My hopes dashed and I look upon the queen who has tried so hard to remedy our lack. Elizabeth is prostrate, her head far back, her hair damp on the pillows. She lies so still I am relieved to see a pulse beating at the base of her throat; it is the only sign that she lives.

"I will inform the king," I say before I quit the chamber. As I hurry along the corridors to the royal apartments my mind churns. A girl, a princess, when we need a prince. It has long been my creed that daughters

247

were as valuable as sons but there should be balance. Sons become kings; daughters become pawns to be bartered to other kings, to produce more sons, more heirs. She should have borne a son. I was certain God would bless us with a boy in our time of need.

Henry will not be pleased. We had banked all our hopes on this. God forbid it but, if anything should happen to Prince Henry … what would we do? What would happen? Would England tolerate a queen? Queen Margaret? Well, it has a ring to it but … the populace would never allow a woman to rule. The nobles would rise up and there would be war again. No lord would follow or swear fealty to a girl.

There will be no more sons now. I am doubtful Elizabeth will bear more children. She is exhausted, tortured with grief, her body dragged down by the sorry state of her mind and she is growing old, well past her prime. We have only Prince Henry and he must be preserved at all costs. I concur with the king's decision that Henry must be kept from danger, screened from contagion. He is the seed of all our hopes for the future – our Tudor dynasty.

Outwardly, my son takes the news well. He says nothing, but turns a little paler and hurries to congratulate his wife on her safe delivery. What he makes of his daughter he keeps to himself. She is a tiny, ailing thing who is christened in some haste in the chapel of St Peter ad Vincula, here in the Tower precinct. They name her Katherine after her aunt who was the first person to receive her from the mid wife.

New furnishings are placed in the bedchamber, soft down for the cradle; a chair for the wet nurse, and furniture for the royal rockers. I swallow my disappointment and visit the queen, hold the child in my arms and bless her as, surreptitiously I assess her mother's health.

The queen is pale and feverish, the film of sweat that has plagued her throughout the pregnancy is increased, her craving for sleep insatiable. It is natural that she should be tired but as the days pass she shows little sign of improving strength. She complains of pain in her belly, headaches so severe she can barely open her eyes. Every remedy I try has little or no affect. In the end when the royal physicians can offer no remedy, another is summoned from Plymouth. I stand at the foot of the bed and watch in fear as he examines the queen for signs of child bed fever. He shakes his head, recommends she be wrapped in a vinegar soaked sheet and promises to return within the hour.

While he consults with the king, I sit with Elizabeth and tell her about the baby.

"Poor little Katherine," she whispers. "She should never have been born."

"Why ever not? She is healthy and gaining strength every day." This is not entirely true but Elizabeth needs comfort, I am anxious to cause her no further anxiety.

"To grow up without a mother must be so ... hard."

"Elizabeth! That is no way to talk. The doctor has great faith in your recovery. This is just a temporary thing ... tiredness and exhaustion are common at this time. You have been through so much. I should never have let you travel so far in such a condition."

"No, Lady Mother. I am not tired. I am sick unto death. I trust you to care for the children when I am gone. Look after all of them, as you have your son. Especially our little Henry ... he was not raised for kingship. I fear he will struggle..." She drifts off to sleep again, leaving me sitting rigidly and with failing hope at her side.

I should have spoken while there was time. I should have told her she had been the best choice for my son. She was a noble queen, a fine wife, a good mother but it is too late now. As the fire slumps and the candles gutter as unknown to us, beneath the pristine sheets of her bed, her life's blood is flowing away.

Barely two months into the new year and I am already sick of it. I sometimes feel as if a curse is laid upon us. First our babies, then our heir, and now their mother, Henry's queen. We have tried so hard yet God has laughed at our attempts to replenish our stock and instead has further depleted it. In trying to right the wrongs of fate we have destroyed Elizabeth too.

I have never seen Henry laid so low. At first he weeps, rants at the injustice of Heaven but then, more worryingly, he slumps into a decline.

While the bells of St Paul's toll the queen's death and the smaller churches and religious houses take up the sorrowful tune, the king sits alone in his chamber and stares into the fire. He will allow no one into his presence; he takes no food for several days and dismisses his chamberers. In the end, driven to distraction with worry, I break protocol and force myself into his presence. Perhaps such disobedience will rouse him to anger and emotion, even the negativity of rage will be a good thing at this time. But my defiance does not provoke him. He lifts his head and stares blankly at me.

"Hello Mother," he sighs as if the weight of the world is upon him. I go forward, kiss his brow, trying not to flinch at the stench of his unchanged linen.

"This cannot go on, Henry," I say quietly. He nods his head slowly in agreement.

"I know. I shall muster myself, sooner or later."

"The time is now, my son. The country needs you. The court needs you. Your children need you and your heir in particular needs you."

He shifts in his seat.

"I would like to sit here forever and just do nothing until it all stops."

My heart lurches to hear my son dismiss life in this way, to give up the fight. I sink to my knees at his side, grasp his hand, shake it a little to emphasise my words, and to make him realise my desperate need for him to stir himself.

"You must not say such things, Henry. I know how you feel. I have been in your shoes. I know the tearing loss you are feeling but it will pass, you will learn to bear it. There is still so much for you to live for, so much to fight for. At this moment our family is down, but we are not defeated. We never will be. Not as long as I have breath in my body."

Our eyes meet. I let him see my pain, my empathy.

"Do you not ever get tired of it all, Mother?"

"Of course I do. We all suffer hard times. It is God's way of testing us. He is challenging us to prove our strength of character. Life has been hard but it has made me strong. It will make you strong again too. Once you are through this bad time and feeling more like yourself, you will remember this day, recall my words and realise I was right."

The fire glows in the gathering gloom, the torches have not yet been lit. I let the silence settle around us, it holds us close in the dark, like a mantle. I breathe deep and slow and feel Henry begin to do the same.

"Did you never once want to give up the fight?"

I allow myself a rueful smile.

"I fought for you. You were my strength, my reason for continuing, despite my fear and exhaustion. At first I fought to bring you home to your Richmond heritage, to the home of your birth but as time went on and York's rule decayed, I wanted more. I knew you would make a better king than Gloucester and once I had raised my goal to include not just Richmond but England too, I could never admit defeat. I wanted to give up many, many times, and often I feared I would fail but I had you to keep me going."

He droops his head, his mouth sulky and his eyes awash with tears.

"You are a woman yet you are stronger and better than I. It was you who put me here, you who keep me where I am. Without you the name Tudor would have remained forever in obscurity."

"And it is up to you to maintain our place on the throne. You must teach your son how to be a good king, as you have been. You must teach him how to rule and then he will have sons and our name, the name Tudor will live for perpetuity. Is that not reason enough to fight?"

He sighs. "Without Elizabeth, York may rise against us."

"Then you must not allow it. You must be strong and determined. Now, I shall call your chamberers, order a bath be drawn and a good meal brought up. A king cannot rule if he is entrenched in despair. You must climb out, rise above it. Once you have washed away the megrim of the last few days you will be strong again. You will be King Henry again."

I am speaking to him as if he is a child but he shows no resentment of it. In his sorrow he has need of me in a way he never has before. I rest a hand on his

252

shoulder, kiss his unwashed hair. "I shall see you at supper."

As I take my leave he calls out after me. "Thank you, Mother."

It is as I am preparing for mass that a summons arrives from the nursery. I put aside my prayer book and hurry there at once, throw open the door to Elizabeth's chamber where her coat is still laid across a chair, her book of hours open near the bed. I tear my eyes from these sharp reminders and cross the room to the antechamber beyond.

The women gathered about the royal cradle cease their conversation as I enter. One of them, a youngster no older than ten is weeping as she folds linen away in the corner cabinet. I search the room, seeking out the child. The tallest of the women turns and I notice with relief that she cradles Katherine in her arms. I smile and move forward.

"How is my granddaughter today?" I ask, holding out my arms.

"Oh, My Lady; I ... My Lady, she is gone..."

For a moment I do not understand. Her words make no sense. *Gone where?* I can see her there, before me in the arms of her nurse. She takes one step closer and I look down at the skeletal features of my youngest granddaughter. Her lips are blue.

The world dips and sways. I close my eyes, brace myself, and fight against unconsciousness while my throat fills with vomit. This cannot be happening. Not now, not so soon after ... we cannot bear it!

June 1503

"What is that in your hand Henry?"

I am reading a story to the royal children, attempting to assuage their grief, comfort their troubled souls but I have failed to capture their attention. Mary is kneeling at the window, her sewing abandoned, trying to establish if the rain has stopped. Several times I have asked her to come and sit down but she is wayward. If she does not do as I say I shall call her nurse and have her removed. She is making my head ache. I put down the book and pick up my needle instead.

Margaret is tense, her face white and more strained than a girl's has the right to be. Soon she must leave the palace, leave England and take her place as queen in the Scottish court. I can tell by the way her fingers clench and unclench that she is as pent up as I. I can well imagine the fears she tries to conceal. She does not want to go. I well remember the day I learned I had to leave my home and travel with Edmund into Wales ... and I was younger than Margaret. I had not yet even begun to bleed.

When Elizabeth was alive she was able to distract her daughter with clothes, shoes and jewellery but now our only new garments are mourning clothes. Her head droops over the collar she is working. We are both practising a new technique demonstrated by Caterina, Tudor roses and Scottish thistles picked out in black and white. Margaret says very little but she is thinking all the time. I know she is, for my mind is also a turmoil of disjointed thoughts.

"It is a partlet," replies Henry, bringing my mind back to the present. "It belonged to mother. It smells of her. I – I took it from her chamber to comfort me."

I should scold him but I lack the heart to do so. Yesterday I discovered him in Elizabeth's chamber where he had been weeping, clinging to the curtains of her bed. I had not realised he had smuggled out one of her garments.

"Why do not you find something worthy to do? The devil finds work for idle hands."

"I am waiting for the king to summon me."

His eyes are desolate at the thought of another day of studying foreign policy.

"That is good. You will learn to be the perfect king ... when the time comes."

"I want to practice at the tiltyard. I have not been allowed to do so for so long, I fear I will forget all I have learned."

"There are other sports you must now master. You must learn to wrestle, to cast the bar, and a prince should always excel at tennis and fighting with the quarterstaff."

"But I will also need to improve my jousting and be taught to fight in armour with poll axe and sword."

"Well, perhaps you will be allowed to run the ring again soon."

"But I want to compete against the others!"

I snip the thread and select another strand. "There is much more to being a king than performing to the crowd, Henry. Your father never jousts ..."

"Father never enjoys himself at all. I intend to be a king more like my grandfather, King Edward. Mother used to tell us all stories about him."

I subdue irritation that Elizabeth spoke over much about her father, who really was nowhere near as good a king as Henry is. I quell the urge to tell the prince of all the things the late queen forgot to mention; his grandfather's laziness, his lechery, his gluttony but ... it is

255

not the Christian thing to do. Instead I adopt a merry smile, cock my head to one side as I answer.

"First you must learn state craft, and then you can perfect your prowess on the field. The ability to fight for the crown is no longer as imperative as it was in your grandfather's day. Your father has changed all that."

He scowls and I am anticipating an insolent remark when a disturbance at the door heralds, not the page we have been expecting, but the king himself.

Margaret and Mary instantly scramble to their feet but Henry follows more slowly. I remain seated and wait to receive the king's kiss of greeting.

I run an assessing eye over him and conclude that he is looking a little better. For that, I must give grudging credit to Catherine Gordon who has lately been his constant companion. On entering his apartments I invariably find them playing cards or sharing supper. I am not certain whether or not she shares his bed, and have little wish to know. She has at last stopped wearing mourning for her traitorous husband and her step is lighter now, her voice bright and merry. I should resent her but... she makes my son happy. I can forgive her very much for that.

Henry stoops over to admire his daughter's needlework.

"You must make me a collar in the same fashion," he suggests and Margaret smiles, quietly pleased at the attention. Mary climbs down from the window seat and offers up her own work for her father's inspection. Henry makes an indefinable sound and I hide my sudden smile. I fear Mary will never make a skilled seamstress. The king wrinkles his brow, groping for appropriate words to praise her uneven stitches and grubby stained cloth.

"She will learn," I comfort him, "or perhaps she has other skills we are yet to discover."

"Let us hope so," he says, moving Margaret's box of silk thread and perching on the settle beside her.

"It will soon be time for you to leave us, Margaret. We will miss you. You are a valued member of our court and family; a credit to our house ... and to your mother."

Margaret raises her head, the muscles of her face undulating as she tries to control an outburst of emotion. I see the tears will not be stopped, one drop falls upon her handiwork and the king reaches out to grasp her hand.

"No, Father, please. I cannot bear it," she cries as she springs to her feet and flees the room. "I really cannot bear it."

Henry stares at me open mouthed. "What did I say to cause that?"

"Nothing, my son. She is overwrought, that is all. We all are and she has worst of all. She is loath to leave us."

"It is the way of the world."

He sighs, turns his head to the window. Surreptitiously I run an appraising eye over him. He is still pale and, I suspect, exhausted despite the attentions of the royal physician and my own attempts to dose him with restoratives.

In the corner, Prince Henry conceals his mother's partlet behind a cushion and sits up straight, one eye on his father. The king sighs again and gets to his feet. "Come along, Henry," he says. "We must be about our business. This will never teach you the rules of kingship."

My grandson kisses my fingers and when he rises, I offer him an encouraging smile. When they have left me, I turn my attention back to my needle and listen to Mary and her nurse whispering in the corner, the birds outside the window. It is so quiet without Elizabeth. With Cecily gone from court there are few women whose company I

257

favour now. I lay aside my sewing and pinch the bridge of my nose. My eyes are growing tired, my head heavy, and as it always does, my mind drifts back down the years to happier days. Days that I had thought at the time were miserable.

<u>July 1503</u>

For almost a year Margaret has been paraded before the world as the Queen of Scotland. Her wardrobe is overflowing with furs and velvets, and she has garments of the softest silks, the finest linen. Even in the depths of mourning her clothes are testament to her position. Her father and I, reluctant that she should grow maudlin, ensure she has little respite in which to mourn her mother.

There are banquets to attend, dignitaries to meet; several times a day she must change her clothes, adorn herself with fresh jewels and always present a calm serenity to the world. She must put aside her tender years and embrace her womanhood, as I did all those years ago.

In an attempt to prepare her for what may lie in the future, I fill her head with advice, warnings and rules. But perhaps I should not worry too much. Since infancy she has been trained for the day she would marry and she should think herself lucky. Some royal women are sent far away to lands overseas where the customs and language are so different to our own. Margaret may feel that the Scottish court is a world away but she is fortunate, only a thin border separates us.

I watch her constantly, looking for chinks in her armour, proof that she is mentally prepared for the challenge. Although she is Scotland's queen I try to instil in her that she must never forget her roots, her Tudor blood, her Englishness.

As far as the world is concerned Margaret is happy to leave us; she puts on a show of welcoming her new role. She must also prepare herself for the indelicacies of marriage. Although I have ensured the union will not be consummated until she is of an age to do so, her new husband may well offer other difficulties.

"In time, the prospect of children will be a comfort to you," I tell her and she wrinkles her brow, embarrassed at the thought of sharing a stranger's bed. "Your children will one day inherit the throne of Scotland. There will be much for them to learn and you will become their teacher, at least in their younger years."

In public she is composed and dignified but in the privacy of my chambers, she lets her guard slip. I witness her tears and hold her while her thin shoulders heave as if her heart will break. But, when the time comes, I am confident she will put such childish fears aside and play her part as she has been bred to do. ·

On the morning she rides away my throat is tight with grief. I cannot help but recall my own journey into Wales, the endless road, the choking dust, my constant longing to turn around and run for home. But perhaps it will not be as bad for my granddaughter. She has her women with her who are familiar and know her requirements, and Henry has organised a lengthy progress for her with many entertainments to distract her.

Each town she passes through will greet her with cheers and waves, each vying with the other to offer the best accommodation, the most extravagant hospitality. It will be August before she crosses the border to meet her husband for the first time. I pray God she finds him to her liking. I hope he is as kind as Edmund was to me.

In spite of the demands put upon him by the forthcoming union with Scotland, Henry continues to languish. When questioned he reluctantly admits that his eyesight is dimming and his digestion upset. This ailment forces him to place much the administration in the hands of his most trusted men, Richard Empson and Edmund Dudley. Recent events have depleted the treasury and it is their job to replenish the coffers and stabilise the economy. Henry's constant fretting at the state of his finances does little to aid his health yet he shrugs off my advice to take more ginger and rhubarb, get himself earlier to bed and to leave more in the hands of his council.

But the deficit refuses to diminish. To the dismay of the younger members of court, in an attempt to make ends meet, he cuts back on entertainments. He no longer has the heart for jesters, fools and masques and if it is at all possible, he keeps to his private apartments.

I hate to see him brought so low and even go as far as to summon Catherine Gordon and tell her to do all she can to bring cheer to the king. She flushes, as well she should at virtually being instructed to take the king to her bed, but she promises to do her best.

Henry's doldrums are contagious and the whole court seems weighed down. I spend my nights worrying for the king's health, for the state of the economy and of our future in general. As well as the running of the court, we are obliged to send huge sums abroad to ensure continuing peace with Philip and Maximilian.

Caterina's future is still not settled and Henry is loath to send her home, or to part with the portion of her dowry already paid. He even contemplates marrying Caterina himself but this is met by outrage from Spain who see it as an 'evil thing' and continue to press for the princess to be married to Prince Henry instead.

I cannot blame them for refusing Henry's proposal and as much as I love him, I can see their point. Although marriage with my son would make Caterina a queen, the privilege would necessarily be short lived. But, should she marry his heir, she will be queen for the rest of her life.

Caterina is Prince Henry's senior by almost six years but such marriages have worked before. By the time they are wed Henry will be full of the vigour of youth and the princess will be a woman in her prime. When the king seeks my opinion on this there is no need for me to contemplate it long before I agree.

"Yes," I nod my head. "There may be some prohibition because she was wed to Henry's brother but we can seek dispensation from the Pope ... I am sure he will oblige."

Young Henry, however, is not so content. With a red face and sweating hands he stands defiant before us.

"All my life," he cries, "I have come second to Arthur. Always second, never first. I am given Arthur's title Prince of Wales, and I like that well enough but I do not wish for his widow. I wish to choose my own bride!"

The king turns purple and, worried that he might suffer an apoplexy, I intervene before he can speak.

"Kings can never choose for themselves, Henry. They must think of the country, the good of the state will come first. Caterina is a fine young woman. She is intelligent, pious and fair and in the prime of her youth; she will give you strong healthy sons and, in marrying her, our relations with Spain will be secured."

"And father gets to keep her dowry!"

The king leans forward, thumps the table and snarls "That is enough!"

Henry takes two involuntary steps backward but his defiance still simmers.

"I should be allowed to choose my own wife."

"What is wrong with the Infanta? Is she not good enough for you? Is she not fair? Is her blood not rich enough? Is her body not well formed and strong?"

For a long moment they regard each other and then the boy mutters:

"There is nothing wrong with her."

Prince Henry, his chin on his chest, casts a resentful look toward his father, a look that makes my heart sink. Henry must fix this. His relationship with his son must be mended at all costs; a king and his heir must sing from the same sheet ... or at least, be seen to do so.

Collyweston - 1504

The endless negotiations exhaust me. As soon as it has been decided the wedding will take place when Henry reaches his fourteenth year, I turn my weary mind to private matters.

The king has ordered work to begin on his shrine at Westminster abbey; a fine affair, fit for the kingliest of kings. Even though I have made similar arrangements for when my own time comes, I find the contemplation of Henry's death deeply troubling. It is better to pretend the day will never come. In recent months, whenever I look at him he seems to stoop more lowly, his diminishing eyesight growing ever worse, his teeth loosening in his jaw. If only I could determine the disease that ails him and find a cure for it but I fear much of it is due to the pressure of running the country, and there is nothing I can do to make that easier for him.

It is a shame he has not inherited my own rude health. I have never been seriously ill, not once in my life if you ignore the months I malingered after Henry's birth. I am fast approaching my sixtieth year and, although my bones ache and I feel the cold more than I did in my youth, I am healthy. I refuse to bow down to encroaching age. The day I begin to creep about the palace like a crone is the day I will be happy to give it all up and let God take me. Without the king's knowledge, I consult his physician but he is equally as perplexed as I.

"I can only ascribe the king's malady to fatigue, My Lady, perhaps if he ate more regularly and cut out those frugal late night suppers."

"He complains that the fayre at the banquets he attends is sufficient to keep his appetite sated for a week. When he is away from the court he prefers to eat lightly."

"Then I am at a loss, My Lady." He raises his hands and lets them drop again. "I will consult my colleagues, perchance they have some suggestions.

July 1504

While I watch Henry anxiously for signs of encroaching death, I fail to notice that I have had no word from Thomas for several weeks. Since I made my vows of chastity our relationship has not altered. We see each other regularly but it has long been his habit to write to me of trivial things. Sometimes his letters contain long winded memories of our early days together or small incidents of humour. Sometimes he sends a recipe for a dish he thinks I might enjoy, or a book he thinks I will relish. When a letter arrives from Lathom, I am expecting another such trivial note.

I break the seal and scan the words carelessly before their import steals away my breath. My hand flies to my throat and Thomas' name tumbles from my lips, tears sting my eyes. My woman comes running as I drop

263

suddenly into a chair, fighting for my next breath as my throat is blocked with sudden grief. She begins to fuss with my clothing, holds out a cup of restorative wine. I shove her rudely away.

I am astounded to feel so lost by this news. *He should have told me,* but perhaps he had no warning. Perhaps God took him as suddenly and as cruelly as he has taken others that I love.

I did not *love* Thomas in the romantic sense but he was a part of the world I miss so much. Slowly, the people who shared those unstable times are leaving. Soon I shall be the sole person at court who can recall the feuding, the uncertainty of civil war. It is strange that I should sometimes long for it all again.

Time passes so quickly now. I wake on a Monday morning and before I know it, it is Sunday again. Almost a whole week has passed without achievement, without any event taking place that is worthy of recall. Having lived in such perilous times, I should be glad of non-events but oh, how eagerly I look back on those days of plotting, those times of uncertainty, the days when my blood surged beneath my skin in a torrent of passion and determination.

I suppose the thing I miss the most is having something to fight for, some seemingly unattainable goal. I have achieved all I set out to do, perhaps my life were better over too. My son is king, my grandson will come after and then, after that, my descendants will form a chain into a future I cannot know, and cannot imagine. The future has no room for me.

I travel back down the years and ponder the past for so long that dark creeps upon me unawares. At some point I must have drifted off to sleep in my chair, for I am woken by a girl coming to light the torches.

"Are you well, My Lady?" she asks, and I stir myself, stretch my limbs.

"Yes," I reply, looking down at the letter that has slipped to the floor. Following the line of my eye she picks it up and replaces it in my hand.

"Thank you."

I scrunch it between my fingers.

"Can I get you anything?"

"No. No ..." I stare at the fire, which is smeeching now she has added more wood. I straighten my legs, my knees stiff and sore. "Well," I change my mind. "You could call my women to come attend to me. It is time I called upon the king."

"It is rather late, My Lady. You slept for some time..."

"No matter. I need to speak to my son."

I find the king alone in his chambers. Outside the corridors throng with courtiers waiting an audience but he has shut himself away from them. For once I do not blame him. Recognising the wisdom of keeping in my good graces, they fall to their knees as I pass through them. At my approach the guards throw open the doors and I sweep into the king's presence. He raises his head from his hand, straightens himself in the chair as if he has been dozing. "Mother," he says. "I was not expecting you."

"No." I wave the crumpled letter in his direction. "I have had some... some rather distressing news."

I swallow down tears, fight for control of my face. Noticing but not commenting on my upset, he gets up and takes the letter, carrying it to the light the better to read it. I watch him squinting at the fine script and wonder where his eye glasses are, or if he is too proud to use them. He lets the letter drop and pulls a rueful expression.

"I am sorry to hear of this, Mother. I had no idea he was ailing."

"He wasn't, as far as I know. Thomas was always too ... too stubborn to call a physician."

My voice breaks at the end of the sentence. Henry places his hand on my wrist.

"I had not realised you cared for him so much."

I give a shaky laugh. "Oh, I do not ... did not ... or so I thought but ..." I swallow some strange blockage in my throat, the pain moving deeper into my chest. "Perhaps I was mistaken. Perhaps I did care ... or maybe, it is just that all death is horrid and there is so much of it in these sorry times. Death is so final. It spells the end ...Thomas and I shall never speak again. I will miss him. He was a good ... he had good intentions and treated me well ... for most of the time."

"It comes to us all, Mother. There is no use in growing maudlin."

I could of course, remind him that he was just now sitting in the dark thinking of Elizabeth but I know better than to do so.

"The world will seem very strange without him."

Henry pulls a chair close to the fire and gestures me to sit. Smoothing my skirts beneath me I lower myself into the seat and wait for him to settle beside me.

"You could remarry now, if it pleases you. I could find you a man of wealth and position."

I cannot hide my astonishment. "Why ever would I wish to remarry? There is nothing a man can offer that would improve my status, my lifestyle – in fact, a man would only be a hindrance. No, I will stick with my vow to live chastely. I may even reaffirm it once Thomas is ... is buried. I expect he left instruction to be interred at Burscough in the family vault."

Henry sighs, rubs his face with both hands.

266

"The news these days always seems to be ill. I crave good tidings like a dog craves a sausage."

"Storms never last. It is always darkest before dawn..."

"Oh Mother! You and your platitudes! Have you heard that Queen Isabella is ailing? She has withdrawn from the government of Spain; I have no idea what will happen now. Trouble heaps upon trouble."

"Is she going to die? Has Caterina been informed?"

He looks at me bleakly, pulls a face.

"I am no prophet, Mother. It has been one death after another lately ... I should tell you, in case you have not heard, that Reginald Bray is ailing again ..."

"Reginald? No, I had not heard. Is it serious?"

He shrugs. "I am not a doctor."

"Well, have you sent the royal physicians to examine him?"

He shakes his head. "I only had word of it yesterday."

I stand up. Suddenly glad of something to occupy me, take my mind from Thomas lying on a cold grey slab at Lathom.

"I shall visit him. We owe that man almost everything, Henry. He supported me for my whole life, or at least from the time I wed Harry Stafford. He was a young man then ..."

"He was well rewarded for it too. I have heaped lands and titles upon him ..."

"And well deserved! He was loyal, intelligent and trustworthy. We owe your crown in part to him and others like him. I shall make the arrangements first thing tomorrow."

Two days later, I am greeted by Reginald's wife, whose name escapes me. She pales when she recognises me and shows me meekly up the dark staircase to the master chamber. Reginald is tucked up in bed with a trio of servants attending to his bodily needs, and a scribe close by, penning letter after letter. The floor is scattered with paper, the candles are burnt low and the fire in need of replenishing. The combined aroma of sweat, wet dog and cold ash fills the air.

"I am so sorry, My Lady," his wife mutters as she precedes me up the stair. "He is a very difficult patient. He will not let a doctor near nor will he allow me to change the bed covers or even refresh his linen. Reginald, look who has honoured us with a visit," she says as she ushers me into the room and hurries to throw open the casement.

He looks up and I recognise the face I have known for so many years. It is obscured now by seamed flesh, bagged below the eye, and pouched at the jawline. Age is a terrible thing and it is painful to reflect that I am not so far in years behind him.

"Master Bray ..." I say, addressing him as I have always done. "How sorry I am to find you so discommoded."

He shoves papers about the coverlet and grasps my proffered hand.

"Lady Margaret ... I am ... I ... totally honoured. To think I should ever receive you here!" He indicates the disorderliness of his chamber. "Get out, get out all of you, I would speak to My Lady alone."

The servants scatter, his wife following in their wake. As she reaches the door he calls after her "Katherine, see that refreshments are sent up."

I remember now. Her name is Katherine; a nondescript soul who has borne him no sons. Master

Bray will die without heirs to leave his amassed fortune. She drops a curtsey and flees the room. An awkward silence falls.

I look about for a seat and lower myself into the one vacated by the scribe. For want of some way of occupying my hands, I shuffle the papers on the table, but I do not read for my eyes are suddenly flooded with tears that I really must not let him see.

"So," he says, "they have told you I am dying."

"No, no, of course you are not dying. It is likely some summer chill and will soon pass."

"I doubt it. I feel God is calling me home."

He pulls his shawl closer about his shoulders. Beneath his gown his body is thin, lacking in muscle, his lower throat coated with wiry grey hairs. The clever, wily politician I met in my youth has turned into an old man, desperately trying to wrangle a deal with God to remain on Earth a little longer. It is a contract that will never be signed. "Why did you come then? You never have before."

I meet his eye, blink a few tears away and try to think of a reason for my visit other than his imminent demise.

"I came to tell you of Thomas's death. I am widowed again, Master Bray. It seems to be my lot in life."

He raises his hands, lets them fall despairingly to the sheet again.

"Stanley has gone? I am sorry to hear that, My Lady, and you ... how are you coping?"

I shrug my shoulders.

"It has hit me harder than I imagined it would. I think it is the culmination of all our recent losses. I feel very alone now, even though Thomas and I were living apart, we have always remained friends."

"Sometimes, My Lady, I think husbands and wives were meant to have separate establishments."

269

The twinkle in his eye makes me smile, I even detect a bubble of laughter beginning in my chest but it is quickly extinguished. Despite the terrors of my past, tomorrows are far more frightening than yesterdays.

I sit with Reginald Bray for some time. He makes no attempt to pretend his death will not come too soon.

"A man knows when his body has had enough, My Lady. The hardest thing is to persuade the mind it is so. Every time I lay back my head and decide it is time to give up the ghost, another thought springs into my mind and I have to struggle up and call back the scribe to make more notes. There are several letters for the king. I am so sorry the good lord has seen fit to summon me before the work is finished on the royal tomb. It will be a fine thing once it is complete – a thing of beauty."

"Just as everything you do is fine." I place my hand over his and feel his fingers tremor beneath mine. I will not let this dear friend slip away from me without me telling him just how valued he is. "You have been an exemplary servant and the best of friends, Master Bray. I will miss you very much and so will the king."

He shakes his head, denying my words and a tear finds its way from the corner of his eye to begin a weary trail down the heavy lines and folds of his cheek. His tongue comes out to moisten his paper dry lips.

"And you have been the best of mistresses. You were a girl when I first saw you, a nervous, skinny young girl but look at you now ..."

"Now I am a nervous, skinny *old* woman," I laugh, to leaven the seriousness of the conversation although every fibre of my body wants to give in to this suffocating grief.

"Oh, you are not nervous! Look at you, you are invincible!" His body shakes with mirth, his face quivering with love. Before this moment I had no idea of

270

the depth of his affection for me. I had always thought he served our family from duty but now, I see obligation to serve has grown into something more and had I taken the time to notice, I would have enjoyed the relationship more. My heart is glad of this death bed confession but the loss of him, coming so soon after the loss of others, finally overwhelms me. I lie my face against our clasped hands and let my tears wash over them.

<u>July 1505</u>

I join Henry in his chamber where he is balancing his account books. The coffers are still worryingly depleted: as fast as money goes in it seems to pour out the other side. It is no surprise when one considers the constant pensions and annuities paid to courtiers and officials, as well as advances to diplomats, and monies spent on buildings, the royal parks, and the wardrobe. It all takes its toll. The king is advised to raise taxes but he is loath to do so since there is nothing the populace hate more but he has no choice.

Henry cut court entertainments some time ago and now makes further reductions in expenditure at the royal palaces. When Caterina approaches him and asks in halting English for money to cover food and clothing, he refuses. There is little I can do to persuade him to reconsider.

He is furious with Spain for the withholding of the remaining portion of her marriage settlement but while the stalemate over her union with Prince Henry continues, neither side will give ground. She has my pity. She is alone in a strange country and her father offers no support; all that on top of the recent death of her mother must be a trial indeed.

"Perhaps we should allow her a little money, Henry. It is not as if she is extravagant, she asks only for food and for money to pay her household."

"I cannot afford it," the king replies. "Until the marriage takes place and Spain pays what is our due, she will have to use her initiative."

"What do you expect her to do? Sell her plate?"

There is no time for reply. The doors are thrown open and Prince Henry enters. I notice straight away that he looks as peaked and unhappy as his father.

"Henry!" I greet him brightly and stand to embrace him, turn my cheek up to receive his kiss. At fifteen years old he already towers above me, but most people do. I take comfort from his stolid strength, his sturdy broad shoulders. He is becoming the image of the perfect prince; we have only to tame his behaviour and he will be ready to rule.

Young Henry is still far too ungoverned; too inclined toward impetuous decisions, spontaneous actions. The king is wise to keep him close. We have both noticed his eye following the prettiest maids of the court and it is a constant battle to keep his mind on his lessons. On several occasions of late he has managed to elude the king and sneak out to the tilt yard to enjoy the company of the young gentlemen that frequent it. I can understand how trying it must be for him to be kept so closely confined but he is old enough now to understand the king's reasons. As our sole heir he is more precious than gold. There can be no risk of injury or contagion.

While the king continues to wrangle with the Spanish over the marriage of Caterina and Henry, I find my mind straying back to the past. In my youth I swore that if I were ever in the position to do so, I would champion the poor, support good causes, give patronage to churches and colleges. I have been true to that promise but now I decide I have not yet done quite enough. I must act before my allotted time runs out. One morning after I have taken confession, I linger with Bishop Fisher in the nave.

"I have it in mind to fund the building of another college or a school, perhaps a great library. Do you have any suggestions?"

He bows his head while he considers and, just as I think he can think of none, he raises his forefinger.

"I have it, My Lady. The God's House College in Cambridge is in need of improvement. The hall is in a sorry state and the library could be expanded and improved. The current building that houses the books suffers quite badly from damp."

"Would you look into it on my behalf? Perhaps we can arrange a visit so I can see for myself what needs to be done."

The day I journey to Cambridge in the company of John Fisher is bright and sunny. The roads are dusty, the meadows full of flowers, the hedgerows replete with ripening fruit, and the birds are busy feeding their young. We stop at a wayside inn where a flustered landlord serves up delicious ale and a chunk of his wife's cake, straight from the oven.

As we sample it, she hovers in the background with her apron over her face and at first I am unsure as to what ails her. Slowly as I consume the last crumb I realise she is tormented by the fact that her labours may not be to our liking. When it is time to move on, a groom assists me onto my horse, I gather up my reins and before I ride off I turn to the woman.

"Your cake was very welcome, Mistress. I enjoyed it very much."

Her mouth falls open, her face turns scarlet as she stutters an incomprehensible reply and makes the semblance of a very clumsy curtsey. The sunshine has brought out the best in me, the pleasure my praise evoked leaves me feeling virtuous and contented for the remainder of the journey.

Bishop Fisher is quite correct, the college is indeed in need of improvement. The exterior looks sound enough but inside the walls are damp, the plaster crumbling, smelling dank and unwelcoming. Apart from anything else, the library is dark and ill-equipped to house the required number of books to cover the new subjects we are planning to introduce.

"We suspect a problem in the roof, My Lady. Moisture is likely finding a way in and seeping into the fabric of the building."

"But, that is easily remedied?" I ask.

"Well, perhaps not easily but it can be done. A new roof should solve a multitude of problems."

As we move from room to room a scribe follows, taking down notes of the changes we suggest. The building is dank and gloomy inside, the chill penetrating my outer clothes, and I am glad when we return outside. I blink into the bright sunshine, crane my neck at the tall buildings in the quadrangle.

"A new gatehouse, as well, I think, Bishop Fisher. This one is underwhelming indeed. An entrance should have presence, something to provide immediate impact and represent the prestige of the establishment."

"Indeed, My Lady and might I suggest, you install your own apartments above to provide comfortable accommodation for when you visit."

"An excellent idea. I do intend to come often ...Oh, and we must think of furnishings and new plate too."

"And perhaps a change of name, My Lady. Something to reflect you as the benefactress. Something like Margaret College or My Lady's College?"

"No. I do not think so. If a new name is required at all, we should simply name it Christ's College. It is more fitting."

For the next few days the bishop and I talk of nothing but the foundation. We discuss the best books, the best supplier of tapestries, and even the purchase of a suitable property where the fellows might take refuge in time of plague. Nothing is overlooked and I find my mind is relieved to be spared the combined worries of court and family for a short time. Half way home John Morton clears his throat.

"I have had another thought, My Lady. I think, to honour you as benefactress, a statue should be made in your image. It could grace the walls of the gatehouse."

His suggestion warms me from within, and a slow smile spreads across my face.

"If you feel that would be appropriate, I am honoured that it be so."

The trip has provided a welcome break from routine and has taken my mind from the pain of losing Thomas and my dear Master Bray. This new project has shown me that the future can still hold promise. I can find interest and pleasure in the current day; all the good times are not necessarily in the past.

*

But my newfound buoyant mood does not last. On my arrival at Coldharbour House I am delivered of a letter from Margaret, now Queen of Scotland. I tear it open and, as I scan the first few lines, a frown deepens on my brow. I move unthinkingly to my favourite chair and sink into it with heavy heart. It is one thing after another. Troubles heaped upon trouble.

I am so lonely, Grandmother, so homesick, she writes. *Each day on waking I think of England and all I have left behind. I am soon to bear a child and I am so afraid, so sickly I can scarce keep any food down. Is this normal? As my belly begins to grow all I can do is think of mother and what befell her ...*

Poor, sweet Margaret. How well I understand her fears. I know how she feels. It seems like yesterday I was in similar vein yet I confided in nobody but kept my terror under a tight rein. I was younger than Margaret and less worldly wise yet my pride kept me strong. I was always determined to fool the world that all was well, even when everything was horribly wrong. With a heavy sigh, I put the letter down. I am so tired, yet I cannot shirk this duty. I will rest for just a short while and then, once I am rested, I will write to my granddaughter and try to instil some Tudor courage into her flagging heart.

Margaret is the least of our troubles. Since Isabella's death, the union between Caterina and Prince Henry has looked more uncertain than ever. Phillip of Burgundy is claiming the throne of Castile, by right of his wife, Joanna. Supported by the nobles of Castile he contests Ferdinand for the throne. Ferdinand, already on the verge of war with the Habsburgs, is now faced with the real threat of civil conflict. To boost his strength, he secures an alliance with France which is to be sealed with a marriage between Ferdinand and King Louis' niece, Germaine of Foix.

It is all such a headache and its effect on us increases when Ferdinand approaches Henry to stand as guardian of the peace between France and Aragon. Uncertain what to do for the best, Henry stalls, partly to preserve our alliance with Spain, partly to see how events unfold. In June, I discover that the king has instructed Henry to make an official protest against his betrothal to Caterina.

It is two days since he made the declaration in the presence of Bishop Richard Fox, the Spanish ambassador and Caterina herself. I am alarmed at this news and I order up my barge and make haste to the king's presence to discover his reason for it.

As usual, I find my son surrounded by advisors. When I enter they make way for me, greet me with bows and false compliments which I accept without comment. Dudley finds me a chair and I hand him my cloak and fan before sitting down. While he looks about for a place to dispose of my possessions, I quickly engage the king.

"I wonder about your decision to have Henry renounce the betrothal. I am surprised you did not consult me first."

With a glance at his gathered council, he quirks his brow.

"You hurried all this way to ask me that? You should not have worried yourself, it is all in hand."

"But the alliance with Spain is vital!"

"I know, Mother. Calm yourself. I have no intention of breaking negotiations. Ferdinand will be unsettled by it, which was our intention."

Bishop Fox steps forward, clears his throat before speaking.

"And Madam, should the king ever desire to break the Treaty of Richmond, the prince's renunciation may well prove useful."

"I see, I see but ...what of Caterina, what must she make of this?"

"That is not our concern. Our objective is to secure the more beneficial future for England. I am beset with problems, not least of all is that traitor Suffolk and his continuing mockery of us. If I ever lay hands on him, I swear he will not see the dawning of another day!"

The king rises so suddenly from his chair that it topples over behind him as he strides from the room. The door to his privy chamber slams and the room falls silent; feet are shuffled, throats cleared in nervous embarrassment. But it is not for me to be shamed by my son's sudden outburst. I rise to my feet, retrieve my cloak and fan from Dudley and follow in the king's wake.

Richmond Palace - January 1506

Outside a wicked storm is raging. It has been blowing hard for several days now, growing worse at night, uprooting trees and stealing the unstable roofs of the peasants. But we are safe behind the walls of Richmond Palace. Although a wicked draft gusts along the corridors setting the torch flames leaping and the tapestries swaying, in the hall while we dine, huge fires burn fiercely in the hearth, maintaining both our warmth and cheer. Replete with supper, we sit back in our chairs to enjoy the antics of the court fools. Watt strums vigorously on his lute, singing nonsense while his companions caper in blatant mockery of our courtly dances. Beside me, the king is mildly amused. He chuckles occasionally but at his side, Prince Henry rolls around in his seat, clutching his belly, tears pouring down his cheeks.

My gaze travels to Princess Mary who is smiling widely until her attention is taken by some disturbance at the back of the hall. I follow her gaze to a messenger pushing through the crowd toward the king's table. When

278

Henry spies him, he leans forward, beckons him closer and the mired man bends the knee before whispering in Henry's ear.

Slowly, my son's face blossoms into delight and I realise that for once the news is good. I exhale thankfully and lean toward him.

"What news, Henry?"

My son turns to me. His sallow cheeks are glowing, split by a wide smile as he lifts his voice above the clamour of the hall.

"It seems we should expect honoured guests, Mother ... Philip and Juana of Castile have made an unannounced visit to our shores."

"Philip and Juana? *Here*? Are you certain it is not some mistake?"

I stand up and he leads me to a quiet alcove away from the hubbub of the hall. He hands me a hastily written letter.

"It seems their ship has fallen foul of the weather and run aground off the Dorset coast. Sir Thomas Trenchard has taken them in. It is he who sends the message. They were en-route to Spain with an army to challenge Ferdinand for Castile when the storm hit, scattering their fleet up and down the coast. It is like a late New Year's gift!"

"Phillip will make a reluctant guest, I think. What of Juana, is she ... well?"

Gossip has it that Juana is rather ungoverned. Phillip calls her mad but, since he craves the rule of Castile, it is to his benefit to do so. I have heard there is little love between them and the gossips say he puts up with her obsessive behaviour for the sake of her claim to her late mother's throne. Henry claps his hands together, rubs his palms like a miser.

"Ahh Mother, I can put this accident to very good use, very good use indeed. Henry!" he calls to the Prince of Wales. "Come with me, we have work to do."

Young Henry casts a regretful look at the entertainments and does as he is bid. With a host of counsellors in his wake, he follows the king from the hall. I hesitate, uncertain whether to follow but in the end, I hasten to my own apartments and summon the castellain, and issue orders to make suitable preparations for the arrival of foreign royalty.

We have, of course, offered hospitality to royals before but this time Henry orders no expense be spared.

"We must not waste this opportunity," he says. "We shall assist with the repair of Philip's ships, help him reassemble his scattered fleet and as we do so, we shall treat him as our treasured guest. Phillip will be in our debt and I will not hesitate to press him to repay us by handing Suffolk into our keeping. Given the circumstances, it will be the least he can do."

Henry sends relay riders to be deployed at stages between here and the Dorset coast to enable news to reach us more swiftly.

The next day Philip's secretary arrives bringing his master's gratitude for our assistance. He begs that we do not put ourselves to any trouble for his master is eager that his reception at court be brief and simple. This could, of course, be taken as an indication of his modesty but henry and I understand that he wishes the indignity of his predicament to remain as quiet as possible. Philip is well aware that his time at court will be more as a prisoner than guest. He knows he has little hope of leaving our shores until Suffolk is in our hands.

The king sends the Earl of Surrey and Sir Thomas Brandon to greet Philip and escort him to Windsor.

"You are to lavish him with attention, lay on the finest food, provide the grandest of accommodation and attire," the king instructs. Philip is to be received into our court as an honoured addition to our palace, a family member. Which of course, he almost is since his wife Juana is sister to Caterina.

Praying that her court clothes are not too outmoded or shabby we send for Caterina to join us at Windsor to make them welcome and assist with the hospitality.

Windsor is the perfect venue for such an auspicious meeting. The old castle is steeped in tradition and Philip cannot fail to be overwhelmed. As the home of the Order of the Garter it will provide the perfect atmosphere to overwhelm the duke with our age old majesty.

It would be untrue to say that my son and I do not take some pleasure at the idea of the proudest knight in Europe coming before us, bedraggled and weather beaten, his valiant army dripping, his ships cast up, broken upon our shores. I send hearty prayers of thanks to God for placing such an opportunity in our hands.

At last things seem to be going our way. Suffolk is among the remaining few of the house of York to plague us; once he is in our hands we will be secure.

The king orders that Philip and his escort pause their journey at Winchester. Once more the king is showing off our connections to the past. Winchester was once King Arthur's Camelot, and with that in mind he lays on feasting and hawking in such style that the duke cannot fail to be impressed. Hopefully he will believe that this is how things in England are always done.

When Henry himself sets out to meet the duke, I send a man in my employ with him, ordering him to send back dispatches, detailing everything that takes place almost as events unfold. So much hangs on this meeting, there are so many things that could go wrong.

My man reports that the king spends an afternoon with Philip watching Princess Mary and Caterina dance. I lower the letter and wonder what the duke makes of his sister in law. No doubt he wishes his wife were as biddable. Apparently Juana has been left behind in Winchester, too unwell, too ailing to be brought to our court. I scribble a note to the king.

I doubt very much that Juana is unwell, it is clear he cannot abide her company and wishes to keep her from our sight for fear we will realise she is as sane as you and I.

I imagine Henry reading it. He will raise his eyes to Heaven and ignore my urging but to me it is imperative that we meet and treat Juana with the respect she deserves.

Henry writes back, a short terse note that speaks of his irritation at my insistent tone but then another, gentler missive arrives.

Our duke ill at ease, he writes, *uncomfortable in the focus of my attention but he can look as unhappy as he pleases, it will not prevent me from pressing for a betrothal between our Mary and his son Charles; it would suit me well for my future grandson to inherit Habsburg.*

My son is astute. Such a match may prove more beneficial than the alliance with Spain, perhaps it was providence after all, that delayed the sealing of the match between Henry and Caterina. If we were to join forces with Duke Philip and aid him in his quest for Castile, Ferdinand would be furious. Henry and I both take pleasure in that thought.

By all accounts, Princess Mary puts every effort into winning Philip's admiration. She excels herself, dancing, singing, and demonstrating her considerable skill at the lute and clavichord. But, knowing men as I do, it will be her golden hair, her charismatic eyes and high pitched merriment that ultimately lures the duke into our trap.

Like her brother Henry, Mary is blessed with a natural ease, a warmth of nature that welcomes everyone as friend ... until you displease her. If Philip's son, Charles is lucky enough to win her as his wife, he will have his hands full indeed. I do not envy him that.

It is hard on me to be left behind, kicking my heels in London while Philip is entertained by king and court. The walls of Coldharbour House seem confining and I itch to join the royal party at Windsor. After a few days of self-inflicted denial, I ignore the leaden skies, the threat of further rain that hangs heavy in the clouds, and order my litter be made ready.

I have travelled just a short distance before I begin to regret it, every bump of the road jolts through my body and chases my ebullient mood away. By the time I arrive they have abandoned the hunting and rain is lashing against the windows, the sky so dark and bleak as to hail the end of the world. I clamber from the litter, damp, uncomfortable and irritable and ascend the steps to the hall. Hurrying to my apartment, my knees and hips aching, I castigate my woman who has been so stupid as to forget to pack my jewel case.

"I will have to face the duke with no jewels," I scold her. "Do you know how important it is that we dazzle this man with wealth and stability? How am I to do that with only a single string of pearls?" I rattle my necklace in her face and she pulls away, shrinks into her shoulders. As I turn away she mutters something that I do not quite hear.

"What was that? Do not mutter. Why does nobody speak properly these days? You all skulk about the palace, mumbling like fools."

She straightens her back, lifts her chin.

"I am sorry, Madam, I merely noted that he will be so impressed by your wisdom he will not notice any lack of finery."

I am taken aback by her words. I had expected insolence but I should not have, she is usually a good girl. I was wrong to be so tetchy with her. It is the pain. It turns the best of us into grumblers. Once my bags are unpacked I will have her rub some salve into my knees, it will ease both my joints and my mood. I force myself to smile.

"You should speak more clearly," I sniff. "Come help me prepare. I shall have to do my best without resorting to baubles and beads. Perhaps I can impress him with piety."

Early next morning, I come from the chapel to discover the king has already taken the duke to the tennis court. I am not in the least interested in the sport but Henry is keen and spends a lot of time there. He no longer plays, of course, but still enjoys a wager. Unfortunately, he is seldom lucky but his hopes of boosting his coffers remains undiminished. I am continually reminding him his purse would be much fatter where it not for his love of tennis but I cannot persuade him from it. I finally discover he and Philip in the gallery. They are lounging on cushions, the king raising the stakes to Duke Philip's increasing bewilderment at the rules.

"Ah, Mother; good morning." Henry ceases his enthusiastic explanation of the game and signals to a servant to fetch me a seat. I ease myself stiffly into it.

"How are you, my dear? Good morrow, Philip. I hope you are enjoying the sport."

"Indeed, My Lady, I am finding it quite ... edifying."

Dorset and Tom Howard are on the court, the ball banging back and forth in monotonous rhythm. We watch for a while in silence while I try to fathom what anyone can find entertaining in such puerile activity. Henry's head swivels avidly back and forth, while Philip looks on with puzzlement. Quickly bored, I stifle a yawn behind my hand that does not escape the notice of our guest.

"You find the game dull, My Lady?"

"I am not a sporting woman. When I was younger I enjoyed the hunt but sadly my bones will no longer tolerate the saddle." I am surprised at myself, I rarely confess to any form of infirmity.

"Ah," he says. "Age takes its toll on all of us in the end."

"Indeed." I sniff and turn my head away, resisting the urge to say what I really feel.

"I confess," the duke continues. "I find the game dreary to watch. Do you play, Your Majesty? I would like to try my hand with a bat."

Henry does not take his eye from the ball.

"Racket."

"I beg pardon?"

"It is a racket, not a bat and no, I can no longer play. I have an ailment of the chest."

The king thumps his own upper body to demonstrate, making himself cough. He waves his arm in the direction of the court. "If you have a mind to play, I doubt Dorset will turn you down. He enjoys a challenge."

Philip rises to his feet, throws off his cloak, strips off his jacket and tosses his hat after it, making me wish I had not missed so many years of Henry's prime.

"I shall do so, Your Majesty," he smiles, his dark face brightening into something more handsome. "You should place your bets on me, Your Grace. I am a man who likes to win."

Henry and I watch him descend to the court and the mummery that ensues. Dorset and Howard stop play, turn to greet the duke with deference. We cannot hear the words of the conversation that passes but shortly afterwards Philip is testing the weight of the racket against his hand.

"Was that a taunt, do you think, my son?"

"Was what a taunt?"

"His remark that he is a man who likes to win."

Henry snorts. "Oh, undoubtedly but he can taunt all he likes."

Side by side, our heads turn back and forth as we follow the ball. Philip is an energetic player, his enthusiasm somewhat outweighing his skill. However, it soon becomes clear that he is no quitter and it is past noon before they begin to show signs of ending the match. I rise to my feet.

"I can watch no more. I must retire, Henry or I shall lack the energy to attend supper in the hall this evening. We must hope Philip's talents at politics match his lack in the tennis court."

Henry kisses the back of my hand.

"We have him, Mother, do not worry about that. We have the duke firmly where we want him."

Windsor - February 1506

Philip has been with us for almost a month and this morning Henry excels himself, ordering no expense be spared. The presence chamber is decked out in cloth of gold, a thousand candles illuminating the dais where the king, Prince Henry and the assembled Garter knights are assembled, all garbed in their best. Everywhere you look are noble courtiers in silk and velvet, some edged with ermine, hung with gold and jewels. Today we do Philip great honour and, amid this carefully constructed timeless opulence, the duke is to be invested with the Garter. Before God he will kneel to kiss our religious relics and swear oaths both sacred and solemn. Oaths that will bind him to our will.

I watch with satisfaction as Prince Henry buckles the garter about the duke's leg and the king fastens a collar of gold about his neck. Philip stands awkwardly tall, his face stiff and red and grave. And then it is Prince Henry's turn to be honoured by the investment of the Order of the Golden Fleece. Adorned in cloth of gold that billows in a rich cloud behind him, he bows before the king and, in fluent French, he makes his oath. Afterwards I notice Philip approach my grandson and offer him his hand.

While the king and I hold only contempt for the duke, young Henry is showing him such friendship that I fear he mistakes our overtures as genuine. Perhaps I am needlessly concerned, I hope I am.

Prince Henry has made such good progress. I no longer fear that he will say the wrong thing or make an outlandish gesture during these public appearances. He draws goodwill from all who meet him; his easy relaxed manner connecting with people, securing their friendship, their allegiance. When the time arrives for him to take his father's place, he will surely be ready, and competent. I watch the two together, Henry hanging on to Philips every word and hope that this camaraderie is an act of diplomacy ... surely it is. It would not do for him to become overly attached to a man we distrust.

I draw my mind back to the present where Duke Philip and the king are about to fulfil the real purpose of the day's event. The signing of the treaty between England and Burgundy.

The gathering falls silent as Richard Fox escorts the duke to a seat at a table and shows him where to sign his name. It is so quiet I can hear the scratch of his pen on the parchment. A sound that is satisfying indeed.

This pact is equally beneficial to both countries. Perpetual friendship will pave the way for further alliance. Henry's betrothal to Margaret of Savoy, and a trade agreement allowing English merchants to import cloth duty free into the Low Countries. It recognises Philip as the king of Castile, spelling an end to our friendship with Ferdinand and aligns us with the Habsburgs. But the real triumph comes when Philip agrees, in demonstration of our newfound friendship, to hand over the person of the Earl of Suffolk at his earliest convenience.

It is almost as if he had a choice in the matter.

It is a few days before Juana arrives at Windsor with her entourage and her reception is very different to that of her husband. Since he arrived, the duke has been reticent when questioned about his wife. When I ask why she did not accompany him from Winchester he offers vague explanations of 'an incident' and even claims to misremember where she is lodged.

"He is hiding her," I tell Henry, watching as he peels the skin from an orange with long sticky fingers.

288

"Either she is raving mad and he dare not let her be seen in public, or he is jealous of her superior status and wishes to keep her away from the adoration of her people."

Henry rubs juice from his chin.

"She is important only until he has made firm his claim on her kingdom."

"But that is unjust! As Queen of Castile she should be received as befits her position, not herded into some backwater as if she were a goat."

"They say she rants and raves at the slightest provocation and hates to let him out of her sight. I heard it said that as their ship went down, she clung to him like a limpet, desperate that they should die together."

"Pwah! That is likely some story. You can believe nothing you hear in a tavern."

"I heard it from a reliable source. I am not in the habit of frequenting taverns."

"But your spies are! Where do you think they heard it?"

Henry peels off a segment of fruit and places it on his tongue. After chewing for a while, he spits a pip into his palm.

"She is expected to arrive in a day or two and I intend to be there to greet her. Would you care to accompany me?"

"I am not sure," Henry wipes his fingers on a cloth.

"They say she is very handsome."

His smile stretches.

"Then there is no need to persuade me further, Mother. I shall look forward to greeting this raving beauty, nothing shall keep me away."

I raise my cup of malmsey in acknowledgement of his subtle pun. The wine flows, sweet and strong, down my throat.

"I shall inform Caterina of her sister's impending visit. A familiar face will be a comfort to Juana after the trials of the last few weeks."

To appease the duke, the Queen of Castile is welcomed to Windsor Castle via the side gate, hustled in through the back door but once inside she is accorded all the respect due to her.

We gather in the great hall where five hundred years of history and tradition bears down upon us. Philip makes no move to greet or introduce his wife but stands languidly back while we go forward to formally welcome her to our realm.

I had feared she would behave immoderately, berate her husband the moment she laid eyes upon him but she is calm and gracious. But the gossips were correct in one respect; Juana is indeed very beautiful. Henry at first seems taken aback by it; he hesitates as if mesmerised and I notice his careful attention to her thick black hair and spirited eyes. Then, with uncharacteristic enthusiasm, he moves forward and embraces her, taking her fully into his arms. A rustle of surprise emanates from our courtiers. Juana's blushes enhance her appearance further and, feeling old and pale, I too move forward to kiss her cheek.

While Prince Henry and Princess Mary make their greeting, I resume my place at the king's side and watch as Caterina takes her turn. The sisters regard each other for a long moment before finally grasping hands and embarking on a rapid conversation in Spanish that none of us can follow. When they show no sign of stopping, I clear my throat and reluctantly they break apart, keeping their hands joined.

"I am sorry, My Lady," Caterina says in halting English. "It is so long since we were together."

Juana, not fully understanding her sister's words, regards me with a smile in her eyes that I cannot fail to return. There is no need of the pretence I exercised in greeting her husband. Juana is quite different. She is indeed exquisite but not at all mad. As she accompanies Caterina and I to the dais, the impression she gives is not one of madness. I realise she is sad, and desperately so.

April 1506

I have not seen Henry this content for many years. His former gloom falls away to be replaced with newfound confidence both in himself and God. He believes Philip and Juana's visit to be a gift from Heaven, a sign of the Lord's approval of our reign. After years of misfortune and uncertainty we are now both convinced of His favour.

As their time with us stretches into several weeks, the king continues to shower the visitors with extravagant hospitality.

"We will dazzle them with splendour," the king says. "Let no expense be spared. Let them think our coffers are so overflowing with coin that we live like this every day."

Although I do not partake in all the activities, I find it exhausting. Each hour is taken up with hunting, tennis, jousting, dancing ... a regime so extreme that even Prince Henry begins to flag. As I feared, our prince has taken a great liking to Philip. The duke's physical strength and prowess at sport throws the king into the shade and, having never showed the least admiration for

291

his father, the prince now strives to spend as much time in Philip's company as he can.

"It means nothing," I tell the king. "The prince merely looks up to Philip. They are not so far removed in age, and share a love of sport and hunting. It is only natural Henry should be impressed."

The king growls something in reply and I steer the conversation to safer ground.

"Henry will forget about him when he has gone and they will be leaving soon, now that the pact is signed and Suffolk safely in our hands."

"Not a moment too soon, Mother. Philip is an overbearing braggart, not at all a suitable companion for a boy of Henry's nature."

My desire to quash the discussion of young Henry has failed. The king's displeasure at the relationship must be greater than I thought. I decide not to inform him that they shared a late supper last evening, or tell him Philip has promised to correspond with our prince after his departure. Once more, I try to turn the conversation to a more positive note.

"It has been an expensive visit but providential, I think. We are now spared the threat of Suffolk – his imprisonment is a great coup. You must be greatly relieved."

"A small weight off my mind, Mother," he says, as if the matter is of small account.

We wave farewell to Philip and Juana as they continue their journey to Castile. I wonder about them as they ride away. Hopefully, they will solve their differences. I have no liking for Philip but Juana has the makings of a good queen, if she can only moderate her infatuation for her husband and concentrate on her social obligations, life would seem kinder. I take Henry's elbow and he assists me back to the royal apartments.

"It is rest I need more than anything," I say, sinking gratefully into a chair. "That visit was Heaven sent but I confess I am glad beyond measure that it is over."

Indeed, the day of the storm was a red letter day for the House of Tudor and as such, before I retire for bed, I make note of it in my book of hours.

The king, pleased with himself and eager to give thanks for the upturn in our fortune, plans to make a pilgrimage of thanksgiving.

"Would you like to accompany me?" he asks. "I intend to travel through East Anglia to the shrine of Our Lady in Walsingham. It is some time since you have been, I think."

"I am weary, Henry, weary to the bone. Perhaps I shall go in the autumn when the sun is not so hot. I would prefer to retire to my estates for a while, if that pleases you. There I will have leisure to reflect and give thanks to God. He will understand."

Cambridge - June 1506

By mid-June I am much recovered and decide to visit Cambridge to discover how the building works are progressing. The road is dusty and potholed, the litter full of flies. I keep the curtains drawn but still they manage to find a way in to buzz irritatingly around my face. My woman is nodding off in the corner and I resent her ability to find oblivion from the trials of the road.

"For Heaven's sake, use your fan with more vigour!" I snap and she jumps to attention and applies herself more proficiently to her task. The flies retreat to the curtain but I know the moment the fan ceases, they will be back to plague me.

I watch a little black beast meander to the ceiling where he halts and rubs his legs together. I am loath to trust any creature that can walk upon the ceiling. *What purpose do they serve?* I wonder idly. *Why did the Lord create the likes of flies and wasps? Was it just to plague us?*

The litter lurches suddenly, and I cling to the seat, narrowly avoiding being thrown to the floor. My woman drops the fan, gropes for it beneath her skirts.

"Are you harmed, My Lady?" she asks as she resumes her seat. "Cambridge cannot be far afield now."

"I can never get used to this hateful mode of transport. In my youth I swore never to use one again but age has a way of rewriting our intentions. I should suffer more upon a horse, I think."

"Yes, My Lady," she says, applying the fan again. "We shall both be glad of this journey's end."

I lean forward, draw back the curtain and peer from the window across the dreary flat landscape. On the horizon, obscured by a haze of heat, the spires of Cambridge are just visible. Groping for my rosary beads I send up a prayer of thanks for a safe delivery.

Taking advantage of the king's recent good humour, Bishop Fisher and I have persuaded him to donate funds to the rebuilding of the chapel at King's College. He promises to join us there, if his schedule allows.

In recent years I have taken a greater interest in Cambridge, the Christ's College in particular but Kings is just as worthy a cause. I am eager to see how the building work is progressing at Christ's, and to discuss the likelihood of my stepson James Stanley being appointed Bishop of Ely, whose diocese includes Cambridge.

Behind us, on one of the household wagons, carefully wrapped in straw and sacking is a portrait of myself as founder. It is a very fine thing, a good likeness I am told, and I am filled with satisfaction at the prospect of my image looking down for perpetuity on the scholars at King's.

We are almost there, the arduous journey almost over. As we reach the outlying streets of the town, I lift the curtain and look out at the shambling houses, the mired road, and a clutch of children playing in the dirt. A small girl removes her thumb from her mouth and points at my entourage and they all turn to stare but they do not wave. Their life is so far removed from mine they might exist on another world. How must it feel to live in such poverty? Is there anything to be done? I let the curtain fall.

"Remind me to speak to John Fisher, about the poverty here. Perhaps we can open an alms house, or something. Those poor wretches have nothing."

My apartments above the gatehouse are welcoming. Mercifully the fire has not yet been lit and the interior is mellow and cool, as my travel-weary body craves. I throw off my veil and pass it to my woman. "I need to lie down, just for a short while."

I sink into the mattress, stare up at the high canopy and close my eyes. I was foolish. A lighter kirtle would have been more comfortable but June is a difficult month to predict. One day is warm and the next is wet but rarely is it as hot as this. When I am rested perhaps I will order a bath be drawn so I can wash away the megrims of the road. I close my eyes ... and dream of nursery days. Edith, Mary and Elizabeth ... we are eating cake before a blazing hearth...

Cake. I can smell cake, fresh from the oven. I sit up and call, the door opens and my woman comes in.

"You slept for so long, My Lady. I know you said a few moments but ... I did not like to wake you."

I swing my legs over the edge of the bed, place my feet on the floor and stand upright, my knees groaning in protest.

"I am sure I could smell cake, or was I dreaming?"

"No, you are right, My Lady. A woman of the town brought cake to the gatehouse and asked that it be given to you. She said you had enjoyed it last time."

"Last time?" I cock my head, remembering. "Yes, I do recall something. I had forgotten. We stopped at an inn, Reginald Bray and I, and while we were there I sampled the landlord's wife's cake. I thanked her for it as we left."

"She must have remembered you liked it and now sends you more."

"How kind of her. Please, send a note to thank her and a small purse to demonstrate our gratitude."

She turns to do my bidding but as she reaches the door, I call her back again. "Ask them to send me a slice now. I find I am quite hungry."

With a laugh, she quits the chamber, her skirts swirling behind her as she hurries beneath the lintel.

When Henry surprises me with a visit a short while later he finds me replete after two slices. "Henry! I am so glad you have come," I say, as he enters. "Try some of this. It is truly delicious."

He takes the proffered plate and pokes it delicately with a forefinger.

"It is not like you to extol the virtues of cake, Mother. Have you found an appetite at last?"

"If one could live on this cake alone, I swear I might grow stout."

296

He takes a tentative bite, chews with appreciation as the flavours burst upon his tongue.

"Mmm, it is good. Where did you get it?"

"From an innkeeper's wife whose acquaintance I made on a previous visit. You should engage her as the royal cook. There is nothing like good solid country cooking ... in my opinion."

He swallows the last crumb. "I must concur. It is very good. Now, are you ready for a tour of the works?"

We stroll companionably about the site, every so often I remark on a detail, or ask for clarification on the purpose of the empty rooms. Bishop Fisher is at my right hand, the king on the other. Henry is silent, pensive.

"What are you thinking, Henry?"

"Oh ... I was just wondering what the life of a scholar must be like. Less ... hectic than that of a king, I would imagine."

"Or that of a king's mother, I am sure." The company laughs gratifyingly but I keep my eye on Henry who seems a little deflated.

The afternoon progresses with discussion as to further improvements and the likelihood of a completion date and then the king and I retire to my chambers.

After watching him stare into the flames, I shift my position, take a deep breath and ask the question I have been trying to avoid.

"Are you going to tell me what is wrong?"

He looks up, startled, and gives a short, forced smile.

"Oh, nothing really. Nothing I can pinpoint."

"You are ailing? Is it your eyes? Are your bowels moving regularly?"

"Mother! I am well. I sometimes just feel ... tired and ... lonely. It seems everyone around me is dying,

297

everyone I trust ... Sometimes I wonder if it has all been worthwhile ..."

"All been worthwhile? What do you mean? Your life? Your reign? Surely you cannot mean your reign?"

"I am just maudlin today. Sometimes I feel so tired and when I look back it is as if my life, at least since I came to the throne, has passed in a flash. I seem to have lacked the time required to do all I had intended. Perhaps I miss ..."

"Elizabeth? Well, that is perfectly normal. I miss her too and so do the children. I had a letter from Margaret the other day and she is missing us all most dreadfully and is not ..."

"Mother, I do wish you would let me finish. I was going to say I miss the freedom I enjoyed as a youth, which is extraordinary when you consider I was an exile, a prisoner for much of it. I had plans and dreams of the things I would do when I came into my own ... Yet, sometimes it is as if I merely escaped one prison for another. I have achieved little I set out to do."

"Nonsense! You have brought peace to our realm. You have rid us of our foes, you have united England with Scotland; you have given England an heir. You are the best of kings, the best of sons..."

I stop, choked by my own sentiment, and dab at my eye with the corner of a kerchief.

"But personal happiness remains elusive. I think perhaps I should take another wife."

"Yes, maybe you should and there is ample time to get more sons. A king can never have enough sons."

"So you never tire of reminding me."

"I suppose Margaret of Savoy continues to refuse you: foolish woman."

"Well, I had never set my heart on her. If she is as sour faced as her portrait suggests she would likely prove an acerbic bed mate. The trouble is none of the suitable women come close to matching Elizabeth in any way. I have a fancy for a pretty, pleasant wife who is as easy to be with as my last."

He means 'easy to manage.'

"You must forget about Elizabeth. Your next marriage will be both diplomatic and beneficial to us; she must be fertile, in her prime."

"And agreeable to the match."

"Only a fool would refuse you but the right woman is out there, you need only to keep looking."

And then, a few weeks later, as if sent by providence, Henry's hopes are raised.

<u>September 1506</u>

Autumn comes early, turning the garden to shades of yellow and gold. I lean on my stick and move stiffly between the flowerbeds. A thin bramble straggles across the path, sprung up from nowhere as is their habit. I itch to bend down, search out the root and pry it loose but, even if my back were strong enough, my rheumatic fingers would forbid it. I prod it in the attempt to loosen the soil but succeed only in muddying the end of my stick. With a huff of frustration I resume my journey, note the flush of late marigolds amid the remains of a clump of chamomile daisy. As I reach the end of the path, I hear my name called and turn to find my woman hailing me from the door.

"What is it? Is something wrong?"

"I do not know, My Lady, but the king has summoned you."

If I were called to anyone but Henry's bidding I would be annoyed but I go as fast as I can and make preparation for a journey to Richmond.

The king is flushed, his cheeks hectic, his eye worryingly bright.

"What is the matter? Are you ill?" I demand without greeting him. He moves swiftly across the floor, takes both my hands and kisses them with delight.

"I am in perfect health, Mother and I have news – news that is both surprising and possibly beneficial."

"What news? What can have happened to put such a spring in your step?"

"Philip of Burgundy – he is dead."

This was the last news I expected, it takes a while for the words to penetrate my confused brain.

"Dead? How? Was he killed? Poisoned?" I ask, immediately suspecting Ferdinand.

Henry passes me the letter and I scan the hastily scrawled message.

"Not intentionally, I think. It seems he ate something that did not agree with him."

"How unfortunate. The marriage between Mary and Charles will still take place?"

"I see no reason why not. It is to the benefit of both parties." Henry's smile widens, a look of uncharacteristic mischief kindles in his eye. "And now, after a reasonable period of mourning, of course, Juana will be free to take another husband."

Realisation dawns. My smile stretches as wide as his. "And we shall have Castile!"

"If I can persuade her to accept me."

"She is not a fool. She will recognise the benefits."

"Unless she is truly as mad as they say."

We laugh, Henry's mirth turning midway to a fit of coughing. The veins on his neck and forehead stand out like ropes and his face turns puce while futilely I pat his back. Belatedly noting the king's plight, a squire

300

hurries forward with a cup of water. When he has the breath to do so, Henry sips it, wipes his watering eyes and, suddenly tired, he slumps into a chair.

Since Henry fell seriously ill a few years ago he has never regained his full health. I am constantly dosing him with pills and potions. In my pocket I have an infusion of fennel, celandine and rose water that I prepared this very morning to soothe his eyes which continue to cause him such bother. But nothing seems to restore his former vitality.

The royal physicians, in their wisdom, have even less success than I. He lies back in his chair, pale from the exertion when a few moments ago he had been scarlet. He looks like a corpse. I turn my head away. His demise is something I dread to contemplate but nonetheless my fearful mind turns to the Prince of Wales.

Unfortunately, young Henry continues to apply more effort to sport and dancing than he does to state policy. If he can find a way of wiggling out of the duties imposed on him by his father's ill health, then he leaps at it. The king and I have both tried to curb his high spirits but although he appears obedient to our will, I do not miss the spark of resentment in his eye. Were we to lift our guard, I fear he would overflow, like a burst faucet or a breach in a dam.

"We should summon the Prince of Wales," I remark, "this news will be hard for him to hear."

Henry arrives some two hours after our summons is sent. He bows low, his hair damp as if it has just been washed.

"My apologies, Father, Grandmother. I was ... in the tiltyard."

At least he makes no attempt to lie.

"Not competing, I hope."

301

"No, Father, just practicing riding the ring."

"You would have been better off at your studies."

"Perhaps but I was with my tutors all morning. I was in need of exercise. I do need some form of release."

Henry is large and powerfully built. I suppose he does need to expend energy. Besides, I have no wish to argue with him, not today. He looks well and hearty and it is hard for me to ruin his buoyant mood, although it seems not to worry the king.

"We have received news from overseas ..."

"And it concerns me?" Henry raises his eyebrows, looks from me to his father, and back again. "Please, tell me what I need to hear."

"The Duke of Burgundy, Philip ... he is dead."

A stunned silence as I watch my grandson's face crumple, his dignity and sense of invincibility decay before my eyes.

"No! That cannot be! He is young – in his prime!"

He steps forward, takes the letter from his father's hand. The edge of the parchment trembles with the depth of his emotion. He looks up at me, his mouth open, his face pallid.

"He *ate* something? Philip – Philip is strong! Athletic – how can a piece of tainted food destroy such a man? Was he poisoned father? Is that the truth of it?"

The king lifts both hands, fingers splayed.

"I know only what is written there. It seems he fell into a fever after partaking of a meal and ... failed to recover."

"I suspect Ferdinand."

The king shakes his head, dabs his lips with a kerchief.

"He had no cause; the treaty was signed giving Ferdinand the throne."

"Juana, then. They say she is mad and thinks herself ill-treated."

"Henry," I step forward to place a placatory hand on his sleeve. "This speculation will not help. Philip is dead. We must pray for his soul and for his easy passing into Heaven."

"I cannot believe this! He was so strong ... he seemed indestructible."

"I know. It is often God's way, to take the strong and spare the weak."

The death of Philip casts Prince Henry down, but the young are resilient and his sadness is soon surpassed by the need for action. I advise the king to allow him a little more rein, to permit him the company of his peers but the king prefers to keep him close.

My informants tell me that despite the king's orders, the prince is often found with the likes of Brandon, Compton and Richard Grey. If they are not practising at the lute and lance, they are writing poetry, exchanging notes of wit and learning. Young Henry likes to laugh; he craves the company of the youthful members of his father's court and shuns the older, staider side. If he worked as hard at his lessons our worries would be considerably less.

He is already skilled at wrestling and fighting on foot with the quarterstaff and, although he is still forbidden to compete, his enthusiasm for the joust is all consuming. Perhaps it is the effect of old age but these days I am more lenient than the king and like to see him happy. Recently, much to my son's annoyance, I gifted the Prince of Wales with a horse and harness that cost me a pretty penny. Now, as I should have seen, he chaffs all the more to partake in the games.

Perhaps we should not worry so much. The prince is popular with commoner and courtier alike; his manner is refreshing in our ageing court, and he certainly adds vigour to any occasion.

Whereas the king is concerned with policy and diplomatic matters, the prince behaves like a king of old, smitten with chivalry and show. I can see that when his time comes to rule, my son's care of the coffers may be undone. Yet, try as we might, our attempts to instil in him a little restraint make little impression. As far as Prince Henry is concerned, the thrill of extravagance outshines the benefits of thrift. I fear moderation will be a hard lesson for him to learn.

While the prince continues at every turn to evade his tutors, the king has not given up hope of securing a second marriage and another son. Ferdinand, still smarting from our treaty with Burgundy, writes that the king's proposal to Juana is not displeasing to her but she is deep in grief and not ready to remarry. Henry fears he has not the time to lose. He begins to negotiate heavily, sending his ambassador so often across the sea that he grows quite green from the ship's motion.

Rumours find their way to our court from Castile. Juana is mad with grief. They say she refuses to bury her late husband but travels about with his coffined corpse among her household baggage. I doubt it is true but if it is, one wonders if she will ever relinquish him. Perhaps she intends to bring his remains with her, prop him up at table, or take him with her to the marriage bed.

Ferdinand insists she is incapable of ruling and promises Henry will be Juana's first choice when her health improves enough for her to remarry. Of course, with Philip out of the way, it suits Ferdinand well to control his daughter's kingdom. Nothing would irk him more than a brood of heirs of English blood. But I think Henry should consider carefully. Perhaps it would be as well to avoid tainting our Tudor blood with the threat of insanity but the king seems unperturbed by the rumours. He laughs off my attempts to discuss it.

"Ferdinand has no wish for her to marry. When I met Juana last summer she was not in any way mad. She was in fact, given the circumstances, quite delightful."

I suspected at the time that the king was impressed by her beauty. It is strange that my son, who has never displayed any unwarranted lust, is on occasion touched so deeply by a woman. I have no knowledge of his experience with the fairer sex in his youth but during his years as king, I have known him show admiration for only two: his wife, Elizabeth, and Catherine Gordon.

Catherine remains his close friend to this day and I have come to value her. Nobody makes him laugh like she does. Very often they are to be found gaming or taking the air in the privy garden. I am certain she has no suspicion of Henry's desire to remarry but her nose will be put quite out of joint if the union with Juana does come to pass. I know for certain the two women will not be friends; Juana of Castile will never tolerate a rival at court.

December 1507

As time goes on and no betrothal is secured, I notice a certain withdrawal in the king. He attends his duties and the court rituals with a lack lustre expression and, whenever he can, he orders his son to take his place. The prince and his household shadow the movement of the king's court, often taking lodgings a short ride from his father's in case his presence should be required at brief notice.

305

The king's chest complaint is exacerbated by continuing gout which, in turn, provokes his increasingly short temper. As the negotiations for his marriage with Juana make little progress, his mood becomes ever grimmer, and even I cannot offer him advice without receiving short shrift.

As ever, falling foul of his favour pains me greatly and I decide to step back a little, and give the king the solitude he seems to require. While allowing Henry to deal with his own affairs, I turn my attention to my grandson whom my spies inform me is himself beginning to yearn for marriage.

I have seen little of Caterina since her sister's unscheduled visit several years ago. She continues to complain of lack of funds, lack of status, lack of adequate clothing. But Ferdinand's failure to send the remaining portion of her dowry is scarcely our fault. The king, having abandoned the idea of a union with Burgundy, continues with little progress to negotiate with Spain. Perhaps he is playing for time, I cannot know for his increasing craving for solitude excludes me from his inner thoughts.

But Christmas brings a short reprieve. Finally, after two long years, the treaty of Perpetual Peace with Maximilian is signed and the king emerges from seclusion and orders Christmas festivities on a scale that have not been enjoyed in England for many a year.

Richmond Palace is festooned with greenery, the fires are heaped with fuel and so many torches burn that night becomes day. The major towns of our realm are lit with bonfires and hogsheads of wine are distributed free to the populace. But wine only sates the public mood so far.

Murmurings of unrest continue to reach us as, on Henry's orders, Empson and Dudley demand ever higher taxes and penalties from those who can afford it ... and it seems those who cannot.

The people grumble against us. I fail to understand why they cannot see it is for the good of England, the security of England. A king cannot rule and keep his country secure if he is not provided with the coin to do so.

I am grieved to see the return of trouble, for the last few years have taken their toll on my son. I pray for him more fervently than I have done since he was in exile. I know he is ailing but it is a long time before he admits it to me.

The moment I hear he has summoned the physicians, I request an audience as if I am a stranger but it is several days until he agrees to see me.

Unsure of my welcome, I enter his chamber, expecting to find him at his desk, as is his usual habit. The instant I see him tucked up in his bed, the counterpane scattered with parchments, some signed, some unsigned, and ink spilled upon the silken sheet, I know the worst. I am looking at a king who is frantically trying to get his affairs in order before it is too late.

"Henry!" I cannot disguise my anguish. Forgetting the pain of my knees I rush across the floor. He lifts his rheumy, red rimmed eyes and I look upon a countenance that is gaunt, hollow cheeked and deathly pale. I cup my face in both hands, my shock all consuming. I had known he was unwell but this ... this is something much worse. Death sits at his shoulder, tainting his breath, fouling his lungs, sinking great talons of agony into his bones. His pain is my own. I am not sure I will withstand this.

"Mother. How are you? I a ...apologise for not seeing you sooner." Even his voice has changed. I swallow my desire to pull him into my arms and adopt my usual acerbic manner.

"So you should be. I have endeavoured to see you several times of late. I had thought I had committed some sin against you."

He attempts a smile but it turns into a wince as he shifts his position.

"You are the last person to commit any sin, Mother. I suppose you realise I am dying?"

"NO!"

The word is out before I can stop it. I close my eyes, brace myself. "I do not believe the physicians have tried everything yet. There will be some underlying cause for your discomfort."

"Mother, mother…" He fights for my hands as I try to slap him away, mortified that he should witness my grief. "They have done all they can. I have some constriction in my lungs …" He breaks off in a fit of coughing, as if to demonstrate his malady. When his kerchief comes away spotted scarlet I clench my tongue between my teeth to prevent myself from crying out aloud.

The pain in my throat is immense. I am robbed of speech, consumed with hopelessness.

"You must be brave, Mother," he says, recovering himself. "Henry will need you. Until he reaches his majority you must act as regent, ensure he understands the … the delicacies of rule."

"I will."

My voice is hoarse. I feel every one of my sixty four bitter years but somehow I will find it within myself to do my duty and fulfil my son's last request.

*

After hearing my confession, John Fisher sees my tears and try as I might, I cannot staunch them. The

308

unspoken pity in his face breaks down my defences. Slowly, I lean forward, slide my arms about my torso and give into all-consuming sorrow. He places a tenuous hand on my back and lets me weep with a grief that shakes my very soul. It is the last time I allow myself the comfort of tears.

Once unburdened, I dry my eyes and order my retinue and chief advisors to be removed to Richmond where I am to take up my role, overseeing the government of the realm.

It is a task I would much rather not be obliged to undertake but I do not fail to acknowledge the irony of Margaret Beaufort, one time insignificant member of the House of Lancaster, ruling over all England.

Greenwich - March 1508

I expect Henry's demise to be rapid but he surprises us all, somehow clinging to life, his mind alert while his body decays. A few days before the March Joust he surprises us all by leaving his bed and appearing again before the court. Well wrapped in furs, he takes the royal barge to Greenwich palace where he meets with the new Spanish ambassador. Ferdinand has finally relented and sent banker's drafts for Caterina's marriage portion. The plans for the wedding between her and Henry can finally begin to move ahead.

"The Prince of Wales thinks highly of the princess," Henry informs the ambassador breathlessly. "He thinks her beautiful and gifted ... as do we all."

I wonder if those present recall the king's proposal that he should marry her himself. I imagine Caterina is relieved to be taking on a fine figure like the prince when she could have found herself sharing the bed of the ageing king. It is clear for anyone to see that his days are few; Caterina will be well aware that she has a very short while to wait until she is made queen.

Miserable to the bone, I sit back in my chair and observe my ailing son as he tries to disguise the severity of his condition. It is a bitter cold day but the pennants snap briskly in the wind and the sun is bright. The young members of court are loud and exuberant, a striking contrast to their king and his mother. Wisely, beneath my thick velvet gown, I am wearing several woollen layers and my woman has placed a warming stone inside my muff. I hope the king is similarly well attired.

He huddles in a thick fur cloak and beside him the Prince of Wales, clad in deep red brocade, watches enviously as his companions, Richard, Earl of Kent, and Henry Stafford, show off their prowess at the joust.

He bites his lip and his eyes narrow with undisguised resentment at his own exclusion from the lists. But the king is adamant. Prince Henry can only ride the ring; he is too valuable to be exposed to the risk of injury. I doubt he will ever learn to put the benefit of England before his own personal pleasures. It will be my job to curb him, and I have no illusion as to how difficult that task will be once he comes into his majority.

The king remains at the celebrations for as long as he can but retires exhausted to his private quarters before noon. Immediately Prince Henry's quiet brooding falls away as he assumes his father's place and begins to act up for the crowd. He is served by the king's waiters, and the king's gentlemen ushers preside over his needs. As soon as he is able, the prince hurries to the tiltyard to join his peers. His obsessive need to outshine all those around him governs his actions and consumes all his attention and, short of forcibly detaining him, there is little we can do. Meanwhile, the king grows weaker each day. Depressed, undernourished and, oblivious to the pain he causes me, increasingly unkind.

Ignoring his grim disposition as best I can, I try to tempt him into good humour by engaging minstrels, challenging him to his favourite pastime of chess, or ordering tasty treats from the most revered pastry chefs in the kingdom. But even my brightest ideas provide him with only momentarily distraction. He soon resumes his former misery; a misery exacerbated by the news that the bankers drafts sent by Ferdinand for his daughter's dowry will only cover a portion of the amount due.

The king is further enraged when he learns that Caterina has sold a large portion of her plate and jewels that should have come into his possession on the death of Arthur. To the disgust of the prince, once again Henry begins to shun Spain and seek other brides for his son. The European marriage market is replete with suitable women; a Habsburg would suit him well perhaps, or Margaret of Angouleme is said to be a great beauty.

Ferdinand and Henry are now head to head, fighting like a pair of ageing stags. The Spanish ambassador attempts to navigate around the king and seeks instead audience with the Prince of Wales. Henry may be ill but he is no fool and ensures his son is kept far from the ambassador. The king has no wish for his son to be persuaded into dealing with the Spanish behind his back.

It pains me deeply to witness my grandson's resentment toward his father increase. He hates the restrictions placed upon him and I fear the rift between them will never be healed. In our company the prince is subdued, speaking only when necessary, his eye lowered and his face sombre in a most uncharacteristic manner yet when in the company of his peers, he is the beating heart of the party.

Oh Henry, if ever a young man needed guidance it is you.

I doubt I have the strength to restrain him. And I, feeling my encroaching years in every movement, know not who to worry for the most; my son who is soon to die, or my grandson who is soon to begin to live.

The royal court divides. On one hand we have those close to the king, full of premature grief, nervous of the days to come, and on the other, the gay frivolity of young Henry's companions. I implore the most learned men, those whose wisdom the prince admires to intercede, draw him back from the frivolous path he is taking. Fisher, Thomas Moore, I even consider writing to Erasmus but although he makes a good show of listening, he heeds no one.

Of course, in public Henry's behaviour is exemplary. He is the master of piety and courtly behaviour but he does not fool me. I know that the instant he is able, he will cast off his chains and soar like an eagle. Those of us who attempt to keep him captive will be shed like moulting feathers. I can only pray he does not attempt to fly too high, or too close to the harmful rays of the sun.

Richmond Palace - April 1509

The year passes agonisingly slowly. The strain of hiding the king's condition from the public increases as he makes fitful recoveries only to be cast down again by the slightest exertion. In February the suffering finally becomes too much. The king closets himself away completely, leaving the country in the hands of his advisors and myself.

As his fevers become more frequent, his anxiety for the future of England increases. "Henry is not ready to

312

be king," he groans, as he clings to my hand with skeletal fingers.

"You have instructed him well, my son." I try to soothe him but as soon as he begins to relax, the demons whisper further doubt into his fretful mind.

"There is so much more he must learn. He is immoderate, rash and too extravagant. After – after I am gone, you must curtail him, Mother. You must continue to guide him."

I close my eyes against the hour of Henry's death, clear the grief from my throat and whisper hoarsely.

"I will, my son. You need not doubt that."

He falls back onto the pillow, still clinging to my hand. We sit there for so long that my limbs grow numb. I long to shift position, move from the chair to stretch my legs, flex my cramped fingers but I dare not let go. To salve my own suffering when Henry has need of me is something I cannot do. I will sit here for as long as I am required.

Henry will not die today. Too often of late I have feared we are entering his last hour only for him to fall asleep and wake again refreshed a few hours later. It is a harrowing time for me, expecting every day to be the one I will lose him but I remember to thank God for each extra hour and to beg him to make my son's passing a gentle one. It seems God is deaf to my pleas.

Some of us die an easy death, slipping from life as effortlessly as passing from one room to another. Others rage against it. They turn away from the open door and shun the kingdom of Heaven, to try to claw their way back to life. To my great sorrow, Henry's death is of the latter kind.

He frets. He cries out against it. He is plagued by the knowledge of unfinished business, incomplete intentions. He summons Prince Henry and subjects him

313

to a list of things a king must do, and a longer list of things he must not.

"Pray with me, son." Obediently, the prince kneels at his father's bedside, rosary beads entwined about their clasped fingers. My grandson and I exchange glances over the sick king's head and I see the boy's fear, his uncertainty. I grope for my own beads, struggle to my knees and pray with them.

For two months the king continues in this way; a purgatory of torture on earth. It endures for so long I even begin to wish God would take him. He is suffering too much. I can bear to watch it no longer.

I stay up all night, praying until the candles are burned low. I creep back to my apartment where, my appetite even less than before, I refuse a light repast. I have just pushed the plate away when the king's servant appears summoning me to the royal bedside.

The acid in my empty gut rises in a bitter tide as I hasten to Henry's apartment and enter a room that reeks with the stench of fast approaching death.

Henry lies like a corpse; the skin on his face as thin and pale as paper. I make the sign of the cross before I approach and take his dry hand in mine. He turns his head stiffly, a grimace taking the place of his once lovely smile.

A sudden image appears in my mind of the day I travelled to join him after Bosworth. The day I laid eyes on him for the first time after fourteen years apart. I had not recognised the tall man who stood with Jasper and Thomas but then he turned to me and smiled, and I knew him at once. How has this day come so fast? Why must I still be here to witness it?

I suppose we all must come to this dark and terrible hour. We all must pass from this world alone, leave those we love behind and cross the threshold into

314

the unknown. We can only have faith that God is waiting to receive us.

My throat closes, my eyes sting with tears I will *not* let fall. Henry gestures to the nightstand where a golden crucifix gleams in the firelight. I reach out for it, pass it into his hands. He closes his eyes, clutches it to his chest and weeps silently, his foul breath gusting in my face.

I reach for his hand. "God loves you, my son. You must trust in him, and he will receive you."

Within hours my son is raving, his fever grown so high it burns my fingers to touch him. Grief lodges in my throat like a stone. When the time is near we summon the prince. He stands at the foot of the bed and looks on, his face flaccid.

"He is beset by demons" Prince Henry cries. "Is it always like this?"

"No. Some pass quietly." I reach for his hand but he pulls away, swallows deeply as he gropes for his prayer beads. The prince spends the next few moments in desperate prayer before looking up at me again.

"Was it like this for my mother?"

"Oh no. No: she passed without being aware of it. It was much easier for her."

This is not true but God will forgive a lie given to ease another's torment. Prince Henry has never fully recovered from the loss of his mother; I hope the death of his father will be easier.

Bishop Fisher moves silently forward and begins to pray, evoking the memory of the glorious virgin to whom Henry has always held a special devotion. The calming words offer him ease and he seems to let go of his earthly troubles; for a little while the king breathes more freely.

315

"Take him now," I pray. "Please God; take him now while he is calm." But God does not listen, for some reason know only unto him, he chooses to draw out my son's suffering. He lets the life drip slowly away, squeezing every ounce of pain from him that he can. But the torment of the king at his passing is nothing compared to my witnessing of it.

His tortured breathing has ceased. His eyes are closed in death and darkness falls upon me like a shroud. A short time ago I prayed for God to take him yet I am so desolate now.

Since my thirteenth year, Henry has been my reason for breathing, my reason for rising each morning. He was living proof of my faith in God's goodness, and the only living creature that I have loved more than I love myself.

The years of struggle, the suffering, the uncertainty, the battle and ultimate triumph of attaining for my son all he deserved, now lie behind me. Those years that seemed harsh as I lived them, now gleam like a lost pearl. I would go back and live it all again for the blessing of the short years I enjoyed with Henry; for the all-encompassing joy of his existence.

Henry is out of my reach. I can do no more for him. His beloved face, his laugh, even his ill humour has melted away. Henry has passed into Paradise. I will never have him back. I am alone. Even God offers me no comfort. Even He has turned away.

Eventually the needs of my body draw me from prayer and I wend a miserable way to my chambers. My women silently help me with my toilette before leaving me alone. I am looking out across the dark garden where a few men are working late, pulling stubborn nettles from

316

the nursery beds. I do not know how long I have been there when a gentle cough announces that John Fisher is patiently awaiting my notice.

"John ..."

He comes forward quietly, as is his habit, and waits for my woman to close the door. His footsteps make no sound when he comes to stand at my shoulder.

"My Lady, I hope I find you well."

I fail to find a positive response.

"I have been better, John. I have been better."

I speak bleakly into the empty shadows. He takes a step closer, his sleeve brushing mine.

"You must not despair, My Lady. The king would not have wanted that. You must look to the future. There is still so much for you to do."

My rosary is crunched in my palm. I attempt to place it on the window sill but I miss and it slides off, cascading over the edge to form a pool of pearls on the floor. John stoops to retrieve it, places it in my hand again, his large palms enclosing mine as if in prayer.

"I can think of nothing."

My voice sounds forlorn; like a child crying in the dark. The heaviness of the last few months weighs on my shoulders, my neck so full of pain I can scarce keep my head erect. John fetches a chair and places it behind me, his hand on my shoulder urging me to be seated.

"Sit, My Lady. Sit down before you fall and let me tell you how much your grandson needs you."

"Henry?" I raise my chin. I had somehow forgotten Henry. The last I saw of him he was stricken not with grief but with the weight of responsibility laid so heavily upon him.

"I was with the prince ... the king, a short time since. He is badly in need of guidance, My Lady ... if you can rouse yourself."

I turn around and notice the shadows behind the bishop's eyes, the silver trace of sorrow upon his cheek.

He is right. Poor Henry, poor flawed, vainglorious Henry will need help, mine and the bishop's too. There will be council meetings to attend, declarations to sign, ceremonies to be arranged.

I draw in breath and release it again. Slowly my shoulders straighten and my mind clears, just a little. Bishop Fisher is right. There is no time to waste in weeping. My time on Earth is not yet done; I have duties to fulfil, promises to keep, and a wayward boy to shape into a King of England.

*

Margaret Beaufort, The King's Mother, Countess of Richmond and Derby, died on the twenty-ninth of June 1509, just a few days after organising and witnessing the wedding and joint coronation of her grandson, Henry and Caterina of Aragon. *'All England for her death had cause of weeping.[1]'*

---

[1] Bishop John Fisher on Margaret's passing.

Author's Note

Margaret Beaufort's remarkable journey did not end at Bosworth where her campaign to see her son King of England was finally realised. Until that fateful day in August she had been a player in the game of war between York and Lancaster but in the beginning, her rise to greatness could not have been foreseen. When the conflict began Margaret was an insignificant figure, her marriage to Edmund Tudor, half-brother to King Henry VI of little moment in the tumultuous events taking place around her. Initially, during the reign of Edward IV, she seemed to accept York's rule, negotiating with the king for her son's pardon and the return of his rights.

There is no evidence that Margaret had any designs on the throne until after Richard III's coronation. It was then that she joined forces with Elizabeth Woodville and began to plot against the king, sealing their pact with the agreement that if Henry Tudor's bid for the throne was successful, he would unite the houses of York and Lancaster by marrying Edward IV's heir, Elizabeth of York.

The initial plot failed and Margaret's part in it could have resulted in the death penalty yet, due to the leniency of Richard III, she was placed under strict house arrest, in the care of her husband, Thomas Stanley. She began the year of 1485 as a traitor to the crown yet she ended it as the most powerful woman in England.

Margaret worked doggedly against King Richard, raising funds and supporters to facilitate Henry Tudor's invasion. In August that same year, her son landed on the Welsh coast, marched across country raising support along the way. In August battle was finally joined at Bosworth where, due to the betrayal of the king's strongest supporters, Margaret's cause was won. She was now The King's Mother but her journey was only just beginning.

Having achieved her goal Margaret may have expected to at last be able to sit back and put her feet up. But the early years of Henry's reign were fraught with uprising, the first incited by John of Lincoln who put forward an imposter in what has come to be known as the Lambert Simnel uprising. This culminated at The Battle of Stoke, in which the king was victorious and the young pretender put to work in the royal kitchens.

The second and more troublesome claimant to Henry's throne was Perkin Warbeck who declared himself to be the younger of the Princes in the Tower, Richard of Shrewsbury. His Plantagenet looks and noble bearing gained him widespread support and his popularity in Europe was the cause of many headaches for Henry.

Warbeck plagued Henry for many years yet after his final defeat was not punished in the usual way but paraded at court as a sort of laughable curiosity. He was later placed in the tower until an attempted escape and alleged plot with long term prisoner, Edward of Warwick, the son of

George of Clarence, ended in a trial for treason. Both men were given the death penalty.

Throughout these continuing troubles, together with the defection of several notables from their court, Henry and Margaret maintained an air of invincible dignity. Margaret's role at court was almost that of a second queen. She was awarded regal status, had rooms adjoining the kings and, on occasion, appeared in public wearing identical robes to the queen. At table she sat at the queen's right hand and was addressed at court as My Lady, The King's Mother. She even took to signing herself nebulously as Margaret R. – an initial that can be interpreted as either Richmond, or Regina.

I expect she rather enjoyed that.

Because of this outward show of pride she is often viewed as overbearing, yet these events are not unprecedented. During the reign of Edward IV, his mother Cecily Neville was afforded similar status and referred to herself as 'Queen by rights.' Margaret never went so far as to use this title, but it was inferred by her treatment at court.

Margaret insisted that things be done properly and put great store in etiquette, ensuring the court followed strict rules. It was Margaret who put forth directions to be followed during royal childbirth. These guidelines were followed not only by Elizabeth of York but by Henry VIII's queens, Catherine of Aragon, Anne Boleyn, Jane Seymour, and her great granddaughter, Mary I.

Every royal event was directed under Margaret's careful eye, from the joy of dynastic weddings to the sorrow of royal mourning. None of us, not even the highest in the land are spared grief and Margaret was faced with many tragic bereavements.

The first came in 1495 with the death of her three year old granddaughter, Princess Elizabeth followed a few years later by the loss of her infant grandson, Edmund. Childhood mortality was high but that does not mean it was ever easy. A king required sons; one heir was simply not enough, it was essential for the Prince of Wales to be supported by brothers. Should anything happen to the heir, another was required to step into his place. This unpalatable fact made the death of a boy even harder to bear than that of a daughter, and the loss Edmund, named for Margaret's husband, Edmund Tudor must have hit the royal family hard.

But fate was not done with them yet and less than two years later, the greatest blow of all came with the death of the recently married heir to the throne, Arthur, Prince of Wales. Arthur was on the cusp of manhood, his wedding to Catherine of Aragon cementing the relationship between England and Spain. His death saw not only the loss of the king's son but political upheaval also.

Henry and Elizabeth were deeply affected by Arthur's death. A few years previously the royal nursery had boasted three sons but now they were reduced to just one; it must have posed quite a blow. The Tudor dynasty was paramount to Henry, Margaret and Elizabeth and one son offered no security, no peace of mind.

There are some suggestions that around the years 1499 - 1502 a breach had occurred in the relationship between Henry and Elizabeth but, whether that was so or not, the couple decided it was not too late for Elizabeth to bear Henry another son. In February 1503, the queen produced a daughter but died shortly afterwards of complications, and her daughter Katherine followed a few days later. Henry was now not just short of sons but also lacked the means of begetting more.

It was Margaret who drew up the ordinances of Elizabeth's funeral and a few short months later had the sad duty of bidding farewell to her granddaughter and namesake, Margaret Tudor, when she left to marry the Scottish king. One way or another, her grandchildren were leaving.

These life events are difficult for anyone; the loss of a family member is always shattering but for Margaret, who set so much store on dynasty and the House of Tudor, they would have been harder still. With each death, it was not just the loss of the family member she mourned, but the diminishing of her future bloodline.

Two years later, tragedy took a further swipe at Margaret; this time with the death of her husband, Thomas Stanley. We know nothing about the relationship between them but they were together for more than thirty years. Often there is a link with people who shared the same troubles, fought for the same goal and Stanley had been at Margaret's side throughout her fight for Henry's crown and during his years of triumph. His loss would have been considerable.

Thomas and Margaret had been on good terms throughout, she kept rooms for him at her various houses and they visited each other regularly. Late in their marriage, her decision to take a vow of chastity is often seen as a clue to the state of their relationship but it probably owed more to her piety and devotion. Chastity was a way of expressing devotion to God, a determination to put aside earthly pleasures. Margaret had been barren for years but it never prevented her from marrying but now she was growing old and did not marry again.

Threats to Henry's crown continued with the Earl of Suffolk's claim to a superior right to the throne. The White Rose, as he became known due to his Yorkist ancestry, cast a further shadow over Henry's troubled reign. The Earl finally took refuge at the court of Burgundy.

Happily for Henry, Duke Philip and his wife Juana, on route to Spain, were wrecked in a great storm and washed up on the south coast of England. On learning this, the king invited the Duke to Windsor where he showered him with elaborate hospitality, refusing to let him leave until he had promised to place Suffolk in his custody. Duke Philip had little option but to agree but he did so on the understanding that Suffolk was left unharmed. Henry kept this promise, sparing his life but imprisoning him in the Tower of London where he languished until 1513 when he was executed by King Henry VIII.

Margaret took great interest in the raising of her grandchildren, overseeing their education and well-being. In the company of the king and queen she observed the marriage of Arthur and Katharine from a small room overlooking the choir at St Paul's. Afterwards, the newly-weds were entertained at her residence at Coldharbour Palace which, in honour of the occasion, had recently undergone extensive renovations. She spared no expense, decking the hall with cloth of gold and ordering the most sumptuous meals and the best entertainers in the realm.

If I am an authority on anything, it is the joy of grand parenting. I know the unexpected joy they bring, the pride we have in each new skill they master. It gave me great satisfaction to discover that Margaret felt the same. During negotiations for her granddaughter's marriage to the King of Scotland, Margaret, no doubt recalling her own painful experience in the begetting and birth of Henry, ensured that the union would not be consummated until her granddaughter was of suitable age. She played a part in choosing Prince Henry's tutors and encouraged his love of music and Latin, as well as encouraging his skill at the joust. In 1507 after watching his prowess at the sport of 'running the ring' she displayed her pride in him by presenting her grandson with the gift of an expensive saddle and harness.

Margaret has many critics but it cannot be denied that she was tough, conscientious and charitable. During her son's last illness, although thirteen years his senior, she assumed much of the day to day running of the country. After his death, in spite of a grief that must have been immense, she found the strength to organise his funeral which was carried out with great pomp and dignity. Margaret, as the most powerful woman in England, took precedence over all ladies present. She was also the chief executor of his will.

By this time Margaret was in poor health and feeling her age yet she had no hesitation in taking a major part in the council designed to instruct the new king, Henry VIII, who was a few months short of his majority. I have little doubt this was more due to duty than pleasure; her son had been the main focus of her love and her overseeing of her grandson's coronation was just Margaret's way of tidying up. She was probably aware that her days were drawing to an end and one can imagine the list of instructions she passed to Henry on her deathbed. It is as well she has no concept of the future of what his reign would become.

She was a forward thinker, conversing with the greatest minds of the day but I doubt she would have embraced the new learning. Although she would have understood

Henry's battle for an heir, she would have condemned his treatment of Catherine of Aragon, and disapproved of Anne Boleyn. Henry's break with Rome would have broken her heart and she most certainly would not have condoned the execution of her beloved Bishop, John Fisher.

Margaret, blissfully unaware of the disasters to follow in the next reign, died in late June 1509, just a few days after the coronation of Henry VIII. She was laid to rest at Westminster Abbey, close to her son, Henry Tudor, for whom she had lived.

'All England for her death had cause of weeping. The poor creatures that were wont to receive her arms, to whom she was always piteous and merciful; the students of both universities, to whom she was as a mother; all the learned of England, to whom she was a patron; all the virtuous and devout persons, to whom she was a loving sister; all the good religious men and women whom she was so often wont to visit in comfort; all good priests and clerks, to whom she was a true defender; all the noble men and women, to whom she was a mirror an example of honour; all the common people of this realm, to whom she was in their causes, mediatrix, and took right great displeasure for them; and generally the whole realm had cause to complain and to mourn her death.'

Other novels by Judith Arnopp

A Song of Sixpence: the story of Elizabeth of York and Perkin Warbeck

In the years after Bosworth, a small boy is ripped from his rightful place as future king of England. Years later when he reappears to take back his throne, his sister Elizabeth, now Queen to the invading King, Henry Tudor, is torn between family loyalty and duty.

As the final struggle between the houses of York and Lancaster is played out, Elizabeth is torn by conflicting loyalty, terror and unexpected love.

Set at the court of Henry VII, *A Song of Sixpence* offers a new perspective on the early years of Tudor rule. Elizabeth of York, often viewed as a meek and uninspiring queen, emerges as a resilient woman whose strengths lay in endurance rather than resistance.

The Winchester Goose: at the court of Henry VIII

Tudor London: 1540. Each night, after dark, men flock to Bankside seeking girls of easy virtue; prostitutes known as The Winchester Geese.

Joanie Toogood has worked the streets of Southwark since childhood but her path is changed forever by an encounter with Francis Wareham, a spy for the King's secretary, Thomas Cromwell.

Meanwhile, across the River, at the glittering court of Henry VIII, Wareham also sets his cap at Evelyn and Isabella Bourne, members of the Queen's household and the girls, along with Joanie, are drawn into intrigue and the shadow of the executioner's blade.

Set against the turmoil of Henry VIII's middle years, *The Winchester Goose* provides a brand new perspective of the happenings at the royal court, offering a frank and often uncomfortable observation of life at both ends of the social spectrum.

Sisters of Arden: on the Pilgrimage of Grace

Arden Priory has remained unchanged for almost four hundred years. When a nameless child is abandoned at the gatehouse door, the nuns take her in and raise her as one of their own.
As Henry VIII's second queen dies on the scaffold, the embittered King strikes out, and unprecedented change sweeps across the country. The bells of the great abbeys fall silent, the church and the very foundation of the realm begins to crack.
Determined to preserve their way of life, novitiate nuns Margery and Grace join a pilgrimage thirty thousand strong to lead the king back to grace.
Sisters of Arden is a story of valour, virtue and veritas.

The Kiss of the Concubine: a story of Anne Boleyn

28th January 1547. It is almost midnight and the cream of English nobility hold their breath as King Henry VIII prepares to face his God. As the royal physicians wring their hands and Archbishop Cranmer gallops through the frigid night, two dispossessed princesses pray for their father's soul and a boy, soon to be king, snivels into his velvet sleeve.

Time slows, and dread settles around the royal bed, the candles dip and something stirs in the darkness ... something, or someone, who has come to tell the king it is time to pay his dues.

The Kiss of the Concubine is the story of Anne Boleyn, the second of Henry VIII's queens.

Intractable Heart: the story of Katheryn Parr

England: 1537

As the year to end all years rolls to a close, King Henry VIII vents his continuing fury at the pope. The Holy Roman Church reels beneath the reformation and as the vast English abbeys crumble the royal coffers begin to fill.

The people of the north, torn between loyalty to God and allegiance to their anointed king, embark upon a pilgrimage to guide their errant monarch back to grace. But Henry is unyielding and sends an army north to quell the rebel uprising.

In Yorkshire, Katheryn Lady Latimer and her step-children, Margaret and John, are held under siege at Snape Castle. The events at Snape set Katheryn on a path that will lead from the deprivations of a castle under siege to the perils of the royal Tudor court.

330

Intractable Heart is the story of Henry VIII's sixth and final wife.

The Forest Dwellers

The People of Ytene are persecuted, evicted from their homes and forced to live in exile from the lands Saxons have inhabited for generations. Life is hard. The Norman interlopers are hated.

Twelve years after the Norman invasion, three soldiers are molesting a forest girl who is fairer than any they have ever seen. Leo stops the attack in the only way he can ...violently. His actions that day trigger a chain of events that will end only with the death of a king.

The Song of Heledd

In seventh century Powys at the hall of King Cynddylan of Pengwern, the princesses, Heledd and Ffreur attend a celebratory feast where fifteen-year-old Heledd develops an infatuation for a travelling minstrel. The illicit liaison triggers a chain of events that will destroy two kingdoms, and bring down a dynasty.

Set against the backdrop of the pagan-Christian conflict between kings Penda and Oswiu, *The Song of Heledd* sweeps the reader from the ancient kingdom of Pengwern to the lofty summits of Gwynedd where Heledd battles to control both her own destiny and that of those around her.

Judith Arnopp has carried out lengthy research into the fragmented ninth century poems, Canu Llywarch Hen and Canu Heledd, and the history surrounding them, to produce a fiction of what might have been.

Peaceweaver: the story of Eadgyth Aelfgarsdottir

When Ælfgar of Mercia falls foul of the king and is exiled, his daughter Eadgyth's life is changed forever.

Sold into a disastrous marriage with Gruffydd ap Llewellyn, King of the Welsh, Eadgyth ultimately finds herself accused of fornication, incest and treason. Alone in a foreign land, her life is forfeit until a surprise night attack destroys Gruffydd's palace, and Eadgyth is taken prisoner by Earl Harold of Wessex.

At the Saxon court she infiltrates the sticky intrigues of the Godwin family, and on the eve of his accession to the English throne, she agrees to marry Harold Godwinson.

As William the Bastard assembles his fleet in the south, and Harald Hardrada prepares to invade from the North, their future is threatened, and the portentous date of October 14th 1066 looms.

Eadgyth's tale of betrayal, passion and war highlights the plight of women, tossed in the tumultuous sea of feuding Anglo Saxon Britain.

All books available on Amazon Kindle or in paperback. The Beaufort Chronicles is also available as an Audio Book.

author.to/juditharnoppbooks

www.judithmarnopp.com